Praise HER MAJ

HER MAJESTY'S ROYAL COVEN

"There's so much humor and sadness here, so much tenderness and compassion and a deep love of women. The book draws a gentle thread through the visions we have for ourselves, the memories from which we build our relationships, and the ways in which we comprehend the present, and then it pulls that thread taut. Superb and almost unbearably charming, *Her Majesty's Royal Coven* is a beautiful exploration of how foundational friendships age, and it expertly launches an exciting new trilogy."
—*The New York Times Book Review*

"*Her Majesty's Royal Coven* is a shimmering, irresistible cauldron's brew of my favorite things: a thrilling, witchy plot; a diverse, compelling, and beautifully drawn cast; complex relationships with real heart; laugh-out-loud banter; and the kind of dazzling magic I wish existed. You won't be able to put it down."
—Lana Harper, *New York Times* bestselling author of *Payback's a Witch*

"Juno Dawson is at the top of her game in this vibrant and meticulous take on witchcraft. Her characteristic wit and grit shine through *Her Majesty's Royal Coven*, which paints a convincing picture of how magic might converge with the modern world."
—Samantha Shannon, *New York Times* bestselling author of *The Bone Season* and *The Priory of the Orange Tree*

"Talk about a gut punch of a novel. *Her Majesty's Royal Coven* is sure to have readers who love witchy stories—and the queerer, the better—salivating from the very first page. . . . This book has more twists, betrayals, and drama than a *Desperate Housewives* episode, and I lived for that. . . . A provocative exploration of intersectional feminism, loyalty, gender, and transphobia, Dawson's *Her Majesty's Royal Coven* is an immersive story about what it means to be a woman—and a witch—and invites readers into an intricately woven web of magic, friendship, and power."
—The Nerd Daily

"Dawson, in an impressive flex, uses the rules of the fantasy genre to make a statement about people of color and LGBTQ individuals and how organizations can exclude and ignore them. Readers who enjoy witches and watching change ripple through a culture will enjoy this series."
—*Booklist* (starred review)

"A femme-forward story of power, morality, and fate that is not shy about its politics. . . . Beyond its politics, what especially makes *Her Majesty's Royal Coven* shine is its impeccable voice. Dawson's conversational, matter-of-fact tone calls to mind writers like . . . Diana Wynne Jones; it's at times funny, at others heartbreaking, but always perfectly calibrated. . . . A thoughtful entry into the witch canon that intrigues and challenges as much as it delights."
—*BookPage*

"Juno Dawson has created your new obsession. *Her Majesty's Royal Coven* is full of her trademark heart and humor, with a delicious slick of darkness. I fell in love with her coven—and I need the next installment now!"
—Kiran Millwood Hargrave, author of *The Mercies*

"Such a joy to read—the world-building is incredible, the writing sophisticated, and the exploration of gender and identity is done with nuance and care. Utterly compelling."
—Louise O'Neill, author of *Asking for It* and *The Surface Breaks*

"The funniest paranormal epic I've ever had the pleasure to read."
—Nicole Galland, bestselling author of *Master of the Revels*

"Look, if the idea of a story about a group of girls living in an alternate England and working for a centuries-old secret government bureau of witches doesn't grab you immediately, I don't know what to tell you. Except that there's also a witch civil war, an oracle that prophecies a young warlock will bring about genocide, and a group of friends torn about how to stop it."
—*Paste*

"Cleverly constructed . . . A gradually building layer of political commentary ultimately reveals a complex metaphor for the UK's sociopolitical climate and mainstream transphobia. . . . An exciting new direction for Dawson. Readers will be eager for the next installment."
—*Publishers Weekly*

"This first adult novel by YA author Dawson (*Clean*; *Meat Market*) is a story of feminism, matriarchy, gender roles, and tradition. . . . Readers who love a big fight between good and evil, who enjoy seeing magic in the everyday world, and those who like their heroines' journeys to include all facets of heartbreak will savor the cut and thrust of this battle."
—*Library Journal*

PENGUIN BOOKS
HUMAN RITES

Juno Dawson is the #1 *Sunday Times* bestselling novelist, screenwriter, journalist, and columnist for *Attitude* magazine. Juno's books include *Her Majesty's Royal Coven*, *The Shadow Cabinet*, and *Queen B*, as well as the global bestsellers *This Book Is Gay* and *Clean*. She also writes for television and created the official Doctor Who audio drama *Doctor Who: Redacted*. An occasional actress and model, Juno appeared in the BBC's *I May Destroy You* (2020). She lives in Brighton, UK, with her husband and Chihuahua.

JUNO DAWSON

HUMAN RITES

★ A NOVEL ★

BOOK 3 IN THE HMRC TRILOGY

PENGUIN BOOKS

PENGUIN BOOKS

An imprint of Penguin Random House LLC
1745 Broadway, New York, NY 10019
penguinrandomhouse.com

Copyright © 2025 by Juno Dawson

Penguin Random House values and supports copyright. Copyright fuels creativity, encourages diverse voices, promotes free speech, and creates a vibrant culture. Thank you for buying an authorized edition of this book and for complying with copyright laws by not reproducing, scanning, or distributing any part of it in any form without permission. You are supporting writers and allowing Penguin Random House to continue to publish books for every reader. Please note that no part of this book may be used or reproduced in any manner for the purpose of training artificial intelligence technologies or systems.

Grateful acknowledgment to Rhianna Pratchett, and the Pratchett estate for permission to reprint an excerpt from *Wintersmith* by Terry Pratchett.

Set in CompatilTextLTPro
Designed by Sabrina Bowers

LIBRARY OF CONGRESS CATALOGING-IN-PUBLICATION DATA
Names: Dawson, Juno, author.
Title: Human rites : a novel / Juno Dawson.
Description: New York, NY : Penguin Books, 2025. |
Series: HMRC Trilogy ; book 3
Identifiers: LCCN 2025005701 (print) | LCCN 2025005702 (ebook) |
ISBN 9780143137160 (paperback) | ISBN 9780593511152 (ebook)
Subjects: LCGFT: Fantasy fiction. | Witch fiction. | Novels.
Classification: LCC PR6104.A8868 H86 2025 (print) |
LCC PR6104.A8868 (ebook) | DDC 823/.92—dc23/eng/20250221
LC record available at https://lccn.loc.gov/2025005701
LC ebook record available at https://lccn.loc.gov/2025005702

Printed in the United States of America
1st Printing

The authorized representative in the EU for product safety and compliance is Penguin Random House Ireland, Morrison Chambers, 32 Nassau Street, Dublin D02 YH68, Ireland,
https://eu-contact.penguin.ie.

To Naṭasha, Nidhi and Nicola

A witch ought never be frightened in the darkest forest...

Because she should be sure in her soul that the most terrifying thing in the forest was her.

—TERRY PRATCHETT, *WINTERSMITH*

WHO'S WHO AND WHAT'S WHAT

HER MAJESTY'S ROYAL COVEN

Established in 1869, HMRC is the official, government-sanctioned coven of the United Kingdom. Young witches are recruited and categorised by their supernormal gifts.

Sentients wield the power of telepathy and telekinesis.
Healers are able to revive living matter.
Elementals can manipulate their immediate environment.
Oracles possess sight backwards and forwards along a linear timeline.
Rare *Adepts* are in possession of two or more of the above talents.

On reaching adulthood, each witch is assessed and awarded a Potency Level from 1 to 7, where 1 is the lowest and 7 is the highest. Male witches, known as warlocks, are registered with the Warlocks' Cabal and ranked similarly.

Note: use of *Necromancy*, or death magic, is not recognised under HMRC law.

THE WITCHES

Ciara Kelly – Level 5 Adept
Renegade witch Ciara previously murdered her sister, Niamh, and stole her identity after spending years in a coma. However, living as Niamh gave her fresh perspective, and she ultimately killed her former ally, rebel warlock Dabney Hale. She came into possession of the all-powerful weapon the Seal of Solomon and chose to destroy it to prevent it falling into the hands of Satanis.

WHO'S WHO AND WHAT'S WHAT

Leonie Jackman – Level 6 Sentient
Leonie is the leader of splinter coven, Diaspora. She narrowly survived Dabney Hale's assault on the mythical Greek Island of Witches, Aeaea.

Chinara Okafor – Level 6 Elemental
Leonie's partner, a human rights lawyer. The couple are based in Camberwell, London. Chinara longs to start a family with her girlfriend.

Elle Pearson – Level 4 Healer
The community nurse recently discovered her 'son', Milo, was, in fact, a physical embodiment of the demon Lucifer. Elle inadvertently turned her cheating husband to stone, suggesting the true extent of her powers is rather higher than her official grade.

Holly Pearson – Sentient (Level TBC)
Elle's daughter, a student and keen artist at St Augustus High School in Hebden Bridge, is an emerging witch.

Theo Wells – Adept (Level TBC)
The mysterious orphan was initially sent to live with Niamh Kelly by former High Priestess Helena Vance. She underwent a magical transformation into a young woman by absorbing Niamh's lifeforce. Rumoured to be the legendary harbinger of Satanis, the 'Sullied Child', Theo was fooled by Lucifer in the guise of Milo Pearson, and was last seen dabbling in necromancy to raise Niamh from the grave . . .

Snow Vance-Morrill – Level 5 Elemental
Helena's teenage daughter left Hebden Bridge with her grandparents following the execution of her mother. She vowed vengeance against Niamh, whom she blames for her mother's demise.

Senait – Adept (Level TBC)
The enigmatic young intersex witch was liberated from a trafficker by Leonie and accompanied her to Aeaea where she appeared to betray the witches to Dabney Hale. She fled the island and her current location is unknown.

Madame Celestine – Level 3 Necromancer
Government name Patricia Umba, the London-based witch is a rival of Leonie and once subjected a seven-year-old Ciara to a demonic 'exorcism'.

Sandhya Kaur – Level 3 Sentient
Executive assistant to the High Priestess of Her Majesty's Royal Coven.

Selina Fay – Level 4 Sentient
The Shadow Cabinet Liaison works to bridge the UK government with HMRC.

Kane Dior Sanchez – Level 3 Sentient
Leonie's friend and colleague at Diaspora.

Emma Benwell – Level 4 Oracle
Head Oracle at HMRC.

Calista
The custodian of Aeaea, the legendary Island of Witches. She lost a hand during Hale's assault on her community.

THE WARLOCKS

Luke Sawyer – Level TBC
Formerly known as Luke Watts and Luke Ridge. Luke's father was the leader of the witchfinder cell the Working Men and recruited his son to the cause. However, Luke's mother was a witch, and he was covertly working against the cell. He fell in love with Niamh but wasn't aware he was actually dating Ciara for several weeks after Niamh's death. Luke ultimately prevented Ciara from using the Seal of Solomon to destroy the world, and she spared his life. His current location is unknown.

Radley Jackman – Level 3 Healer
Leonie's brother is the leader of the Warlocks' Cabal. He very nearly died at the hands of Dabney Hale.

THE MUNDANES

Jez Pearson
Elle's husband has been cheating on her for some time. Elle learned the truth from Ciara, and was undecided on how to proceed when they both discovered Milo was not really their son.

Conrad Chen

Niamh's fiancé was seemingly slaughtered by Ciara during the first war. However, once Ciara's amnesia was cured by the Seal of Solomon, she remembered that she had spared him. Ten years ago, she wiped his memory and left him stranded on a beach in South Wales.

SUPERNORMAL ENTITIES

Gaia – The Great Mother

The great feminine divine is revered by all witches, and although she has many names, witches of the global west mostly refer to her by this title. They believe Gaia is an all-powerful goddess who created all of existence and imbued witches with their gifts as her guardians on earth. As Gaia formed the earth, countless entities found themselves tethered in her new reality. Witches call these beings 'demons'.

Satanis – The Demon King

Sometimes called Satan, he is the most powerful of the demons trapped in Gaia's created reality. He seeks to destroy Gaia's creation and break free of this prison. Before the written word, early witchkind split the mighty demon into three weaker beings: Lucifer, Belial and Leviathan, and imprisoned them. Their whereabouts are long since forgotten.

Lucifer

The Demon King of Desire. Lucifer has been manipulating the witches for decades appearing in various guises including Milo Pearson, and Ciara's supposed lover, Jude Kavanaugh.

Belial

The Demon King of Hate. Appears to humans as a monstrous bull. Belial exploited Helena Vance's latent hatred of trans people to hasten the fall of HMRC.

Leviathan

The Demon King of Fear. The return of the Beast was foreseen by oracles. It is said the Sullied Child will lead him from his prison and into this reality, heralding the end time. Leviathan has no one earthly form, instead manifesting as a witch's worst fear.

IN MEMORIAM

Niamh Kelly – Level 5 Adept
   Niamh was murdered by her sister and her soul transferred into Ciara's corpse. She was buried in Hardcastle Crags in Hebden Bridge.

Annie Device – Level 5 Oracle
   Elle's grandmother. The former Head Oracle was murdered by Helena Vance so she couldn't warn the witches of her plans to kill Theo.

Helena Vance – Level 5 Elemental
   The disgraced High Priestess was exploited by Belial and ultimately executed under witch law in the Pipes at the Grierlings prison estate.

Rev. Sheila Henry – Level 3 Sentient
   The founder of Witch Pride was murdered by witchfinders. Luke gave the cell her identity, believing it would cast suspicion away from Niamh and Theo.

Moira Roberts – Level 4 Sentient
   The Chief Cailleach of Scotland was killed by Dabney Hale during his raid at the House of Hekate.

Julia Collins – Level 4 Adept
   The former High Priestess of HMRC was assassinated by Ciara during Hale's insurgence of 2011.

Zehra Darga – Level 2 Sentient
   The archaeologist was killed during Hale's raid on Aeaea.

Dabney Hale – Level 6 Adept
   A former lover to both Ciara and Helena, the arrogant warlock sought to undermine female superiority by siding with the forces of Satanis. Ciara broke his neck.

HUMAN RITES

25 YEARS AGO . . .

Leisureland – Galway, Ireland

A witch squatted over the entrance of the ghost train, a long talon beckoning unsuspecting children into her lair. She had mushy-pea-green skin and a hooked nose with a wart on the end. She wore a pointed hat and had stringy black hair.

Niamh Kelly felt sorry for her.

It was the second week of the summer holidays and September was unthinkable. For redheads Niamh and Ciara, it was a turquoise sky, Factor 50 sort of day. A dance remix of 'The Boy Is Mine' pounded from the Crazy Mouse and the air was nigh sticky with candyfloss and toffee apples.

But where was their dad? Niamh couldn't keep the hot yellows of panic out of her aura. It made little sense. He'd told them he'd wait while they both paid a visit to the toilets, but when they'd emerged, he was nowhere to be seen. They had nothing to fear here, she reminded herself; they'd been coming to Leisureland their whole lives – it was in Salthill, only twenty minutes from their home in Galway.

'He can't've gone far,' Ciara snapped, belying her own anxiety. She took her sister's hand. 'Come on. We'll go wait by the ticket office.'

'Maybe he went into the men's toilets?' Niamh said. 'We should stay here.'

Ciara tugged on Niamh's arm. 'No. He said if we ever got lost, to go to the exit.'

The girls passed under the swing chairs as they swooped and dipped overhead. They'd tuned out the joyful screams and laughter. A funfair is a mighty noisy spot for a sentient; a cacophony of nervousness, bravado, much-too-late second thoughts at the top of the Big Dipper. The wee psychics had never consciously learned to phase out such background din, it was as natural to them as exhaling.

'When did he say that?' Niamh grumbled.

'Years ago, when we were little.'

They were still little, but less little than then. 'He never said that today.'

Timid sparrowgirl Niamh would be the death of her. 'Niamh, don't be a baby.'

'Can I help you girls? Are yous lost?'

The twins turned to see a smartly dressed woman looming over them, silhouetted before the bright sun. Older than their mother – so old—she wore a trench coat and a woollen beret in the same shade of Barbie cerise, even in the sweltering July heat. 'You girls need help?' She spoke with a local accent. Her lipstick was fuchsia pink and there were waxy flecks of it on her sharp, uneven teeth.

'We can't find our dad,' Ciara said.

Ciara! She could be anyone.

'Good golly, Niamh Kelly,' the woman said. 'You don't have to worry about me.'

It took both girls a second to realise she had overheard a message meant only for Ciara.

'How do you know my name?' Niamh asked. All around them, children ran between the rides, their parents keeping them in check. Any one of these mums or dads could help them. Niamh told herself they were quite safe.

'How do you think?' the woman gave them a theatrical wink. She had a big nose; Niamh tried not to stare.

You're a witch, Ciara said.

'I am,' the woman said aloud. 'I met your mammy once on Inishmaan before you two were even born.' She smiled again, and there was something familiar about her. 'I told her all about you twos.'

'Can you help us find our da?' Niamh asked.

'I certainly can. Come with me,' the woman said.

Ciara gave a shrug and followed after her as she made her way along the gangplanks between the rides and stalls. Their mam had always said they should find a kind woman to help them if there was ever an emergency. Niamh wondered if she was from the little local coven, though the thought didn't quite sit right. Being adepts, all the Galway witches had fussed over the twins since they were toddlers, yet they'd never met this woman.

Ciara, wait.

Her sister stopped.

'Girls, come along now. He's waiting for you.'

'Dad?' Ciara said.

'That's right. Just this way. I'll take you to him.'

Who is she? Niamh asked Ciara.

I can't read her, Ciara replied. They stood together, shoulder to shoulder, concentrating.

The witch looked back, her expression hardening. 'Now, girls, it's very impolite to go snoopin' inside someone's mind without permission,' she said sharply. Her nails were long and filed to a point, the same searing pink as her lips. 'We'll have to teach you some manners.'

'Who are you? What's your name?' Ciara said. 'We shouldn't talk to strangers.'

'But you know me already . . .'

The twins were so good at muting the noise of mundane life, they were slow to realise Leisureland had fallen quiet. The swing chairs hung diagonally in mid-air. The Big Dipper was suspended upside-down in the centre of the loop. A clown blew giant bubbles which waited, frozen, between gleeful statue children.

'How did you do that?' Niamh asked. She'd never seen anything like this.

'I can do whatever I want, I'm a god,' the woman said. 'Now stop asking questions and come with me, you precocious little bitches.'

She grabbed a wrist in each hand and hauled the twins towards the park exit. They dug their heels in, but she was stronger than she looked.

Niamh and Ciara Kelly had always known this day would come. They had used their considerable gifts to heal, to speak, to learn. Now they would have to use them to *fight*. The twins didn't need to communicate. They'd thought about this moment often.

Niamh twisted her bones; Ciara pushed as hard as she could.

The woman didn't budge, but she did let go of them. The girls grasped each other and ran for the waltzers. 'You foul cunts, that hurt!'

Ciara and Niamh held hands and used a trick they'd used since they were five or six. They called it *No*. They wrapped a barrier around themselves. At home, it worked well at stopping Mam or Dad manhandling them towards the bath.

The woman came up against their shield and stopped. 'Let me in.'

'Fuck off,' Ciara said.

Niamh looked to her. Oh, Ciara'd be in *trouble* if she told Mam she'd said that word.

'Come with me now and I'll make it painless,' the woman said. Her voice was deep now, deeper than any man's. Her skin turned a mottled olive green, and lank raven hair poured over her shoulder and back. Warts bubbled and burst across her hooked nose.

Neither Kelly girl said a word.

'One day I shall be whole once more, and you'll wish you'd taken a quick death here today. You have no idea of the horrors to come; the torment you'll deliver unto each other.' Her haggish cackle drilled through their skulls. 'Bye for now!'

The girls flinched as the waltzers clattered past them, the

Tamperer featuring Maya blaring from the sound system. What *is* she going to look like with a chimney on her head?

Brendan Kelly hurried over, concern creasing his face. 'Girls! What did I tell you about wandering off? You want to give me a heart attack?'

The twins looked to him blankly. They couldn't recall how they'd come to be by the waltzers when they'd only just stepped out of the toilets. They apologised sheepishly. The magenta woman was nowhere to be seen.

Neither Ciara nor Niamh would remember a single second of the exchange.

25 YEARS LATER . . .

Theo - Hebden Bridge, UK

'Who are you? *Really?*' Theo asked the boy she had previously known to be Milo Pearson. Now, she wasn't so sure.

Behind his face, there was another, and another, and another, and she recognised none of them. Men, women, children. She'd never known an aura like it. She couldn't read him anymore, his mind a mirror in which she could see only herself.

Together, they walked the nature hike through Hardcastle Crags. It was late, and cold, bitterly so. The dark was very close, and she could scarcely see where he was leading her.

'I'm Milo.'

Theo stopped walking. 'You're not. How are you doing this?'

He turned to her, his eyes glinting like mercury in what sparse moonlight found its way through the canopy. 'Do you want to see Niamh again, or not?' He didn't even *sound* like Milo any longer, his voice older than the valley. 'Follow me. We're close.'

Theo could have found her way to Bluebell Meadow alone in the dark. Even after all this time, she still felt Niamh; something like a mournful hymnal amongst the trees. The night was oddly silent; no owls; no badgers. Even the wind seemed to hold its breath in anticipation.

'Can you feel her?' the boy who looked like Milo asked. 'She's still here. Just.'

Theo wrapped her arms around herself like a shield. 'So what?'

'Don't be coy, Theodora. You know why we're here.'

'You're wrong,' she said defiantly. 'I won't. I can't.'

With dancerly, fluid movements, Milo took her hands in his and squeezed them tight. 'It's time you understood your part in all this. You aren't like other witches.'

Theo laughed, half-embarrassed, half-sarcastic. *You're not like Other Girls* was the reddest red flag.

'You know this,' Milo said, stating facts. 'You have untold power. This is what you were made for. You are a tiger, not a sheep, so stop dressing like one. It doesn't suit you.'

Theo tried to focus, to ignore the strange watchfulness of the night forest. What did he mean? *She* knew nothing of her childhood, of her parentage. She couldn't resist the question. 'What do you know about me?'

Milo smiled. He strode away, deeper and deeper into the woods. 'So. Story-time. Once upon a time, the witches tried to kill us, but they failed. They split us, and since that day they spoke of one who would reunite us.'

'The Sullied Child.' Theo was more than familiar, thanks, but this only confirmed her worst fears. 'Is it me?'

Even in the darkness, his teeth gleamed, great white shark. 'All in good time. There's work to do.'

She stopped stubbornly in her tracks. Theo knew what work he spoke of. 'I told you, I won't. It's forbidden! It's unnatural.'

Annoyance flared in Milo's eyes. 'Idiot. You are a witch. You are nature herself.'

She shook her head.

He tried a more caramel tone. 'Don't you want her back? She was taken from you on the whim of a mad woman. Everyone you have ever loved was stolen from you, Theo. It doesn't quite seem fair.'

She fell into step alongside him and looked into his eyes. For the first time she entertained the notion. 'But what if . . . what if she comes back . . . wrong?'

He shrugged off her concerns. 'Piffle. Old wives' tales. It's well within your grasp.'

Necromancy. The unspoken art. So taboo, it was impossible to know what might happen because no one dared leave evidence of their handiwork. But Theo knew, without question, that she would rather have no Niamh at all than a lumbering zombie. The physical body had been in this grave for *weeks*. The *real* Niamh, her soul, well that was what hurt Theo's heart. The notion that Niamh's sentience was *here*, amongst the snowdrops and holly, seeing all this unfold, was too much to bear.

The trees thinned as they reached the privacy of Niamh's glade. They waded through brittle, waist-high brambles, until Theo stood roughly where she was buried, a smooth pebble the only clue to her final resting place. It was engraved with a CK for Ciara Kelly, the woman who had killed her twin and stolen her body. 'This wasn't even *her* body,' Theo said. 'It's Ciara's.'

This detail didn't seem to trouble her guide. 'Technicalities. With both Ciara and Niamh on the physical plane, the soul transfer will become perilously weak. They will revert within moments. Nature will right itself.'

That made sense. Whatever dark spell Ciara had used to commandeer her sister's body was grossly unnatural – there's a lid for every pot, and Ciara had switched lids. Perhaps this was justice.

All this was moot, though, because such magic was far beyond Theo.

'Here,' Milo said, and *The Song of Osiris* floated from his position to hers. 'This was meant for you.'

'I don't know how,' Theo said, exasperated, hoping he didn't think that admission was her agreeing to this.

'Let the book show you how, and let love guide your hand.' He opened his palms, some sort of pacifying motion. 'You did love her. You can bring her back.'

Theo looked from the book that hovered before her, to the grave. 'Where is she?'

'The between space,' Milo said. 'When the physical body perishes, the soul lingers just outside of our reality.'

'And then where?'

'And then nowhere. Nowhere at all. Would you like me to tell you Gaia created some celestial members' area? This is all there is, all there ever was. *This* is Gaia's creation, and the rest is a fiction. You get one chance, and Niamh's was taken from her. Unless you save her.'

Theo turned her attention to *The Song of Osiris*, and it opened itself, the pages flicking of their own accord. The bible-thin paper was covered in red, scrawled script. She had tried to read it, but it made scant sense.

'I don't want to,' Theo sobbed, hot, frustrated tears on her cheeks.

'Why are you lying?'

And she was. She did want Niamh back, more than anything. More than she'd even wanted to become a girl.

'Let it in,' Milo told her.

Theo trained her sentience on the book and found it did seem to speak. Lots of voices were contained in the pages, all whispering over each other at once. She couldn't focus on a single message. *Stop*, she told it, *I can't hear you.*

The chatter ceased for a second and then the red ink – blood – lifted from the pages and into the night air. It formed a swirling mist of scarlet tendrils that lingered a moment before swimming towards Theo. She felt the entity, the song, reaching out for her with inquisitive whiskers. With her mind, Theo made contact, trying to understand its message.

The red mist slithered over her lips, into her eyes and ears.

And just like that it all made sense. Suddenly, Theo knew precisely how to bring Niamh's soul out of the realm of shadows, and into Ciara's corpse below. Milo smiled ever so slightly, stoically triumphant.

The power locked in Hardcastle Crags lifted Theo off her feet. She stabilised herself a metre or so off the earth, feeling a tsunami of radiance ripple through her. She'd never felt anything like it, well, at least not since *that* night on the bank of the beck. Her hair whipped around her face, getting caught in her mouth.

This was the first step. She needed this much power. She drank in the vitality of the forest. It was soul nectar, and she lapped it up.

The power was for her sentience. She needed to feel far beyond Hebden Bridge. She needed to feel more than just the living; she needed to feel the dead.

Suddenly, it was as if she held one of those blacklights up against reality. Now there wasn't just the tell-tale signature of life, there was *more*. A new layer of vision. She was joined by four, maybe five phosphorus, shifting spirits: cloudlike wraiths. Hardly tangible, obliquely humanoid, they were little more than wisps on the air, drifting aimlessly through the woods.

Souls. Souls or ghosts? Ghosts. She was seeing *ghosts*.

They were everywhere; in the trees, drifting across the meadow. Some of them were more indistinct than others, like they were fading away. Theo swallowed hard. This was where the dead went.

Can they feel anything? she asked Milo.

Nothing on Earth, he told her.

It didn't take her long to find Niamh in the crowd. The shape looked nothing like her, but it *felt* exactly like her. Theo felt the kindness, her sloping thoughts, her quick humour. It was *her*. She also found she could manipulate this strange matter as she would anything corporeal. She seized hold of Niamh's essence, because it definitely wasn't the same as her radiance, and directed the energy towards the grave.

It takes more than that, Milo told her. *If it was that simple, we'd all do it.*

Before her, a slender, needle-like dagger emerged from the now empty pages of *The Song of Osiris*.

You know what you have to do. Remember the sacrifice she once made for you.

Oh. Of course there's a catch. Isn't there always?

A life for a life. It seemed fair. Although it felt a lifetime ago, a few chaotic months ago, in these very woods, Niamh had offered herself to Theo entirely. She wouldn't exist, least of all in her current form, without her. Now it was time to repay her. Maybe, Theo thought, this was always foreseen by Gaia. The reason for things. *This* was why Niamh had so flippantly offered her a home that day in Manchester.

But didn't he just say you're the Sullied Child? Doesn't he need you yet? This voice of reason was drowned out by the myriad of otherworldly voices still swirling through her skull.

Theo joined in with them. Her lips moved, uttering some strange language she'd never heard before. The sounds were hardly human, noises unlike anything she'd heard, raking at the back of her throat. Her eyes were wide and black like obsidian.

She took hold of the hilt of the dagger and ran the blade along her pale forearm diagonally. She screamed in pain, although could barely hear herself over the ringing in her ears.

Blood sprayed from the wound, forming the same nebulous, shifting cloud that had emanated from the book. It gathered over the burial site a moment, before spiralling downwards and into the earth.

The pain in her arm subsided, but Theo weakened at once. She felt the tug of the grave, thirstily gulping up her offering. It wasn't just her blood it was draining; it was her radiance. The skeletal remains below needed something, something living.

Theo's head lolled forwards, and the ground came up at her fast. Still Niamh suckled on her. It was like a magnet, pulling her down, down, down, and there was nothing she could do to stop it now she'd started. She felt her knees connect painfully with the earth, and she bowed to the grave.

The cool dirt felt good on her face. Her vision went grey and gritty, all TV static for a moment, until blackness swung in like finale curtains.

Niamh

All at once, the sun set behind the caldera. They'd travelled here for the sunset and it didn't disappoint. The sky turned indigo and lilac, the sea was liquid gold and the sun seemed to melt like ice cream on pie. Gaia was here, truly, Niamh could feel her. *Mother.* Without warning, tears pricked her eyes. Over the table, Conrad squeezed her hands. Neither said anything as they watched. Words weren't good enough for it anyway.

She dared to look away from the lightshow. She wanted to see Conrad's face. At the same time, he looked to her reaction. They caught each other. He smiled and she physically felt the love balloon in her chest. They couldn't really afford this holiday, but sitting on the cliffside terrace of the cocktail bar in Fira, she found she didn't have a care in the world. In all the billions of people on this planet, they had found each other. How lucky they were. How very lucky.

'We should just do it,' he said.

'Do what?'

'You know what! What are we waiting for?'

Niamh smiled, toying with him. 'What? Right here in Greece? In the bar?'

'Soon. I mean it.'

She wasn't going anywhere and neither was he. What was the rush? She was twenty-four, he was only two years older. *Wife* felt like a very grown-up thing to be. They had all the time in the world.

All at once, the sun set behind the caldera. They'd travelled here for the sunset and it didn't disappoint. The sky turned indigo and lilac, the sea was liquid gold and the sun melted like ice cream on pie. Gaia was here, truly, Niamh could feel her. Without warning, she felt tears prick her eyes. Over the table, Conrad squeezed her hands. Neither said anything as they watched. Words weren't good enough for it anyway.

Wait.

Something was wrong. Didn't she just do this?

All at once, the sun set behind the caldera. They'd travelled here for the sunset and it didn't disappoint. The sky turned indigo and lilac, the sea was liquid gold and the sun melted like ice cream on pie.

Niamh looked to Conrad, but it was Luke Watts holding her hand over the table. Luke smiled, and she physically felt the guilt balloon in her chest. Even after everything that had happened, a second chance. How lucky she was. How very lucky she was.

'Luke?' Niamh said.

'Time to go home,' he replied. 'I'll see you soon, Niamh.'

The sun sank all the way behind the dormant volcano and the bar, the bay, the island went black.

'No!' she yelped, but it was too late.

Very black. Total black.

The air was cold, damp, in her nostrils. Earthy somehow. Peaty.

She tried to talk, but found she had no mouth, no tongue. *Hello?* she instead used her powers to speak into the endless darkness. All there was was turgid blackness, solid, slick like leather. Niamh listened.

She wasn't alone in this void. She was aware enough to know that. There was something behind her, and overhead. Something breathing down her neck, not that she had a neck to breathe down. *Who's there?* She tried once more. It was big, whatever it was. Coolly smooth; eellike. There was something right next to her.

She wished it away, this thing looming over her.

And then she was in Annie Device's garden. Better. Much better.

Here, it smelled of garlic and mint and geranium. Here she was safe. Light, again. Eyes sore, hay fever spongy. Even witches get hay fever. The spring sky, cornflower blue, was powdered with cartoonish clouds, and starlings chirped, wise enough to keep off the ground in these cat-filled parts.

Theo, in her old body, hunched and elbowy, was playing with one of Annie's kittens next to the well. She ought to warn her about that well – it wasn't just a well. Next to her, on the bench, Annie patted Niamh's hand. 'You can't be here, sweet Niamh.'

'But I am,' Niamh said, confused.

'No,' the old woman said kindly. Her hands were soft as old silk. 'You aren't. Neither of us are, not really. This is merely the Afterglow.'

'What's the Afterglow?'

'Gaia is kind. This is her parting gift to her daughters. A memory to bathe in, just a while.'

When Niamh looked now, Theo was herself – in her female form. She levitated about a metre from the grass and was covered head to toe in gore and mud. Her eyes were wide and wild, black and equine. Darkest magic coursed through the girl. Niamh gasped. 'What's happening? Annie? What is this?'

'You're not done yet, sweetheart. You never were. It wasn't your time. And I'd know, remember.' The oracle tapped the side of her head with her index finger.

That sensation. Knowing you're in a dream. Not wanting it to end because the other side of sleep is less pleasant.

But this never happened. She remembered this day in Annie's garden, but this wasn't how that day had gone. And that was when Niamh understood.

She wasn't in Santorini *or* outside the watermill. She didn't know how or why or when, but she was dead. This was death.

She looked to her friend, whose blind eyes were fixed just past her. 'Annie, did you know? That all this would happen?'

'Leviathan will rise,' was all she said.

Niamh was once more surrounded by nothingness.

Endless, limitless, impenetrable black.

She realised what was so awful about this place: the total absence of life. From the moment she'd been born, Niamh had been immersed in the full richness of Gaia. Sea spray; lemon juice; dogs snoring. Mown grass; the shock of first frost; rainbows. And now she was gone. Void. Devoid.

That didn't mean she was alone in the abyss. She did not have eyes to see, or skin to feel, but she could *sense*.

The thing circled her once more, a shark swimming these black waters. *What are you?* she asked it.

The shadow said nought. It didn't need to. She knew.

And suddenly she felt again.

Away she went from this placeless place. Good, she didn't believe in hell, but . . .

Cold. Very cold. Damp. A toe. A thumb. Ears. It was *so* cold. Why was death so fucking cold? A throat: so dry, so thorny, it hurt.

Her body ached all over, tender somehow. Bruised, overripe. She was laid down. Even this stillness was sore on her back, her thighs, her rear. Her hips and spine creaked, cranky. She felt very, very tired. She wasn't quite awake yet, but aware of the day beyond sleep. Niamh knew she must now wake up, however little she wanted to. The alarm was pealing.

She found she could move her limbs. It hurt. Bones clicked and clacked. Her muscles were stiff. Only then Niamh found she couldn't move *far*. Only an inch or so either side of her shoulders and feet. She was stuck. No wonder the air felt so stale, so musty. There was something in front of her face. With frozen fingers, she pressed something wooden and wet, inches from her nose.

This was no duvet and she was not in bed.

She was in a box.

There is a word for a box they put people in.

Oh fuck.

Fucking hell, no.

She tried to call out, but there was dirt or dust, something gritty, in her mouth. She coughed and spluttered, spat it out as best she could. Her tongue was like dry suede.

Panic fluttered in her chest. She couldn't breathe. No, she could, but not well. Who would do this to her, shut her in . . .

Oh goddess.

She pushed harder on the sodden wood, tried to roll over. Her knees bumped against the same wooden surface. She tried to use her powers. She was weak. Her stomach and head felt hollow.

She felt the velveteen purple-black of Theo's aura. Theo was close. *Theo . . . Theo help me.*

She pushed and kicked, but each gesture was weighed down by saturated clothes.

Stop, she told herself. Panic was futile. Panic would only make this worse. She could do this. She could feel roots, plant life. Worms and millipedes and earwigs writhed close to her. She was underground. She was buried. *Be reasonable, be rational, Niamh.* In the olden days, witches had slept underground to commune with Gaia – it had been restorative, in fact.

And Niamh could use that.

She screwed her eyes shut and *breathed*, really breathed in as much radiance as she could. Down here, even in the darkness, the earth teemed with abundance she could use. She drank it in. This was Gaia.

Better. Soon, Niamh felt this body hum with power. *This* body because it didn't feel right. It felt like she was wearing it back to front, or with both arms in one sleeve. Something was amiss – besides the obvious fact she was six feet under. She lay still and focused on the hard packed soil overhead. It was matter, she could move it.

Move.

She pushed and pushed with her mind, splintering first the soggy wood panels and then driving earth and ballast skyward. She powered on with gritted teeth until she felt a lick of fresh, frosty, night air on her lips. Finally, she opened her eyes. She could *see*. Moonlight.

With a final thrust, Niamh shattered what remained of the wooden lid, splinters flying skywards. Her path clear, she floated this body out of the grave. Her *grave*. Fucking hell. *What the fuck did I miss?* Panicking, her ascent wasn't graceful, she lurched like a puppet on wonky strings.

Her bare feet landed on cool grass, ungainly, and she toppled forward. She was weak, but the ground felt real and solid, reassuring. She continued to harvest power from the soil. She needed these feet, these legs, to work again.

Niamh looked at her hands, her fingernails and arms. She was dirty, covered in thick grey grime. She was wearing a simple, white cotton dress, although that too was black with dirt, and sodden from rainwater.

She drew herself upright, spine complaining, and took an uncertain step. Every joint seemed to rub and grind, and Niamh pulled more radiance from the forest. She was in Bluebell Meadow, deep in Hardcastle Crags. She remembered nothing of how she got here. She had been here . . . when she fought Helena. She almost *killed* Helena, with bees. It was all to . . . to save Theo.

Theo. Where was she? She had sensed her close at hand.

On cue, Niamh saw the girl vanish into trees on the other side of the clearing. She tried to call her again, but her throat was too dry. She coughed, and limped forwards, trying to catch up to her.

Every step was laboured, requiring toddler-like focus. One foot placed deliberately in front of the other. Confused, exhausted, a little sob found its way out of her mouth. She needed help; she needed someone to explain.

Up ahead, she heard distant voices. Thank the fucking goddess. She just hoped they were friendly, whoever they were. She couldn't go much further. Lurching from tree to tree for support, she lumbered forwards. 'Help me,' she rasped.

She sobbed some more. If she gave up, if she folded, no one would find her for hours, days even. With what muddled sentience she had, she sensed familiar auras. Elle, Leonie . . . and someone else. 'Please . . .'

The forest around her thinned out into another clearing, sheathed in a lacquer of silver moonlight. Niamh drew some strength from an ancient elm and found the momentum to stagger forwards.

A familiar, uncannily familiar, voice spoke. 'Theo, what have you done?'

Ignoring the rough terrain underfoot, Niamh tumbled into the dell. She found herself face-to-face with . . . herself. This other Niamh wore her mauve woollen winter coat; her skinny jeans; her battered Converse. But the other Niamh's hair was shorter, and sported a wiry white streak through the front.

Behind Theo and the other Niamh was Leonie, Chinara and Elle. All stared her way, slack-jawed and dumbstruck.

'Help,' she whispered. 'Help me.'

'Niamh?' said her doppelganger. 'How?'

Niamh had enough left in her tank to recognise this other woman was her sister. She would know the iridescent aura anywhere. Ciara was here. How? She ought to be rotting in a hospital bed. Seeing her on her feet for the first time in almost a decade was like a firework going off in Niamh's mind. A lot of feelings, a lot of colours and bangs, but . . . good. Yes, it was good.

Her sister was alive. Her sister was here.

And then Niamh remembered something she'd thought a dream: her visit to the safehouse in Manchester; feeling the gemstone hidden in Ciara's comatose hand, and then . . .

And then Greece. Greece ever since. How long had she relived that treasured moment? What had Annie called it? The Afterglow.

It made a sad sort of sense. Her sister had . . . *done something* to her. And now here they were.

Niamh knew from experience what would happen next: her sister would flee. She would run and hide, anything to avoid admitting responsibility for whatever the fuck had happened here. And Niamh was in no state to stop her. She could only hope that

Leonie or Chinara got to her first. Now she was amongst friends, Niamh gave herself permission to let go. Her legs went to jelly. She could rest, they would take care of her.

But as she teetered forwards, Ciara did not run. She stepped *towards* her, not away. Niamh fell and Ciara reached for her. Niamh crumpled into her arms and Ciara lowered them both to the grassy floor.

'You're alive,' her sister breathed into her mud-caked hair. 'How?'

Niamh was too weak to answer. She heard Leonie demand answers of Theo, but it felt a million miles away. She clung to Ciara, resting her head on her shoulder.

She felt a warmth flowing through her. Ciara was healing her, channelling radiance through her skin and bones.

It was more than that though. Niamh felt her radiance being displaced at the same time, flowing into the other body. This was new. She felt almost liquid . . . human honey. It felt right though, natural.

Ciara held her tightly, crying gently against her hair, rocking her like a baby. She kissed her forehead as she wept. Niamh gripped her back.

The spell broke. The Kelly sisters went home.

When the rushing sensation subsided, Niamh opened her eyes. A frail, filthy woman who looked just like her lay in her arms. The pitiful thing in her lap blinked up at her, her lips crusty and split. 'What now?' she rasped.

PART I
NOW

LEVIATHAN WAKES

abashed, the devil stood,
And felt how awful goodness is, and saw
Virtue in her shape how lovely; saw and pined
His loss.

—MILTON, *Paradise Lost*

THE BEACH HOUSE

Snow - Cornwall, UK

Snow waited on the terrace. Far below, white spray fizzed against the cliffs. The sea was furious tonight, churning and swollen. A storm sailed towards Boscastle Bay, a dark broom of rain sweeping across the horizon. She'd know, she was the one who'd summoned it. Snow's brow furrowed as she focused, pulling the Atlantic front off-course and inland. She wanted the storm to make landfall.

She wanted to show her visitor what Snow Vance-Morrill was capable of.

She knew she wouldn't have to wait long. The visitor came at about the same time every night. A few lamps shone inside the beach house, and fairy lights swung in the wind overhead, entwined around the pergola.

Soon, the terrace door creaked open, and Helena joined her at the table next to the hot tub, her heels tapping efficiently across the stone tiles. Her mother kissed the crown of her head and smoothed down her white-blonde hair. 'Goodnight, my love. Sorry I'm late. You know how it is, got stuck at the office again.'

Snow looked into familiar, milk-chocolate eyes, but wasn't fooled for a second. 'I know you're not her,' Snow told her.

'So? Does it matter? I can be.'

'But you're not. It's not real.'

Her mother's mouth curled at the edges. 'Then why is it you wait out here for me every night?'

Snow couldn't quite put her reasons into words. It was better than the nothing she had?

Helena reached out for Snow's hands, making sure – the way she always used to – that she hadn't been biting her nails. 'Oh, Snow, give it a rest. Always whining. Your Dior tote isn't the real deal either, but you still take it to the beach.'

It was true. Whatever this thing was, it sounded like her mother, looked like her mother, even smelled like her mother – of Pomegranate Noir and hazelnut lattes. They'd bought that fake Dior together, on their final holiday to Tulum. How could she know that if she wasn't really Helena Vance?

'How was school today?'

'Like it matters?'

Helena sighed. 'I don't suppose it does, but I never settled for second best and nor should you.'

Snow was flunking. After they'd been forced to leave Hebden Bridge, she'd transferred to an all-girls school in Truro last September. Uniform aside, it was a carbon copy of her old school in Manchester, but she'd sleepwalked through the entirety of the first term. She had made no real friends; girls hated her because she was prettier than them, and she didn't care to enter into flirtations and hand jobs with spotty white mundane boys who thought they were drill artists because they owned a balaclava. Lessons washed over her, a diluted gruel of oxbow lakes, covalent bonds and iambic pentameters. It was very hard to care when she had a much greater purpose than passing her GCSEs.

She was a Level 5 elemental now. That was the only grade that mattered to her.

Each afternoon, as soon as the bell rang, she'd either train with Diana Bell, a witch from the local coven, or head out to sea and practice alone. Concealed by cloud cover, she'd pull vast, spiralling columns of water into the sky, steering and directing them. To much bafflement from locals and the weather forecasters, she'd light up the sky with pulsating sheets of lightning. She'd learned to absorb the bolts, harness them, and channel the current out through her hands.

The way her mother used to.

'I'm so, so proud,' Helena told her now. 'You know that, don't you?'

Snow closed her eyes tight, forcing back tears. She was so tired, it felt like there was cement in her head. 'But you're not really her,' she said again.

'Would you prefer I looked like this?' an Irish voice chirped.

Snow opened her eyes again, and now Niamh Kelly sat across the table from her. The woman who murdered her mum, all smiles, and red hair, and velvet hippy shit. Her hands curled into fists under the table. 'No, I wouldn't.'

The outside lights dimmed a moment, and her mother was back with her once more. 'I speak with her, you know. In the beyond.'

Snow sat up straighter. 'How? Can I see her?'

'You can't. But rest assured she wants nothing more in this world than for you to be the most powerful witch of your generation.'

Snow believed that, but grimaced. 'Theo is stronger,' she stated matter-of-factly. 'So is Leonie. And Chinara. And Niamh.'

Helena smirked and took a sip of her merlot. 'Well, then. What are we going to do about that?'

POSSIBILITY

Niamh - Hebden Bridge, UK

There's a scene in the film *New Moon* where a semi-catatonic Kristen Stewart sits in a bay window and watches the autumn roll into winter while Lykke Li sings mournfully. It was all Niamh could think of as her duvet ripened. It would be hysterically funny – if she were able to leave her bed.

Doctor, doctor, I think I'm a pair of curtains. Then pull yourself together.

Yet she could not. It was all white-grey sky beyond her damp November window. This mortal world was monochrome compared to her technicolour dreams on the other side.

She flexed her fingers, checking she still could. Never before had she noticed how people are fruit, rotting imperceptibly. Peach fur skin puckers, the flesh softens. The thought plagued her waking hours.

Instead, she filled her head with *Friends* on Netflix. Ten seasons, two hundred and thirty-six instalments. Sure, it was almost violently homophobic, but that's what nineties babies had been forced to navigate. Her laptop rested on the duvet, just inches from her face. Every few episodes, the concerned streaming platform checked in with her that she was still alive, and if she wanted to continue the binge. She honestly wasn't sure how to answer. Truly it was novocaine for her mind; the familiar scripts keeping her on the right side of hysteria. The quiet of night reminded her of that dreadful abyss; sleep was just that bit too similar to death. She daren't embrace it. She let the episodes play as she slept.

She had taken to her bed after the night in the woods, almost two weeks ago. Since then, she'd walked as far as the toilet, and washed her hair once, when the follicles hurt against her pillow. Niamh knew she ought to leave the cottage, there was nothing physically wrong with her, but the world was much too big. She felt its weight, its *realness*. All the clash and bang. Bin-lid cymbals. The soft-focus memories of the Afterglow were fading fast, but it hadn't been real, not like life was real. To be alive is to ache, digest, yawn, itch, belch. There had been none of these hard edges in her gentle Santorini dream, only the languid glow of love.

Is that what heaven is? A bubble bath of your finest memories? Niamh couldn't dwell on that either, because if she'd found heaven, and lost it . . . that didn't bear thinking about.

All she knew was there were monsters, real and otherwise, waiting outside her cottage. Safer to enjoy 'The One Where No One's Ready' for the four thousandth time.

She couldn't do it. Too much to contemplate beyond her bedroom door. She had died, and now she was back. Much too big.

One morning, the seventeenth since her absurd resurrection, Niamh awoke to something she hadn't smelled in a really long time.

Was that *bacon*? Had Theo started eating meat? It smelled really good. Maybe Niamh should throw the towel in and start eating meat too. Fuck morals, where had they got her? Murdered is where.

She was just curious enough to venture downstairs. Downstairs didn't seem so scary today.

Pushing off the now wretched duvet, Niamh swung her legs out of bed and rummaged in the thin, grey morning light for her Ugg boots. She found one, then the other, and checked her tit wasn't hanging out of her nightie before leaving her room. The air was fresher the second she opened her bedroom door. Yes, it was time to leave the bubble and the stench of cat-food breath. Already she felt faintly embarrassed for being holed up for so long. Something in her had shifted this morning.

Niamh padded down the narrow stairs, stooping so as not to hit her head. Theo had kept the cottage spotlessly tidy. Of course she was on her best behaviour, the little witch just raised the dead for fuck's sake. Her houseguest had been ferrying food to her bedroom three times a day, but had very much tiptoed around Niamh. Niamh was aware she hadn't been giving out very inviting vibes – on any level.

On these food runs, Theo had tentatively filled her in on what she'd missed in bite-sized vegan nuggets. Ciara had masqueraded as Niamh for almost three months, and what a busy three months they had been. Dabney Hale was dead. That was good, probably. Luke was missing and, twist, a witchfinder. That was less good, but paled into insignificance when you considered that Milo Pearson had actually been Lucifer in disguise the whole frigging time.

Niamh received these missives as if they were episodes of a TV series she'd skipped while on vacation. Numb, impassive. They didn't feel real. When would this strange anaesthesia wear off? This was *real*. Santorini was *not*.

Niamh hovered at the foot of the stairs, looking into the kitchen. Theo was indeed at a frying pan. 'Are you cooking *bacon*?'

Theo jumped, surprised to see her vertical no doubt. 'Fakon,' she said, regaining her wits. 'Vegan bacon.'

'But . . . it smells . . .'

'Exactly like the real thing,' Theo said with a shrug. 'Witchcraft, I guess. You want some?'

Suddenly Niamh was hungrier than she'd ever, ever been. A welcome surprise. That, at least, felt real. 'I absolutely do.'

Theo made the sandwiches with thick tiger bread and HP Sauce, alongside steaming mugs of tea. They ate in silence and

Niamh had wolfed down the butty before she could dwell on how she'd made it as far as the dining room table without having a meltdown. She also established that Tiger was fine, still at Mike's house just down the hill. Her former veterinary partner used to pamper the dog silly, and Niamh had no doubt he was enjoying the stay.

She became aware of Theo's inquisitive mood. Niamh's powers were fine, it seemed, she just hadn't cared to use them much. The girl was simply dying to ask. 'Go on then,' Niamh said.

'What?'

'Theo, you'll explode if you don't ask.'

Theo looked at her, properly, for the first time. After a second, she blurted out, 'Are you a zombie?'

Oh, OK. Not the one she'd anticipated, but fair enough. 'Do I look like a zombie?' Theo hesitated. Ouch. 'Darl, I get it, I need a shower. No, I am not a zombie. At least, I don't think so.' She didn't. As soon as she and Ciara had switched back in the forest, she'd felt no worse than she would with a mild case of flu. Her funk was mental, not physical. 'Is it my turn? How did you do it?'

Theo looked deeply, deeply ashamed. 'I honestly don't know,' she confessed. 'Something took over me when I read from the book. I wasn't in control. Milo . . . Lucifer . . . tricked me.'

Enchanted objects can contain demonic entities. It sounded a lot like Theo had invoked something to enhance her already phenomenal powers. Niamh washed down the last of her crusts with a glug of tea. 'You shouldn't have done it.'

Theo frowned. 'I don't regret it.'

Niamh fixed her in a stern stare. *Annoyance* was new, and also welcome. 'Well maybe you should, Theo. I taught you better than that. The natural law . . .'

'But now you're back,' she protested. 'What Ciara did was wrong—'

Even hearing her sister's name was enough to make her slap the table with her palm. 'Please don't make me invoke *two wrongs don't make a right*, because I will.' Theo was being childish, but then, she was a child. 'Life isn't fair. Not everyone gets a happy ending. I died, Theo, and that was Gaia's plan for me.'

'What if it was Gaia's plan for me to bring you back?'

Niamh stiffened. They both knew that it wasn't *Gaia's* plan. If her hunch was right, they'd played right into the hands of someone much worse. Niamh couldn't even begin to understand why Lucifer was so fucking keen to have *her* of all people back in the land of the living. It made no sense whatsoever. If anything, Ciara had done him a favour by removing a powerful adept from the world.

'Am I going to be in trouble?' Theo asked, her voice almost comically girlish.

'Yes. I should think so.' Niamh wouldn't lie, but nor would she feign anger. She reached over the table and took her hand. 'But you know what? It is what it is.'

Theo blinked. 'It is what it is?'

'Yep. *Love Island* philosophy.' Niamh shrugged. 'I am here now, and what's done is done.' Really, it did boil down to that. All those days in bed, she'd tried to figure out how she felt about her death, and her return, but what she felt about it was almost irrelevant. She was back, like it or not. She was close to boring herself, wrestling with it. 'I've got your back, Theo. Come what may.'

Theo covered her face and started to cry. 'I'm so sorry.'

Niamh pushed her chair out and circled the table to hold her. 'I know.' Niamh really did feel it. The bubbling conflict of being a teenage girl. Theo's aura was dusky-rose pink – gratitude and love – mixed with swamp-green regret and guilt. It was a hideous combination. 'I'm sorry too. Shutting myself away was a bit dramatic. It was very Kristen Stewart—'

'In *Twilight*?'

'Very that. I just needed some time upstairs, to . . . adjust. I am back. I'm here. I am not a zombie.'

'But are you glad I did it?'

Fuck. Again, she would not lie. 'I don't know. Depends what happens next.'

Theo seemed to accept this answer.

'Tell you what, let me shower and then how about we go for a walk into the Crags? It's a nice enough day.'

Theo agreed to this plan, apparently delighted to have her friend back. No doubt she felt somewhat off the hook too. The girl needed Niamh to forgive her, and so she would. Niamh remembered how much reassurance she'd relied on at that age. The *am I getting this right* of being fifteen. She remembered once thinking she'd said something that could be construed as a bit racist to Leonie in 2001, and it haunted her even now.

Niamh went to the bathroom and peeled off her nightie. She looked herself over in the mirror above the sink as she brushed her furry teeth. The new white streak in her otherwise ginger hair wasn't awful, but it would take a lot of getting used to. It was white, pure white, like a skunk's markings. Her sister had also cut a lot of her hair off while she'd possessed her body. Niamh could funnel some background radiance into making it grow back faster, but that was wasteful of nature.

Niamh reached for the shower control and pulled it on. She wanted a hot, hot shower to blast the grot off her body and out of her skull. She stepped into the water and let it blast her full-frontal in the face.

Better. It was time to wake up again. Theo needed her, hiding wasn't an option. She'd allowed herself a few weeks, but she also knew that sometimes the ubiquitous 'self-care' can all too easily turn into hermitage. It had happened before, after all. That was how all this had started; Niamh Kelly, in cosy, self-made isolation, hiding or unwilling to treat her festering wounds. She'd come too far to give in. Elle needed her. And Leonie.

And Ciara.

The skin on Niamh's neck prickled.

She opened her eyes and wiped the water out of them. 'Hello?'

The oddest sensation. As if someone were in the bathroom with her, right on the other side of the flimsy shower curtain.

'Theo?'

There was no response. But Niamh felt it. There was something in the room with her, sharing her air.

She had to see it. Whatever it was, she needed to see. She teased the edge of the shower curtain with her fingers. Steam swirled around her legs. Holding her breath, she tugged the curtain aside and stuck her head through the gap.

The bathroom was empty. Distantly, she heard Theo clattering around downstairs. No one was there.

She wasn't alone though. She felt *watched*.

KITCHEN SINK DRAMA

Leonie - London, UK

The worst thing in Leonie's life was the lack of space for a dishwasher in their flat. That *might* have been a *slight* exaggeration given the septic abscess of the society she lived in, but a dishwasher would have taken the edge off. When they'd bought this place, back in 2015, they'd told themselves that they'd remodel the admittedly poky kitchen to allow for one. Of course, that had never happened. She had founded and launched a coven, but she still hadn't fixed their kitchen.

As a result, and because Chinara did, like, ninety per cent of the cooking, the washing up fell to Leonie. She *loathed* it. The mere thought of food scraps touching her hand was enough to make her queasy. If nothing else, it gave her time to listen to Capital Xtra on Alexa. While she still mourned the loss of Choice FM, the early evening host, Khadija, was part of the Black Mass community and her taste in music was *chef's kiss*.

Chinara strode into the kitchen barefoot, carrying a dirty mug. 'I wish you'd do a sweep before you start,' she said, placing the cup next to the sink for Leonie to wash.

'I'm in charge of washing, not sweeping.'

Chinara slid her arms around her waist and rested her head on her shoulder. 'Just having a small hug.'

'Have a big one if you want.'

Leonie felt Chinara press her body closer, felt her breathe

through her hair, her lips nuzzling the exposed strip of skin along Leonie's shoulder.

'What you doing back there?'

Chinara did not reply. After ten years, this was how to keep things sexy. Know when it's time for jokes and when it's time for solemn, serious fucking. Respect the sex. Treat it as something holy and magical, because isn't it? The body making pleasure within. To orgasm is to experience something transcendental.

Leonie felt Chinara's fingers slide under her waistband and into her knickers. Expertly, Chinara circled the area, but didn't rush in. The thrill was all in the anticipation. In making her want it. Instead, Chinara's lips moved up to her earlobe, which was cheating. The whole body can be an erogenous zone, but Leonie's ears and nipples were her Achilles heel. And now she was powerless.

Wet, in any case. *Now* she was ready. Chinara's fingertips moved in for the kill, and Leonie was hungry for them. Even knowing what was coming, her body reacted with surprise, and Leonie almost jack-knifed into the soap suds towering out of the sink. She gasped loudly, a shocked *oh!* as a wave of pleasure spread from her middle.

Chinara's hand wasn't a mundane hand. She'd been the first elemental Leonie had ever fucked, and the way she deployed her gift had been mind-blowing the first time she'd sent an imperceptible charge through her clitoris. Just enough to stimulate her.

Soon, her whole body felt electric, and Leonie was lost to the physical. With Chinara pressing herself against her back, Leonie prepared to come. She built up and let herself go. Fuck what the downstairs neighbours thought.

She came back down to earth and Chinara withdrew her hand from her pants. Present again, Leonie twisted round and kissed Chinara and the lips. 'What was that for?'

'Services to dishwashing.'

Leonie smiled and reached for the clasp on Chinara's work

trousers. But Chinara gently took hold of her wrist. 'I got my period today, it's OK.'

Leonie wouldn't have cared, but Chinara didn't like it. Her girlfriend gave her another kiss and returned, somewhat smug, to her paperwork in the lounge.

Leonie, however, frowned and felt a new and unfamiliar panic as she ran a calendar in her mind.

THE WEIGHTED BLANKET

Elle - Hebden Bridge, UK

For the most part, Elle was *coping*. What did that even mean? To cope; to be able to manage the bullshit the world is throwing at you without lying down in a foetal ball on the floor, even though that's precisely what she had *wanted* to do every day. Most days, she didn't give in, but today was different. She would not cope today.

She could hear Holly pottering around downstairs, but she couldn't get out of bed. She knew it was psychosomatic, but Elle simply couldn't bring herself to lift the duvet.

It was winter, and still dark long after seven. She could hear a callous rain tapping against the window. A day, if ever there was one, to give up. But mums cannot give up. If Mum gives up, who feeds the kids? Washes and dresses them? Elle had had two reasons to get up every day for almost seventeen years.

Although, it turned out, she hadn't.

It was like a scream inside, a banshee. The last time she'd felt this fury, she'd almost killed her husband. Perhaps it was best if she stayed here forever. If something happened to Holly, she'd never forgive herself.

The problem was that the spell hadn't *entirely* lifted Lucifer's lie. Elle kept forgetting what she'd forgotten. As her head loaded up each morning, she did what she always did: she ran through all the things she had to micromanage that day; the packed lunches, the afterschool clubs; what needed to be in the washing machine today to be dry for tomorrow. Each morning, she factored Milo into those plans; was it a football day? Had he done his homework? Was it parents' evening?

But Milo had died over sixteen years ago. On the Tuesday of the thirty-eighth week of her first pregnancy, she couldn't feel her baby anymore. As a witch, she'd known, she'd *known* the second his heart stopped beating. As a healer, it was the most sickening irony she'd ever experienced. Had she been aware of the umbilical cord wrapped around her son's neck, she could have probably fixed it. But she hadn't been aware, and so she hadn't acted. She'd been induced, and delivered his tiny, bruised dead body. She'd produced milk that no infant ever drank.

It was the worst pain of her life.

And it had all been erased.

In its place was the illusion of a teenage son. Fantasy and reality kept colliding, but by looking meticulously through photo albums, it was clear the cuckoo had arrived in their nest last spring. Just before Theo had. Until then, it had just been her, Jez and Hols.

Now it was just her and Hols.

When the coven had fixed Jez after her little . . . mishap, they'd done it very effectively. Lucifer's spell had been wiped from his head and he'd remembered history correctly. He'd remembered the miscarriage. It had been as if Jez was a pin to prick her lovely bubble. Her grandma always used to say the truth was more powerful than any lie, and slowly, horribly, the grim memories had trickled back to her. The cat was out of the bag.

For Jez, it had been like living it again. He hadn't been able to cope. No wonder he'd gone.

About a month ago, she had entered the bedroom to find him shoving Calvin Kleins and socks into an overnight bag. *I need some time away love, to get my head straight.*

Elle had known then it was over. He was trying to soften the blow. No one ever means 'a break', they mean a break-up with a returns policy.

As far as Elle knew, he was renting in that newbuild block of flats in Hebden town centre. She didn't know if *Jessica* was with him or not, she didn't want to think about it. As she'd always feared, it was finally all too much for him. As the fake memories of a live-and-kicking Milo tried to re-enter his mind, he'd given up. It was the final straw. Living with two witches was one thing, a demonic entity masquerading as his dead son was another.

Elle almost laughed. Almost. She reached for the bedside table for her packet of choc chip cookies. The empty packet fluttered to the carpet with nothing to anchor it. God, had she really eaten all five of the big, soft American-style biscuits already? She briefly wondered if this was how crackheads felt. There was a weird triumph in this little rebellion, of eating a real cookie instead of a cardboard Go Ahead low-cal excuse. All these things she had denied herself.

Maybe she'd get really, really big. She'd have a hot treacle sponge and custard after every meal like it was school dinners. She'd have chips instead of salad. The yummy mummies at yoga would mutter *Gosh, didn't she let herself go*, and then she'd eat them too and get even bigger.

There was a gentle tap on her bedroom door. 'Mum?'

'I'm fine,' Elle called back. She didn't want Holly to see her like this, tearstained and surrounded by cookie crumbs.

Undeterred, Holly entered the stuffy room. 'Are you ill?'

'No,' Elle said. 'Yes. I don't know.'

'Is it depression?' Holly asked in the same way you ask about a burst appendix. If only; you could remove an appendix.

'No!' Elle blurted out. Depression felt very final, and she simply wouldn't name this feeling in case that made it real. That said, could Elle imagine feeling happy ever again? Nope.

Her daughter hovered next to the bed. Elle stared at the ceiling. 'We need to go soon,' said Holly. 'I made you some tea.' She held out a steaming mug.

Tea could cure almost everything – but not this. The thought of getting to Manchester and putting on a brave face was simply too much. 'Just put it down somewhere.'

Holly made a space on the bedside table and put the cup next to a blister packet of sleeping pills. Zopiclone. Elle was tired all day and then she climbed into bed and found herself wide awake, her mind almost vibrating with questions, with what ifs. 'Mum, come on, we'll be late.'

'I'm not going,' she confessed.

'But what about Auntie Niamh? It's her big day.'

'She'll be fine.' To tell the truth, Elle found Niamh uncomfortable to be around. It was ghoulish, unnatural. However normal she looked, she *felt* very different. And, in a way, this was all her fault. All their fault. Ciara, Niamh, Theo.

'She needs us, Mum.'

'I can't,' Elle said, and it really did feel like the truth. She could just about manage Holly and the house and her shifts at work, but being a witch on top of that felt too much.

Holly suddenly swept in and yanked the weighted blanket clean off the bed. 'Move.'

'Holly!' Elle quickly pulled her nightie down.

'I mean it. Don't you think this is what Lucifer wanted? It was meant to destroy you. Don't let it. Get up. Prove him wrong.'

Elle sat up. Even in the gloom, she saw her reflection in the mirror and it wasn't pretty. She looked old; more and more like her own mother with every passing day. 'Why would Lucifer possibly want to fight me? I'm a nobody.'

'No you're not. You turned Dad to stone. You were someone enough to create a fake brother for me. Don't you wanna know why?'

'Not especially.'

Holly drew herself tall. She must get this defiance from her great-grandma, because it certainly wasn't from her mother. 'Look, I could probably put you out cold, you know?'

'Don't you dare talk to me like that.' Elle now stood. Yes, Holly was taller than her now, but she'd still get a clip round the ear if she wasn't careful.

'You can either go to the memorial looking like a shitty old nappy . . .' Holly waved a hand over her crumpled demeanour. 'Or with a pencil skirt and a winged eye. Which is it? Look, I'll go without you otherwise and . . . I'll get my nose pierced while I'm there. And buy drugs. And become a sex worker. Actually I won't, I'll just give it away for—'

'Oh for crying out loud, OK!' She sighed. Maybe Elle *had* needed that stark reminder. She was still a mum, and there was always mumming to be done.

WOMEN'S MONTHLY

Leonie - London, UK

By some minor miracle, Leonie had managed to get a GP appointment within the week. She sat in the waiting room, leafing through a tattered copy of *Elle*, and thought of their Elle. She hoped she would attend the memorial that afternoon. It was Niamh's first big event, and they'd all agreed to go along in support. But though she was three hundred miles from Hebden Bridge, Leonie was still able to hear Elle's anguish. It was a howl, a sad, sickly wail. And Leonie didn't know how to help.

The waiting room of the Camberwell Medical Group was packed and moist. Too many damp bodies with wet umbrellas. Babies wriggled and screamed in prams or their parent's arms. The man next to her coughed a phlegm-filled cough, and Leonie shied away from him. It was giving sauna of sickness, and she wasn't here for it.

She wanted to cry; she really did.

Obviously a lot had been said over the last decade about 'unprecedented times'. Leonie had, all her life, longed for society to change, BUT NOT LIKE THIS. It made her almost nostalgic for the days of Helena's HMRC, the Before Times. Life felt increasingly like a *raft* she was clinging on to. Nothing felt solid. Leonie couldn't ignore what was happening in the north anymore, not when it affected her friends so closely.

She checked her phone: 9:15. She was keen to get going. After this check-up, HMRC was going to teleport her directly to Manchester, where she'd reunite with Chinara.

There was a strange swooping sensation in her head every time she remembered Niamh was back. A month had passed since that night in Hardcastle Crags, but she was still struggling to adjust. She hadn't even properly processed the notion of her being dead in the first place when Theo had . . .

And that was when her stomach cramped every time. What Theo did was *not* OK. But who cared!? Niamh was back! Yay! But no, forbidden necromancy was very, very bad. What a fucking rollercoaster. Leonie felt tipsy on it.

'Leonie Jackman?' Dr Hamidi poked her head out of her consultation room.

Leonie gathered her things and tossed *Elle* back on the pile. As soon as the office door was shut, Dr Hamidi – Samiya – relaxed a little. The doctor was an occasional visitor to Black Mass and one of Leonie's most reliable donors at Diaspora. 'Take a seat, Leonie, what can I do for you?'

Samiya was one of those heroic healers, hiding in plain sight within the NHS. As long as she didn't pull any miracle-level shit, she'd get away with it. Leonie liked Samiya a lot, she'd taught her so, so much. For many Muslims, witchcraft was strictly haram, but Samiya, and others like her, were finding a way to reconcile what they were – witches, queer people – with the god they felt in their hearts. Samiya had told her once that she used her gifts for good, for the community, and she saw that as doing Allah's will. She was made this way for a purpose.

'What seems to be the problem?' the doctor asked her once she was seated.

Leonie sighed. Who enjoys this sort of chat? She had few boundaries in the first place, but still. 'I haven't had a period in . . . well, not since like October. I think.'

'Is that normal?'

'Nope. Usually, I'm like clockwork. Although I didn't notice . . . with everything that's been going on.'

'OK, hop up onto the bed for me.' Leonie did as she was told, swinging her feet off the floor. 'Are you on the pill?'

Leonie half-laughed. 'No.' Unless semen had gone airborne, she felt safe.

'Worth asking.' Samiya asked if she could lift up her top – a vintage Chicago Bulls jersey – and Leonie gave her consent. The doctor held out her hand and traced the air over her abdomen. She frowned a little and then repeated the process with *both* hands. They glowed with an inner amber as they scanned her body. 'Leonie, is there any chance you could be pregnant?'

This time, Leonie really laughed. 'No. Still very much a lesbian.'

The doctor reached for a doppler and passed it to her. Leonie looked at her as if she'd handed her a snake. 'Have a listen. I don't quite know how to tell you this, but – you're pregnant, Leonie. There is a heartbeat within you.'

IN MEMORIAM

Niamh - Manchester, UK

They were seconds from starting, when the doors opened onto the rear terrace at HMRC. At the podium, Niamh held her breath. Was it her? Holly Pearson entered the rose garden first, with Elle right behind her. Niamh instantly felt ten times better. That morning, Holly had told her it wasn't looking likely, but Elle was here, and now this all seemed a little more achievable.

As you'd expect, Elle looked immaculate, wearing a heavy wool coat, in houndstooth, and with her hair neatly tied back in a low bun. The world could well be ending, but Elle would put on her own brand of armour: a flawless winged eye and a Ruby Woo lip.

Niamh gave her a nod and Elle returned the gesture. *I love you, Elle Pearson.* Their love went unsaid, but it's nice to hear, always.

Niamh waited a moment to let them find a place in the rows of fold-out chairs. Only a handful of witches were gathered in the wintery garden of Her Majesty's Royal Coven. For one thing, it was too cold for the glittering frost on the domed oratorium roof to have thawed, but for another, there were worryingly few of them left. What an awful thing to be doing two weeks into her new job. A job she wasn't sure she wanted in the first place.

Theo, Leonie, Radley Jackman and Chinara were on the front row, next to Seren Williams from the Bethesda School of Dance. Next to her was Selina Fay, the Shadow Cabinet Liaison and next to *her* was the one Niamh was really worried about: Alyssa Grabowski, the High Priestess of Coven Intelligence America.

For her first formal engagement as High Priestess, this was A LOT, but Niamh felt she really didn't have a choice. There was no one else to do it, and they'd been very good with her phased return-to-work over the last couple of weeks.

Seren had been caretaker while she'd recovered, but Niamh *was* officially selected by the coven last summer. If she refused the call, there was no obvious candidate to replace her. Except Leonie, but Leonie would rather die. Those were her exact words.

There had been no pomp. No ceremony. After what had happened at the House of Hekate that would be in *very* poor taste. And now, for the first time since the bad old days of the war, Niamh wore the official Westwood cape of HMRC. It was heavy, pencil-grey wool, fastened diagonally over the chest. She'd always hated them: too authoritarian; too . . . cabin crew somehow. It just needed a matching beret to complete the look. As it was, she'd put her hair up and bothered to apply some make-up for the first time since her return. She wasn't ready for this, but she could fake it, and if she was able to fake it, she figured she was getting better.

She might have felt more prepared if she were able to sleep properly. Each night, she couldn't quite shake a lingering sensation that she wasn't alone. She'd taken to sleeping with a nightlight app on the phone, but the shadows in her room felt like a congregation. Every night this week, on the cusp of sleep, she'd awakened with a start, quite sure there was someone at the foot of her bed.

Even now, she knew she was alone on the little rostrum they'd erected for her, and yet . . . right in the corner of her periphery, there was *something*. She dared a glance over her shoulder. There was nothing there. There never was.

She hadn't told anyone of her unease, still hoping it would subside in time. People had enough questions about her current state – everyone was curious to know if she was a zombie, it seemed. While she'd avoided that fate, Niamh was starting to wonder if she'd sustained some other damage in transit. While she was reluctant to employ the term 'PTSD' because it had become overused to the brink of meaninglessness online, she couldn't help but wonder if it was apt. She'd come back from the dead – did she really think there wouldn't be any long-term side effects?

On the front row, Grabowski cleared her throat impatiently. Alyssa's face was impassive, although that could just be the Botox. Her face was taut, her hair styled in perfect blonde waves. She wore white, only white, always, and Niamh found that very odd. How did she not spill?

Focus. Crisp December air. Cashmere scarf. Her grandma's old red leather gloves, as supple as skin. Go-time. She just had to get through the next five minutes and then everyone could get inside for mulled wine and mince pies.

To Niamh's right was the new memorial. A sleek obelisk of black marble; chic yes, but how many people in HMRC had approved this design and failed to notice it looked like a stereotypical witch's hat? Mortifying. And it was engraved with far too many names. Shamefully, Niamh didn't recognise many of them, but a lot she did: Annie, Sheila, Moira, Irina.

Helena.

Niamh had insisted on her name being added at the last minute. She was a victim too, whatever anyone said. They'd all been played, like pathetic tiddlywinks in a game none of them knew was underway.

In total there were sixteen names on the slab. Most had fallen at the attack on the House of Hekate in October. All victims of the new War of Satanis. No one mentioned that only one side of the obelisk was engraved. The other three were nice and blank, ready for more names.

She sensed her audience becoming restless. No more delays. Niamh unfurled her creased notes. Helena would not have needed notes. She cleared her throat. 'What an awful first duty,' Niamh said, her voice wobbly. 'What a sad thing to have to do, but I think we have to. We can't pretend this isn't happening, and to do so would be fatal.' As Niamh said that she saw Leonie flinch. Her friend had been reluctant to join this fight until it had almost claimed her brother, but now she was here, fully. That was all that mattered.

'Even on such a bleak occasion, it's good to be here,' Niamh went on. 'Back in the land of the living.' She faked a wry laugh. It was supposed to be a harmless joke, but Alyssa sat up stiffer. She was not amused. Niamh felt her cheeks redden and hid behind her notes.

'For over a hundred years, we thought we were the top of the food chain. Women, elevated. Maybe we grew arrogant; maybe we got bogged down in power struggles and politics, I don't know. But I *do* know all witches, all women, have a common enemy. There are ancient forces moving against us, against the natural order. And they are winning.'

Elle couldn't look her way. There was a panicked mutter within the rows of witches.

'It's true. Some of our most powerful women are dead.' Niamh gestured at the totem. '*I* was dead, for fuck's sake.'

An even louder chatter. This time, Alyssa did flinch, perhaps at her choice language. Theo blushed a deep salmon-pink shade.

'We can't pretend that it's business as usual anymore. We cannot ignore the catastrophe coming over the hill. It would be easier, so much easier, to hope it'll all go away, or to spend our days arguing about what makes a perfect witch, but there isn't time to be perfect. Perfect is going to kill us. This is the reckoning. Look at the charter of 1869. Earlier! Look at the diaries from the Tudor days. The prophesies, the legends. We always knew Satanis would come for us.

'*This* is what Her Majesty's Royal Coven was started for.'

The vigil complete, the HMRC board reconvened in the conference room on the fourth floor. The room smelled of over-stewed coffee and Biscoff pity-biscuits. Theo sat stiffly at Niamh's side.

Drinking hot water with lemon was Alyssa Grabowski, at the opposite end of the table, her entourage fussing over her. The American High Priestess was an adept too, though unlike Niamh, she had mastery of sentience and sight. She spoke with a placeless accent, although Niamh knew that was only because her ear wasn't attuned to regional variances like she was here. 'It's such an honour to be invited to your coven, thank you sincerely for your hospitality.'

'Thank you for coming,' Niamh said, though she knew when she was being buttered up. The delegation hadn't been *invited*, strictly speaking.

Sandhya entered the boardroom and closed the door. She gave Niamh a curt nod. 'Everyone's verified.'

Alyssa stiffened. Just outside the room there was a team of sentients screening every attendee. Every witch, eighteen of them in total, had been assigned five secret sensory prompts to memorise. Niamh's had been the smell of cut grass; a unicorn; the feel of Velcro; the taste of wasabi and the sound of windchimes. After Ciara, after Milo, no one was taking any chances. Niamh felt these measures were futile. The lie that was Milo Pearson had been so cleverly woven into their lives, they'd have given him the sensory cues the same as any *real* person. Ciara was worse. Fact was, they *should* have been able to recognise it was Ciara at the driving seat and not Niamh. A thorough sentient *could* have done it. The coven had failed.

'Thank you, everyone, for bearing with us. Obviously, in light of recent events, we've stepped up security.'

Alyssa intervened. 'I'd like to, if we may, circle back to your intel.'

'Of course.' Niamh heard Leonie very clearly sigh internally and wondered if the other psychics in the room could too. It was Niamh who had wanted Leonie to come. As the High Priestess of the second largest coven in the UK, it felt appropriate. Her friend was distracted though, only half-focused on the meeting. She was slumped next to Radley, finally back at work after his ordeal in Russia.

Alyssa continued. 'While I applaud the energy of your words earlier, I wanted to drill down into the facts. Now more than ever, I think they have to trump feelings. Hyperbole is exciting and all, but we, as leaders, must retain core values.'

Niamh clung to the core value of not screaming in her face. What did her words even mean? It was difficult to fathom amidst all the corporate jargon. Once more, she thought to channel Helena's detached professionality. Fake it until you . . . feel alive again. 'I appreciate I'm still adjusting to . . . well, everything . . . but we have multiple accounts of what occurred at the House of Hekate, in Russia, on Aeaea, and in Hebden Bridge.' That was also why Niamh had asked Elle to attend this meeting. She was technically the key witness. 'I have no doubt that we're dealing with a demonic presence unlike anything else recorded. We've had a team scouring the oracle archives, and we think this is the attack they have foreseen for generations. Satanis is rising, attacking Gaia herself. We need every coven in the world to unite to—'

Alyssa held out a finger. 'See it's that sort of emotive language we need to be mindful of.'

'I think that's just facts, actually,' Leonie added.

Alyssa checked her dossier over. 'OK, let's explore the facts. Dabney Hale is dead. We can't verify his motivations. Helena Vance is dead; we can't ask her either. From what I can tell, two powerful witches – ex-lovers, no less – went rogue, and the matter is resolved.'

'My son wasn't human.' Elle finally spoke. Her normally animated face was emotionless and it chilled Niamh to see her this way. 'It wasn't even my son. My son died before he was born, but that *thing* was living in my home for months.' Her eyes glistened. 'I fed and clothed him. I shouted at him for leaving plates under his bed. His trainers stank. And none of it was real. Who could do that? *What* could do that?'

Alyssa nodded with a very studied portrayal of sympathy. 'The bedevilment you experienced was unprecedented.' There was that word again. It rather absolved everyone of responsibility Niamh felt. 'The question remains – was it an isolated occurrence?'

'It was Lucifer,' Theo announced, and Niamh swore the delegates around the table physically inched back. The poor girl was quite the pariah.

Alyssa, instead, smiled. 'If I had a dime for every person who claimed to be in league with Satanis, I'd be a very rich woman indeed.'

'But it was,' Theo insisted, and Niamh patted her hand.

Alyssa now glared at her insolence. She apparently wasn't used to being challenged, which raised misgivings for Niamh about her entire coven. Helena hadn't liked being challenged either, and look how that turned out. 'How much is verified by your oracles?'

Niamh turned to Emma Benwell, still serving as Head Oracle. The last few weeks had aged the poor girl, she looked exhausted. 'The reverie is in turmoil. Our covens agree on this. The timelines are at a nexus.'

'Go on,' Niamh told her.

Emma blanched a little. 'As you know, we see the past as a single stream, but the future diverges into many possible rivulets. But now it is as if . . . as if the threads are drawing to an end. The river isn't flowing towards an ocean of possibility. They are heading towards a moment very close to now.'

'And what is beyond this moment?' Alyssa prompted her.

'Nothing,' Emma said. 'Nothing at all.'

Niamh had goosebumps, but Alyssa only smirked. 'That's not what I'm hearing from our oracles on either coast. In fact, they have flagged concerns that the panic in the European covens is polluting the reverie. Doom-mongering. Project Fear. It's so important to keep an open mind to blue-sky thinking.'

What did that even mean? Was this about money? They *did* need money from the US coven, but more than that, they needed *witches*. Niamh leaned forward. 'Alyssa, we need you.' It pained her to say it, but it was true. 'What lies ahead is on a global scale. This won't be like Dabney's uprising. We're dealing with a threat who can go anywhere, can appear as anyone, dead or alive.'

'And yet he didn't,' Alyssa said, her veneer starting to fray. 'He appeared as a teenage boy in a rural town in England. Wouldn't Satan manifest in the Kremlin or the White House if he could?' Niamh internally silenced a cheap comment about Trump and urged Leonie to do the same. 'And that brings me to what I believe is the actionable point.'

'Which is?'

'We came to offer help. We have a wonderful facility in Arizona for teenage witches and warlocks.'

'A facility?' Niamh could scarcely keep the horror out of her voice.

'It's one-of-a-kind wilderness retreat—'

'I'll stop you right there,' Niamh said, feeling a powerful crimson terror swell in the girl at her right. 'Theo's going nowhere.' The rising reds were quelled.

Alyssa slid a glossy brochure over the conference table. 'I'd ask you consider all your options. You don't deny Theo's transition is what started the current turmoil.'

'Which transition is that?' Leonie asked pointedly.

Alyssa sniffed. 'Into her witchhood, obviously.'

Niamh took over. 'Theo Wells is a minor, and was inducted into Her Majesty's Royal Coven. No one is suggesting she is in any way responsible for the actions of the adults around her.'

'They are,' Radley said suddenly. Every neck twisted to look his way. 'That actually *is* what a lot of people are saying. With respect, Niamh, you're not listening to everyone.'

'Rad, no,' Leonie said, looking faintly mortified on her brother's behalf.

'It's true,' Radley replied. 'People are talking. It's not what *I* think, but maybe . . . it's not something to dismiss so hastily.'

The temperature in the room seemed to drop, and Niamh realised Rad was only vocalising what a lot of witches in the room were thinking. She looked around the boardroom and no one was willing to look her in the eye. They were all very happy to scapegoat the fifteen-year-old for everything that had gone wrong in the last twelve months.

Niamh massaged her temples. 'I understand it would be easier for us all if shipping Theo off to Arizona made all this go away, but it won't.'

Selina Fay took a sip of her coffee and spoke. 'Miss Wells must appear before a disciplinary panel. It's in the constitution.'

Theo's panic fizzed up once more. Niamh spoke for her. 'Fine. But she is a minor. I will represent her in that matter.'

She felt Theo's gratitude, but Niamh fought to shield any doubts. Theo had performed an act of necromancy. Her fate was out of her hands now. She didn't want to offer false hope.

Alyssa seemed ever more satisfied. 'But you confirm there will be an official inquest?'

'Yes.'

The American smiled to expose her perfect terrace-house teeth, and it had all the warmth of a dead shark. 'Very well, to the next point of business. How is your sister, Dr Kelly?'

INCIARCERATED

Ciara - Manchester, UK

She was alone in the communal showers. The pitter-patter of water echoed off the tiles.

The fuss around transgender women in women's prisons was faintly amusing to Ciara Kelly, presently residing in the women's estate. There were zero trans women incarcerated at Grierlings, and it was a good job because the cisgender women here were scary as fuck. She rubbed some shampoo over her scalp. Her new Mia Farrow haircut wasn't by choice, it was to stop someone grabbing her hair if, or when, she got jumped in the shower block.

Ciara had never fucked with routine, but now it was all she had to monitor the passage of the days and weeks. This is why they call it 'doing time', she had established.

Alarms sounded at eight in the morning. Her cell was unlocked and, unless she was in confinement 'for her own safety', she was allowed to join the slumped procession to the canteen for breakfast. Every inmate wore a grey elasticated tracksuit and plimsols. Drawstrings and laces were a suicide risk.

Breakfast was porridge, toast, cereal or fruit. Coffee and tea were served at lukewarm tongue temperature so they couldn't be used as a weapon.

In daylight hours, prisoners had access to the women's garden, the library or the workshops where they could make inert magical items for mundane idiots, such as cauldrons, brooms and wands. They were shipped from Grierlings to tourist tat shops in witchy towns and villages like Pendle. There was a prayer room, and one could make appointments to speak to the prison therapist, a painfully dry woman called Paula who mistook colourful shoes for a personality.

In the evenings it was a garlic-heavy dinner, and then the TV and games room. Well, it was for everyone else, Ciara couldn't go there because everyone wanted to slit her throat. She'd pretty much snapped their spiritual leader's neck. She wasn't winning the Miss Grierlings pageant anytime soon.

What was it now? A month? More? It was, she told herself, by choice. She *could* have fled that night at Hardcastle Crags. Probably. Once she had been back in her rightful body, she'd been weak and feeble, her muscles atrophied from her bedbound years in the safehouse. Even so, with enough will, she could have gone into hiding – she'd done it enough times before. For reasons even she couldn't quite comprehend, she had submitted to her fate and HMRC had carted her here.

Every week, she hoped for a visit from her sister. Nothing as yet. She'd been so weak that night, barely conscious. Now there was much she needed to say, and it was long overdue.

How the fucking-shitting-sweaty-hairy bollocks was she meant to tell Niamh that Conrad was still alive, and living somewhere in South Wales. Do Moonpig do a card for that? Every time she thought of what she'd done, she almost hurled. She steadied herself by holding the water pipe.

There was no hot water in the shower block by mid-afternoon, but that meant it was usually deserted. She'd got used to tepid showers by now, and at least they woke her up. She hadn't slept soundly since she'd arrived, even if she was in solitary confinement. She didn't trust the wardens to not let someone into her cell.

The shower block was as disgusting as one would imagine; the very worst council-run swimming-pool changing room. Pubes and plasters in the drains. In fact, it was reminiscent of the old pool at St Augustus High School. The water in that pool had been *lime green*. She'd had a period every week for four years to dodge those PE lessons.

Like everything at Grierlings, it needed knocking down. The original prison block – now the women's estate – and the Pipes were built in 1874, not long after the foundation of HMRC. As part of their deal with the mundane government, they'd agreed to construct a prison strong enough to contain any witch or warlock who didn't play nice. The second residential block was specially added after Hale's rebellion to house his followers.

So, while Ciara was detained in the wing with all the high ceilings and cornicing, nothing worked properly. The drains were blocked. The eggy smell of rotting hair and soap never abated. The water pressure was an insipid dribble. Perhaps for the best, given how cold it was.

Ciara quickly rubbed caustic shower gel over her body before rinsing. She was scared to even close her eyes. Once they were shut, she was in the dark, no longer able to sense her surroundings telepathically, like a mundane. She loathed it. Worse by far than the imprisonment was the fact they'd stripped away her power. She *was* a mundane in all but name.

The irony that her neutering was achieved partly through the use of *White Sorbus* in their water supply wasn't lost on her. Karma is a bitch.

The Victorian pipework clanked as she shut off the pathetic trickle, and she wrapped a threadbare towel around her shivering body. She returned to the pegs where she'd left her robe and slippers and found they were gone. Oh, this game again. Schools and prisons are worryingly similar, she found. 'Very funny,' she said aloud. 'I'm totally fine with walking back to my cell in a towel so you can shove them up your arse.'

Ciara headed for the exit, but found the considerable bulk of Monika Barta blocking her path. Arms folded, face grim, like a bouncer outside a provincial nightclub.

'Why so salty?' A nasal American voice echoed off the mildewed tiles. Ciara turned back and found Cassidy Kane perched on one of the rickety benches. 'I only wanted to talk. You've been avoiding me for weeks.'

Ciara shrugged. 'Because you're annoying as fuck, Cass. At least before, I was off my face. Not sure I can handle you sober.'

Monika grasped Ciara by the shoulders and shoved her back into the changing area. The showerheads dripped loudly, but Ciara couldn't hear anyone beyond the bathroom. 'You might want to be nicer to me, Ciara. Like, right now, I got some friends to start a fight in the TV room to distract all the guards. I'm quite influential around here.'

'You're influential *everywhere* because you're rich as *fuck*. Your parents still sending you pocket money?'

Ciara saw a flicker of annoyance in Cassidy's mouth. She'd always been so easy to get a rise out of.

Cassidy Kane, like Ciara, had been a Dabney Hale groupie during the rebellion. From what she could remember from their time together at Millington Hall and, later, the Hotel Carnoustie, Kane was a Connecticut Kane. A very old, very wealthy witch family who'd gone over with the Mayflower and later made their fortune in shipping. Did Cassidy know she was a screaming cliché? The bored little rich girl, mad at Daddy for providing all the money, but none of the affection? Probably, but trust fund kids only rebel knowing there's a golden safety net ready to catch them when they fall; it's how they test their parents love.

'I haven't seen my parents in almost ten years,' Cassidy said.

'Whose fault's that?'

Now Cassidy rose and walk towards her. 'Yours, apparently.'

Ciara actually laughed. 'How'd you figure? I was flat on my back for the best part of a decade. We both made our choices, I reckon.'

Cassidy eyed her. 'Well, sweetheart, recent events have shed a different light on things, haven't they. Given how you snapped Dab's neck and all?'

Ciara tried to dart past Monika, but the great thug simply held out an arm and Ciara was shoved over. Her butt smacked painfully onto the wet floor, and she got back on her feet before they could kick her. Clutching the towel around her chest, she cowered away from Cassidy and her sidekick. 'You don't know shit, Cassidy. Dabney Hale was going to end the whole fuckin' world. You included.'

Cassidy and Monika shared a sly grin. 'We know, you stupid cunt.'

For the first time, Ciara was surprised. 'What?'

'He told us.' Cassidy raised a hand and Ciara was lifted off the tiles so fast, she felt her neck sprain. The next thing she knew, her back slammed against the ceiling. The invisible hand released her and she plummeted back to the ground. She would not scream. She landed awkwardly and scrambled back onto her knees. She wouldn't cry either, but it hurt. It really hurt. She was stark bollock naked, her thin towel now on the other side of the room, but nudity was the least of her worries. What they'd done was *impossible*. Grierlings was fortified with layer upon layer of anti-magic measures. They should be as impotent as she was.

Ciara dared to look up at them as they laughed. 'How?' she said through gritted teeth.

'Nothing is impossible,' Cass said, somehow reading her mind. 'Where there's a will, there's a way. How do you think half the inmates are junkies?'

Ciara rolled onto her rear and pushed herself against the wall. Both her knees bled. Her left wrist throbbed and she couldn't heal it. So how could they?

'Dabney shared with those who stayed loyal to him, Kiki.' Ciara looked deep into Cassidy's eyes and saw something richly golden swirl and shift in her blue-grey irises. Her voice changed, no longer sweet and candied. This was deeper, older. Ancient. 'We are everywhere, child.'

Cassidy rose off her feet and glided over to her position. Her fingers locked around Ciara's throat and lifted her off the ground once more. Ciara felt the back of her head make contact with the bathroom wall.

'Join us. We are legion.'

Ciara could scarcely breathe, let alone speak, but she managed to hiss, 'Get fucked.'

The demon wearing Cassidy's body snarled. 'You could have been a god.'

Ciara found herself oddly hysterical. 'Yeah, well, you could have brushed your teeth.'

The Cassidy inside Cassidy winced, and Ciara took the opportunity to headbutt her. Ciara's forehead made contact with Cassidy's nose and she felt a satisfying smush. The grip on her neck loosened and Ciara flopped to the tiles. Monika was about to deliver a kick to her ribs when the bathroom door was kicked open.

Light from the corridor flooded the dingy shower room. A male guard filled the doorway. 'What the fuck are you doing?' he barked. 'We're on fucking lockdown, get to your cells. Quickly!'

Ciara fought to get her breath back. She could tell the guard that Cassidy was possessed by some demonic force, but would he believe her? Probably not. Could the demon take control of him too? Probably.

As she filed out of the room, Cassidy threw her a final icicle glare. *Join us, child.* The sotto voice filled Ciara's head. *You wouldn't want to be against us.*

As the prison officer demanded she get dressed, Ciara leaned on the bench, shaken. Not for the first time, she craved a reality where Niamh had finished her off ten years ago at the Hotel Carnoustie. Knowing what she knew now, that would have been a mercy.

There was a fight coming, and Ciara couldn't do a thing about it. She didn't know when Satanis was going to come for her, but he was going to *punish* her for her betrayal. She didn't like to admit it, even to herself, but she was scared. This was going to hurt.

THE SIZZLING LOUNGE

Niamh – Manchester, UK

If she'd been worried it was going to be awkward, by the third glass of Sauvignon blanc, her fears were banished. This was FINE!

It wasn't, not remotely, but she planned to drink through it. She'd come back from the dead. If anyone dared deny her a wine or two, she'd destroy them.

She raised her glass and peered over the feast. The table was piled high with silver serving dishes and pillow-sized garlic naan breads hanging from skewers. After almost thirty years and nine billion curry nights, it went without saying that rice, naans and chapatis were for sharing. 'To us,' Niamh said. 'For getting through today.'

Everyone – Leonie and Chinara, Elle, and the girls, and Radley – toasted back. 'You smashed it,' Lee said over the din of the restaurant.

'High Priestess suits you,' Chinara added, toasting with a mango lassi.

Elle, always the lightweight, was already looking a bit glazed after a glass and a half of Pinot blush. 'I'm sorry I've been ignoring all your texts,' she said. 'And turning up at HMRC at the last minute was very drama queen, even for me.'

'Shut up, you daft cow. I should have checked in on you more,' said Niamh.

'No,' Elle said emphatically. 'I should have been there for *you*.' She took another mouthful of rosé. 'Not your fault my son was secretly Satan, was it?'

The table was silent for a dreadful second, before Niamh almost spat her wine over Leonie. They broke. Every paranoia, nightmare and anxiety boiled over and everyone creased – even Radley. Other diners looked their way. Laughter was so, so inappropriate, but that somehow made it ever funnier. 'And I'm sorry you had to grieve for me!' Niamh added, dabbing her tears with a napkin before mascara ran down her face. 'What a waste of time, honestly.'

'We mostly grieved *Ciara*, in fairness,' Leonie added. The most sober person at the table – Lee hadn't touched a drop of booze. Something about antibiotics. Niamh resisted reading her, respecting her privacy.

'Still,' Niamh said, picking through what was left of her aloo gobi for any bits of cauliflower she'd missed. The Sizzling Lounge, not far from Piccadilly station, was frenetic, the air thick with sitar, and the fatty, meaty smog from the signature hot plates. It was so busy there was no need for Lee or Niamh to shield their conversations. 'Then I had you all worrying I'd gone *Pet Sematary* on you. Sorry I shut myself in my bedroom for so long. I know you were all worried.' She took a breath. In truth, she still hadn't found the words to describe how she felt. 'I just . . . I just needed to get my head on right.'

'Not literally I hope,' Chinara said with a grin.

Niamh pretended to snap her head on straight.

'Same!' Elle shouted over the din and everyone loudly protested. 'I feel so daft! I just needed a night out with my girls! Honestly, I feel better than I have in . . . well, since . . .'

Holly looked at once both mortified to see her mother getting increasingly merry and relieved to see her out and about. Elle was right though. It wasn't just chapatis they were sharing. Niamh absorbed a little bit of radiance from each of her friends, feeling herself clarify on a cellular level. A witch needs her coven. She should have figured that one out sooner.

'I don't think any of us have anything to apologise for,' Radley said, seated on the other side of Chinara. 'How could we have known?'

'Um, the oracles?' Niamh added.

'Ciara killed one, Helena killed one,' Leonie said, sipping her Diet Coke. Niamh noted she'd hardly made a dent in her biriyani. This time, she gently tried to read her. Her mind was like charcoal; impenetrable.

'We were *fucked*,' said Elle, whispering the last word.

'The point is, what do we do now?' Chinara said. 'If the *special relationship* between our covens and the US is on the rocks, we're the resistance. We are it.'

'Then we really *are* fucked,' Leonie said. This thought had entered Niamh's mind also. HMRC was the oldest coven in the world, and one of the largest, but she didn't want to stand alone against Satanis.

'Why us?' Theo finally spoke. She'd barely said a word other than to order her curry.

It was a good question, and she didn't have to elaborate. Every single one of them must have thought it. 'Maybe we're cursed,' Holly said. 'You think?'

'It had crossed my mind,' Niamh said. 'Did one of us take an enchanted crystal out of a crypt or something? Can I kindly ask you to fucking put it back. No judgement, just put it the fuck back.'

There was more laughter and it was its own kind of magic. It was healing. She felt high on sisterhood. It was worth being back, if there were to be nights like this. Little worries, like tadpoles, kept trying to wriggle back into the forefront of her mind, but – for tonight – she kept them at bay. The drink was helping, at least temporarily.

Radley briefly checked his phone. 'Ah, Niamh, that's Nick. He's on the team I have searching for Luke Watts, or Ridge or whatever he was called.'

'Not now, Rad. No shop talk.' Leonie pointed at her brother. 'I'll confiscate your phone. Relax.'

Niamh, though, sighed. 'Any leads?'

'Not as yet.'

'Keep me posted.' Theo looked her way and offered a psychic wash of sympathy. Honestly, Niamh could have done without that slice of information on waking up. *Oh, by the way, the last guy you shagged a) shagged your sister in a manner of speaking and b) he's also a witchfinder!* Niamh downed what was left of her wine, doused the fury in her stomach.

There was no passage of time in the Afterglow. As soon as she'd come round in the woods, she'd wanted Luke there. She had wanted to seek refuge in his big arms, where everything felt safe. The thing she'd liked most about Luke was his rock-solid normality. He was her anchor.

But it had all been a lie. He'd lied and lied and lied. She wanted him found. She wanted to hear it from his lips. She remembered well enough the long, lazy summer before she'd visited Ciara in the safehouse. The nights she'd used his chest as a pillow, the slow, deep fucks on a Sunday afternoon while Theo was at dance class.

All that time, he'd somehow hidden that secret from her. It stung, and she was humiliated. She should have seen it. Girlish infatuation had dulled her sentience.

And still, she missed him. No, that wasn't true. She missed the *fantasy* of him. The Luke she thought she knew didn't exist.

He was a *fraud*.

A blaring horn snapped her out of this spiral. A car screeched by the restaurant's steamed-up windows, briefly illuminating the street outside. At first, Niamh thought nothing of the silhouette looking in through the window, and returned to the conversation.

But when she looked again, the figure was still there. She frowned and rested her wine glass. The outline was thin and tall; too tall, far taller than any human would be. It loomed over the table nearest the window: a couple enjoying a date, but they seemed entirely blind to the form only inches from them. Whatever it was, it didn't move, slender fingers pressed up against the frosted glass.

Niamh felt *that* feeling again. She felt it at night, and she'd felt it in the black hinterland between life and death. She reached out with her mind, and there was nothing but an unnamed fear; a sense that something absolutely awful was going to happen. Suddenly, she was nauseous, the wine turning in her tummy.

Not wanting to cause a scene, she stood smoothly. The form remained, unflinching. He – was it a he? – didn't move at all, and Niamh wondered if there was simply a structure outside casting an odd shadow up against the restaurant.

'Are you OK?' Theo asked quietly.

'Yes,' Niamh lied. Whatever this thing was, she didn't want Theo anywhere near it. She worked double-quick to shield her anxiety from her. 'I just need to make a quick call.'

Niamh collected her phone and her coat and headed for the curry-house exit.

She stepped outside into a bitterly cold night. A choppy wind yapped around the street. She pulled her hair out of her eyes in time to see a hunched shadow sweep across the wall of the alleyway aside the restaurant. Ready to fight, Niamh followed.

She turned into the passage. Steam swirled from the noisy extractor fans. Back here there were only dumpsters and bags of garbage. Niamh sensed well-fed rats, a fox. The fire-escape door to the kitchen had been propped open with a broken restaurant chair. She could hear the chefs shouting at each other inside; pans clattered. Nothing out of the ordinary.

And then she saw it. Against the wall stood her watcher. It was *real*. She felt vindicated for a second, and then only scared. Niamh was frozen, her feet refusing to move another inch down the alleyway.

It was hidden amongst the shadows, too thin to be human, head too large. Long fingers at the end of longer arms flexed. It was nude, skin like dull rubber. Streetlight gave its skin an oil-slick sheen. There was no discernible face, no mouth, no eyes, and yet it seemed to look right at her.

Her mouth fell open stupidly. Had this *thing* been in her cottage for all these weeks? Had it been in her room? In her bed? She staggered to the bins and managed to scrape back her hair before vomiting over the trash bags. Lumps of poorly chewed cauliflower and potato splattered over plastic. It burned her nostrils.

She drew herself upright before it could flee, tried to read it. But she couldn't, of course. Because it wasn't human.

What are you? She dared to ask. *You've been following me.*

It didn't respond. She wasn't even sure if her thought waves had penetrated its thick skin. The wretched thing backed into the wall and melted, absorbed into the graffiti-covered brickwork. Gone.

Niamh reached for the wall and puked again. Because she *knew*.

When she'd come back from that black place of despair, she hadn't come back alone. She'd brought a hitchhiker.

WHAT TO HEXPECT WHEN YOU'RE HEXPECTING

Leonie - London, UK

Chinara blinked expectantly, and Leonie realised it had happened again. She hadn't heard a word she'd said. 'Sorry, what?'

Her girlfriend frowned. 'For Gaia! What is wrong with you lately?'

Thank G she was an elemental and not a sentient, or she'd have known exactly what was wrong. 'It was noisy,' Leonie shot back. The turd-brown Bakerloo line was one of the oldest in London, and it did rattle and shriek as it trundled through the underground network towards Central. That said, Chinara was sitting directly opposite her and the carriage wasn't even that busy.

'I asked who it was you were meeting?'

'Some student witches from UCL.' Leonie didn't relish lying to Chinara, but the alternative made her want to puke. Sometimes literally. Turns out 'morning sickness' can strike at any time of day or night, without warning. Yesterday, the sugary smell of churros cooking outside the Southbank Centre had made her hurl into a bin. The sooner this was over with the better. This, meaning the nightmare she couldn't wake up from. Teeth falling out, unexpected examinations, and phantom babies – the triumvirate of fucked-up dreams, and one had just come true. According to

Dr Hamidi, she was somewhere around two months pregnant. If Leonie stared hard enough in the mirror, she thought she could see the beginnings of a bump in her abdomen. Or maybe she was just sticking out her tummy, it was hard to tell.

It was impossible. She was a gold-star lesbian, and she was pretty sure she'd remember having sex with a man. And, craziest part, that was the scariest thing about it. *If* she'd hooked up with a dude, she'd get it. *If* she'd been raped, she'd understand. But neither of those things had happened.

Which left only one thing: Dabney Hale. In October, she *had* been violated by a man, only not like *that*. Hale had used the Seal of Solomon to hex her entirely, turning her into his personal puppet. And now this. Too much of a coincidence to ignore.

If she was the host for Dabney Hale's mutant reincarnation baby, she didn't want Chinara to know. Chinara *really* wanted a baby. Always had. But Leonie couldn't have this one. She wouldn't.

She shuddered, even on the sweltering Tube train. This was some next-level *Omen* shit. What was inside her? Maybe Theo wasn't the Sullied Child after all.

Too late, she realised Chinara had said something else, and she'd missed it again. She apologised and she saw an all-too-familiar glimmer of exasperation in Chi's face. She was the grown-up; Lee was the fuck-up. She often questioned why a premier league woman like Chinara Okafor put up with her, and now here she was about to abort a baby when all Chinara wanted in life was to be a mother.

Leonie hoped no one ever realised exactly how selfish she really was.

Chinara disembarked at Embankment, but Leonie stayed on the Tube until Regent's Park. Again, given her sexuality, she'd had precious little need for contraceptives, the morning after pill, or abortions. In a world which reviles queer women, it was nice there was that bonus. This meant she was embarrassingly clueless about the whole process, however. Samiya had been helpful.

Because neither Leonie nor her GP could quite pin down *when* this impossible conception had taken place, the doctor had referred her to a specialist clinic near UCL for a surgical abortion. There were witches there, Samiya assured her. Their kind had always been on hand to help women in need.

Leonie now walked through the tourist-packed streets of Marylebone in search of the right address. This was the London Americans thought of as London. The brownstones and stoops were straight out of a Richard Curtis movie; red phone boxes and zebra crossings. Not *her* London at all. A number of the smart townhouses had plaques next to the front door suggesting they were clinics: dental, Botox . . . abortion.

Fifteen-minute procedure! Painless! In and out!

Leonie had been an abortion cheerleader her whole entire life. When Helena had gotten unexpectedly knocked up only a few months after meeting Stef Morrill, she'd been right there at her side, offering to go with her to a clinic if that's what she wanted to do. Even as a teenager, observing the fight for reproductive rights, Leonie had known how she felt. It was a no-brainer; it was the most obvious feminist cause there was: the right to make decisions about your own body.

That said, did she actually *want* to experience an abortion? No, of course not. What a fucking faff. Smear tests were awkward enough. Again, she told herself *if* this blob growing inside her had been the handiwork of some random man, she wouldn't have given two shits. Men spaff potential babies down the drain every time they wank, why would she give it any more thought than they do? What made this that much more troubling was she wasn't wholly sure what was growing inside her was . . . normal.

After the Milo revelation, all bets were off.

To make matters worse, it was starting to rain. Horrid, sleet-like pins blew into her face. Too windy for an umbrella, all she could do was pull her hood over her braids and cling to it to keep it up. 'For fuck's sake,' she muttered, shouldering the onslaught.

Leonie spotted the clinic on the other side of the road. A handsome townhouse next door to an artisanal bread and cake shop. Maybe she'd get a cronut once this was all over. Least she could do for herself. She'd been warned to bring a sanitary towel with her and that she'd be kept for a while afterwards. She'd be sore, but that should be on a par with PMS cramps, and she'd tolerated those since she was twelve.

If she'd worried about not being able to find the place, she needn't have. Even in the bitter weather, a clique of women stood just yards from the royal blue front door, armed with flyers and judgement. Leonie felt her resolve harden. How *dare* they. There were three of them, all women in their fifties or sixties, with an air of grandmotherly concern. Wolves in M&S clothing. What was it about having choice these women didn't enjoy?

Leonie felt a hand grasp her arm. She whirled round, ready to punch the protestor in the face. It took her a second to realise this wasn't a rogue pro-lifer.

It was *Senait*.

Lee's eyes widened. She was too stunned to speak. She'd spent a lot of time – and Diaspora money – trying to track this little bitch down. They do say you always find something when you stop looking. Leonie relived the head-spinning panic of *that* morning on Aeaea: waking up to a massacre and realising her sidekick had vanished without a word of explanation.

The biting wind tore around them and the sudden storm made sense now; Senait was causing it. *Why* she couldn't say.

Leonie shouted over the weather. 'OK, you better fucking start talking.'

In the squall, the younger woman was oddly calm. 'Don't go in there,' Senait said, corkscrew curls whipping across her face as she shook her head. She looked exactly as she had back on Aeaea, wearing the same outsized denim jacket and baggy combat pants.

Leonie glowered at her through the deluge. 'So, like, what? You sold us all out on that island to come be an anti-abortion protestor?'

She brushed off her jibes. 'Just don't go in there, OK? It's important.' Her tone softened. 'Look, promise me. Please?' Senait turned to leave, but Leonie seized hold of her frame with her mind.

'Oh don't you fucking dare,' Leonie said, lifting the girl a couple of inches off the floor. Luckily, with the rain, most people had darted off the street in search of shelter. She turned her round and carried her back down to earth. 'You owe me a massive fucking explanation. You owe every woman on Aeaea.'

Her eyes filled and her voice trembled. 'I know! Believe me, I know. But I can't. At least, not yet.' She meant it, Leonie could tell. The girl was terrified. Of who?

'Why? Why not?'

The wild weather abated a fraction. Senait looked genuinely repentant, but big doe eyes weren't going to get her off the hook. 'I can't explain. It's complicated. I will though, soon.'

Leonie pulled her close by the jacket and snarled in her face. 'People *died* on Aeaea, you know?' Leonie thought of proud, beautiful Zehra Darga, the archaeologist who'd unearthed the Seal of Solomon before being severed by one of Hale's dickhead foot soldiers. 'That was your fault. You led Hale right to them.'

'I know! I didn't want . . . I didn't have a *choice*, you have to believe me.' Leonie tried to read her, but her mind was as chaotic as the tumultuous sky above. Nothing about Senait had ever made sense. Her reverie was a strange collage, a scrapbook of scattered memories more than a timeline.

'Did you know what Hale was going to do?'

Senait was about to argue, but seemed to change her mind. She nodded.

'You left me there.'

'I had to,' she said. A tear ran down her face. 'That was the way it had to be.'

'I'm just gonna ask this one fucking time. Are you working with Lucifer?'

'No! Fuck no!' she said in her odd Yorkshire/Lancashire hybrid accent. 'But I was sent here today to tell you to stop. Again, no choice in the matter.'

'If not him, who are you working for?' Senait said nothing. 'I could fucking force you to tell me, you know?' She reached for her head, ready to wrench the truth out of her mind.

Senait pulled herself out of Leonie's grasp and almost squared up to her, puffing out her chest. 'Go on then. Torture me.'

Instead, Leonie scowled. Senait was an adept; part oracle. 'How did you even know I was going to be here? Did you dream this? Did you know about . . . did you know?' She couldn't bring herself to say *baby* or *pregnant*.

'Kinda.' She didn't sound sure. The rain fell as swooping drizzle now. Both women were soaked to the skin. 'Look. If you want to know what's going on, go see Madame Celestine.'

From bad to worse. How was a necromancer going to help? 'You know her? Did *she* send you?'

Senait pulled her wrist out of Leonie's grasp. 'Leonie, let go, please. I can't be here.' She looked very lost, and very sad. What else was new? From the very first time they'd met back at Domino's glorified strip club in Italy, Senait had been an orphaned little kitten. Question was, was it all a very skilled act. 'But I'll see you soon.' She backed away.

'Senait!' Leonie called after her. 'Hold on! Who the fuck are you?'

But Senait's particles were already scattering, like golden glitter in the wind. She teleported away, the doe eyes the last thing to vanish.

Leonie stood in the street alone. She looked over her shoulder and the clinic door. Belligerent, she strode towards the Centre. It'd take more than a cryptic visit from a known bullshitter to stop Leonie Jackman.

So why then did her hand stop just short of ringing the entry buzzer? 'Fuck,' she said, pressing her forehead against the now wet door. 'FUCK.'

THE WAR ROOM

Niamh - Manchester, UK

In an attempt to trick herself into believing that she was not living through the end times, Niamh peppered office days such as this with little treats. She'd started that day with an iced vanilla matcha latte – she found the colour pleasing more than she liked the grassy taste – and a cinnamon bun. The bust of her wool dress was still covered in sugar. She'd dressed smartly: a shift dress with opaque tights and sensible boots. Today she had to be a Grown-Up.

They had turned a glass-fronted conference room on the fourth floor into what she called her War Room. A place where 'her' people: the oracles, supernormal security, the warlocks, could bring any whiff of a clue. The walls were now a collage of strange newspaper clippings and internet printouts.

MYSTERY FLU CULLS SEABIRDS
COASTAL RESIDENTS COMPLAIN OF 'DEATHLY' ODOUR
HOPPING MAD! SUSSEX VILLAGE INFESTED WITH FROGS
EMERGENCY ZOO APPEAL FOR 'DEPRESSED' PRIMATES
PAKISTAN: DOCTORS BAFFLED BY SCREAMING CHILDREN
OAK TREE DEVASTATION 'UNEXPLAINED'
NO CLEAR CAUSE OF FOREST FIRES
RECORD CALIFORNIA RAINFALL IN NOVEMBER

It was all over the world. If you scratched just beneath the surface, the natural order was starting to unravel. And this was just the beginning.

Niamh paced the room. Still two hours until Theo's inquest began. She couldn't focus on anything except a strange orange-brown stain on the carpet under the desk. Had someone died in here?

Jen Yamato from Supernatural Security was seated at the table today. The cop who had done exactly what Helena had told her to do without question. Niamh couldn't decide if that was a good thing for her or not. Regardless, she was highly efficient at her job, so she stayed – for now. Next to Jen was Nick Bibby from the Cabal, Selina Fay from the Shadow Cabinet, and Emma Benwell, Head Oracle.

And beyond the glass, on the other side of the office, was a shadow that shouldn't be there. As worker bee witches buzzed about their coven duties, the shadowman waited.

Niamh turned resolutely away from it. 'Do we have *anything*?' she asked her team, exasperated.

'Nothing new from government,' Selina reported. 'The Prime Minister requests he be kept informed.' Niamh understood that equine Tory shiteater Guy Milner was facing a no-confidence vote within his own party. Coven matters were probably the furthest thing from his mind.

'Jen, please tell me we have something on Leviathan?'

She shook her head. 'We're calling in grimoires and scrolls and prophecies from every coven in the world. They're being checked into the archive as we speak.'

Emma spoke next. Niamh liked her. She had a calming influence on her coven-within-a-coven. Today she wore a loose silk shawl in a soothing jade over her bald scalp. 'Aeaea,' she said. 'In our dreams we see sand, and sea, and sky. A temple on a mountain. A lighthouse. The women, they await.'

'They survived?' Niamh understood from Leonie that Hale and his mercenaries had ransacked the Greek island to get to the Seal of Solomon.

'Some of them.'

'What's the relevance of Aeaea?'

'The library on Aeaea is rumoured to have the most complete volumes on the history of witchkind. Far pre-dating the covens,' Jen told her, taking a tiny puff on her watermelon Lost Mary. Niamh would overlook the vaping indoors for now. Everyone was stressed enough.

'Can we ... go there?' Niamh asked.

'We don't know how,' Emma said. 'Its location has remained a secret for millennia.'

'Great.' Niamh flopped into her seat at the head of the table and rewarded herself for not screaming with a pink Mr Kipling French Fancy. 'Nick? Anything from the Cabal?'

'We're still looking for Luke Ridge. He can help us identify any surviving members of the witchfinder cell.'

Niamh stiffened on hearing his name, but didn't want to be seen to express any emotion over him. She was very new to this High Priestess lark, but she knew enough to know women in leadership positions have to be twice as perfect as any male counterpart to even get by. 'Good,' she said brusquely. 'Keep me posted.'

She glanced through the glass into the thrumming office. The obsidian shadowman still lingered, unseen by anyone but her. 'Emma?' she began.

'Leviathan will rise.' The oracle's voice was one of many, ringing through the annals.

The three officials looked puzzled. 'Yes?'

'Rise from where?'

More bafflement. The oracle went on. 'We don't know. It could be a figure of speech or a reference to where our ancestors banished him.'

The only time Niamh had felt fear, *physical fear*, like this was the very first time Irina – RIP – had shown her the oracle's apocalyptic vision of a fallen Manchester. A great darkness looming over the devastation, concealed by ash and smog. Her first glimpse of Leviathan on earth.

She didn't want to look towards the shadowman again, lest she draw attention to herself, but she was starting to wonder. Why wasn't it doing anything? It just . . . waited.

She stood suddenly, startling the others. 'I'll be in the archive if anyone needs me.'

All hail Leviathan, demon king of fear! Render men infirm of intention with thy infernal screams.

Niamh set aside the tome, resting it with the countless others she'd spread out on the floor of the basement. She liked it down here. While the archive room was windowless and somewhat musty, it reminded her of the library reading rooms back at UCD. The study desks were dark oak and the bookcases had locked glass doors to protect the antique texts and antiquities they held. The room even smelled of old pages and ink.

She indulged a minute of nostalgia for those days in Dublin with Conrad. How had she ever qualified as a vet? Gods: the reading, the essays, the all-nighters, and how she'd partied too. When did she sleep back then? And yet she'd still somehow got a distinction. If she could do that, she could do this.

She picked another volume out of the leather shipping crate. She had dismissed the junior archivist checking the loans in, wanting to be alone in the cellar.

Half-alone. She couldn't *see* the shadow, but knew it lurked close by. The invisible umbilical cord only stretched so far. Niamh exhaled, trying to rid herself of a lingering nausea. She knew what she *ought* to do. She *ought* to tell Leonie and the coven. She *ought* to quarantine herself away. But she couldn't bring herself to tell anyone. It was as if the leech – yes, that was the right word for it – was the embodiment of everything shameful she thought of herself. The time she'd let her first boyfriend come in her face because she thought that was normal; the times in her life she'd stopped eating to be thinner; the rancid lecturer she'd flirted with to get a better placement, and the worst of them all: when she'd told her mother what Ciara was doing in the garden, knowing precisely what would happen.

To tell *anyone* about this parasite would be to strip off in public and spread her legs. She simply could not.

Perhaps what she needed was a necromancer. She knew of only one operating in the UK: Madame Celestine – Leonie's nemesis down in London. A visit was worth considering. If anyone knew what breed of ghoul was haunting her, it might be her.

Niamh rummaged in the crate for a copy of *The Song of Osiris*. She'd put every coven on alert, praying there was more than one copy. Alas, there wasn't one here. She did find a slim volume titled *The Living and the Dead: A Witch's Guide*.

The wall lights dotted between the glass-fronted bookcases flickered. Niamh hoped it was only old wiring. She examined the contents page. 'What Lies Beyond,' she read aloud.

Gaia's reality exists of earth, air, fire and water. All is matter. What awaits beyond the physical realm is the great mystery. No witch can say for certain what the state of death entails.

'Well, I fucking can,' Niamh said and threw the book aside.

There was a far easier way to get answers she wanted. The Demon King of Want. Maybe it was time to call on Lucifer. She laughed to herself. That was how he got you! Sneaky fucker. He waits until you want something so badly, you'll give him your soul in return.

There was a knock at the archive door. 'Come in.'

Sandhya Kaur entered. 'Niamh. They're ready for you.'

She took a deep breath. The shadowman, the leech, would have to wait. Now she had to fight for Theo's life.

AFTERSCHOOL SPECIAL

Theo - Hebden Bridge, UK

It was really hard to care about their GCSEs when the world was ending. Theo and Holly went through the motions at the after-school homework club. It was held in the library, and Elle would collect them at the end of her shift to drive them home. Theo held a copy of *The Highlands Grimoire* inside her Biology textbook while keeping one eye on her phone. Today, in her absence, HMRC would decide her fate over what she did in the woods.

In a lengthy written testimony, Theo had said how sorry she was for what she did, but it was lip service. She was sorry about the process, not the result. Thinking about the ritual did make her feel queasy, grubby almost, but she could not be sorry that Niamh was back.

The days in which Niamh had festered in her room had been very, *very* concerning, but worries about her coming back as Frankenstein's monster were all but dismissed. Theo had even heard her singing along to Girls Aloud on the radio that morning. Zombies don't do that.

Theo had done something that no witch on record had ever done; she'd brought someone back from the realm of the dead as good as new. Not bad for a rookie. She would have to learn to bury that pride deep because it seemed the witching community had a highly visceral reaction to the fifth discipline of their art. Hopefully her handwringing letter of penance would do the trick.

'Your thoughts are so noisy! Relax!' Holly said, very much phoning in her art homework. She sketched what seemed to be a half-woman, half-serpent creature, bare-breasted and rising out of a lake or something. Not her best. 'As if they're putting you in Grierlings. You're fifteen.'

Theo cast a glance at Miss Ramsey, the librarian, and shushed Holly. She could only shield them so much. 'They might.' The only way she might avoid it is on a technicality. Necromancy wasn't illegal because, according to Her Majesty's Royal Coven, it didn't exist. The coven had been denying its existence since 1869 to keep the mundane government off their backs. How could she be guilty of something that isn't real? By making it a crime, they would have to recognise it. That loophole could save her from anything too serious. That said, there *were* rules about misuse of supernormal powers; underage use of supernormal powers; the use of invocation or demoniac entities, and she was guilty of all three. She was definitely in trouble.

Her fate, once again, rested in Niamh's hands. 'Maybe I should just go to that place in America,' Theo said. All this drama wasn't fair on Niamh, and perhaps it would get her a million miles away. It did seem that people near her got hurt, whether she meant them harm or not: Luke, Annie, Sheila, all those kids back at her old school. All this shit had started going wrong the day she rolled into Hebden Bridge. She was the Bad Seed, the Unlucky Penny, the – let's go there – the Sullied Child.

'Don't you fucking dare,' Holly snapped. 'If you leave me here alone after everything that's happened, I'll kill you myself.'

Theo shushed her again. The library was in the old school chapel and voices really echoed up and around the vaulted ceiling. 'But then you'd be alone anyway?'

'Shut up. You aren't going to some conversion camp and that's that. As if things aren't bad enough.'

Theo checked her phone again for any updates. Nothing. 'Is it still weird at home?' In Theo's eyes, Holly was astounding. How she hadn't had a feral breakdown was beyond her. If anything, the last couple of months had *made* Holly. It was like watching her grow in fast-forward.

'What do you think? Although at least Mum's back at work. She's in her pretending nothing's wrong era. I don't know which is worse.' Holly added some shading to her snake-woman. 'It's so mental, Thee. I remember Milo being this pain in my butt for my entire life, so my whole life is wrong. He wasn't there. But he was. It's like there's two versions on top of each other. In one, Mum and Dad told me I'd once had a big brother who died. They loved him, and every year we celebrated his birthday. He has a grave in Todmorden. But then there's this whole other version where Milo was this annoying wanker with smelly feet and awful taste in music. They both feel, like, equally real. I can't tell them apart.'

Theo said nothing. Milo had done a very convincing job. She too had to keep reminding herself that nothing, not once single second of their time together had been what it seemed. She'd fallen for it, hook, line and sinker. What did that even mean come to think of it? If it was a fishing allegory, it worked. She'd been got.

'What about your dad?' Theo asked instead.

'Fuck him,' Holly said. 'He's worse. Not even like we can blame the devil for that one; he's just a shit husband.'

'And father,' Theo added.

Holly nodded. 'I can't believe he left Mum to deal with this on her own. I hope he has an anal prolapse and dies.'

She didn't think that, not really, and Theo didn't even need to use her powers to know that. Holly did care, and that was worse. Theo took Holly's hand over the table. Each fingernail was painted a different colour of the Pride Progress flag. 'OK, but what about *you*?'

'What about me?'

'Are you OK?'

Holly thought about this. 'Yes. I'm fine. Do you know why? I'm a mega powerful queer witch. I'm ready to kick some demon ass.' She paused. 'OK, that sounded less shit in my head.'

'You're also very pretty,' Theo added for good measure.

'Aw thanks, hun, you too, obvs.'

'I think you might be my hero,' Theo told her best friend.

Holly accepted it, albeit bashfully. She looked out from under long lashes. 'In the words of Kelly Clarkson, *What doesn't kill you makes you stronger.*'

'I'm not a hundred per cent sure she's the one who said it first.' Theo smiled.

'Have you found anything?' Holly asked, nodding at her extra-curricular reading.

Theo checked no one was looking their way and slid the grimoire towards Holly. 'There's a binding spell that sounds interesting.'

'Bind Lucifer?' Holly said sceptically.

To hear Holly say it aloud was faintly embarrassing. A circle of salt and a waft of a smudge stick wasn't going to help them this time. 'You're right,' she conceded.

Theo rested her head on folded arms, hoping inspiration might come. There had to be *something* she could do to help. Not for the first time, she imagined ending her own life. There was a strange comfort in these musings, an illusion of control over her own being. Sometimes, late at night, on the precipice of sleep, she'd mull on *how* she'd do it. On a good day, she envisaged weeping mourners at her funeral, how much they'd appreciate her heroic sacrifice. On bad days, she was left with the humbling notion that no one would much care, or worse, be grateful that she'd fixed a gnarly problem for the coven.

She sat upright as if she was on a tack. Spidey-senses tingling. The library was warm and she was with Bestie, but something wasn't right. An instinct as old as the earth told Theo to be alert. She was prey and a predator was close.

'What's wrong?' Holly asked.

At the other end of the library, away from the tidy bank of study desks, were the bookcases. They came up to about head height, but Theo had straightened just in time to see Milo Pearson glide between two rows. He threw her a loaded look over the top of the fiction aisle and cocked his head; he wanted her to follow him.

She blinked.

'Theo? What is it?'

'Nothing,' Theo said, masking her shock. If Holly wasn't able to see him, she wasn't about to tell her who was visiting. She wouldn't let harm come to Holly. 'Just gonna pop to the loo.'

Milo looked over his shoulder as, with swan-like calm, he walked from the main hall towards the Sixth Form Quiet Area in the next room. Theo understood she was being summoned. Finally. She hadn't seen him since the night in the forest, but she knew he'd be back for her. Clearly they had unfinished business. He'd *used* her. Her ego was beaten to a pulp, but he was the only one with any answers.

Theo followed, trying to match his cool.

She entered the adjoining corridor that led to the Sixth Form room. Milo was ahead of her, but now the hall stretched before her. As he prowled away, the narrow corridor seemed to grow longer and longer. 'Hey! Stop!' she called. Milo looked back over his shoulder and smiled. 'Asshole,' she muttered under her breath.

He was getting away. The further he went, the longer the passage extended, telescope-style. Theo broke into a run to catch him up. But as she did, the whole hallway rotated like some carnival funhouse. With a cry, Theo toppled onto the wall, falling to her hands and knees. She gripped a faded Stonewall poster for support and it tore. The tunnel continued to roll, and Theo flopped onto the ceiling, spiralling onto her back.

'Stop it!' she screamed. She clambered back to her feet and started to stagger down the ceiling. The corridor continued to spin, but she tried to keep upright. 'Milo!' No, she would not call him that name. Poor Milo Pearson never was. This thing was a fake. 'Lucifer! I know what you are!'

By way of a response, the school hall now tipped vertically, and Theo fell onto her bottom. The corridor was now a slide and gravity ran its course; Theo plunged down the chute. 'Holly!' she cried instinctively, but it was no use.

Down and down she went. Somehow it was looping, she slid past the entrance to the library, two, three, then four times. 'Stop!' she screamed again. 'Stop it!'

The end of the corridor was black in front of her, gaping like a mouth ready to swallow her whole. Theo covered her face with her arms and braced for a crash landing. She was ejected from the slide and into darkness. Her feet hit the ground and then her ass followed. Ow. A moment of shock, and then mostly nothing. She wasn't badly hurt from the fall, but she'd feel it tomorrow. If she got a tomorrow.

She opened her eyes, and saw she was in a different classroom in a different school. She knew this place all too well. It was Balgreen Park, her old school in Edinburgh. The 'special school' she'd been sent to when she was twelve, just as she was learning who, or what, she really was.

Whether this was real or not she couldn't say. Her former classroom was a burned-out shell. Now, the walls were blackened, and the air was acrid. Flecks of ash idled downwards like snowflakes. It certainly *smelled* real. Around her, the furniture, smaller than she remembered, was incinerated; the metal chair legs twisted, fused and melted.

'Quite a mess you made,' the thing that looked like Milo said. He was perched on the charred remains of the teacher's desk. 'A wonder no one died.'

Theo glowered at him through the murk. 'How are you doing this?'

Lucifer shrugged. 'I can do anything, I'm a god.'

'That's not true.' Theo fought to keep her voice steady and brave. 'Demons can't do shit in the real world. That's why you need witches to do your dirty work for you.'

He chuckled. 'And there's always someone more than willing. Like Ciara; like Helena. Like *you*.'

Theo wondered if her powers worked here. She tried to lift him off the desk. Nothing happened.

'Nice try,' he said. 'That won't work here.'

'Where am I?'

'A little snow globe of my own creation. Do you like it?'

'Am I asleep?'

'Daydreaming, maybe.' He gestured to his left and she saw herself sitting with Holly in the main library. As Holly did her homework, Theo rested her head on a pillow of her folded arms. Her eyes were open, vacant.

'Pussy,' Theo hissed. 'Come face me in *my* world, where I can kick your ass.'

Now he really laughed. 'Big words for such a little girl.'

Theo crossed her arms and moved closer to him. Could he hurt her here? She had no idea, but he'd brought her here for a reason, and he could have killed her like a hundred times and hadn't yet, which suggested he wanted something from her. Demons *need* witches. Even the biggest of them. 'Who are you? Really?'

A tilt of his head. 'You know who I am. You felt me all syrupy in your guts, didn't you?' He smiled. 'You *wanted* him. I saw your fantasies. The sweetest of all were the ones where he held your hand, or messaged you an X to wish you a good night. How charmingly PG.'

'Oh, fuck off.' She felt herself flush. She was such a basic bitch. Strip away her transition, her powers, and she was just another teenage girl who'd fallen for dimples. Fucking idiot. But then, the mirage of Milo Pearson had been a ballistic missile designed for her, a hormonal timebomb. Lucifer was the demon king of want, and he did it very well. 'It's your fault. You used me,' Theo said.

'Everyone wants something, Theo,' Lucifer said with a swipe of his hand. 'You wanted to be used.'

It was cruel. She had been an easy mark. A transgender girl, an orphan no less, simply starved of lasting love. He'd allowed her to *believe* that she could be loved, wanted, *claimed*, in the same manner as any other girl. And she'd fallen for it. Simp behaviour.

'Of course, now things have changed somewhat,' he went on.

'Your desires have shifted. If it was unconditional love you yearned for then, now it's *knowledge*. You're parched, my dear.'

Theo said nothing. She was suddenly very interested in the tip of her shoe.

'It's the big question, isn't it?' The voice changed. Now it was a female voice. Theo looked up and saw a young woman swinging her legs under the desk. She was slight, with jutting collarbones and olive skin. Her raven hair fell in lank curtains about her hollow cheeks. Her bare arms were covered in bruises, and her teeth were yellow. Theo recognised this woman from her nightmares. It was her birth mother. 'Just who the fuck is Theo Wells? Everyone's dying to find out!'

'Go away,' Theo said. She didn't want to see this woman.

She spoke with an odd, placeless accent. Not Scottish, but like she'd been living in Scotland for a while. 'Excuse me, I'm still your mum and you won't talk to me like that, young lady.'

'Stop it!' shouted Theo, plugging her ears with her thumbs.

Lucifer shifted back to his Milo form. 'Better? You prefer Thirst Trap Lucifer? I can be anything you *want*. That's pretty much my whole brand.'

'I'm going now,' Theo said, wondering if she could walk her way out of this strange oubliette.

'But don't you want to know? Who it is you are?'

She turned back to look at him. She sighed. 'Do any of us know that? Really? I'll take the long way round like everyone else has to. I'll go to therapy.'

Now he really laughed. 'You are so fun. I do like you, you know. You talk like they talk in TV shows. Everything you know, you know from Netflix.'

One question had plagued her since the night when she'd learned the truth. If he was as powerful as he said he was, he already knew. 'Are you my father?' she asked, her voice now pathetically small.

Milo/Lucifer shook his head. 'Nuh-uh. That's not how it works. You want, I want. Tit for tat.'

'A deal with the devil? Ground-breaking.'

He laughed some more. 'Theo, I can make you the most powerful witch there has ever been: greater than Circe, Morgana, Amina, Sheba, Rihanna. I can tell you how you came to be, and how every single second of your life has been a breadcrumb to this moment.'

'But . . . ?'

He smiled. 'Well, that's the deal.' He clasped his hands in a mockery of a prayer. 'I am going to need your body. And it does have to be you.'

'*Why?*' She had never sounded so exhausted her whole life. It was almost a beg.

Lucifer just smiled knowingly.

Theo wiped away a tear. 'You are never getting me. Ever.'

Without warning, Theo was hurled up against the ceiling. She felt her back crack into plaster. It hurt, for real. 'Don't try me, you little cunt,' Lucifer snarled at her from below.

'You don't scare me!' Theo lied, stuck to the ceiling.

'You *will* submit to us,' he barked. 'Or every last person you love will die.'

Theo screamed. 'Just kill me! Go on! Kill me because I'm never giving in ever again!'

He pushed her further into the ceiling, so much so the plaster cracked, dust raining down. And then he released her. She squealed as the classroom floor came rushing up at her and—

'Theo?' Holly asked, poking her with the tip of a biro. 'Are you asleep?'

Theo fell out of her library chair, clashing noisily with the side of the desk. Some Year 10 boys laughed at her and Miss Ramsay shushed them all again.

'What? No.'

Holly pursed her lips. 'Then what was I just saying?'

Theo was about to tell her everything but then stopped.

Holly peered at her. 'Theo? Are you OK?'

Theo swallowed and nodded, shielding her thoughts. She would not involve Holly. She believed every word Lucifer had just told her. What if Holly was the one he chose to suffer? Or Niamh? Or Elle? The problem was she had fallen in love with these people. She had more to lose than she had ever had before.

So maybe it was time to take herself far, far away.

QUE SERA SERA

Niamh - Hebden Bridge, UK

Niamh ran into Elle – almost literally, given how tight the car park area was – in the drop-off zone at St Augustus. The school was hardly recognisable since their time. 'The Pit', a secluded, tree-lined slope where the naughty boys and girls (Leonie) had gone to smoke at break was now a state-of-the-art sports hall for one thing. It was also so, so much smaller than she remembered. Once upon a time, they'd called this 'Big School'. Now it seemed like a neglected, dusty dollhouse they'd briefly played with.

She perched on the bonnet of Elle's Fiat as they waited for the girls. It was a cold evening, crisp and clear, as the sun set. Niamh's favourite sort of winter day. She could only just see over the top of her chunky knit scarf.

'How did it go today?' Elle asked, still in her nurse's uniform. It was great to see her back in the world once more.

Niamh had come to the school directly from the committee hearing at HMRC. Three and a half hours; excruciating. 'I'd better speak with Theo first.' Elle nodded, and Niamh changed the subject. 'What about you? You're looking better, Elle.'

'Ninety per cent bronzer, but thanks.'

Niamh took her hand. The pair exchanged healing energy, just a drop, but it felt nice. 'You're amazing.'

'Niamh, I think I'm a single mum. Gods, I'm a statistic. I'm thirty-eight and single. This was not in the plan.'

'There was a plan?' Niamh asked wryly.

Elle smiled ruefully. 'I can still hear my gran in my head: *Only Gaia sees it all, Elle.* She was right. I was an idiot.'

'No you weren't. The oracles didn't see this coming, how could we? But being single's not as bad as movies taught us, you know. We've got each other. Cinderella, Snow White, Ariel – where were their girlfriends? The poor wee lasses never stood a chance.'

'What about Luke?'

'What about him?' Niamh was annoyed at the annoyance in her own tone.

'Are we single ladies together?'

'Yes, Beyoncé, we are. I don't even know where he is.' If Luke was the new plan to replace her old plan, both plans were now torn to shreds. One dead, one lost. 'If he knows what's good for him, he'll stay hidden.'

Elle frowned. 'But didn't Ciara say he helped to—'

'I don't care what my sister has to say on anything,' she snapped and felt bad for snapping. 'Luke lied.' And that was that. His lies hurt a lot more than she cared to admit. Like some anaesthetic wearing off, she was starting to feel these wounds. What her sister did. What Luke did. What they did *together*.

Enough to make her feel quite nauseous.

Holly and Theo ambled down the school driveway towards the car park, taking their sweet time. They all chatted for a moment, finalising plans for next week's Winter Solstice, before Niamh and Theo bid Elle and Holly farewell and ambled quietly into the car.

Niamh couldn't believe they were already facing down 21 December. For one thing, that meant she'd been back for almost two months. It still felt very new, like she was still learning to walk, talk, chew. She pulled her Land Rover out of the drop-off zone and set off up the hill towards Heptonstall village. It was rush hour and Hebden Bridge was a clogged bottleneck.

'Go on then,' Theo said nervously when she couldn't wait a second longer for the verdict.

Niamh reached out gently with her senses. Theo was even tenser than normal, her psyche tight and black like a liquorice stick. Inwardly, the girl had barely changed since she'd arrived months earlier. 'I won't keep you in suspense. We're not shipping you off to America, look at it that way.'

She sighed deeply. 'Maybe you should?' Theo squirmed. 'If it's safest.'

Niamh shook her head. 'I'm not sure it is. The CIA won't even admit there's a threat. Alyssa Grabowski can fuck off back to her wellness ranch, whatever the fuck that is. Sounds like a cult. I don't like her.'

'So what did they say?'

'It wasn't that bad – the Board of Directors isn't so scary. We spent a lot of time talking about whether or not you *knew* Milo was Lucifer.'

'I didn't,' she argued, but Niamh saw the slightest cobalt twinge of a lie in her. She chose to ignore it.

'I think we came up with a solution – if you're open to it?'

'What is it?' Her voice sounded taut in her throat. She was even paler than normal if such a thing were possible.

'OK,' Niamh started, pulling the car into the turnaround to head up the hill. 'Two things. First of all, when you finish at St Augustus, you have to attend the Bethesda School of Dance in Wales.'

'What?'

'It's the only school for witches and warlocks in the UK, and it's not much of a school – more like a residence. The headmistress, Seren Williams, can supervise you as you hone your skills.'

'And I'd get to, like, dance?' Theo said hopefully.

'Every day. It's an ancient tradition.'

Theo's aura lit up, joyful daffodil yellows. 'So my punishment is I have to go and do something I love doing? OK. Yes? What was the other thing?'

Niamh grinned, but felt weirdly nervous, like she was about to propose. 'This is the bigger one. They want me to register as your legal guardian.'

'What?'

'I would be responsible for you. Like a parent would be. I'd make sure you finish school, attend craftwork sessions, and then get you to Bethesda in one piece. And it would be binding until you turned eighteen.'

Theo stared at the dashboard for a second, then looked to her with something like bewilderment. 'Wait. Are you saying you're *adopting* me?'

Niamh let out a short, high laugh. 'Well yeah, I guess.'

'How is that punishment?' As an orphan herself, Niamh was very aware of *Annie Syndrome*: all waifs and strays are tormented by the fantasy of a Daddy Warbucks turning up and claiming them.

'Would you rather go back to Grierlings?'

'No! I . . . I just really thought they were gonna . . . well, I don't know. I thought they might stick me in the Pipes.'

That was a whole other conversation. Niamh wanted that wing of Grierlings demolished entirely. Niamh dropped back into second gear as they approached the sheer hill up to the village. It was curious, her reactions felt sluggish somehow, like she was still fighting off the fug of, well, death. Would it wear off? Or was there some permanent damage? Niamh pressed her foot down harder. She would simply keep going. That's what you do.

'Don't you think, Theo, you've been punished enough? You were kept in a cage; you were hunted like some poor fox by Helena; you were fucking poisoned by Ciara for weeks. And that's not even touching on your time in the care system before you came here. In fifteen years, I think you've been through more than most people have been through in their whole lives.'

Theo just nodded, unable to speak for a moment or two. 'Are they making you do this? Do you *want* to do it? Be my guardian?'

'Yes,' Niamh said without hesitation. It was the same snap reflex that had led her to volunteer to home Theo last spring. Gods, all that was less than a year ago. It felt like an infinity. 'If I've learned anything this year it's not to plan a fucking thing. Did I think this was where my life was headed? No. But here we are. And I'm happy you came, I really am.'

'But . . .' she trailed off.

'What?'

'People . . . people keep getting hurt.' The girl was tearful. 'If it weren't for me, Annie and Sheila would still be alive.'

Niamh took her eyes off the road to look at Theo. 'No. That is not your fault. What Helena and Luke did is not on you.'

As she refocused on the traffic jam, a black flash whipped in front of her vehicle. She slammed on the brakes and Theo rocked forwards. 'Sorry!' Niamh cried.

'What is it?' Theo looked out through the windscreen.

'Did you see that?' Niamh tentatively asked.

'What?'

Niamh saw it, the leech, crawling between the brake lights ahead. As night fell, it returned. Even when she couldn't see it, though, Niamh sensed it. She was never entirely alone.

'Niamh?' Theo prompted again. So, Theo couldn't see it. That was oddly reassuring for some reason.

'It was a fox,' she lied. 'It was fast.'

The car behind then honked its horn, long and extra-angry, and she moved off, and so did her shadow.

They finally broke free of the High Street jam and started up the steep hill to Heptonstall.

'Look,' she told Theo, keeping her eyes fixed on the road. 'I believe that everything that's happened, happened *to* you, not *because* of you. We're all being used. It's not our fault. It's not your fault.'

A tear ran down Theo's cheek. She wiped it on the end of her sleeve.

'Shall I tell you about my life before you rocked up?' Niamh said, keen to concentrate on Theo and not the entity outside the car. 'I went to work every day. Sometimes seven days a week. I told myself it was because I was needed, but *I* needed *it*. If I was in that cottage by myself, I was grieving Conrad, or Ciara. You can really get drunk on that kind of morose. Sometimes I went out with Elle, and I visited Annie every week, but that was about it. I was keeping Luke at arm's length because I felt so guilty for fancying him. Every night, I'd microwave some shite, or just have a bit of toast, and watch boxsets of shows I'd already seen until I fell asleep on the sofa. It was *fine*, but I wasn't living. Not really. I was stuck on a loop. And then you came along. You were like a demolition ball through that cottage, but maybe I needed it. This sounds like a line from a bad YA novel, but maybe I really did have to die to—'

Theo laughed. 'Don't! Don't say it!'

'Well, darl, it's true. This is what's happening. Right now. None of us have a choice.'

'But you do have a choice. You did have a choice. You could have left me in Grierlings with Helena.'

Niamh shrugged. 'Yeah, well,' she said, 'I'm not a cunt.'

They both laughed as the Land Rover crunched down the gravel in the lane outside the cottage. They were home, where they were meant to be.

Long after Theo was asleep, Niamh went out into the garden, armed with everything she needed. A bundle of sage smouldered in her left hand. It wasn't a smell she particularly enjoyed (slightly sweaty?) as the smoke billowed into her face, but it was still the best herb for cleansing. Stepping confidently, even in the dark, Niamh walked barefoot around the perimeter of the garden. It was cold, and a neon moon suggested there'd be a keen frost in the morning, but the bite of the air served to revitalise her. As she went, she stooped to press tiny chunks of garnet into the soil with her thumb.

Each fragment was imbued with her intention. A furious, red command to KEEP OUT. It had taken her much of the night to charge each stone, but – although it was symbolic – she now felt *officially* responsible for the girl who slept upstairs.

Niamh wouldn't even be here if it weren't for her, so perhaps they shared in that responsibility. Niamh and Theo were bonded by law and magic.

She completed the perimeter of her garden, creating a loose forcefield. She felt it hum its low, grave warning to anyone who might trespass. *Keep out.* Alone, these charms would only do so much, but might buy her some time until she figured out a more permanent solution. There had to be a way to vanquish her shadow in a manner which didn't involve her going back to that dark void. She couldn't go back. She would not.

There it was. In the grazing fields beyond the boundary wall. Even in the dark, Niamh could make out a hunched figure with emaciated arms and legs, about fifty paces into the night. It seemed to be growing more solid, although there was a certain liquidity inherent to the entity. Either way, it now had form. Its head hung limply to the right on a scrawny neck, as if it were considering her. But as Niamh's head moved, so did the entity's.

She stared it down. *Understand this. I will kill to protect her*, she told the malevolent thing.

And she meant it. Ciara had that part right.

SOUL FOOD FOR THOUGHT

Leonie - London, UK

Nan's Kitchen sometimes felt like the last bastion of authenticity in Brixton. When everything else had become a Gail's Bakery or a fucking Five Guys, Nan's still served good, old-fashioned Caribbean food to actual Black people. Not just people: witches, warlocks, and their allies too. The restaurant was just off Electric Lane, partially concealed from mundane eyes with a few well-placed charms. Leonie had not lived personally the fabled glory days of this part of London, but it was important that something of its culture was protected.

She entered the restaurant and her mouth, praise be, watered. At least jerk chicken and mutton curry weren't turning her stomach. Yet. Something to be thankful for. When had she last eaten? She'd been running on adrenaline since the bizarre encounter with Senait. Like, what the fuck?

She hadn't told anyone, even Chinara, about the meeting. They'd have the girl in Grierlings in seconds – she was wanted over the incident on Aeaea – and despite everything, Leonie had a crumb of doubt she was clinging to. Nothing about Senait made sense, but Leonie was a mighty sentient and she knew the pus green of hatred, the murk of deception, and the glaring scarlet of violence and none were present in the girl. Whatever she'd done, Leonie *cared* for her. It made no sense whatsoever, it was entirely beyond reason, but she didn't want her locked up.

What's more, she *believed* her. Leonie had not gone through with her termination. Yet. Goddamn it. It was supposed to be easy.

Temi, behind the bar, gave her a nod as she shook the shit out of a cocktail shaker with muscular arms. The *thought* of rum, however, did make her nauseous. Fuck this.

Leonie knew pretty much everyone here. They were nearly all witches, or warlocks. Temi was in the Diaspora coven, while her mother – Nanette – came to Black Mass regularly. Leonie leaned over the bar and gave Temi a peck on the cheek. 'Sabrina said Celestine was here?' Yes, she'd had an oracle track her target down like some sort of stalker. She'd spent all day searching. She was getting desperate.

Temi nodded towards the basement stairs. 'Go on down, babes.'

Leonie stopped briefly to say hi to a warlock couple she knew from Diaspora, and headed through a beaded curtain to the cellar bar.

The music was quieter here, and it was darker, only candles in Gü ramekins lighting the space. Normally this was overflow from the restaurant upstairs – further booths for diners, but tonight there was only one table occupied. Nan was with Madame Celestine and one other woman of around the same age. A mother's meeting if you will. Leonie felt a sudden pang of homesickness for her own mother. No, not homesickness – *guilt*. She'd not visited Leeds in almost a year, even with all the time she'd spent in Yorkshire.

The women drank punch and read the cards. Celestine held court, as imposing as ever. Nan and her friend looked guilty, like schoolgirls who'd been caught behind the bike shed, and it almost made Leonie smile.

'I don't want trouble,' Leonie began, holding her hands up in surrender.

'I'd like to see you try some,' Celestine replied, not looking up from her spread. She turned a card with her cherry-red nails. *The*

Empress. Figured. Celestine was truly the High Priestess of this community. Leonie was what she'd ever been: an upstart, an agitator, an activist, a northern transplant above all else.

'I need your help,' Leonie said through a clenched jaw.

Celestine and Nan exchanged a wry smile. Nan spoke to her silver-haired friend. 'Come on, Mona. I'd better make sure my fool daughter isn't drinking the bar dry. Let's leave them to it.' As they passed at the foot of the stairs, Nan gave Leonie's hand an encouraging squeeze. *Good luck, babe.*

Celestine gathered her cards with a swipe of her palm and begun to shuffle them. Her fingers were adorned with rubies and turquoise. 'Why is it the Baby Queen only comes to me when she wants something?'

Leonie shook her head. It was true. Hot, oily tears of frustration pressed hard on her eyes, but she didn't want to cry in front of Celestine. She didn't want to prove her right; that she was, had always been, swimming well out of her depth. 'There's something wrong with me. Like, really wrong.' *Rosemary's Baby* wrong.

Leonie stepped into the feeble flicker of the tealight on her table. In a second, the satisfied smirk fell from Celestine's face. She uttered something under her breath in her native French. The older woman slid off the banquette seat and backed away towards the restrooms.

'What? What is it?' When necromancers are afraid, that can't be a good thing. But she was – the mighty Madame Celestine *was* scared; Leonie saw it all over her face.

Only then her expression softened. Leonie had never seen her face so gentle, so open. Tentatively, she inched closer. With quivering hands, she traced Leonie's aura. Suddenly, Celestine fell to her knees, her skirt fanning around her. She bowed deeply, pressing her forehead to the tiles.

'What are you doing?' Leonie cried. This was somehow worse than being mocked. 'Get the fuck up.'

Celestine gazed up at her, awed. 'You are with child.'

'I know! *That's* what's wrong.'

'Did we see this in you?' Celestine seemed to talk past her, to no one in particular. Skittish, her eyes scanned the room, and Leonie wondered if a necromancer is ever truly alone. *'Bébé reine,* that's what I called you. I wonder if they knew, the spirits. Baby queen. And now here she is . . .'

Leonie crouched to her level and seized her upper arms. 'Celestine! What are you talking about? Are you OK?'

Celestine's eyes were wild. 'She is in you.'

'Who is?' Leonie spat.

'Your child is the most blessed Mother.'

A hot tear found its way out. 'What? Celestine, please . . . I'm so, so scared. I know you fucking hate me but, please! Please help me.'

Celestine cupped Leonie's face in her hands. 'Do not be scared, child. This is a beautiful gift.'

'You don't understand. I didn't . . . I never . . . there isn't a father. I . . . is it Satanis?'

'No! Of all that is good, no!' Her trembling fingers reached towards Leonie's abdomen. 'Can't you feel it, girl? The power growing inside you? Terra Mater, Dame Nature, Asase Afua, the Great Mother!' When Leonie was too stunned to reply, Madame Celestine gave her all the clarity she needed. *'Gaia!* This child is the daughter of Gaia herself.'

15

YULE

Elle - Hebden Bridge, UK

Whether it was called Christmas, Winter Solstice, or Saturnalia, or Yule, Elle had always loved the run-up to 25 December more than the day itself. Throughout her childhood, her grandmother had gone to great lengths to teach her the true meaning of the midwinter celebration.

In ancient times, thousands of years before anyone decided it was Jesus's birthday, the feast marked the beginning of a period of fasting that could last well into spring. The cattle or poultry had to be slaughtered and cooked because many farmers couldn't afford to feed them through the famine months. While that explained the celebration meal, Elle loved the fact it signalled the promise of lengthening days and shorter nights. That was something to celebrate, now more than ever.

But while Annie had always made this time of year special, her mother had made Christmas Day itself miserable. Elle's childhood memories were of watching *Top of the Pops* and that awful Dudley Moore film while her mum ranted that the kitchen was too small to cook a proper turkey dinner. If her dad tried to help out, he'd be yelled out of the room. No wonder he'd run off with his secretary. Funny, and awful, how history repeats. Was nagging genetic? Her mother had been a bully, and Elle had been so desperate to control her spouse she had turned him into a garden gnome. Elle feared she'd focused so hard on not becoming her grandmother, she'd become her mother.

This thinking wasn't good for her. Elle instead focused on the majesty of the night.

As the sun set over the Pendle Hills, the witches made their 21 December procession, carrying their paper lanterns. It had been organised by the cosy Hebden Bridge coven, this year as a memorial to Sheila Henry. They were mostly older witches, retired from HMRC duties. Elle had always been so scared of getting older, but these women seemed to have a lovely life with their book club and lunch dates and wine tastings. Perhaps ageing was something to look forward to, not run from.

There were about twenty witches this year, trundling up the path towards the copse. It was enough to make Elle suspect *everyone*, not just her, wanted to burn the last twelve months and herald a new, and hopefully better, year. They didn't wear robes for winter solstice, just coats and scarves: this way they didn't need to shield from mundanes – locals just thought they were hippies.

They gathered at the highest point of the hill, Elle alongside Holly, Theo and Niamh. Leonie, Radley and Chinara had come up too. They had decided at the last minute to spend mundane Christmas with Leonie's mother, and Elle was delighted to see them in person.

Sheila's widow said a few words and they lit their lanterns, setting them free into the night sky. Fashioned from withies and paper, they would burn up, and the ashes would scatter harmlessly. They were beautiful, serene. On the still, frosty night, the lanterns drifted upwards diagonally, weaving around one another, flickering a soft amber glow.

Farewell to a fucking dreadful year. Elle exhaled deeply, her breath forming a cloud. Farewell Jez; farewell, Helena; farewell, Annie; and farewell, Milo. Her poor, sweet, innocent little boy. She had to let him go all over again. Holly looped an arm around hers and Elle allowed herself to cry as she watched her lantern get smaller and smaller until it was a new star in the sky.

Elle had always loved an open fire. She watched the fire burn; the rush and twist of it up the chimney breast; the snap and crackle of the kindling. It was hypnotic. Odd that witches should be so drawn to the thing sometimes used to kill them.

She was cold to the bone. Even after twenty minutes next to the hearth in the Pendle Inn, Elle still couldn't feel her fingers. Like Annie had done in previous years, Elle had organised a buffet at the inn for everyone after the procession. Yes, the pub had a tacky little witch on the sign out front, but so what? Normally, Leonie would make a stand about how the state-sponsored execution of twelve people shouldn't be a tourist attraction, but tonight she just sat awkwardly in the corner, drinking tea. Apparently, she'd been down with a stomach flu for a couple of weeks and wasn't feeling very well. Elle had offered to scan her for signs of a virus, but Leonie had resisted fuss emphatically.

So instead, Elle sat by the fire and watched as people piled their plates high; she'd move once she could feel her toes in her trainers again.

Radley Jackman, carrying a plate of chicken wings and mini burgers, slid into the armchair on the opposite side of the hearth. 'Great spread,' he told her.

'Nothing to do with me.' Elle had only paid the deposit and left it to the pub. That said, organising the event had gone some way to keeping her head busy. Too much time alone with her thoughts was dangerous right now.

'How are you holding up?' Radley asked.

What to say to that? She'd been raised not to be a moaner. 'Yeah, I'm OK, thanks. How are you? Are you all better?'

'Physically, yes.' He sighed. 'Mentally, Gaia only knows.'

Elle couldn't imagine what Hale had done to him in Siberia, and she certainly wasn't going to pry. 'Rad, I'm so sorry.'

He shook his head. 'I was a fool. I underestimated what we were dealing with.'

'*You* were a fool? At least you didn't think Lucifer was your son for the best part of a year.'

They both stifled a laugh. Inappropriate, but what else could you do? 'I . . . I don't know if it's my place to say, but I . . . I was furious when I heard Jeremy had . . . walked out. I don't know how he could do that to you.'

Wow. No one had really mentioned Jez *or* Milo so far. The elephants in the room. Elle shrugged. 'I don't know what to tell you, Rad. I think I always knew . . .'

'What?'

Elle took a soothing mouthful of mulled wine from her cup. It was just sweet enough, the clove cutting through. 'That sooner or later . . . that it couldn't last. I couldn't hide what I was forever. Annie knew. She sat me down before the wedding and asked if it was wise to marry a man – a boy, let's be honest – who didn't know what we are.' She admitted to the most shameful part. 'That day I told her that I wasn't a witch anymore.'

Rad smiled kindly. 'I'm not sure it's a position we can resign from.'

Elle nodded. 'You can say that again. I wasn't much older than our Hols. And I was in love. I thought I'd won the lottery.'

Elle almost *felt* him gather his nerve. *Oh god*, Elle thought as Radley sat up straighter. 'You ought to be with someone who sees you for exactly who you are.'

And what, pray tell, was that? A woman who almost killed a man in a vengeful tantrum. She wasn't sure what she was, so she didn't see how he could. Elle took another sip of her mulled wine. 'Maybe.'

'Maybe one evening, we could get some dinner? I'm in Manchester all the time at the cabal. I could come over to Hebden?'

After fourteen years of marriage, this was so alien to Elle, but she couldn't deny it felt good. Radley had asked her out when she was fifteen, and she'd laughed at him. She wasn't proud of it, but he *had* been a nerdy eleven-year-old at the time and it was unthinkable to date someone in a year *below* you at school. Only the really weird, guinea pig girls did that. It was nice to know that he still carried a torch, and that her exterior at the very least was still – to someone – desirable.

Elle stared into her mug. 'Maybe,' she said again, hoping it would buy her some time. Alas, Radley knew what maybe meant and it read all over his face. She quickly corrected herself. 'Not, not maybe as in *no, not ever!* Maybe as in *my head is a total mess*.' She would need to fully accept her husband had gone for good before she could so much as contemplate a new one. Despite it all, she kept forgetting Jez was gone, would find herself looking at the clock at 6 p.m. each evening wondering why he hadn't walked through the door. That needed to stop.

Also, there was a chance right now that she would accept his offer simply to compete with Jez. *You moved on, so did I!* That wasn't fair to poor, sweet Rad.

'Understood. It's an offer that comes without an expiration date.' He leaned in. 'After everything we've been through, and everything we're yet to experience . . . I think we've definitely earned a nice meal and some good wine.'

Elle was about to remind him they might not have as much time as he imagined, when there was a noticeable change in the vibe. Radley craned his neck round and Elle followed his gaze to where she saw a man from the Warlocks' Cabal pull Niamh away from the buffet.

Radley set aside his plate and rose. Elle, being nosy, followed suit.

'Nick?' Radley began. 'What's wrong?'

That was his name: Nick Bibby. They had met a few times in passing. He was quite hunky, in a dad-bod way.

Nick greeted Radley. 'We have intel on the surviving witchfinders. I thought you'd want to know, both of you.'

'I thought most of them died at the House of Hekate?' Niamh asked.

'Most. Not all,' Radley told her. He steered them away from the party towards their fireplace retreat.

Nick continued. 'Our source told us a new cell has formed out of the younger members who were left out of the attack in October. Potentially very dangerous. Hell-bent on revenge.'

'The father's sons, naturally,' said Radley wearily. 'It never ends, does it?'

'Well, where are they?' Elle demanded.

'They've been holding meetings in Bradford or Doncaster.' Nick paused, turning to look at Niamh. 'And they're making plans.'

'They're going after Luke,' Niamh said with resignation, having read his mind. 'I think we better get to him first.' She looked to Rad. 'Find him.'

THE NIGHT BEFORE CHRISTMAS

Leonie - Leeds, UK

It was a relief that Leonie didn't have to travel back to their childhood home on the Belle Isle. After many years and a lot of therapy, she was woman enough to admit there was trauma from those years. Her father leaving them to start a life with a new (white) wife, and new (white) kids. Her mum palming them off onto HMRC when she was told they were 'special'. Even before those events, Leonie and Radley were already outcasts because they had a Black mum and a white dad: taboo even in 1990.

Nowadays, Donna Jackman (why she never got rid of her dad's surname she'd never, ever know – but then, neither had she) lived in a smart Victorian terrace near Roundhay Park. It had lovely bay windows and a back yard with enough space for her mum to put out a deckchair and read her thrillers in the summer sun. Leonie took comfort in the fact her mum, although alone, had a nice house and a nice life and a one-eyed cat called Frida.

The night of Christmas Eve, Leonie had asked her mum to do her hair and so, the way they had when she was little, Donna styled Leonie's hair with Shakin' Stevens and Wham! playing on the radio. Leonie sat in the kitchen on a dining chair with a towel over her shoulders while Donna removed the overgrown braids she'd had since the autumn. It was time for a change.

'Been a long, long time since I've done hair professionally,' Donna told Chinara. 'Twenty-five years at least.' Even so, her mother's fingers were just as nimble as they'd been back then; Leonie could hardly feel her working. As the hours ticked on, Donna chatted away to Chinara, who watched from atop the kitchen counter, drinking some eggnog. Vile stuff, even without morning sickness. 'I gave it up to do office work when the kids went away. More money, better hours,' she told her.

Leonie winced. She and Rad had not 'gone away'. They had been told, by some friendly witches, that they were going on a magical adventure. Instead, they'd been sent to live with white people who schooled them, strictly, on how to conform. Chinara knew this, of course, but said nothing. No need to make her mum feel guilty this Christmas.

Once her hair was free of the braids, loose and curly, Donna asked what Leonie wanted her to do with it—knots, twists, rows? 'Cut it. Short,' she said.

Donna protested; after all, Leonie did have gorgeous hair – but Leonie insisted. She wanted it off her neck. It was only once Donna got to work with the clippers that she realised, with grim resolve, that the last time she'd worn it like this, it had been the war.

When Donna finally handed her a mirror, it was almost midnight. Leonie admired herself, turning her head side to side. Her mother had blended the sides, but left her a wave of curls on top, spilling towards her brow. It was very lesbian, and Leonie approved. 'Do you like it?' Leonie asked Chinara, who had never had more than a centimetre of hair in the whole time she'd known her.

'I do,' Chinara said with a smile.

The vegetables were already chopped and sat in pans of salty water ready for tomorrow and so Donna kissed them both goodnight and went upstairs, shouting. 'Be asleep by twelve, or he won't come!'

'Santa. Family legend,' Leonie told Chinara as she tipped much of her eggnog down the sink. 'I told you that shit was disgusting.'

Chinara turned to face her. 'Why aren't you drinking?' she

said in a way that suggested she'd been sitting on the question all night. 'You love drinking. Are you sick?'

The time had come, then. Leonie had known it would be unavoidable. She was a big fan of booze, and the notion she'd get through solstice and Christmas without a single drink was wild. The only other option would be to claim she was going sober, but it was possible Chinara would find that claim harder to swallow than the truth.

'Sit down,' Leonie told her as she returned her chair to the kitchen table and sat.

'Oh my god, what's wrong?' Chinara was ashen.

'OK,' Leonie started. 'Would I lie to you?'

'No,' Chinara said without flinching.

'Good, because I need you to believe something really fucking insane.' She felt like she was on the rim of a clifftop, ready to fall. And here came the plunge: 'Chinara, I'm pregnant.' A white-hot flare shot through Chinara's mind, but Leonie carried on because what she was about to say was so fucking wild, she might chicken out. She blurted it all out in one breathless splurge. 'I went to see Madame Celestine and she thinks I'm carrying some sort of divine gift from Gaia.'

She waited. She waited to be called a liar, a cheat, a whore. She steeled herself to lose the love of her life.

Chinara's nostrils briefly flared and then she said. 'OK.'

Leonie waited for more, but nothing came. 'OK?' Chinara was so still, as still as Christmas Eve, and it made Leonie want to cry. 'You're not angry?'

'Of course not.'

'And you believe me?'

Chinara didn't break her gaze as she pulled her chair closer. 'You may be many things, my love, but you are not a liar.' Leonie crumpled onto her shoulder. She cried and cried, and felt her stroke the new buzzcut. She didn't think she could love this woman any more, but Leonie felt her heart expand on all sides and fill up with even more love, bubbly like pink champagne.

Chinara waited until she was all cried out. Leonie wasn't sure if that was minutes or hours. Chinara wiped away her tears with a gentle thumb. 'Now. Tell me everything. Start at the beginning. Leave nothing out.'

So Leonie did. Everything, although that wasn't much. She told her how, when she was on the incredible lost island of Aeaea, on the night before Hale had massacred many of its inhabitants, she'd had a dream unlike any other. A dream about a vivid jade serpent, how they had communed, become one entity in a lush tropical rainforest.

The gory events that followed had driven it from her mind, but at the time, it had been the most visceral dream of her life. She had *felt* it.

That had been almost three months ago.

She also told her how she'd worried it was something Hale had inflicted on her, about the random encounter with Senait outside the clinic in London, and then Madame Celestine's extraordinary reaction. It was long after midnight when she was finished. Santa didn't come anywhere near the chimney.

'That's everything I know. I know it sounds unhinged.'

Chinara sat back in her chair, processing. After an agonising silence, she said, 'No more or less unhinged than a twin killing her sister and then stealing her body; or Lucifer masquerading as a teenage boy; or Helena murdering Annie. These are unhinged times, so it seems.'

Leonie wiped her eyes on some kitchen roll. 'But I'm *pregnant*.'

A smile formed in the corners of Chinara's mouth. 'A baby isn't so scary,' she said. 'We wanted a baby. We always wanted a baby.'

The baby that existed in their blue-sky conversations over dim sum wasn't the same child as this one. 'I don't know if we wanted *this* baby.'

Chinara stood and held her hands over her waist. 'May I?'

'Of course.'

Her girlfriend placed warm hands on her abdomen. Leonie wasn't sure what *she* was feeling for, but Leonie *could* feel something sentient. It wasn't the same as when she was around children, but it was a . . . something. There was a *something* developing inside her. A potential.

'Do you believe Celestine?' Chinara asked. 'That this child is from Gaia?'

'I don't know, but I don't have any other way to explain it.'

Chinara said wistfully, 'Maybe every child is a gift from Gaia.'

Leonie didn't buy that; most children are very annoying. She definitely preferred Holly as a teenager. Either way, Leonie felt something unwind in her spine. She'd been holding this all in for weeks now. She'd assumed, honestly, that Chinara would leave her. To cheat would be one thing, but to shag a man would be unforgiveable. To not use protection, leaving them both vulnerable to STIs, would be a betrayal further, too. At least, that was how she'd envisaged the worst-case scenario. As the anxiety left her body, she felt light-headed, dizzy almost.

'How can you be so calm?' Leonie asked her.

'How do I *appear* so calm?' Chinara corrected. She took a couple of laps of the small kitchen, choosing her words carefully. Typical lawyer. 'I've always taken great comfort in Gaia. She was Mother. You can understand why I'd want a replacement.' Chinara's mother, back in Nigeria, had disowned her on discovering she was a witch. 'I do not believe she has a plan for us, that would be boring, but I do believe she gave us these powers, and that she sees us. I think she has blessed us before, and so I don't question that she would bless us again.'

Now that Leonie had told Chinara, it felt suddenly very, very real. She was *pregnant*. 'Oh fuck. Are we ready for this? With everything that's happening? What if *this* is the Sullied Child? Did you think of that?'

'Stop.' Chinara took her face in her hands tenderly. 'Listen, my love, if we wait for a *good time* to have children, we will be waiting forever.' She paused as if remembering herself. 'But this is your body, your choice. Maybe this is not our time.'

'Are you ready?'

She didn't hesitate. 'Yes. I have felt this for a long time. I want to be a mother. I want to give myself over to something wholly, and be selfless in that. Gaia gave us life, and now I want to do the same.' She looked at Leonie gently. 'The only question is, are *you* ready?'

Leonie knew Chinara hadn't meant it as a barb – but it was true that Leonie *had* lived selfishly, her whole life. She did things because she wanted to do them, because they brought her joy, or challenge, or satisfaction. She had constructed the Leonie of her dreams, and she liked it the way it was.

So Leonie said nothing. She did not have the answer.

THE LAKE

Luke - Coniston Water, UK

Luke had had better Christmases. Like in '96, the year it snowed. While the turkey was in the oven, his father had driven him and his mother up to Boone Hill and they'd gone sledging in a rusty wooden toboggan. On that day, there had been no fights, no raised voices, no terse silences. Only laughter and damp mittens. That's the magic of Christmas.

The summer after that picture-postcard day, Luke's father had murdered his mother because she was a witch.

This year, apart from a pathetic flurry of snowflakes at lunchtime, the day had been like any other he'd experienced since moving to the caravan park. He'd had a Dr Oetker frozen pizza for dinner. Tragic, but there would have been something even worse about preparing a turkey dinner for one. The Christmas holiday families had departed following New Year's, and he was alone on the Ribbon Park estate once more; no one wanted to stay in a static caravan overlooking Coniston Water in January. He thought, though, that it was beautiful; every morning, the view outside his window surprised him. The vast lake had infinite colours, moods; some days it was a foreboding jet black with slate-grey skies; other times it was frosty, ethereal and misty.

He could feel nature here. The witches were right. It was motherly, feminine and reassuring.

He'd been here since he left Hebden Bridge. He banked on the

Working Men's Club assuming he'd gone further. As it was, it was only a couple of hours' drive from his home town to the Lake District National Park. Luke had been nothing if not prepared. Predicting the day would come when he might need to get far, far away from his father, he'd paid a ne'er-do-well in Huddersfield to knock up some fake ID some years ago. It had cost him twenty-five quid and a trip to an off license to become Tom Brooks.

'Tom Brooks', caretaker, had seen the crude, hand-painted job advert tied to a cattle gate as he drove northwards in November. The owner of the campsite had gladly agreed to cash-in-hand, and that was that. A winter in a faded static caravan, from where he'd plot his next move.

Because Niamh had been his entire plan. He wasn't sure what else there was.

Tom, Luke, whatever, opened the door and let the January air into the fusty mobile home. It had rained overnight, and the sky felt cleansed and purified. An odd luxury, to choose your own prison. For he *was* punishing himself – no one had forced him to flee Hebden Bridge, or denounce his identity – but he had more than earned it. His actions had led to the death of Sheila Henry, an entirely innocent woman.

He had not lost a minute of sleep over the death of the man who'd killed her: his father. Luke had always thought he *must* have loved his father, in amongst all the hate, but no. He hadn't cared one jot, and was glad that he wouldn't hurt anyone else ever again. On that respect he only felt the tidy satisfaction of a case closed.

Sheila, though, was something else. He could not sleep for the shame, and the horror. Countless times he had replayed her final moments in the derelict warehouse. The brutality in which she'd been snuffed out, a bolt arrow through her skull. Her poor wife. The kids she mentored. The coven.

Luke asked himself the same question he asked every day: *Should I kill myself?* No was the answer today, and every day preceding it. That felt like a get-out-of-jail-free card, and he wouldn't play it. Nor would he turn himself over to the Working Men's Club for a pasting. He wouldn't give those cunts the satisfaction.

The insomnia was making him quite sick. He'd lost all appetite for anything except coffee and beer, so he'd lost weight. He felt tired all day, wired all night. So exhausted was he now, that he was becoming prone to strange hallucinations during his waking hours. Sometimes this would take the form of blurred vision, or inability to judge depth. Sometimes he could no longer remember the names of common objects when he was talking to campsite guests.

But worst of all was when he saw Sheila. Sometimes he saw her waiting outside his caravan, blood coursing over her left eye. Sometimes he saw her inches under the black water of Coniston Lake. She was waiting for him to save her, but he could not. All he could do was watch her die, over and over again.

He gave his burner phone a cursory glance. Nothing. He didn't really know why he'd got it. He'd thrown his old one into the river on his way out of Hebden Bridge, and with it all his contacts; he hadn't wanted the temptation of reaching out to Ciara. She'd let him go, and told him she never wanted to see him again. And anyway, he'd come to think that Ciara was human methadone. She looked like Niamh, but that was where the similarity ended. Luke craved *Niamh*, not Ciara, and she was dead.

Everyone he had ever loved was dead.

Leaving the caravan door open, Luke filled the kettle and set it to boil. Maybe he'd drive into town and get something to eat. All he had in the kitchen was a stale loaf of bread and the dregs of some peanut butter on the sides of the jar. He was imagining an egg butty when he heard an engine, and tyres crunching down the track. Weird; he wasn't expecting guests until the weekend.

He stuck his bare feet into his wellington boots and stepped outside. There was only one way in and out of the caravan park; a bumpy dirt road he'd spent much of the winter trying to maintain. Sometimes cars got stuck in the gully when they tried to pass. Now, if he squinted, he saw a gleaming black-and-red Golf bump down the lane towards him, at speed. Poisonous colours, like some spider or Amazonian frog.

The boy-racer car told him at once he'd been found.

His heart sank. The witchfinders had done their job.

Luke saw another vehicle, a white Transit van, some way behind the Golf. With the lane blocked, there was no other option; Luke ran for the lake.

The caravan park had its own jetty. The rowboats were stowed away in the shed, waiting for spring, but Luke had left the one motorboat ready at the little harbour. Of course he'd planned an escape route, he wasn't a fool.

Behind him, he heard car doors slam as he ran. Looking back would only waste time. The wellies were cumbersome, but he made it to the jetty. He thudded into the boat, and tugged the mooring, but it wouldn't budge. *Fuck.* Somehow, it was stuck on the cleat.

He felt a shadow over him for a second and cursed again; it was too late. The form made contact with his shoulders – someone launching themselves, kamikaze-style, from the gangplank above. It was an awkward rugby tackle, but it was enough momentum to tip them both out of the boat and into the freezing winter waters.

The ice cold tore all the breath from his chest. He was only underwater for a second before surfacing. His attacker had drifted away, but was back on him in a heartbeat, trying to push him under.

Through mouthfuls of lake water, the other man spat, 'You fuckin' bastard, you fuckin' killed my fuckin' dad.'

He knew the voice. Young John Ackroyd. Luke *had* broken his nose, and drugged him, but he hadn't killed his father. *That* one wasn't on him.

As his face broke the surface, Luke gulped in as much air as possible. He focused on not panicking. John was going to try and drown him. He had to conserve his air. That said, Luke was head and shoulders taller than John. Instead of trying to swim away,

Luke now clung to the skinnier man. If today was his day to die, he'd take one last misogynist bastard with him when he went.

Coniston Water was black and cold. Under here, he didn't know which way was up. Silt and pondweed swam around them. Luke screwed his eyes shut and clung to John's coat.

In the darkness of the lake, Luke felt strong hands around his body. They looped under his armpits and tugged hard. Eventually, he became aware of his ankles scraping against the lakebed. Frigid morning air hit his face, and he was dumped on the bank. He opened his eyes and saw only vast white sky. He coughed up a lungful of lake onto the shore.

'The fuck you do that for?' John rasped. 'I had him!'

Luke sat up and saw John and another man wade out of the shallows.

'The hell you did! And don't you fuckin' move,' his rescuer told Luke, jabbing a rifle in his face. Not much of a saviour.

Luke couldn't move, even if he wanted to. Violent shivers shook his frame. Hyperthermia might kill him before the Working Men did.

There were four of them from the looks of things. John was joined by Keith Barrett – one of his father's oldest friends – and two younger men he didn't recognise. It was Barrett who held the gun. 'Get up,' he commanded.

Dripping wet, Luke pushed himself to his feet.

'Get your hands up,' Barrett added. 'If you try owt, so fuckin' help me, I'll blow your head off.'

'I'm not going to try anything.' Luke knew when he was beaten. He couldn't take on four of them, not frozen stiff. He raised two trembling, raw hands.

'I could have killed him,' John protested.

'You weren't supposed to. Now get warm,' Barrett told the other two wet men.

'He *killed* my—'

'Johnny, shut the fuck up or I'll shoot you an' all.'

John scowled.

'I didn't kill anyone,' Luke told Barrett. 'Definitely not Mick Ackroyd.'

Barrett winced slightly. 'A lot of good men died on Halloween.' They were not good men, and it was good that they were dead. 'You fuckin' sold us out to the bitches, mate.'

Luke shook his head. 'They didn't need any help from me.'

John lunged at him, but his colleague held him back. Barrett ordered them both to return to their car. 'What you did was worse,' Barrett muttered. 'It's in their nature to be witches, you *chose* to betray your brothers.'

'My mother was a witch,' Luke said. 'You might as well kill me too.'

Barrett frowned. 'You kidding? As if we'd kill you. Fella, you know the name of each and every witch in Hebden Bridge. One way or another, we'll get them out of you.'

Shit.

They could torture names out of his mind. He knew they had at least one warlock on their side. Luke wondered if killing himself might have been the smartest idea after all.

'Now move yourself. Into the van. I want you alive, but I can shoot you in the dick or summat.'

Hands still aloft, Luke only took a couple of steps towards the Transit when he found he couldn't move his legs. Barrett nudged him with the tip of the rifle. 'What yer stoppin' for?'

The air grew notably colder, a bitter wind howling in off the lake. Luke smiled, despite his shivers. To his right, Coniston Waters froze over, the water solidifying with a satisfying groan. The surface glittered with frost.

'What's so fuckin' funny?'

Now he grinned, broadly. 'You're so fucked,' he said.

Barrett looked confused for a second and then the rifle was ripped from his grasp. The gun boomeranged into the trees on the perimeter of the caravan park. 'What the fuck?'

The younger man drew a hunting knife from his leather jacket, but that too was snatched clean out of his hands by an invisible force.

Ice bit Luke's face. Then more. Soon they were being pelted with hail the size of golf balls, as if the white of the sky itself was attacking them. He flinched, but still couldn't move to shield himself. It was hard to see more than a metre or so in front of himself, and he could scarcely hear the witchfinder's cries over the wind.

'Get out of here!' Barrett called to John and his friend.

'I can't move!' John yelled.

A static caravan flipped over, landing squarely on top of John's Golf. It compressed like a can of pop.

Then, through this arctic maelstrom, Luke saw a glimpse of flame red hair. Arms at her side, she emerged from the trees, levitating a metre or so off the ground. Leonie was at her side. They came in to land, walking towards him. Over his shoulder, he could just about make out the lithe silhouette of Chinara Okafor suspended over the great, frozen lake. The storm swirled around her petite frame, but her eyes burned like lightning through the storm.

Impassionate, business-like, the witches on the lakeside approached the witchfinders. With only the lightest of touches to their heads, the Working Men crumpled into heaps on the floor, unconscious. They took two each. Only Luke remained standing.

The hail stopped, and Chinara glided to the shore. Luke found he was able to move once more. The witches had him surrounded, and he knew he was no safer with them than he was the witchfinders. They had just as much cause for vengeance. One way or another, it was payback time.

Leonie and Chinara, hung back, leaving Ciara to deal with him. In fairness, she did say she could only offer him a head start. That was their deal.

The redhead approached him, still sporting the white stripe in her hair. Her green Doc Martens scrunched on the wet sand. 'Thank you,' he said, getting his breath back. 'For what it's worth, they were going to torture me to find more witches. You probably just saved a lot of women.'

'We've been looking for you,' she said, almost resigned.

'To kill me?'

The witches looked to one another. Eventually Ciara spoke. She sounded resigned. 'No. You're of use to the coven. We can use you as bait to draw out any remaining witchfinders,' she said, voice unnervingly steady. 'But there's something else you should probably know, too.'

'Ciara? What is it? What's up?' Luke asked.

She took a deep breath. 'Well, that's the thing,' she said. 'I'm not Ciara. Not anymore.'

He was very, very cold, his mind sluggish. So it took Luke a long moment to realise what that meant.

A WOMAN SCORNED

Niamh - Manchester, UK

Luke hunched over a bucket of puke. 'Finished?' Niamh asked curtly. Teleportation was quite the ride the first time, especially for mundanes.

While the pistachio tinge to his skin told a different tale, he said he was, and she gave Sandhya a nod. Her assistant took the full bucket from him and went to dispose of it. Way outside her remit, the woman was a gift from Gaia.

Luke was cuffed. They were in the concrete gymnasium in the basement of HMRC, surrounded by what was left of the Supernormal Security division, and the women looked *pissed*. All their fury at what had happened last Halloween was syphoned into this one man. They wanted to rip his arms and legs off.

'Go,' Niamh told them.

Jen Yamato stepped forwards. 'But this man . . .'

'This man *fucked* my *sister*,' Niamh said coolly, and that was all the explanation needed. Her witches left her to it.

The training room was comically huge for the two of them to be having this confrontation, but he was trapped in here. It was windowless and fortified. It felt safer than anywhere else in the offices. Her footsteps echoed throughout the gym.

He looked up at her, dumb. 'How?' he asked finally.

'Theo.'

'Good for her.'

'Is it?' she said cryptically.

She glowered at him, circling as he knelt before her. There were two people but *three* shadows in the cellar. Hers, his, and the third, thin silhouette arching across the ceiling. The leech was still attached. Closer all the fucking time.

'You're . . . back. That has to be good.'

Niamh shook her head. 'Death defines witches as much as life. We are agents of nature. What Theo did stands against everything I believe in. It was my time to go.'

Luke frowned. 'How can you say that? What Ciara did—'

'Was no worse than what I did to her. You don't know us, Luke. You don't know me. You never did.' She had a vinegar sting in her mouth. 'And I certainly didn't fucking know you, did I?'

A pause. 'I'm sorry.'

'Oh fuck off.' Niamh reined in her fury. At times like this she felt too small a vessel for her firepower. She was a nuke, ready for someone to push the button. '*Sorry* is for children.'

'Do I get a chance to explain?'

'Explain *how* you lied or *why*?' He flinched, unable to meet her gaze. Nope, thought not. 'We spent every night together for three months.'

'And every night it got harder to come clean.' He looked remorseful, but he must be quite the actor. 'I am a different man because of you.'

Niamh's arm jutted out and, with a yelp, Luke skidded the length of the gym until he came to a rest up against the wall. 'Sorry,' she said. 'See? Sorry is bullshit, isn't it?'

He rolled back up to a seat. 'Do your worst. I deserve it.'

She'd never enjoyed a pity-party. 'I didn't bring you here to kill you, Luke. I brought you here because the coven demands justice for Sheila Henry. *I* demand it.'

'I'm not arguing. It was Ciara that let me go free.'

The wrong button to push. 'Well, soon you and your fuck buddy will be back together . . .' That response was childish, but somehow easier than expressing how she really felt about either of these individuals.

'How is she?' he asked, voice full of concern.

'Are you kidding me?'

He was quite genuine. 'She saved the world, you know? We owe her one.'

'Ciara saved the world . . . *from Ciara*.' Niamh laughed. Aloud, and a lot. She couldn't help it. She felt like she was going insane, like there was a spoonful of jelly where her brain should be. 'My sister murdered me, but you think I owe *her* one. Got it.'

It prickled most of all because she was pretending Ciara didn't exist and that made her weak. She was letting her rot down in that prison, ignoring her requests to meet, because she was a coward. The sentence for Ciara was the Pipes. She and every witch at HMRC knew it. So why was she foot-dragging? This was rhetorical thinking; she knew precisely why. Niamh knew only too well that almost killing your sister didn't bring any sort of comfort. Funny that.

'I think we're done here,' Niamh said sadly.

'Wait,' he said. 'Please, Niamh . . .'

'Why?' She laughed bitterly. 'Goddess, I feel DERANGED. This time last year, I was just a vet.'

'You were never *just a vet*.'

'I was!' She became aware that she wasn't blinking. She must also *look* deranged. 'You know, not so long ago, the biggest worry in my life was where I was going to watch *America's Next Top Model* because I didn't have Sky. I'd have to go round Helena's! Now Helena's dead; I'm dealing with you, and *her*; I've somehow adopted a teenage girl. I'm a high-functioning zombie, and the end of the fucking *world* is coming up at us, and no cunt believes me.'

She stopped short of confessing *and I'm also being followed by a malignant shadow that makes me want to scream and hide and pull my eyes out of their sockets so I don't have to see it*. Right now, it loomed over them both, stretched across the ceiling.

She took a breath.

'Everyone is looking at me like I'm in charge, but, Luke, I was just fuckin' dead. And the only two people who'd actually know what to do are *still* dead.' She gave a laugh, though it wasn't funny. 'But I'll keep on pretending. That's what grown-ups do, isn't it? We pretend we know what we're doing and hope we don't get found out.'

And silence fell between them, heavy.

'I have to go,' she said finally.

Luke looked up at her with familiar blue eyes framed by familiar black lashes. 'OK. If this is the last thing I say to you, I want you to know that everything I did was because I loved you.'

That made her want to pop his head off like a dandelion. She held her tongue. Strode to the exit and summoned the Supernormal Security women back into the basement. *Love* was as cheap as *sorry*. Words aren't things. Fool's gold.

Jen entered first. 'Get him to Grierlings,' Niamh told her. 'I never want to see that man ever again.'

But even as she said it, she took one last look at his handsome face, and traced it in her mind.

NIGHTGUESTS

Ciara - Manchester, UK

A dream realer than any dream. She remembered curling up with Jude Kavanaugh in halls of residence, her first year at Durham. The room was smaller than her cell now; breeze block walls covered with tatty pictures of Richey Manic and Courtney Love. The window was jammed shut but she'd never felt too hot, even snuggled like penguins in her single bed. And now she knew why.

He wasn't real, and never had been.

'It wasn't so bad, was it?'

Ciara opened her eyes, and felt his arm wrapped around her chest. It was bliss, for a split second, and then repellent.

With a cry, she threw herself off the narrow prison cot and onto the hard, cold tiles. She scrambled into the corner of the room next to the steel toilet. Even in the gloom, she saw the pale, naked form of Jude reclining under her bedsheet. He propped himself up on an elbow, gave her a cockeyed smile and patted the empty space next to him on the bed. 'Come back to bed. I know you like it from the side . . .'

'How the fuck are you doing this?' she cried. 'The prison—'

'You can't imprison an idea, Ciara. I'm on your mind. What can I say, I'm memorable.'

'You're *Lucifer*!' Ciara spat.

'If you say so. I never named myself.' He sat up straighter, the thin bedsheet resting in his lap. He was exactly as she remembered, muscular, sleek as a jaguar. His golden hair was bed-messy.

Ciara tucked her legs to her chest, some sort of shield. 'You can't be in here.'

He inspected his nails. 'I'm everywhere. The hunger in every human heart.'

'But Cassidy . . . how?' Her power had come from somewhere.

'It's a *building*, Ciara. A few charms and potions aren't going to keep you safe forever. Is that why you're hiding in this squalid hole? Are you hiding from me?'

'I don't have a lot of choice in the matter.'

He smiled. 'Oh come on, it's me you're talking to. I know you. Intimately. Ciara Kelly can do anything she puts her mind to.'

Clever little Satan. But she was ready for him now. That flattery might have worked on Ciara Kelly at nineteen, but it wouldn't now. Jude was a fictional creation – a precision tool tailored specifically to exploit her weakness, a bad-boy rebel for the wayward twin. A Clyde for her Bonnie, a JD for her Veronica. She'd been a fool to fall so easily. 'Leave me alone. You aren't even here. You aren't even real.'

Ciara eyed the plexiglass window in her cell door and thought about calling for the guard. Would they believe her? She was all alone in her cell – solitary confinement for her own safety. He could kill her, make it look like suicide.

'Shout if you want. They won't hear you,' Jude, Lucifer, said nonchalantly. 'This is a courtesy call. I came to offer you a choice.'

'And what's that then?'

'Dabney Hale served his purpose. He found the crown, and you destroyed it for me.'

Ciara sat up a little straighter. Outside her window, the moon was a brilliant pearl in the winter sky. 'The Seal of Solomon.'

Jude sighed. 'He was useful to a point. He didn't lack ambition, did he? But I oft suspected he wouldn't quite get us over the line.'

Ciara prayed she'd remember all this come the morning. She'd somehow contact Niamh – force her to talk to her. But she feared he could easily wipe it from her mind. 'For what? The comeback tour? Is Satanis finally getting the band back together?' That was always the prophesy: witches had split Satanis in three, eons ago—Lucifer, Belial and Leviathan. He'd been threatening a return ever since.

Jude laughed and it made Ciara ache. *He isn't real.* 'Something like that. There was a narrow window of opportunity with you two – his narcissism, your nihilism – but that was all Plan B, to tell you the truth. Not that you didn't come in very handy in other ways . . .'

'You used me.' She hated how *weak* he had made her. 'Did I ever make a choice? My whole life?'

He looked to the ceiling, considering this. 'Yes. You are full of bad choices. I more like to think I had a hand in raising you. I had a word in your mother's ear, you know, when she was pregnant. It was almost too easy.'

Ciara said nothing. Her fucking mother. While there was blood in her veins, she would never be free of her. She'd had nothing but time to mull on everything that had happened last year, and she had some inkling of what Satanis might be planning, but she certainly wasn't going to tell him what she knew. In case she was wrong. In case she was *right*.

'Look. As arrogant as he was, Dabney was right about one thing. This *is* the end, Ciara. The Age of Gaia is drawing to a close. Life as you understand it, reality itself, will be forever changed. A dark dawn breaks on the horizon. Your choices are thus: you can join me, embrace ascension to a demonic form, or you can die as a mortal as the earth burns, drowns and splinters.'

She couldn't not ask. 'Why would you give *me* the option?'

He swung his legs off the bed, the sheet somehow shielding his modesty. 'You won't believe me, but because I like you. Not everyone can ride a demon like you can, Ciara. You're something else.'

She rolled her eyes. She rolled her eyes at motherfucking Satan. 'Sure. I bet you say that to all the witches.'

He shook his head. 'Mock if you want, but you've become so much more than just another pawn on the board. You *are* special. Isn't that what you always wanted? This moment was foreseen for the ages. The stars aligned, if you like, and what a star you turned out to be.' He looked deep into her eyes, the way he used to do when they made love, and for fuck's sake, she believed him. 'You've earned it, Ciara. You've earned a place in eternity. We couldn't have done this without you. You destroyed the one thing that could have stopped us.'

A cold, horrid feeling gripped her stomach. He could be lying, but there was a definite satisfaction in his tone. She'd so casually turned the Seal of Solomon to dust at Halloween, like kicking over a sandcastle. 'You're lying.'

'Not this time, my love. But like I said, you'll be handsomely rewarded. Come with me, Ciara. Become a dark goddess.' He held out a masculine hand. 'What's left here for you? Just take my hand, and you become what you always knew you were – more than them. More than *her*. The last woman standing. Show them all. Show them your nature. Become Satanis herself . . .'

She observed his outstretched hand. It might as well be a Big Red Button and, even as a little girl, there wasn't a Big Red Button she could walk past without smacking it. Detonator. It was in her, the hunger for the blast, the glee of seeing things fall apart. Jenga! Timber! Boom!

But no.

'That sounds like hard work, to tell you the truth,' she told him. She clenched her teeth so hard her jaw hurt. 'Maybe you don't know me at all. I'm a pussy, Jude. I got fucked-up while Dabney and Helena did all the heavy lifting, and where are they now?'

His smile faltered. She remembered that too. He didn't like to be wrong.

'How do I know this isn't all part of your Big Plan? Maybe you still need me. Who else have you got to do your dirty work?'

Wounds opened up on either side of his forehead. Blood trickled down his cheekbones as two curling bony horns emerged from his skull. They soon framed his face, like a ram. 'You'll find out soon enough.'

Ciara awoke on her sad little cot, alone. She sat up, checking the dark corners. Outside her cell window, it wasn't even a full moon, and it was overcast.

She remembered the dream though, and knew it was no dream. He was coming, and he wouldn't be alone.

Ciara went to her door and, for the first time, ran her hands over the lock. There had to be something she could do to get out of here. She had to warn Niamh.

THE WITCH'S FORUM

Niamh - Manchester, UK

WWCD? What Would Ciara Do?

It was a little after 2 a.m. as Niamh made her way through Hardcastle Crags. Seemed as good an idea as any she'd had thus far. She allowed the night-time forest and the winter moon to charge her. She felt ready. In a weird way, she was less nervous for this than she was for the hearing tomorrow. *That* really triggered her IBS.

She found her way to the spot where they had buried Ciara's body: Bluebell Meadow. She was making it up as she went along, but it made a sort of sense. This was where they had come back into the world together.

The dell was hard-packed and frozen; brambles bare and glistening with frost. Niamh cleared an area and knelt atop the gravesite. With gloved hands, she unpacked her kit-bag: purple candles for communion, a salt circle for protection. It felt counterintuitive to summon this *thing* that was stalking her, but ignoring it wasn't working either.

What Would Ciara Do? She'd talk to it. Now if only Niamh had spent most of her formative years messing around with demons.

She opened the book and, slightly embarrassed at how not . . . *witchy* it was, shined the torch from her phone over the page she'd folded the corner of. *Summoning a Demonaic Entity*. 'OK, here we go.'

Niamh followed it like she would a Gousto recipe card. She'd taken a small ceremonial dagger from the archives, although she knew that any old knife would have done the trick. Within the circle, she etched the sigils into the soil – painstakingly copying the designs from the spellbook.

All done, she wiped the blade with an anti-bacterial cloth to get the mud off before pricking her finger. She squeezed a few droplets of blood over each sigil, remembering her Nana Hobbs's warnings: *Never trust a witch with plasters on her fingers, she's been up to no good mark my words, girls.*

Hardcastle Crags came alive. On the dangerous side of the salt circle, Niamh heard twigs snap and branches shiver. Her heart ferreted. She wasn't alone. Little voices: *Witch, we serve; How can we help you this night?; Let me know you, child.* Fireflies glittered from the naked trees. They weren't fireflies.

A frigid wind cut through the meadow and Niamh steadied herself, sinking her fingernails into the soil. 'Where are you? Show yourself.'

Ignoring the lesser demons teasing at the edge of the barrier – a hedgehog that wasn't a hedgehog; a series of fat moths – Niamh looked across the dell. There was her leech.

'Here. Come to me. Now. I command you.'

The shadowman was drawn closer. Tonight, it was shaped like a tadpole; a human torso dwindling into a thin mertail, connected to the earth. It resisted, trying to pull back. For the first time, she heard the apparition; it almost squealed. Focusing her mind, Niamh reeled her fishy in.

'What are you?' Niamh asked.

It did not reply. Instead, its petroleum head split, a mouth fell open, jaw gaping unnaturally wide. It did not speak, it roared. A hot belch like shit and rotted meat blasted Niamh in the face and she recoiled, vomiting at once. She remembered she *must* remain in her *Zisurrû*.

She heard a buzz. Fat bluebottles spilled from the shadowman, penetrating her safe circle. The flies swarmed her and all she could do was curl into a foetal ball. 'Stop!' she cried, but soon pressed her lips together as the flies entered her mouth, little legs on her tongue.

How naive she'd been. She'd thought it was as easy as using the phone book. She'd called and *he* had answered.

'Don't hurt me,' she whispered. 'Theo needs me.'

Becoming aware of a second presence on the other side of the barrier, she dared to open her eyes. Ciara crouched, catlike, just outside the *Zisurrû*. She wore pleather hipsters and a barely-there strappy handkerchief top. Niamh recognised it as the clubbing outfit she'd most envied, back in the day. She'd never have the balls to wear it. 'Nice try, babes. What were you gonna do? Cut it off with your little knife? It's not a skintag.'

This was not her sister. 'Lucifer?'

She blew her a kiss. 'I'll see you soon enough, darl. If you try it again, you'll regret it.'

With that, the demon that looked like her sister burst into flames. Niamh screwed her eyes shut but couldn't get the stench of flesh out of her nostrils. It smelled of barbecue drippings and burned hair. She begged for it to stop.

When she opened her eyes again, Niamh was alone in the woods, bedraggled and muddy. She had rarely felt so powerless in her entire life.

Niamh slipped the claret robe of the High Priestess over her normal clothes. She hated this fancy dress stuff. This wasn't what a witch was. They might as well shove a pointy hat on her head. A witch was something like rain or grass, not velvet and gold.

The exertions of the previous night had left her dog-tired as she changed in the antechamber off the Forum. She checked herself over in the mirror. She'd pass as professional, her hair neatly tied back. The leech waited in the reflection alone, pressed like a spider in the corner by the door. After last night, it was almost sulking, she could feel it. 'I'll try again,' she told it, and it retreated up the wall onto the ceiling.

There was a polite tap at the door. 'Come in,' she said, and Radley Jackman entered, wearing his own cape.

'I apologise, I thought I heard you talking to someone?'

'Nope, all on my lonesome,' she lied.

'They're ready for you,' he told her.

Niamh nodded. She could ignore her requests no longer. It was time to face her sister. Their day in court, at last. 'I'll be there in a minute.'

The Forum was a circular chamber in the same wing of Grierlings as the Pipes. Built at the same time, it was a grim venue, sanitorium-like with its tiled walls and floors. The laurel-green hue only added to this austere, clinical feel. The dome lights which hung from the high ceiling were modern, of course, but they barely dented the gloom of the chamber.

The judicial witches took to their podiums, all facing inwards to the centre of the bullring. Members of the community were allowed into the viewing stall which ran around the perimeter of the hall. Niamh threw a quick glance to Theo, Leonie, and Holly and Elle where they waited in the front row. This wasn't a mundane court of law; there was no jury, because they had their own brand of justice.

The founders of Her Majesty's Royal Coven had agreed to the charter with Queen Victoria and the Prime Minister of the time, William Gladstone: the witches were entitled to their own laws, provided they police their own. *That* was how and why witches still executed those who would betray the coven.

Niamh took the stairs onto her rostrum, careful not to trip on the cape. She was directly opposite Priyanka Gopal, representing the board of HMRC. To her left was Radley, and to her right was Selina Fay from the Shadow Cabinet. Next to her was Ute Schnell, High Priestess of Hexenzirkel in Berlin. Niamh had always liked Ute from afar. She'd been in post since 1979, as unflappable and no-nonsense as her flat shoes and grey bowl cut. She nicely offset the witch to her left: Alyssa fucking Grabowski. The American

Priestess had flown back especially, and Niamh couldn't help but feel this was a judgement on her judgement.

It was procedure to have a sister from an overseas coven adjudicate a coven trial, but that's what Ute was for. Alyssa had volunteered.

Maybe it was fair. Niamh could hardly be expected to be partial at this hearing. The accused was her sister. And had murdered her fiancé. And her. But had also saved the world. It was complicated.

Niamh felt sick, but she also felt *sure*. Of one thing, at least.

'Everybody rise!' demanded the forum leader, a wiry witch who'd been in the post as long as Niamh could recall. Jean took her role *very* seriously. 'We witches gather here today for the inquest into Special Case 258: Her Majesty's Royal Coven versus Ciara Kelly.'

A mechanical grind rumbled far below them, and a grate opened at the centre of the forum floor. A cage ascended into the courtroom from the bowels of the building. It was archaic. There *had* to be a more modern way to strip a witch of her powers. Niamh saw Theo looking on from the gallery and was reminded of how Helena had kept her in a cage once too.

It was tall and domed: an adult-sized birdcage sprang to mind. It was roomy enough for Ciara to stand fully upright. Niamh tried to keep the surprise off her face. She looked very different to Lucifer's apparition in the forest. Since she saw her last, her sister had cut off all her hair, and sported a nasty purple bruise to her cheekbone. She'd been hurt. It was hardly surprising given what she'd done to the rebellion's poster boy, but to see her sister swollen and injured sparked some playground ember instinct to wade in and defend her. Even after everything, their childhood remained how it had been.

Fuck. Niamh knew at once she'd made a grave error. She ought to have seen Ciara privately before today. Even the thought of sitting opposite her had made Niamh feel like someone was wringing her intestines. Her dithering had left her unprepared and weaker for it. Like, what the fuck where they meant to say to each other after all this time? *Hey there, sorry I murdered your fiancé! LOL it's OK, I shouldn't have put you in a coma for a decade either! Truce?* The forum rendered those conversations impossible.

Jean barked again. 'The Forum also calls forth the witness Luke Sawyer.'

Sawyer? Interesting. His mother's maiden name. Luke Watts, Luke Ridge, Luke Sawyer. He'd had more names than she'd had hot dinners.

A second cage was winched up into the Forum. Luke, taller than Ciara, did have to hunch a little. 'Well, why's he in a cage?' Niamh asked. 'He can't do anything!'

'That we know of,' Radley interjected. 'He is witchborn.'

This was insanity. She'd *know* if he had powers. Although he had somehow shielded his entire backstory from her, a Level 5 Adept. Fuck, maybe he *was* a warlock. Her mother would be so proud.

Niamh regarded the sorry state of both prisoners. 'Are you both OK?' She sighed. What else was there to say?

Luke nodded.

Ciara said, 'I've been better. I've also been worse.' Her tone was pointed.

Her sort-of ex and her sister in cages before her. This was ridiculous. 'Let's get on with it,' she said, opening the leatherbound folder on her platform. 'Ciara Louise Kelly, you stand accused of murdering a sister witch, misuse of supernormal abilities and the most serious charge of betraying your coven. How do you plead on these matters?'

Her twin didn't flinch. 'Guilty.'

'Great, well there we are then. Case closed.' Niamh made a great show of slapping shut the file.

'The punishment for betraying the coven is death by fire,' Alyssa spoke out.

'Thank you, I'm aware of that. We recently toasted our High Priestess.' Niamh glared at the American. 'And it's for that reason that my first act as High Priestess is to urgently review the use of the Pipes and capital punishment in general. It's draconian and has no place in modern witch culture.'

As a kerfuffle broke out, she briefly caught Luke's eye. He looked *proud*. She ignored him. She'd had him put in a sort of comfortable confinement in Hale's former lodgings at Grierlings – for his own safety and theirs – but it was a temporary measure. He was a knot she couldn't untangle.

'With respect, you can't unilaterally change centuries of tradition,' Selina Fay added.

'Why not? *Tradition* is the worst reason to do anything. It's not even a reason, it's an excuse.' The civil servant wilted under her gaze. She saw Ciara smirk slightly. 'I'd remind everyone here that I was elected to make coven decisions.'

'Then what do you propose?' Radley said.

Niamh hadn't got that far. All she knew was that it was wrong to execute people, whatever their crime. She also knew this was a convenient moral excuse she was telling herself because she couldn't resign her sister to death.

She gestured at the caged pair. 'They aren't going anywhere, are they? Look. I hate this whole place. I don't understand its purpose. Do we just lock people away? Forever? Some of the people here pose no threat to the coven whatsoever. Is this experience changing them? How? Or are they locked up here so we feel good about ourselves? We're hurting them because they hurt us? It's not working! I still feel shit about everything they did!' Alyssa grimaced at her zesty language. 'The existence of Grierlings is beneath us witches. I understand my sister did heinous things, but there has to be a better way . . . for her, and for us.'

In the gallery, Theo and Leonie both clapped loudly. 'Tell. Them.' Leonie cheered.

'Great,' Alyssa chipped in. 'Again, do you happen to have any suggestions or are we just virtue signalling?'

Niamh had one suggestion, but was pretty sure Alyssa didn't want to hear it. Luckily, Ciara spoke before Niamh could tell her counterpart to shove it. 'I'd like to speak with my sister in private,' she said, wrapping her fingers around the bars.

'Absolutely not,' Jean snapped.

Ciara looked up at her. If it weren't for the cage and the *Sister's Malady* in the air vents, Niamh would have known precisely what she wanted, but as it was, it was a moot point. 'It's too late, Ciara.'

'Niamh, *please* . . .' She shot her an urgent look.

Niamh didn't want to do this in front of an audience. She didn't want to do it at all, which was why she hadn't visited her in jail. She felt the weight of stares, everyone waiting to see what she'd do next. 'We have got to stop this game, Ciara. Too many people have been hurt. I think it's better that you remain here. I'll make sure you're safe, but you can't be free. At least not now . . .'

'For the love of Gaia, Niamh! Do you ever shut up?' Ciara shouted. 'You've got to listen to me, all of you. Satanis isn't coming, he's *here*! He is right here, in Grierlings!'

'What do you mean?' Radley asked her.

She glared out from between the bars, eyes almost silver in the low light. 'Lucifer came to me in my dreams.'

'Impossible,' Jean said. 'Grierlings safeguards against such entities.'

'Try telling Satan that. Not a big fan of sticking to the rules. Funny.'

'Ciara!' Niamh stopped her. 'Enough. What do you know?'

Ciara glowered up at her, her green eyes framed by tired red circles. 'I can help you. But not like this. Get me out of here and we can fight this together.'

'You've gotta be fucking kidding. No way.'

'Really?' Even now her sister milked her moment. 'I'll tell you where Conrad is.'

The Forum fell silent. Niamh wondered for a moment if she was imagining things. 'I . . . what?' Her heart beat in her ears. Conrad was dead, cremated and scattered in Santorini at sunset. She knew exactly where Conrad was.

Ciara tried to speak quietly, but acoustics of the vast dome were working against her. 'Look, I *was* planning on telling you in private, but you didn't give me a chance.' She winced as she said, 'Conrad isn't dead.'

Niamh was too winded to even respond. Her mouth gaped and she looked helplessly to Leonie.

'Ciara, what the fuck?' Exasperated, Leonie called from the gallery.

The room was spinning. Niamh felt the floor tip and she had to grasp the podium to stop herself from falling. Ciara didn't once take her eyes off Niamh. 'We've got a *lot* to talk about, sister.'

CON-FESSION

Ciara - Manchester, UK

Niamh hadn't said anything in a very long time.

Ciara had been allowed to accompany her sister to the Head Warden's office in the Men's Block so they could use the computer there. If they were outside of this hellhole, Ciara could have unravelled the spell she cast all those years ago, but as it was, Google would have to do.

It was all there in screaming colour.

> **MYSTERY MAN FOUND ALIVE IN SWANSEA**
> **STILL NO CLUES IN MYSTERY MAN CASE**
> **WHO IS 'JOHN DOE'?**
> **POLICE BAFFLED BY AMNESIA MAN**

'This can't be real.' Niamh was as sickly pale as any redhead had ever been.

'I'm sorry,' Ciara repeated for . . . actually, she'd lost count of how many times she'd said it. Niamh was seated in the wheely chair, and Ciara paced behind her. She was glad of this brief taste of life outside Grierlings, even in this dour, nicotine-bronzed office with its plastic plants. Nicer yet to be alone with her sister, at last.

Niamh rubbed her temples, hands propping her head off the desk. 'But I saw him. I saw his body in the cottage. There was so much blood.' She spoke like a robot, not taking her eyes off the pictures of Conrad.

There had been a public appeal, naturally. His pictures were released to the press. But while the power of the media is strong, Ciara was stronger. The clever little spell ensured Niamh blithely ignored the news reports coming from South Wales. Only now, when forced to look, did she see. 'It was all a glamour. None of it was real.'

Niamh now turned to look at her, a bitter scowl twisting her features. 'You couldn't do that; you aren't that powerful.'

'It wasn't just me. I invoked a demon,' Ciara admitted. She recalled her final visit to the cottage, the entity that had slithered from the shadows into her body. 'I . . . I think it was Lucifer himself.'

Her sister said nothing. Ciara really missed the days when she'd thought the whole Satanis thing was a story to scare little witches.

'It was so powerful, Niamh. I've never felt anything like it. I rewrote reality for fuck's sake. Only I knew the truth.'

A tear trickled out of the corner of Niamh's eye and she wiped it away before it could roll. 'But why . . . ? Why would you do that?'

Ciara found she didn't have an easy answer to that one. 'He sent me to *kill* you.'

'I wish you had.'

Ciara crouched at the side of the chair. 'As if I'd do that.'

'You *did* do that.'

'I didn't mean to!'

'So you decided to kill Conrad instead? That's so much worse, Ciara.'

'No! I had nothing against Conrad. I liked Conrad.'

A tear ran down Niamh's pale cheek. 'So then *why*? For fuck's sake.'

'Just remember how . . . sick I was back then, OK? I wasn't me.' Ciara took a breath. 'I . . . it was just meant to be a joke.'

Niamh pushed the chair back, and Ciara fell onto her arse,

banging her head on the desk. 'Get away from me, you fucking psychopath.'

'I *told* you, I was out of my mind!' Ciara snapped, bored of tiptoeing around her. 'Pot, kettle, black! You ripped my soul out, remember?'

'Because you killed my . . .' She stopped. Reality was starting to reassert itself. What Niamh thought she knew, she did not. What was it they called it? *The Mandela Effect*: false memories shared by swathes of people, each swearing they believe occurrences that simply never happened.

It was fair though. To Niamh, Conrad had been dead. It'd been real enough to make her kill. Almost.

Niamh stopped and drew a long breath. 'OK. Enough. Enough tit for tat bullshit. Where the fuck is he? What did you do to him?'

Awkward. She pulled herself upright using the desk. 'I, um, left him on a beach. He remembers nothing, and anyone who remembered him thought he was dead. I made sure if he showed up in the press, you'd forget it as soon as you saw it.'

'But *why*?' Niamh asked again, chipping away at her.

It all came careening out of her throat like some screaming genie freed from her bottle. 'Because I was jealous of you! I wanted to hurt you. Death wasn't enough, I wanted you to feel the same pain I had felt my whole fucking life!' Ciara yelled like she'd never yelled before. 'Happy now? There, I said it.'

Niamh was silenced. Ciara regrouped, embarrassed at the soft pink flesh she'd just shown.

'Anyway. I was doing you a favour!' It was an approximation of the truth. 'Dab would have killed him sooner or later. I put him out of harm's way if you think about it. Even Dabney believed the spell. Everyone but me.'

Even Niamh couldn't deny that. Dab would have hurt anyone who stood in his way. Niamh's tone softened. 'Jesus fucking Christ, Ciara. It's been *ten years*!'

She leaned over the desk. 'And whose fucking fault is that?' she retorted. 'When you came to the Carnoustie, I knew it was over, we all did. You'd caught Dab. I was going to tell you the truth, and undo the spell. I swear to Gaia. Only you severed me before I got the chance.'

A horrid silence followed.

Niamh came back to the computer. The news cycle had moved on quickly and there were only the official police pictures to look through. John Doe – a nod to his American accent – was found on the Gower Peninsula in South Wales, stark-bollock naked. The cuntier parts of the internet thought it was a hoax, or that it was an elaborate marketing campaign for an HBO series.

Nope, it was just her spell.

Niamh touched the computer screen. His face was as handsome as ever, if more bewildered than usual. 'Did you hurt him?' she asked in a small voice.

'Not physically.'

Niamh's bottom lip trembled and her eyes were wide. It reminded her of the weeks immediately after their parents died, how they'd tried to not cry to keep each other strong. 'Do you know where he is now?'

Ciara sighed. 'No. Not exactly. The spell was so strong, I created a memento mori, inside my head – only the opposite, I guess. A knot in my mind to make myself remember he *wasn't* dead. Only then, when you attacked me, I lost it. I lost *everything*. I only remembered when the Seal of Solomon fixed me up again.'

Ciara swallowed, watching Niamh. They had bigger things to worry about than Conrad Chen, she knew. Every time she remembered Jude's – Lucifer's – taunts she felt acutely sick. But this was her sister.

'Look, I think I can help you find him. I wanted to make sure I didn't lose him. But I can't do it in here. I can't sense shit in here.'

Niamh considered this. 'How do I know this isn't just some scheme to get out of here?'

Ciara gestured at the images on the screen. 'Hello?'

'This is fucking insane.' Niamh stood and walked to the office door.

'Where are you going?'

'Away. Before I fucking sever you again.' Niamh slammed the door shut behind her so hard the walls shook. The door locked, sealing her in the office until someone came for her.

That could have gone better, Ciara mused, slumping into the empty swivel chair.

22

SLEEPOVER

Elle - Hebden Bridge, UK

Elle cooked. Lentil lasagne. She liked the challenge of vegan cooking. She also liked setting the table with the nice rattan mats and candles, even though it was just Lee and Niamh. It felt like a FUCK YOU to Jez. She could still be the hostess, even if she wasn't a wife anymore.

Was his Child Bride living in his new flat with him? According to her spies, yes. Did she care? Also yes, but she mostly found it really sad – for both of them. Jessica Summers was twenty-four years old, and Jez was forty. There was a whole Milo between them. What on earth did they talk about on a night? Did people think he was her father when they went out? Mortifying.

Anyway, it was kind of Niamh and Leonie to come over on her invitation. Niamh had brought Theo, obviously, but she was upstairs doing whatever it was Holly and Theo did up there. Elle had assumed a post-mortem would be necessary after Ciara's hearing, but she hadn't anticipated just HOW necessary.

She flitted in and out of the kitchen to the dining room, making sure everyone had enough to drink. Lee wasn't drinking because she was on antibiotics, but she kept Niamh's glass topped up. Finally, when the vegan cheese had performed some attempt at melting like regular cheese, she carried it through and placed it at the centrepiece of the table.

'Sweet Baby Gaia, I needed this,' Niamh said once they were eating.

Leonie patted Niamh's knee under the table. 'We've got you. Today was a *lot*.'

Elle washed down some garlic bread with Sauvignon blanc. Did Jessica have such solid friends? Doubt it. They'd been friends since before that little trollop was born. They'd been friends since before she'd met Jez, even. She was confident their friendship would outlive Jez and Jessica's fling.

These women were now officially the loves of her life. 'Have you decided what you're gonna do?' Elle asked Niamh.

'I'm gonna drink a lot more wine,' she said before ruefully adding, 'I don't know. I'm so angry.'

Leonie and Elle shared a subtle look and Elle knew what she meant. She couldn't see the problem. 'But Conrad is alive!' she said. 'Isn't that amazing?'

Niamh almost flinched. 'Yeah, of course . . . but he's been missing for ten years. So much has happened. His dad died a couple of years after he . . . vanished and his mum remarried. Am I meant to explain all that to him? I . . . I'm older now too. With HMRC, and Theo, and everything . . .' She didn't mention Luke, so Elle didn't ask, though she was dying to know how she felt about him being back on the scene. They waited for her to go on. 'Ciara has made a fucking mess here. I don't know what to do. What do you think I should do?'

'Go get him!' Elle decreed, again not really seeing the issue.

Leonie was more thoughtful. 'It's Con. You loved him and he loved you. Ciara took that away.'

Elle saw Niamh's lip quiver. 'Forever?'

'No!' Elle said. 'She can undo the spell, can't she?'

'In theory,' Lee said.

'Things can go back to how they were before.'

Niamh shook her head. 'How? How, Elle? Helena, and Annie, and Theo, and . . . what Ciara did to me. I don't think *I* can be the same as I was before.'

'We're all older,' Leonie said matter-of-factly. 'We all weather. But did you ever stop loving him?'

Niamh didn't hesitate. She shook her head.

'Then that's all that matters.'

Elle couldn't hold it in a moment longer, she had to know. Annie had always said gossip was a drug, and yes, Elle was a junkie. 'I don't know if I'm allowed to ask this, but what about Luke?'

Elle's carefully considered mood lighting flickered as rage tore through Niamh. 'What about him?' The framed pictures on the mantelpiece rattled.

'Steady there, Red.' Lee placed a hand over Niamh's.

'Luke is nothing. Luke can stay in Grierlings until we figure out what to do with him. I don't even want to talk about him.' She abruptly changed the subject. 'Elle, how are you? Theo told me about Jez . . .'

'I don't want to talk about him either,' she said, although she really did. It was *all* she wanted to talk about. Scenarios played over and over in her head. There was the one where a car fell on him while he was at the garage, and it crushes him to death. There's the one where Jessica cheats on him with a younger man and he tastes the shame. The worst of all, though, was the one where he came home and asked for forgiveness. In that skit, she'd make him suffer on the sofa for a few weeks, but then she'd start the work of moving past his betrayal.

She would take him *back*, and for that, she *despised* herself. What a weak, pathetic creature she was.

'Stop!' Both Niamh and Leonie said it at the same time. In this state, she was no good at hiding her thoughts. Who was she kidding; she'd never been any good at it.

'Elle,' Leonie began. 'What you have been through . . . is unspeakable. *Of course* you want Jez here to take care of you.'

'Don't feel bad about that,' Niamh added.

'This is our fault,' Lee went on. 'We could have told you a lot sooner.'

Elle poured herself more wine. 'You didn't do anything wrong.'

'We could have stopped him,' muttered Leonie, knowing full well that broke coven law. You can't just use witchcraft willy-nilly on unwitting mundanes.

'We can help you,' said Niamh. 'Let me take some of the anguish.'

Elle smiled kindly. 'Haven't you got enough of your own, love?' That made them all laugh. What a mess. What an absolute fucking mess.

It felt to Elle like they were entering a new era. If their twenties had been about girlish freedom, and their thirties had been about establishing themselves as women, their forties felt like an unknown proposition. Truly grown-ups. They knew themselves now. But what to do with that knowledge? She knew one thing now that she hadn't when they were sixteen: these friends were her friends for life. They were going nowhere. That, if nothing else, was reassuring.

Elle cleared their plates and served some apple crumble for dessert. The exchange went some way to clear the air, and she knew not to mention Conrad or Ciara again tonight.

'OK, my turn,' Leonie announced once pudding was out of the way and they'd retired to the lounge with a cafetière of coffee. Decaf, obviously; they weren't students anymore. A sniff of caffeine after 3 p.m. and Elle would be awake all night.

Leonie took a deep breath. 'Confession time. I came up under slightly false pretences.'

This time Elle glanced at Niamh. This didn't sound promising. What NOW?

Leonie sat between them on their big leather sofa and took one of each of their hands. 'OK, what I'm about to tell you is a lot, and I'm gonna need you to keep an open mind.'

'Jesus, spit it out,' Niamh told her.

'I'm pregnant, BUT,' she jumped in before either of them could say a word, 'it's not what you think.'

You could spread the silence on toast. 'What do we think?' Elle said, aghast. Donor sperm, if she had to guess.

'I . . . I'm pregnant with Gaia's baby.'

Niamh withdrew her hand and looked like she was trying to figure out the punchline. Elle instead had the strangest sense of déjà vu. It was as if she'd seen all this in a film or perhaps in a dream.

'Is Gaia some woman you know? Are you her surrogate?' Niamh asked uncertainly.

'No! I mean, like, actual Gaia.' Leonie looked rather sheepish. 'I told you it was a lot.'

'You're not serious?' Niamh said, but Elle was already on her feet. 'What are you doing?'

'I'm getting our Hols,' she told them.

She had not seen these images on television *or* in her sleep. She had seen them in Holly's GSCE Art sketchbook.

The three women stood at one side of the dining table, waiting for Holly to explain herself. 'Well?' Elle asked.

Holly just shrugged. Theo too scoured the pictures, and Elle saw she was just as surprised as the rest of them.

The piece Elle had remembered was sketched in smudged charcoal and was undeniably Leonie. Elle hadn't realised when Holly had first shown her it because of the shorter haircut, but now it was clear. It was Leonie, and she was cradling a swollen, pregnant belly.

'When did you draw this?' Niamh asked.

Holly looked at the date. 'October.'

Elle shared a glance with Niamh and Lee. 'Before the coronation,' she said.

'October. That was around the time I think it started,' Lee murmured, not taking her eyes off Elle's daughter's artwork.

They flicked through the pages of the sketchbook. A collage of magazine images showed a red-haired woman with two merging faces, back-to-back like Janus. An earlier piece – this one in vivid orange and red wax crayons – depicting a woman on fire. 'And this was last year . . .'

'Helena?' Lee breathed.

'I don't know!' Holly said, exasperated. 'I can't help what shit pops into my head!' Elle told her to watch her language.

Niamh took a deep breath. 'Holly, we might need to do some further testing on you. Are you aware you're seeing things which haven't happened yet?'

'No,' Holly said, suddenly curious.

'Do you think she's an adept too?' Theo asked. Both girls now seemed excited, gripping each other's hands.

But Elle's heart sank. She couldn't help it. Being an oracle looked so hard: the hair loss; the visual impairment. Not that it had ever bothered Annie. 'Another adept? I thought you were supposed to be rare!' Elle asked.

Niamh shook her head. 'Maybe.'

'It'd be a helluva coincidence,' Leonie said, turning back to her portrait.

'I didn't even know this was you!' Holly said. 'And look! Not everything I draw comes true.' She leafed through the book. 'Here's Charmander marrying Squirtle while holding a pansexual flag.'

'Hols, your great-grandma was one of the most legendary oracles of all time,' Leonie said. 'I'm not surprised you got a bit of her mojo.'

'And your mum is a lot more powerful than she lets on,' Niamh added. Elle flinched, remembering that awful day in the garage. Sometimes Elle thought the power inside them didn't always come from a place of 'love and light'.

Niamh took Holly by the shoulders. 'Never be afraid of your own strength. Own it.'

And now Holly looked to Elle. How things had changed since that night up in her bedroom when she'd sliced into her hand to prove she was a witch. That evening felt like a hundred years ago; the memories of some other, much more naive, woman. Right now, her daughter needed her again. 'I'm proud of you, Holly. I am. An adept. Annie would have loved this. She always knew you were special. Well, of course she ruddy did.'

Holly smiled bashfully, her shoulders inching down. Her daughter was becoming a woman, and a witch. She, if nothing else, was real. Lucifer couldn't take that away from Elle.

Still, as she remembered Holly at bath-time – in a buggy, on her first day of nursery, the endless sodding *Peppa Pig* – a part of Elle felt like she *was* losing her daughter. To this *thing*, a thing none of them ever chose. *Witchcraft*.

Leonie looked over her portrait once more. 'You saw this?' Holly nodded. 'It looks like I'm about to get a lot bigger.'

'You're gonna keep it?' Elle asked. If there was a more tactful way of phrasing that, she didn't know it.

'Yes,' Leonie said.

'Are you sure?' Niamh put in.

'It's a gift from Gaia.'

'Girl, you return gifts all the goddamn time,' said Niamh.

Leonie laughed before sobering. 'While that is true – sorry, Elle – this feels right. Don't get me wrong, I've been back and forth, but Chinara helped me see things differently. I can't explain it.' She stroked Holly's drawing tenderly. 'This was meant to be. I don't know why, but I trust Gaia. She made me who I am and she didn't make mistakes. Black, lesbian, witch. I have to trust her on this too.'

Elle wished she felt that intimate with Gaia. Maybe she'd spent too long pushing that feeling away; the warm glow within when you're alone at night. That feeling that you're not quite alone, but in a good – not creepy – way. To her, that sensation was Gaia, and for thirty-odd years, she'd been wishing it away.

'But . . .' Elle said tentatively. 'What was the gift for?'

'What?' Lee looked confused.

'Is Gaia just giving out presents now? Like . . . why? Feels a bit random.'

Her friends looked to one another. Leonie could only shrug, her mouth forming an upside-down U. 'I don't know. I didn't really think that part through. Maybe she saw how much Chi and I wanted a baby?' She didn't sound at all convinced.

'Dare I ask what else you've drawn?' Niamh angled the book away from Leonie.

Elle hadn't thought that far ahead. From Holly's face, the enormity of all this hadn't even started to sink in. She went from vacant, to concerned, to downright fretful in less than a second.

'What?' Leonie prompted.

Holly wilted. 'Well, we did a lesson on Goya . . .'

'Oh fuck,' Niamh said.

Neither of them exactly art fans, both Elle and Leonie asked for clarification. Instead, Holly flicked to the last page.

It was a double spread, depicting a massacre. Haunting charcoal figures – bodies – were piled on top of each other, horror etched on their twisted faces. The pyres burned, throwing plumes of thick smoke into the air. And, emerging from the fog, a faceless, horned figure loomed over the destruction.

'Right then,' Leonie said. 'Great.'

'I saw this too,' Niamh said. 'Irina Konvalinka showed me this right at the beginning.'

'We were warned,' Leonie agreed.

'Leviathan will rise.' Niamh had never sounded more defeated.

Theo shrank back.

Elle knew the first part of that prophecy. They all did. *The Sullied Child would take him by the hand, and Leviathan will rise.* She considered Holly's artwork. If her visions came true, they were in trouble.

Elle felt acutely sick. Instinctively, her hand covered her mouth, but, luckily, she kept her crumble down. She would not lose another child. She could not. When Satanis came for them, she *would* save her daughter.

But how? She felt like a flea standing at the bottom of Everest. Niamh and Leonie's lips continued to move, but Elle could only hear her own thumping heartbeat in her ears.

Elle possessed an awful, terrible power. She had almost killed Robyn Jones in the Methodist church. She had *very* nearly killed Jez. But she couldn't *control* whatever darkness it was she contained. And she was going to fail Holly unless she figured out how to.

There was something inside her, something pulsing, something red and livid. Every time her mother had told her to be a Good Girl, every time she'd sat up straight, every time she'd worried about disappointing Jez, it had fed. Elle was bloated on a thousand swallowed words. She'd bottled it for so, so long but it was time to release it: her rage.

It was time to be a witch.

WATCHFUL WAITING

Snow - Hebden Bridge, UK

Snow watched their lovely dinner party from the top of the neighbour's roof. She crouched on the tiles alongside a birdshit splattered chimney stack like some gargoyle. Elle lived on a cringe middle-class cul-de-sac where all the Barrett houses were identical, and the grass was plastic. The people were plastic too, so smug with their big cars and bigger TVs.

Snow saw them moving around through the front room windows at Elle's. She had known these women her entire life: *aunties* in name, all of them. Elle was her guide-mother. Witches don't get christened, that would be absurd, but Elle had sworn to protect and raise her if anything ever happened to her mother, just as her mother had for Holly.

Instead, the three women at that dinner party had sent her mum to her death.

Snow turned now to Helena, who sat casually beside her, the evening breeze ruffling her chestnut hair. 'Shall I torch it?' Snow asked. 'They're all in there. We could do it right now.' The thought of Theo's skin and flesh burning was irresistible. This was all her – *his* – fault. Everything had started when that freak got to town.

Helena beamed. 'While you score definite marks for enthusiasm, now isn't the time.'

'When is? It's been weeks. I'm *ready*.'

'I know you are, my sweet girl, but don't forget about the other one.'

'I'll kill Ciara too.' Snow made the extra effort to sound tough, but she meant it. When the time came, she wouldn't flinch. The way they hadn't hesitated to put her mother in the Pipes.

'I know, but it won't be easy while she's in Grierlings.'

'How do we get in?'

'I'm working on it,' Helena said. 'But I'm going to need you to do something first, Snow. It's a big ask, and it won't be pleasant.'

Snow watched shadowy forms move around in the light coming through the blinds at Elle's place. 'I don't care. I told you. Whatever it takes.'

'Whatever it takes?'

'Yes.'

The entity that looked exactly like her mother smiled. 'Excellent. Then I'll need you to meet a friend of mine . . . he's called Belial, and he's very important.'

HOW DO YOU LIKE YOUR EGGS IN THE MORNING?

Niamh - Hebden Bridge, UK

How she had missed waking up to the polite chatter of pots and pans in the kitchen, the kettle tooting on the stove, the aroma of fresh black coffee in the pot. She floated down the cottage stairs lighter than she had since . . . well, since she died.

Luke stood with his back to her, teasing fried eggs off the bottom of the frying pan with a spatula. She liked them over-easy so they didn't have a trace of that spunk-like globbiness on top. This all meant the hens must have laid – the only time she ate eggs was when she knew they'd been nowhere near a cage.

'Morning!' he said. He wore yesterday's boxer shorts with a Foo Fighters T-shirt. 'Coffee?'

'Please,' she said. In the fallow period between Conrad and Luke, she'd scarcely bothered with breakfast; most mornings just getting a flat white on her way to the clinic. Now she found herself ravenous as she woke, her appetite adjusting to her handsome new chef.

She slipped her hands around his waist and rested her head on his broad shoulders. 'How did you sleep?' she asked.

'Like a baby. There's something about your bed.'

'Or maybe it's just me,' said Niamh with a smile. 'Who knows what my sentience is doing while I sleep . . . ?'

He grinned. 'You giving me sweet dreams? I love that.'

She laughed. Only then something chilled at her core.

This wasn't at all right. Luke was in Grierlings.

Nor was she dreaming. He was warm. His T-shirt smelled of Ecover detergent. She released her hands and took a step away from the imposter. 'Who are you?'

The man in her kitchen turned round. Oh, he looked like Luke, but he was both ice cold and burning hot at the same time. A cruel smirk curled his lips in a way that Luke would never. 'I thought we should catch up properly after I saw you in the forest the other night.'

With a glance, Niamh summoned all five of the knives from the magnetic block on the counter. Even the bread knife. They hovered around her like drones. She turned them, aiming them at the doppelgänger, pointy end first. She launched them at him, and they passed right through him as if he were gas, clattering off the stove splashback.

'Good one,' he replied calmly. He took a step towards her and she backed into the kitchen table.

'Get out.'

'But we haven't had a chance to talk, what with you being dead and everything.' He took an insouciant sip of his coffee. 'I met you only once, when you were a little girl at Leisureland, not that you'd remember it. I knew your mother and your sister very well indeed.'

Niamh tried to remain calm. If she couldn't hurt him, maybe he couldn't hurt her – or Theo, who was presumably still upstairs. Demons were weak on the physical plane; that was why they so relied on witches or warlocks to do their bidding. 'Just leave us alone, you smarmy motherfucker.'

He made a show of looking offended by her language. 'I'm not here to cause trouble, I'm just here to collect.'

Niamh said nothing, refusing to play along.

He came closer. He didn't just look like Luke, he smelled like him. Unfussy soap and deodorant. 'You have something of mine,' he breathed. He looked past her into the lounge and she followed his outstretched finger. The shadow was under the sofa, pressed into the dark. Its white eyes peered out of the darkness.

Her leech. 'What is it?' she breathed.

Luke, or Lucifer, grinned. 'A friend of mine. I think you know his name. Why do you think I went to so much trouble? Do you have any idea how long all this took?'

'Are you going to tell me your evil plan?' Niamh said, trying so hard to be Buffy. That's what you do in the face of the Big Bad; you don't sob, or run, you do a sassy quip.

He shrugged and pushed himself up onto the kitchen counter. His hairy legs swung against the cupboards. 'Sweetheart, *you* were the plan.'

'What?'

'You all were!' This was all so much worse in Luke's deep Yorkshire growl. She used to find such sanctuary in it. 'Dabney, Helena, Ciara. Nudging them so gently along the path they thought they were making *choices*. Getting Ciara to kill you; getting Theo to bring you back. Everyone had to be in the exact right place at the exact right time – for him.' He nodded at the thing under her couch.

'Tell me what it is.'

'You. Know.'

Niamh took a deep breath. The nebulous dread she felt now in the pit of her stomach was what she had felt in Irina's vision, what she'd felt looking at Holly's picture last night. Pure, oily terror. Fear. 'Leviathan.'

Lucifer made a 'hmm' noise and helped himself – somehow – to more coffee. 'Not *quite*. But it will be soon enough.'

Niamh scrutinised him. 'The witches who defeated you—'

He looked affronted. 'Excuse me, we were not *defeated* . . .'

'They *split* you.' Unlike him, Niamh hadn't had her coffee yet, and her mind was performing gymnastics to keep up with him. 'Into three entities, and they hid you in different places, so . . .' Oh. It suddenly made sense. *This* was why necromancy was outlawed before laws were even written down. Her fore-sisters didn't want anyone opening doors they'd locked. Where better to hide something you never wanted anyone to ever find. 'They hid him *in death*.'

Lucifer smiled and gave her a jovial wink. 'Very good, top of the class. I myself was sawn in two and sent as great mountains of ice to the north and south, frozen . . . until humanity let me melt. My brother Belial was shot into the heart of the sun, until humanity pierced the bubble around the skies. My brother Leviathan was plunged into the endless abyss of death. Well, his *essence* was, in any case. And to bring him back from so very far away, I needed a powerful conduit. An adept. Three in fact. You, your sister, and the child. Thank you so much. I appreciate you.'

'Fuck you,' Niamh said.

'Oh, just say when and I'll rail you so hard you won't walk straight for a week.' He looked her over hungrily. Niamh felt suddenly naked in her satin slip. 'Not now though, eh? Now I just need my shadowy little pal over there . . . oh, and Theo.'

'No.'

Lucifer shrugged. 'But she's mine too. I made her for this.'

'Get the fuck out of my house.'

'We need her, Niamh. But I have an offer for you. Give her to us and you'll be spared. You'll be the High Priestess of Hell and the others will be your coven in eternity: Ciara, Leonie, Elle, Holly. Annie and Helena are already waiting for you. You'll be the queens of the damned, and you shall feast on the souls of humanity like nectar.'

Niamh stared him down. 'Did that work on witches in the sixteenth century? Because I'm not feeling it.'

'Easy Way or Hard Way, Niamh. I will spare the witches who bow down to Satanis, or they can burn with the mortals. Just one girl in exchange for all the witches. More than fair, I think.'

Niamh took a bold step towards him. She didn't have to be a vampire slayer, because she was already a witch. Fighting isn't always fists and she sometimes forgot her own strength. It was difficult, like looking for a reflection in a dull spoon, but there was something to read. Her whole body resisted, repulsed as if she was trying to read the worst, most perverted and heinous thoughts in the worst person on earth, but she persevered. She had to do this for Theo. She read him *hard*, mining the onyx that was his soul. 'There are . . . words,' she said, digging into the darkness. 'To banish you.'

A flicker of annoyance crossed Luke's face. She pressed harder and her head throbbed in pain. She was reading a demon.

'Ancient Sumerian?' Niamh said, gritting her teeth. 'I don't understand them, but I can copy them.' Not taking her eyes off his eyes, she recited the words he was desperately trying to hide from her. Strange sounds, beautiful syllables and stops, tripped off her tongue. She had no idea what she was saying, but as the sounds flowed from her lips, she saw him flinch away.

'I made her,' he said again. 'She is *mine*.'

'Get to fuck,' Niamh said, and repeated the incantation, louder this time. Somehow, she now understood what she was saying: *Sister Ki, fortify my heart with the contentment of the now. Silence my ears to the avarice of the Wanton One. Let me not be led astray. Cast him to the darkest pit of man.*

Lucifer flew at her, grasping her throat. He lifted them both off the floor. How was he doing this? He shouldn't be able to touch her. This had to be in her head. She kept on reciting the words of banishment.

'I want you to remember this,' he hissed. 'When every last bitch is sliced from cunt to mouth, I want you to remember you made this choice, Niamh Kelly.'

And he was gone.

Niamh knelt on the kitchen tiles, rubbing her throat. She didn't realise Theo was standing at the foot of the stairs, bleary-eyed and in her tartan pyjamas. 'Niamh?' She yawned. 'What are you doing?'

Niamh stood and crossed to her, wrapping her in a hug. 'I'm not going to let anyone hurt you,' she told her.

'What?' the confused girl said.

'I'm sorry.'

'What for?'

Niamh spoke as she jogged up the stairs. There was a big day ahead and she was still in her nightgown. 'I've been sleepwalking. I wasn't properly back. Well, I'm fucking back now.'

Theo followed her upstairs. 'Niamh, you're freaking me out. What just happened?'

'I got a wake-up call.' It was that time again. 'We're at war.'

Theo needed her in the present. No more delays. No more distractions. No more thinking it over. It was time to deal with the other man she'd been avoiding so she could *focus*.

'I'm going to find my fiancé, and then I'm going to kill Lucifer. How does that sound?'

Theo thought a moment. 'Yeah, pretty good.'

25

PURE SHORES

Niamh - Gower Peninsula, Wales

Because Leonie was pregnant – something Niamh was still struggling to wrap her head around – they had to travel the mundane way. The three of them sat in the back of the armoured truck; one of Grierlings' prisoner transports. Niamh, Leonie and her twin sister, just like old times.

'Road trip! What're we playing?' Ciara smiled, woozy from the drugs they'd pumped her full of. *Sorbus* solution and good old Valium. Her eyes were glassy, unfocused. A prison guard, a grey man of indeterminant age who smelled of Camels and Extra Strong Mints, drove in merciful silence, Radio 5 Live on quietly.

This would be a much easier mission if they could trust Ciara to use her powers to track him down, but Niamh didn't trust her as far as she could spit her, so that was the end of that. It was only because she was High Priestess that she'd been able to get her sister day-release at all. Despite the risk, Ciara was still the best shot they had at finding Conrad. Leonie was more powerful than either of them, and that was why she was along for the ride; if this went south, Leonie could take Ciara, Niamh was certain of that.

'Maybe we shouldn't talk?' Niamh suggested as the truck rolled out of the Grierlings compound and she felt her own sentience return.

'It's a five-hour drive,' Leonie put in.

'What about the licence plate game?' Ciara said.

'There aren't any windows,' Niamh replied dryly. It was going to be a long, long drive.

Six hours and two service station wee stops later, their driver brought them to a standstill and opened the rear doors. Brisk, saline sea air hit her as Niamh stepped down from the truck.

The driver had parked in a layby atop the cliffs overlooking the coast, and the view was at once both beautiful and brutal: jagged, rocky outcrops zigzagged, coves like gums around teeth. It was a biblical sort of a day, a brown sea surging towards the beach in muscular glugs. A wild wind slapped hair around Niamh's face, and she drew her coat tighter.

This was where she'd brought her fiancé. It was alien, remote.

'Why here?' Lee asked, looking to Ciara.

'Why not?' Her sister shrugged. She was a little more alert now. 'I wasn't myself. I was off my tits. It wasn't my choice to make, not really.'

Niamh thought to what Lucifer had said back at the cottage – how they'd all been manipulated. Even so, she couldn't regard Ciara as a victim in all this. Perhaps Ciara still possessed some sentience because she looked at her now, shrewdly. 'You know I could have just killed him. That's what Dabney sent me to do. I was meant to kill *you*, remember.'

Niamh had filled them in on her breakfast encounter on the endless drive down. 'You might *think* you chose to spare me, but *he* needed me. Everything that happened has happened because he was pulling our strings.' She glared at her sister. 'But that doesn't get you off the hook.'

Ciara just rolled her eyes.

'It's so fucked,' Leonie said. Her friend now had an undeniable bump, which she absentmindedly shielded with her hands. 'We've all been played. All of us.'

'We couldn't know,' Niamh said.

'Still,' Ciara added, 'it doesn't feel good. All our Girl Power was bullshit.'

It was true. The anthem of their whole lives, from Barbie to the

Spice Girls, had been *Girls can do anything*. Now it felt like an illusion; a pink-hued marketing strategy dreamed up by a man. By *the* man. Since they were in pigtails and jelly sandals, they'd been dancing to Lucifer's beat, their carefully considered choices stage-managed by their horned Svengali.

Why them? It didn't seem fair. Every child wants to be special, but – as she got older – Niamh craved a kind of normality. Now, more than ever, she wished she were a mundane woman, with worries no greater than the monthly DFS repayments on a corner sofa. That'd be a weird luxury.

Leonie stroked her tummy. 'Do you think he's responsible for this somehow?'

'Do you think that?' Ciara asked.

She shook her head. 'It feels . . . good.'

'Good enough for me,' said Ciara.

Niamh wasn't sure she shared her confidence, but one problem at a time. 'Come on, let's get going. He's not going to be out here, is he?'

They took the van into Swansea, the nearest city, and left it there with their stony driver.

'This would be so much easier if you just let me lift the curse,' Ciara said as they walked a somewhat downtrodden high street. It was populated mostly with empty retail units or vape shops. 'He'd remember who he was and, like, head to Hebden, right?'

'No!' Niamh snapped.

Leonie pursed her lips. 'He's been under a spell for a decade,' she said. 'Can you imagine the shock? It might be like waking up a sleepwalker. We don't want to kill the poor guy.'

Niamh felt hopeless. This was only the beginning. *John Doe* could have gone anywhere in the world in all that time. They could be tracking him for *years*. The busiest shop looked to be a branch of Greggs, and Niamh's stomach grumbled. She could go for a vegan pasty. 'Let's start in there.'

Leonie took the lead. She entered the bakery, and, at once, every mundane in the shop put down whatever they were about to purchase and walked back out, their faces vacant. Leonie strode to the counter where a man with an undercut and a topknot in a hairnet was serving. 'Hello,' she said brightly.

'All right, love, what can I do for you?'

'We're looking for a man.'

'Aren't we all?' Ciara added under her breath.

Leonie ignored her. 'There was a famous man with amnesia. Do you remember? They found him naked on Three Cliffs Bay.'

The man – Huw according to the name badge he wore – stared into space a second as Leonie rummaged through his memories.

'You do remember? It was a big deal, wasn't it?'

'They call him John Doe, no?' he said sleepily.

'Do you know where he is?'

He winced and shook his head. 'No, love. You'd be best off asking Glynis. She knows everyone she does. Works down the Mumbles.'

Leonie released her grip on his mind. 'Thanks, Huw, *love*. Three vegan pasties, please.'

Named after the headland on which it was built, the adorable-sounding Mumbles was a world away from the high street, although only a twenty-minute drive along the coast. It reminded Niamh of Hebden Bridge, not only with its narrow, cobbled streets, cottages, tearooms, pubs and gift shops, but also with its vibes. She could live here, and so, she suspected, could Conrad. A crumb of hope.

There was a dainty Victorian pier on the southernmost tip of the peninsula and that was where Leonie had established they could find Glynis; in charge of the fish and chip shop opposite. Seagulls lurked outside, waiting to dive-bomb unsuspecting tourists. Niamh drove them away, although they complained noisily as they went. She ducked out of the way of a dirty protest.

'Let's try again, shall we?' Niamh said to Lee as they stepped inside, greeted by the aroma of chunky chips and vinegar.

'Your turn.' Leonie gestured for her to take the lead.

The lunchtime rush was over. Only the remnants of a golden-oldies coach trip were seated inside the restaurant, washing down their lunch with milky tea. This time Niamh approached the woman on the counter. 'Hello, we're looking for Glynis?'

The woman, who looked more than a little like Shirley Bassey, regarded them with suspicion. Niamh comforted her. *We don't want trouble, we're friends.* Her face softened. 'I'm Glynis. Who's asking?'

'We're looking for an old friend. A man was found on the beach a long time ago. The papers called him John Doe.'

You can trust us.

Glynis's face lit up, and Niamh felt her insatiable thirst for gossip. Quite natural; girls are taught at a young age the lucrative trade in secrets. 'He's not Doe anymore! He changed it to Gower, after where he was found. John Gower they call him. Johnny to his mates.'

'He's alive?'

'Well, of course he is, love, he's not old, is he?'

Niamh felt powerfully drunk, actually staggering backwards. Leonie caught her and took over on her behalf. 'Do you know where he is?' she asked.

Niamh couldn't work a charm any longer. She took a seat at a Formica table and put her head in her hands. Ciara watched from the window seat. Did she feel guilty? Niamh couldn't even read her sister in that moment.

Conrad was alive. All she'd wanted for ten years. But your most outlandish wishes aren't meant to come true, there's a reliable comfort in their impossibility. It was more than her brain could take.

'Who did you say you were?' Glynis asked, her face wrinkling.

'We're his friends,' Leonie purred. 'We've been looking for him.'

This seemed to confuse the older woman even more. 'He's been lost ten years.'

'So have we, Glynis. Now, where is he?'

'He lives in Langland Bay. He owns some holiday cottages.'
'Is that far?'
'No, just over the hill, doll.'

By now, to Niamh, it felt like they were all sitting amongst sand and silt on the seabed. Glynis's words were echoing and distant. The sound of the ocean filled her head like a conch shell.

Ciara came and sat opposite her. 'Niamh, he's OK,' she said softly, reaching for her hands. Niamh withdrew them, tears pouring down her face. Ciara handed her a too-shiny napkin. It scarcely absorbed a thing.

Leonie turned to them. 'Come on,' she said. 'She won't remember anything if we go now. I think I got a grip on where we need to go. She knows his cottage.'

Ciara and Leonie swept out of the shop, but Niamh found she couldn't walk. 'Wait! I don't know if I can see him.'

For the first time, Ciara's expression hardened. 'Niamh, get it together. Lucifer took him from you.'

'*You* took him from me.'

She raised a single brow. 'So fucking take him back.'

She made a point.

Ten minutes later, the prison truck was parked up outside a charming beach house overlooking the bay. It was painted in a gentle nautical blue with pristine white doors and shutters over the windows. The view from the attic must be breathtaking to wake up to. But then Conrad had always had excellent taste.

Leonie ensured both they, and the van, were cloaked from mundane eyes. Once more Niamh found her feet rooted to the spot. 'Is this where he lives, or one he owns?' she asked.

'I don't know, but this was the one inside Glynis's head,' Leonie said. 'I'm sure of it. I recognise that.' On top of the house was a distinctive swordfish weathervane, pointing northerly.

'Let's take a look.' Ciara took a step towards the driveway, but Niamh grasped her arm.

'No. Let me go alone. Please.'

'He won't know who you are,' Ciara said.

'Even if he sees me?'

She hesitated and then shook her head. 'Not until I break the curse. At least, that's my guess. It's not like I do this on the regular.'

Niamh felt nauseous. Even knowing what she knew, the memories of finding Conrad's 'murdered' body in the cottage kitchen felt real. She remembered frantically searching for his pulse, cradling his stiffening limbs. She remembered his funeral, the suit he wore to be cremated in. It was dizzying to reconcile what felt like two truths within her, but it was getting easier – to distinguish between truth and lie, fact and fiction.

Fact: Conrad was alive.

'Keep me hidden,' she told Leonie. 'I don't think I have the strength.'

Leonie promised she would, and Niamh started a slow walk up the sloping driveway towards the home. It felt like a cortège, like she was, once again, approaching his coffin. She could almost smell the powdery perfume of the lilies and lilacs atop his casket. *Fiction.*

The beach house garden was neat, tall pampas grass bowing to her in the breeze. There was a front terrace with a swing chair for watching sunsets. She dared not enter the house, even invisible. Instead, she made her way down the side of the house, past where the inhabitants had stored some paddleboards and oars, and continued to the rear of the property.

She froze as she heard a voice from within, deep and masculine. It reverberated through the walls. Her heart somersaulted. She knew that voice. Real, this was all real. It was like bringing something out of a dream. Her life as Niamh Kelly Version 1.0 had stalled on the day he 'died', and now it would start again. Would she revert to being that carefree child of twenty-four with all her Pinterest wedding ideas, the one whose heart was soft and unbruised? Was that even possible?

At the back of the house was a lawn and a deck with a covered hot tub. She smiled; Conrad had always been obsessed with the idea of getting a hot tub, believing them to be the height of decadence.

Careful to keep her footsteps ghostly light, Niamh crossed the deck to glass bifold doors. With all the reverence of Christmas morning, Niamh pressed her fingers against the cool glass, squinting inside before quickly withdrawing them; they might not be able to see her, but they would see her phantom fingerprints.

A male silhouette moved on the other side, beyond the open-plan kitchen diner, in the living room. Niamh gasped, hand covering her mouth in reflex. The shoulders, the shape of his head, his haircut the same as ever. He wore cargo shorts and she recognised his shapely calves.

It was him. It was really him.

Only then, the door to the lounge opened, and a woman entered. She was shorter than him, her hair tied in a swinging ponytail. Niamh sensed the cornflower blues of home, comfort, security.

Without ceremony, this woman gave Conrad a fleeting kiss on the cheek and handed him the toddler she carried in her arms. He embraced the child as only a father could.

MY BAD

Ciara - Langland Bay, Wales

'So you're pregnant with Gaia's baby?' Ciara shook her head. 'That's nuts.'

'Right?' Leonie said nothing else, and then they both cracked up. They were waiting on the pavement at the front of the beach house, chatting. It felt good to laugh, Leonie thought; she had done so little of it lately. 'I feel good though. Maybe it's hormones or something, but it feels *right*. I'm having a fucking baby.'

Ciara eyed her gentle tummy bump. 'You starved your Tamagotchi to death because it was, and I quote, "a needy little fucker".'

Leonie's eyes widened as she remembered. 'Jesus. And I used to make my Sims ignore their babies too. Fuck is wrong with me? Hopefully Chinara will keep her alive.'

'It's a her?'

'Yeah. A daughter of Gaia.'

'You can read your own foetus? That's fucked.'

'No! It's more like a . . . development. I can feel a development. Pretty fucking weird, to tell you the truth.'

'Science fiction, honestly. Never me.' Ciara felt twenty years catch up with her all at once. She *saw* Leonie; the faint crow's feet around her eyes, the odd grey hair in amongst her curls. They were *grown-ups*. Ew. 'You'll be an amazing mum,' Ciara told her. 'Not a regular mum, a cool mum.'

Leonie laughed, getting the reference right away. 'I hope I stay me,' she said. 'I still want everything I have now. Diaspora, and my friends, and my life.'

'You will, assuming the world doesn't end,' Ciara said, confident for someone who had no idea what she was talking about. Leonie had just voiced precisely why she *never* wanted children. Too much to sacrifice. She was too selfish, and knew it. Better than being too selfish, and *not* knowing it. 'I don't know anyone who knows who they are like you do. You've always known who you are. You won't lose that.'

Leonie looked genuinely grateful. She had opened her mouth to reply when Niamh came thundering down the driveway towards them. 'Let's go,' she said.

'No one home?' Ciara asked, but Niamh just kept walking in the direction of the truck. She looked stricken.

Leonie turned to the house; her gaze distant. She was reading it. 'Ah fuck.'

'What?' Ciara awaited an explanation. Niamh said nothing, instead climbing in the back of the van. 'Will someone tell me what's going on?'

Leonie took hold of her wrist. She spoke solemnly. 'Ciara, he's not alone in there. There's a woman and . . . and their two kids.'

Ah, fuck.

If the drive down had been bad, the drive back was nails-on-blackboard excruciating. It was after midnight when they pulled through the gates to the Grierlings compound. Leonie had returned to London by train, so it had been just the two of them and their silence all the way back.

Niamh remained with her while they waited for the prison guard to remove her ankle tag. Very Lindsay Lohan circa 2011.

'What are you going to do?' Ciara asked when the silence became too much to bear.

'I'm going to teleport back to Hebden Bridge,' Niamh replied.

Ciara rolled her eyes. 'I meant about Conrad.'

'I know you did,' she said curtly. They sat opposite each other in the drab waiting room next to the warden's room. There was a plastic monstera plant in the corner, and some crimped magazines on the coffee table for visitors. It smelled of Nescafé powder. Niamh sighed. 'There's nothing I can do, is there? I feel so stupid. It never entered my head that he'd have moved on. Because I didn't.'

'That's not true.' Ciara's face scrunched as if it were obvious. 'I know because I found it very hard to pick up where you left off when I . . .' *Stole your body?* 'Became you. Theo, the coven. Luke. You weren't where I left you. Not at all.'

Niamh considered this a moment. 'If I was different, it was because of grief, Ciara. His death changed me on every level. And it wasn't even real.'

Ciara leaned forward and said, all jokes aside, 'Go get him. Let me lift the spell. He has a choice. Let him decide.'

'I can't.' Niamh screwed her eyes shut.

She was going to cry again, and Ciara hated how much it pained her. She asked, very gingerly, 'Is this about Luke?'

Niamh sat bolt upright, like she'd been shocked through the ass. 'What? No! It's about *Johnny Gower*. He has two children, Ciara. He has a wife.'

'So? I don't give two shits about some mundane woman I never met. *Johnny Gower* isn't real. He's *Conrad Chen* and he's in love with you.'

Niamh shook her head. Even drugged off her tits and under the influence of Grierlings, Ciara swore she could feel the absolute defeat pulsing off her twin: brown-grey, like a muddy puddle. 'He was a decade ago.'

Isn't *making amends* or *taking responsibility* one of the Twelve Steps? Ciara was grown enough to own her actual fuck-ups. *This* one was a hundred per cent on her. 'If I hadn't cast that spell, you'd still be together.'

'You can't know that.'

'No, I do,' she admitted. 'Like, it pains me to say this, but you were perfect together.'

Niamh shifted uncomfortably.

'You really were. I knew that no one had ever loved me the way he loved you. I could sense it, remember? It was so pure, so . . . warm.'

'You had Jude,' Niamh said sheepishly.

'Who was literally Satan. Good one.'

'We didn't know that then . . .'

Ciara was bone-tired. Where was the guard to get this thing off her leg? 'Niamh, listen to me. Do you have any idea how annoying it was? You got everything you ever wanted, including the hot fiancé.'

Niamh's face twisted into a scowl. 'So you took it from me? To spite me? Because you were jealous?'

'Yes.' Oof, that one smarted. 'Happy now?'

Niamh eyed her in disbelief. 'No! Not even close! I swear to Gaia, you're still a fucking child in there. It's like you mentally stalled the day Mum and Dad died.'

Ciara was about to argue back; say how Niamh's temper tantrum had cost her nine years of her life. But no. One of them had to break the record or the tune would never change, going round and round in circles forever. Ciara would prove her wrong and be the adult. 'You're right. I wanted to hurt you.'

Niamh's mouth hovered open like Ciara had just uttered the last words she expected to hear. 'Well,' she began, sounding more exhausted that enraged. 'You did. Job well done.' Niamh stood, heading for the exit.

'Hurt people hurt people.' Ciara slathered her tone with irony, but she meant every word.

Niamh paused. 'I am aware of that, Oprah.'

'Can I ask one thing before you go?' Her sister hesitated in the doorframe, so she continued. This could well be the last time she saw her in a long, long time. She had no control over when Niamh would return. 'Did you know?'

Niamh turned back; shoulders slumped. 'Did I know what, Ciara?'

Her voice was small, wobbly, but she would not cry. 'What Mam did to me?' She bit the inside of her cheek in case. It hurt and she tasted blood.

Niamh said nothing for a second, and Ciara was sure she was going to deny it. After a torpid moment, she sighed deeply and said, 'I . . . I didn't understand what was going on. She was so . . . fixated on you. I . . . was a little jealous. You were the special one. It was like she didn't even see me sometimes.'

Ciara was speechless. She couldn't truly believe that. Could she? Fuck it, a tear got out, running down the crease of her nostril. 'If that's true, you should be grateful. I wish she hadn't fucking seen me.'

Niamh looked guilty. 'I . . . our mother died, and I . . .' She staggered over the words. 'How could I think badly of her? Even though . . . I knew something wasn't right.' Another pause, and then, 'Sorry isn't enough. But I am sorry. For what happened. I can't undo it.'

She fucking *had* known. Ciara wiped her tears away. What was the point? Miranda Kelly had been dead for over twenty-five years. She couldn't hurt her ever again. What mattered was now. 'You had Conrad first. You licked it so it's yours. Go get him.'

Niamh didn't look her in the eye as she left.

FORGET-ME-NOT

Niamh - Hebden Bridge, UK

As much as it ached to say it, Ciara was right. There was a sentence she never thought she'd entertain. Four days had passed since their trip to Wales, and despite her intentions, she'd thought of little else at a time when she needed her head in the game.

She and Theo had breakfast at the kitchen table. Coffee in the cafetière, bagels and peanut butter and jam. The good shit: Bonne Maman. 'What are you gonna say to him?' Theo asked.

Niamh shrugged. The coven oracles seemed to think that Ciara's spell could be broken by presenting Conrad with enough evidence of who he really was. Ciara's illusion was strong – strong enough to persist for a decade – but the truth was stronger. It had been enough, after all, for her sister to simply tell her he was still alive for the magic to begin to unravel.

Seeing him with her own eyes had only confirmed what in her gut she knew. Being confronted with his old passport, photos and videos *should*, in theory, be salient enough to dispel Ciara's web of lies.

'I have no idea,' Niamh said with a sigh. 'But none of us have ever had a choice. Ciara was manipulated into everything she did.' Her brain knew this to be factually true, even if her heart hadn't got the memo. Ciara had always taken a twisted satisfaction in her shit choices, even when they weren't entirely her own, and that was hard to let go of. 'Conrad had his memories violated, and he deserves to get them back. And then he can make an informed choice. It's not for me to play goddess.'

Theo put her bagel to one side. 'Do you really think none of us had any free will?'

Niamh knew where that was going. 'That's not what I meant. I knew what I was doing when I brought you here; when I gave you all my power in the woods. I made a choice. No one forced my hand. But . . . it's more we were *placed*? The only reason Helena was even High Priestess was because Lucifer had Ciara kill the old one. Every action had a consequence. Like that game we used to play where you'd write one line of a story and then pass it on to the next person to complete.'

'But who put me in front of Helena in the first place? Me! What I did to my old school. That got this shit started. This is all my fault.'

'It absolutely is not,' Niamh said firmly. 'You were a child, remember. If anything, we are *all* victims. We got gamed. And now it's our move. We strike back.'

Theo seemed to mull on this for a moment.

'You'll be late for school if you're not careful, darl.'

'Do you want me to come to Wales with you?'

Niamh shook her head. 'It's like a superhero film . . . this is something I have to do alone.'

Theo gave her a squeeze from behind. 'I hope . . . I hope it goes how you want it to go.'

Suddenly, Theo recoiled, like she she'd been stung by a wasp. Niamh looked round to see her frowning. 'What's wrong?' Theo almost looked her up and down. Niamh felt a chill on the nape of her neck. 'Theo?'

'Nothing,' Theo said. 'I-I just remembered I didn't do my Physics homework.'

Niamh smiled. 'Use your powers and make Mr Fisk think you did. I won't tell anyone if you don't.'

Theo smiled and picked up her rucksack, but Niamh frowned. The girl wouldn't look Niamh in the eye; nor could Niamh read her. She sighed: a problem for when she was back.

As the coven teleported Niamh back to Wales, there was an awful second of blackness between leaving and arriving: it felt like a glimpse of the void she had found herself in on her journey back to the living. She rematerialised close to Conrad's home, breathless with panic, and keeled forward, running her fingers through the grass verge, still damp and dewy. She was solid, she told herself. She was fine.

She had been paranoid that the witches who sent her here would notice the dreadful shadow that followed her. If they did, they hadn't said anything. That's how polite women are; you don't mention a zit or a bit of facial hair, you do tuck in a label. Thems the rules.

But follow her it had. The leech hung to the side of the street, pretending to be the shadow of a willow tree. Niamh saw it still. It had even teleported with her. What did Lucifer mean when he said it both was and wasn't Leviathan?

One worry at a time. The time would come when she'd rip that shadow in two, but not today. She hoped it could read her intent. She hoped fear itself was able to fear her.

She hoisted her weighty satchel of evidence onto her shoulder and walked towards the house with feet of wet clay. Every footfall was forced. How to do this? Tactful and solemn, the way she'd break bad news to owners of dying pets, or ripping off the plaster? With magic, she could do it very quickly indeed if she so chose – literally ram the truth into his head. That's what Ciara would do.

At the front door, she took a final deep breath and knocked the brass mermaid, her tail clacking. Footsteps padded down the hall.

'Hello?' The woman waiting on the doormat looked confused. Niamh almost laughed. *Of course* she was a redhead. Conrad had a type. Her hair was shorter than her own, secured in a cute knot at the nape of her neck. She wore Lucy & Yak dungarees over a striped Breton. 'Can I help you?'

'Can I come in, please?' Niamh asked, sending her an overwhelming desire to acquiesce. 'I, um, have some information about your . . . partner.' There was a wedding ring on this woman's finger, but Niamh couldn't bring herself to say husband.

'Is he OK?' Her already milky skin went deathly white.

Niamh realised the woman thought she was from the police. 'Yes, yes! As far as I know. Is he not home?'

Niamh sensed the instant rush of relief pulsing through the woman. 'He just popped out to the tip. He'll be back any minute. Come on in.'

The woman led her through a white, airy house, all exposed beachy boards and rattan rugs. Sure enough, there was a framed wedding picture in the hallway: black-and-white, bride and groom laughing amidst a shower of rose petals. 'Ignore the mess,' she said, gesturing at a smattering of toys. 'My youngest couldn't go to nursery today. Bit of a temperature.' She spoke with that sing-song South Wales accent. 'Sorry, what did you say your name was?'

She was strong, her mind resisting Niamh's subliminal control. 'My name is Niamh Kelly.'

'I'm Cari. Are you with the police?'

Niamh stood in the lounge, not sure how to drape her limbs, as Cari filled the kettle at the sink. She hadn't even offered a drink, but that's just what you do, isn't it. 'No, nothing like that. I knew your husband from university.'

'From before he was found?' She stopped. Now Niamh had her full attention. 'You know who he was?'

Niamh nodded. There was a gurgle over a baby monitor resting on the breakfast island. Cari listened a moment, satisfied with the following quiet.

'But that's huge, that is,' Cari said, eyes wide. 'What was his name?'

Niamh hesitated. 'Maybe I should speak with him first?'

'Of course, of course. You're right. Can I get you a tea? Or a coffee? I've only got instant, the Ocado is due later.'

Niamh accepted the offer, mostly for something to do with her hands. This was excruciating. A shopping list of dilemmas was building up: *So I reveal the truth to Conrad, great. Then he has a choice, which is also great because neither of us has ever been given a choice. Let's say he remembers his deep love for me and comes home. That's the ideal. Isn't it? But then I'd have Cari and two children to deal with. I could do what Ciara did; render them blind to the fact Conrad has ever been in their lives. Only, that's impossible because two kids are evidence that there must have been a sperm at some point, so I'd have to create some fictional history to resolve that in Cari's mind. Well, this is a hot fuckin' mess.*

And what about Luke?

His face suddenly bolted across her mind. Intrusive.

What about him? That fucker could fester as far as she cared. Let him remember what he did. Every time she thought even slightly warmly of Luke, she forced herself to consider instead lovely, kind Sheila Henry. She was punishing herself as much as him.

'How long have you been with . . . John?' Niamh asked, picking the scab. No one had cheated, but it felt as a soiled as a betrayal somehow. But then, what she'd done with Luke . . .

'Let's see,' Cari said. 'If we were married six years ago this May, we met, yeah, about eight and a half years ago.'

Fuck this shit. 'Oh wow,' Niamh said, blinking back a sudden sting in her eye. 'A long time.'

'Yeah, well, I met him not long after he turned up really.' Cari filled two mugs with steaming water. 'Is oat milk OK?'

Niamh assured her it was. 'So, how did you meet?'

'Oh, I'm a psychologist,' she said lightly. 'Amnesia, like *total* amnesia you see on TV, is basically a myth, so I was part of a team at Bangor University who researched his case. We worked on the assumption he was probably faking it all, but no. He's one of a kind.'

I'll fucking say, Niamh thought until there was a gentle noise from outside. A car door closing.

'Ah, that'll be him.'

Seconds later, the front door opened and footsteps ambled down the hallway. Niamh almost puked. She felt acid chunks halfway up her oesophagus and swallowed it back.

Almost ten years, and here he was.

'God, the queues at that place get worse,' he said from the hall.

'John!' Cari called. 'There's someone here for you.'

'What?' he bellowed. He seemed to be stumbling around, pulling his shoes off perhaps.

She lovingly rolled her eyes. *What's he like, eh?* 'Can you just come here please, babe?'

He wandered in from the hall, idle as a summer cloud. Barefoot, he wore jeans and a grey sweatshirt, rolled to the elbow. He was stockier than he'd been in his twenties. His face now had a pleasant softness to it, but he still looked younger than his thirty-six years, even with a fleck of silver in his black hair.

He gave her a curious once over. 'Hey,' he said. Even his accent had subtly changed. When they'd met, he was all California, mingled with Dublin, then Yorkshire, and now, it seemed, Wales.

'This is Niamh,' Cari said, and Niamh scanned his face for a grain of recognition. She'd clung to the hope that seeing her would be enough, that the bubble would burst. 'She says she knew you . . . from before.'

'What?' he said, his face falling slack.

A weighty silence was interrupted by another snuffle over the baby monitor. 'I'll go see if she's OK.' Cari gave him a tender good luck kiss on the cheek as she passed him.

He didn't take his eyes off her, but it was a cool, clinical glare. 'You knew me? Did I know you?' Conrad – John – came to the lounge and sat in the armchair. Niamh mirrored him, perching on the sofa. There was a coffee table, a neutral zone, between them.

'Yes, you did. Very much so,' Niamh said. *There*. In his mind, a little bit of their past started to leak in, like sand through a clogged hourglass. She could sense mere crumbs. She'd have to make a bigger hole in the dam.

'Well . . . who was I? What was my name? God, I'm so sorry, this is all such a shock. I have so many questions.'

His face. His kind, loving face. Niamh wanted so badly to reach over and stroke those cheeks.

She wanted to cry.

Why?

Because now she was in his head. How noisy, and joyful, and colourful, these years had been.

The rose petals at the wedding had been blush pink and peach and cream, like raspberry ripple. A pianist played 'You Are So Beautiful' by Joe Cocker as she'd walked down the aisle. Niamh felt, *felt*, his sheer plunge of relief as their first child, Betty, was pulled from Cari at the end of a torturous birth and placed in his arms to cut the umbilical cord. How *fierce* his urge to protect that helpless, gooey pink thing had been. The painting she made for him on her first day of nursery was a brown splodge, but he treasured it. It was framed.

They swam with sharks in Cape Town. They euthanised a sick dog, a Maltese, and cried that night in bed. They went to a cooking class and made paella, but it was horrid. He ran after a toddler as she smeared shit down a wall, and then laughed as they recounted this story to Vik and Sal, their parent pals.

These things. These things in his head were *real*. John Gower was no fiction.

While Niamh had wept alone in a stone cottage, he had been at Glastonbury, dancing to the Foo Fighters after trying MDMA for the first time. Even with the chemical incentive, that euphoria was real.

His life had rolled forward as hers had stalled.

'What's wrong?' he said, and Niamh realised tears were streaming down her face. 'Please, just tell me. However bad it is, I want to know.'

Niamh wiped away the tears. 'OK.' She sniffed, and it wasn't pretty. 'If it meant losing your wife and children, what about then? Would you still want to know?'

His expression twisted into one of near disgust. 'What? I don't understand. There's nothing on this earth you could say that could make me love them less.'

It felt like he had his hand around her heart, squeezing it like a sponge. 'But if it changed everything?'

'Nothing would ever change that. I owe my life to Cari. She made me who I am, and . . . well, do you have children?'

Why does that question always feel like a fucking blade. 'No.'

'Then you just can't know, sorry. It's like a whole new type of love, I swear. So just please . . . tell me.'

Niamh felt the well-rehearsed words ready to take to the stage: *I am your fiancée. We dated for six years. You were my first love. Remember Santorini?*

Instead, Cari came back in, holding a sleepy-looking infant to her chest. What an adorable thing she was too. Would they have had children? Is this what they'd have looked like?

John stood and joined his wife. Niamh instinctively rose too. 'What is it?' Cari asked. 'What did she say?'

Ciara had, on a cruel whim, destroyed her life that day ten years ago. One life, blown to smithereens. Niamh would not make it five lives. 'Nothing,' Niamh gasped. 'I said nothing.'

They both frowned, dazed. She had already begun her work.

She backed towards the hall, wrapping around their minds like smoke. 'You will remember nothing of this. I was never here.'

As she got to the front door, she could already hear John telling Cari about the queues at the rubbish dump. She closed the door softly behind her.

Niamh took some time to walk along the coastal clifftop path, a grizzling winter sea gnawing at an equally grey sky. The coven would collect her from here when she was ready. She did not look back at the beach house as she went, but she left John Gower with one thought to keep.

You were loved.

THE KNIFE

Theo - Hebden Bridge, UK

'I can't do it now, everyone's watching!' Holly despaired. The page of cartridge paper attached to her easel was blank.

Mr Breen let a few students, arty types (*adj.*, Queer), hang out in the art room over lunch because they could be trusted to not trash the place. The worst *they* behaved was a bit of bickering over who got to cast their music to the speakers. Right now, it was just the pair of them. Theo assumed more would turn up once they'd hit the canteen, but for now, they were safe to talk.

'What's in your head?' Theo asked her.

'Do you have any idea how much shit pops into my head all day long? How am I supposed to know what's a vision and what isn't? I mostly think about Dalla from *iDoll* to be honest.'

Theo gave her a look. 'Dalla? I thought your bias was Eun-Ji?'

'Exactly! I change my mind all the time. Either way, I don't think it means I'm gonna marry a Korean idol though, does it?'

'So how did you do it before?' Finding out she was an adept must be a trip. Theo was fortunate, in a way, that she'd found out about witches and adepts at more or less the same time.

'I don't know . . . there was just some stuff I wanted to paint or draw.'

'So maybe *those* ones are visions or premonitions or whatever?'

'Oh great. My intrusive thoughts have meaning. Fun.' Holly

chewed her end of her pencil. 'Do you think my hair will fall out? Do you think I'll go blind?'

These thoughts had, of course, crossed Theo's mind. 'Maybe. Would it matter?'

'No. How cool was Annie?'

'Exactly.' No one was cooler than Annie. 'Being an oracle is cool as fuck. Like, hello, you can see backwards and forwards *across time.*'

'I'm basically Gaia.' They were interrupted by a pair Sixth Form students entering the studio noisily, and shut up at once.

Theo thought she should get some food too, but she was nervous, and when she was nervous, her stomach shrivelled up like a prune. 'What're you nervous about?' Holly asked.

'Don't read me!' Theo whispered, although the Sixth Formers were far too interested in each other to care what a pair of uniformed lower-schoolers were discussing.

'I couldn't help it. What's up?'

'Nothing,' Theo lied. 'Well, Niamh went to get Conrad today. I'm worried about her.' That was true enough to throw Holly off her other concerns. Who knew what life would be like now Conrad was back in the picture. Selfishly, Theo thought she might be a lot less welcome in the poky cottage. It's funny how you can't pick what's freaking you out. Theo knew she should be most concerned that Lucifer had singled her out for fuckery, but no, she couldn't face the thought of losing Niamh. *That* was what kept her awake at night.

'Don't sweat it. Let's do something after school. We could go steal make-up from Superdrug or something,' Holly suggested.

'No,' Theo said, not entirely sure if she was kidding or not. 'I should see how Niamh got on.'

That was a lie too.

Theo was a very good liar. So good, it scared her a little.

After the bell went at 3:15, Theo headed for Hardcastle Crags instead of home. It was cold, and even this early in the evening, it was getting dark. Spring felt like it was years away, thoughts of lazy barbecues in the garden impossible for many reasons. The summer, any future summer, was on the other side of what lay before them all.

Not dallying, but unafraid in her beloved forest, Theo made a beeline for Annie's old cottage – the watermill. It was her conversation with Holly earlier that had given her the idea to come here. Annie, a woman who saw the future, had never seemed scared of her, even at her worst. That had to be worth something. And anyway, her decrepit watermill was empty and no one would see her, which was exactly what she needed for this meeting.

Last autumn, the sale of the cottage had fallen through. It was as if Annie's force of will had been holding the former watermill aloft: as soon as she died, the structure started to subside towards the beck. The firm who'd wanted to turn it into a holiday home had pulled out.

So now the building was waiting for the garden to swallow it whole like a great green whale. Theo had to beat a path towards the front door. Soon, the cottage would be hidden to anyone who didn't know it was here.

The house was locked, naturally, but it took almost no magic to force open one of the windows; the frames were black and rotten. Theo, as flexible as any dancer would be, slipped through the gap with ease, feeling very Catwoman.

Without all of Annie's furniture, and books, and her plethora of cats, the watermill only reeked of damp. Theo tried the light switch and found the electricity no longer functioned.

No sooner had the thought to light a fire entered her head than the hearth came alive with a woof. As the flames settled, Annie's time-worn settee and coffee table emerged from nothing.

Theo braced herself. She hadn't expected it to be so easy. She had come here to summon him, and there he was. She hadn't even needed to prick a thumb. Milo sat in Annie's old armchair, always one step ahead, whatever she did. He wore some very slutty short shorts and a Nike tank top, gold chain at his neck, just the way she recalled. 'That was quick,' she said, testing the old sofa. It certainly *felt* solid. She tentatively sat.

'Well, I know what you want, don't I?' Lucifer replied.

'You tell me then,' Theo said, trying to imagine how Leonie would act in a situation like this.

'You saw it.'

She had. This morning at the cottage, she'd witnessed it. Niamh had *two shadows*. They were equally dark, but only one had made sense given the pale January sun coming from the kitchen window. The other had been pointing the wrong way. That was why she'd needed to speak to Lucifer right now. She was so done with him calling the shots and deciding when and where they met. If he wanted her so fucking badly, he could show up for her. Because this wasn't just about Theo anymore. Niamh needed her. 'Does Niamh know it's there?'

'She does,' he replied.

Theo frowned. 'Why didn't she tell me?'

'The same reason you didn't tell her.'

Touché. Because they wanted to protect each other. Theo moved on. 'OK. What is it?'

'I think you know.' He was so fucking smug. If she thought for a second she could kick him in the face with her Docs, she would.

She'd had all day to worry about it, and yes, she knew. 'It came back with her.' Lucifer nodded. 'I brought it back when I brought Niamh back.' He nodded again. 'That's why you showed me how to do it.'

With an almighty crack and rumble, the cottage walls fractured and split, dust and rubble raining down on her.

She gripped the arms of the impossible chair. 'What are you doing?'

'Showing you the future.' A gale battered the cottage and she could scarcely stand upright. She shielded her face against the dust. As the house crumbled around her, he held out a hand to her. She had no choice but to take it.

'Make it stop!' Theo cried, screwing her eyes shut.

The walls ground apart, tumbled down like sand, to reveal they were standing on the crest of a hill. The whirlwind died down and she heard only birdsong. Theo opened her eyes to see a lush, green valley, birds soaring over the canopy. 'Look again,' Lucifer said.

They weren't birds. They were *Pterodactyls* soaring on leathery wings. 'What the hell?' Theo said.

'Not hell,' he said. 'Heaven. Everyone always assumes the worst of us, but *demon* is a word you gave us. You call Gaia a goddess, but in what way is she different to us? She's only more controlling. She imprisoned us here. But we have *such* plans for your reality.'

'Jurassic Park?'

He laughed heartily. 'Anything you want. You made this possible. If you want the dinosaurs back, let's do it! It's the least we can do to return the favour.'

Theo wasn't impressed. Yes, the tropical air felt wonderful on her face – the air damp and refreshing. It was very beautiful. No concrete and steel and smog, only trees and animals. As far as she could see from this vantage point, the earth almost hummed, throbbed, with abundance, and it was tempting. Well, duh – that was his whole brand.

'I'm not helping you. This is fiction.'

'It doesn't have to be. The world is what you'll make it. You're the one, Theo. Not *sullied*, but splendiferous.'

Theo looked to him. There was a feeling inside her that felt a lot like pain. Oh god, was this her heart breaking?

He confirmed what she'd always known. 'You know it's true. You always knew it was true. Your whole life you've felt like an aberration, but that's because you are one of a kind. You aren't a witch, Theodora, you're so much more. You will become Leviathan Incarnate, my child. That is what you were made for. Like a blade is made to cut, you were made for this. It is your nature.'

'TAKE ME BACK!' she screamed, the words hurting her throat. 'TAKE ME BACK!'

'With you we close the circle, my child. The age of man is over.'

'Then it's a good job I'm a woman.'

He chuckled again. 'This is the last chance I grant you to spare those you love. Accept your birthright, Theodora. I won't ask nicely again.'

'Get that thing off Niamh.'

He stepped to her and cupped her cheeks in his hands. For a second she thought he was going to kiss her, but he instead nodded slowly. 'You can and you will. Don't you see? Only you can do that. It came back with her, but *you're* the vessel it needs. Give yourself to me, Theo. Submit. You have twenty-four hours to accept or I start killing your friends.'

A cool wind coiled around them. 'You can't actually *do* that!'

Something dangerous sparkled in his blue eyes. 'Is that so? Watch me.'

Everything was gone: Lucifer, the jungle, and sky, and Theo was once more in Annie's cold, bare cottage. She hugged herself tight. This wasn't fair. None of this was fair.

A knife is made to cut.

Theo had run her whole short life. She was bone-tired.

TABULA RASA

Niamh - London, UK

Fool's Spring Niamh's grandmother had always called it; those days in late winter when there's just a glimmer of spring in the air and everyone prematurely celebrates the shift of the seasons. *Don't pack away the thermals just yet*, she'd remark. Still, it was nice enough in London for her and Leonie to get hot chocolates and idle along the South Bank.

She had travelled directly from Wales to London with a specific request in mind that only Leonie could help with.

'Are you sure?' Leonie asked her for about the fiftieth time on their short walk alongside the Thames. They'd just strolled under the bridge outside the BFI, where there was a second-hand bookstall. Niamh had browsed for a minute or two, her hands leafing through the yellowed paperbacks, but her mind stayed always on Conrad.

'No,' Niamh confessed, avoiding her friend's gaze by looking down on some hipster types mudlarking below on the riverbank. 'God, Lee, I don't know. I just couldn't do it. It seemed so cruel.'

Leonie said nothing, and Niamh wondered if she was riffling through her thoughts. She occluded her already frantic head.

'Whether he's Conrad or John, he's moved on. I can't wish his wife and kids away.'

'Do you think he'd choose them?'

Yes. And that was the worst part of all. Even Niamh Kelly, High

Priestess couldn't compete with what he had back in Wales. 'I don't know,' she lied.

'So what are you going to do?'

Niamh stopped and looked to the Somerset House side of the Thames. 'Leonie, make me forget.'

She pursed her lips. 'Niamh!'

'Do it! Just . . . make me forget. It was easier when he was dead.'

'You don't mean that.'

'But wasn't it? I was moving on – finally. I was building a life with Theo and—' She stopped short of saying Luke's name. 'Conrad moved on, why can't I?'

Leonie wrapped her arms around her in a bear hug. She had quite the bump now, even through her neon orange puffer jacket. 'Because *he* didn't have to grieve. That's the difference.' That much was true. 'But you did move on. We all saw it. I remember how broken you were at first. It was hard to watch, but you did come out of it. Time moved on. No one can stop time . . . except good ol' Gaia.'

Niamh shook her head. 'It's not fair.'

'It's not.'

'Please, Lee. Just erase him.' Niamh was so tired of being the Good Witch. All her life she'd had these powers and played by the rules. All the pets whose lives she could have extended well past their sell-by dates. She'd been so restrained. She'd earned a bonus.

'No,' Lee said firmly. 'Don't ask again. I'll tell you why, too. We are who we are because of our scars.'

'That rhymed.' Niamh gave her a sour look.

'You have lost so much. We've *all* lost so much. But it makes us harder, stronger, tough and chewy.'

'Lee!'

'I'm serious, even if I'm rhyming. We're gonna need thick hides for what's coming down the tracks.'

She had a point. Niamh nodded. Some twat on an e-scooter almost collided with Lee so Niamh gave him a gentle psychic nudge into the nearest bollard.

Leonie went on. 'I cannot imagine what you're going through right now, but time keeps on keeping on. You'll heal. You did it once before. Remember last summer? You and Luke were tight. You were *happy*.'

Niamh carried on walking, her oat hot chocolate now cool enough to sip. Whenever Luke came up, she felt like her stomach twisted at a right angle. 'You can't build a home on a lie. Me and Luke; it was make-believe.'

Leonie frowned. 'Was it?'

'He lied.'

'But you *were* happy. I didn't need to be psychic either, it was all over your fuckin' face. Your puss was well fed.'

'I'm gonna slap you in a minute.'

'I'm just saying . . .'

'Let it go,' Niamh said archly.

'OK, *Elsa*, whatever, but happy is rare and regret is common as fuck. Remember that.'

Niamh took a deep breath and people-watched for a minute or two as they walked in companionable silence, arm in arm. All these busy people rushing past, with no clue about the world they lived in: the goddess who'd made them, and the demons who were betting against them. Both of the High Priestesses Niamh had grown up with, the late Julia Collins and Helena, had spoken of their responsibility, but Niamh hadn't ever dwelled on it. It's something people say when they're in charge of things – head-teachers, prime ministers and such. Niamh felt it here, though, in the throng of London Town. The witches were all that stood in the way of humanity and demonkind. Niamh was responsible for these people, each of them small but massive. They had MOTs, and Hinge dates, and clandestine affairs, and pregnancy scares, and a hundred episodes of *Dr Pimple Popper* stored on their TiVo. Niamh had to fight for their lovely mundane lives. That was the deal; Gaia had given them great gifts, but they weren't for nothing.

She took extra care to hide her thoughts. The shadow wouldn't be far from her, and she didn't want Leonie to know. Not very empowered thinking, but now that she was pregnant, she simply wouldn't risk her.

'I should really get back,' Niamh said eventually. 'Theo is with Holly, and no doubt I'll have to recount the entire day to Elle at some point.'

Leonie nodded. 'Good luck.'

'And to you.' Niamh wiped a chocolatey smear off Leonie's chin with a gloved thumb. 'You know you don't *have* to involve Diaspora.'

'I know. And thank you for not commanding me to.'

'I'm not Helena.'

She smiled ruefully. 'I owe my coven the truth. Fight or die! The end is nigh!'

Niamh exhaled. 'You rhymed again.'

But Niamh didn't leave just yet; there was a lot to digest. So much so, they extended their stroll well past the Globe.

THE FIGHT

Leonie - London, UK

'What about Gaia?' Leonie asked, through a mouthful of tteokbokki.

'Bit on the nose maybe,' Chinara replied.

It was funny how quickly the blob growing inside her had taken on a face, a future. Leonie had decided she would let her daughter pick exactly what she wanted to wear. They'd try to tackle capitalist gender head-on – no pink anything until she was old enough to choose it for herself.

'What if we went with something gender-neutral?' Chinara suggested.

'Like Alex or Sam?'

She rolled her eyes. 'Well, yes, but with a bit more poetry than that. What about Rain, or Sand?'

'What about something Nigerian? Or Bajan?'

'Maybe. We have time, we'll think of something,' Chinara assured her. She returned to her bibimbap. They were in Jeon's, their favourite Korean place in Soho. It was the exact balance of trendy serving slates and cheap and cheerful charm. Laminated menus with little pictures of each dish.

'And we really need to decide on Jackman-Okafor or Okafor-Jackman, or do we really fuck it up and go for Jackafor?' Leonie added with a wink.

'Well now you're just being absurd.'

'Okaman?'

Chinara paused, chopsticks aloft. 'Actually, I do quite like that, but let's get through tonight before we make any enormous life decisions, shall we?'

Leonie didn't say it was a night tailor-made for grown-up decisions. This was perhaps the most grown-up she had ever felt, not that it didn't make her want to drag her heels more than ever. Perhaps the *knowledge* that you're actively hiding from responsibility is what makes you an adult. 'We should get the bill,' she told Chinara.

They walked from Frith Street to the theatre where they – for now – held Black Mass. The derelict theatre was due to be refurbished any day now. The pandemic was far behind them (she hoped), and this was to be the new home of *Showgirls: The Musical*. A search for a new venue for Diaspora was already well underway. Leonie would prefer something in South London anyway, but she'd miss the faded grandeur of this place.

Doomy whispers had travelled around their community: This was about the busiest she had ever seen a Black Mass. *Leonie is making a statement. Something about the Sullied Child.* Congregants packed the aisles and, from the stage, Leonie could see silhouettes gathered at the back of the stalls. The Royal Circle was no longer structurally sound, or she was sure that would have filled up too. It was *noisy* with both nervy chatter and skittish thoughts, almost more than she could stand. Her hand shielded her tummy, unconsciously.

She wanted all the backup she could get around her tonight. The whole Diaspora board sat behind Leonie on grotty old sofas from the changing rooms: her most trusted deputies, Kane Dior Sanchez and Valentina Goncalves, who had essentially run the coven while she'd been in Hebden Bridge for most of the last year; Chinara; Sanam, the treasurer; and Sabrina, their oracle. Radley had come down from Manchester too, and she was really very touched at the gesture. Or he was just keeping tabs on her, but she'd take all the moral support she could get.

His response to her pregnancy had been one of disbelief, but in the absence of any logical explanation, he'd quietly accepted it. She suspected he'd given up on ever trying to change her mind somewhere around 1998.

Leonie crossed to her lectern and checked her mic. Her voice boomed around the theatre and an expectant hush fell over the audience. It was time. It was past time, in fact.

'I remember standing here, almost a year ago, but – somehow – I feel ten years older. I mean look at me; I've *aged*.' There was a polite chuckle from the stalls. 'I told you back then that the concerns of Her Majesty's Royal Coven had nothing to do with us here. I was wrong.'

There was understandable chatter from the crowd. She saw Madame Celestine amidst the audience, face unreadable. Leonie held up a hand. 'I know, I know, that was pretty much the whole point of Diaspora. But if you can't admit you're wrong and do a bit of back-pedalling . . . well, you end up like fuckin' Twitter.' Another ripple of laughter.

'Everything HMRC does affects us whether we like it or not. Listen. We – *I* – ignored the warning signs. Some international covens are still ignoring them. I wanted to believe that some dusty old-white-lady prophecy had nothing to do with us, nothing to do with Diaspora. But there won't be an inch of progress for witches of colour on a burnt-out shell of a planet. The future of the environment is our future too. Black lives, women's lives, queer lives all hinge on the fate of our planet. No fucker is gonna respect your pronouns when we're fighting to breathe, fighting for water. You get me? I believe all of Gaia's creation is at stake. There are forces, demonic forces, that seek to destroy everything that we are – witches and mundanes alike.'

Leonie sensed a ripple of panic. She'd always been able to take a crowd with her, but if they spiralled off into fear now, she'd never get them back. 'I would never, ever enlist you the way HMRC enlisted us ahead of the war. This is a choice. I feel, as a witch, and as a woman, that I am powerful. I have a skill-set that can do some good. I can help. Tomorrow I'm going to Manchester to meet with the High Priestess to discuss our next steps.'

'*We're* going,' Kane added heroically behind her, gesturing at the rest of the board.

'I don't know what the next steps will be. I know that some of you fought the last time. I know some of you lost people last time. You don't have to answer now, but if you think you could lend your power to the cause, let one of us know.' She felt she had sold them a promise, and just betrayed them, even though she knew it was right. 'I need you to know one thing: this isn't us helping HMRC. It's us helping ourselves.'

Now Leonie saw some emphatic nods as some applause started. She'd done what she had to do.

Still. She couldn't help but hope none of them came with her.

They got off the night bus at Peckham Road and prepared to walk the last couple of blocks. The streets were dark and empty at this hour, save for a savvy fox going through some garbage that had been dumped next to a wheelie bin. Leonie linked her arm through Chinara's and huddled close to her. It was so cold tonight, it almost hurt to breathe. 'Do you think I did the right thing?'

'Yes,' Chinara said without hesitation. 'You gave them a choice we never had.'

'We don't have a choice, not really. If we want a world on which to raise this little one . . .'

'Gaia sent us that child for a reason.'

'I wish she'd sent us more thorough instructions.'

Out of nowhere, a mild wind cut down Havil Street; the vague promise that comes when you step off the aeroplane on some foreign tarmac. The stars even cut through the murky orange light pollution they were accustomed to in London. The air was static and tinged with sulphur. A teleport, incoming.

Gaia is always listening, Leonie thought even as she asked. 'What's happening?' She held her partner more tightly.

'I don't know,' Chinara replied, pulling away. Defensively, both her fists erupted into flames. Leonie, in turn, made sure no one could see them, sending out a powerful urge to the nearest homes to get away from the windows.

Lightning crackled before them, skittering across the street and licking the lampposts. That wasn't usual for teleportation. Was it an elemental? Something else?

As if something sliced through the night, a gash opened up in the air before them. Both witches recoiled. This was unlike anything Leonie had ever seen. The slit widened, and through it she saw another night. This one was balmy and came accompanied by the chirrup of crickets.

A lone, hunched women stepped through this fissure, from the beach to the concrete of South London. She wore a white cotton dress and turquoise jewellery. Her grey hair hung over her shoulder in a single, thick plait, almost to her knees

'Calista . . .' Leonie breathed, hardly able to believe it. Her heart soared way over the crescent moon. How dearly she'd *hoped* the old witch had survived Hale's assault on Aeaea, but she'd had no way of knowing. She'd left the woman hidden in a secret vault, with no way of reaching out to check they'd all made it. She ran to her now. 'You're alive! I'm so glad to see you!'

She went to embrace her, but Calista didn't look so overjoyed at the reunion. She said nothing.

'What happened?'

'Child, this has been foretold since the first word. Since the first letter. Leviathan will rise and Satanis will be as one.'

Leonie looked briefly at Chinara. 'We know. I've gathered my coven. We're ready to fight.'

'I pray you are right.'

'Tomorrow we're going to the north to begin talks with HMRC and—'

'No you are not!' Calista snapped as the tropical wind continued to waft through her hair. 'You don't understand, child. Leviathan has *risen*. He *awakes*.'

31

JAILBAIT

Ciara - Manchester, UK

Was this it? Not *just* the meagre offerings of the Grierlings library, but Ciara's fate.

As for the purgatorial library, there were no fewer than twelve copies of *Where the Crawdads Sing*, yet not a single edition of *The Bell Jar*. It was a musty room, rising damp staling the pages. It reminded her of the municipal library back in Hebden Bridge: Calderdale Council logos and mustard-brown sofas unchanged since 1975. She and Niamh had often gone down on Saturday mornings as girls, where they'd take to a beanbag and binge sugary *Sweet Valley High* or *Point Horror* paperbacks.

Ciara rejected the singing crawdads. She'd take a *Bridget Jones* for nostalgia. She'd sell a tit for a *Valley of the Dolls*. Perhaps now was her opportunity to see why posh girls like Jilly Cooper. She had nothing but time.

Which led to her sole nagging, ruminative thought. *What do I do?* She'd unburdened herself of Conrad Chen – morally if not magically. He was for her sister to worry about now.

But that made Ciara herself the last loose end. Dabney Hale was dead, and the coven would deal with Lucifer without her. They'd made that very clear. Her sister wasn't going to stick her in the Pipes because her sister wasn't an actual dictator. So that just left her here to rot. Forever? Gods, a frightful notion.

Ciara was ever less certain of the goals of this building and those like it. Was she meant to reflect on her wrongdoing? Well, duh, she was fully aware that using demons to off Irina Konvalinka was on the naughty side. That reflection had taken half a second. Was it to stop her doing further wrongs? That it did, she supposed. But in a world with sentients, it was possible for them to look inside her heart and realise she had no desire to harm anyone . . . else. For now.

Only then an ugly voice whispered in her mind: *But you did.* And that was the crux of it. Elle, Leonie, Niamh – none of them would have killed to keep a secret.

Which meant there was something deeply wrong with Ciara Kelly. Screw loose or whatever. So maybe she did belong in this joyless hellhole.

The door to the library opened and Cassidy Kane and her burly sidekick, Monika, sauntered in like they were about to take her lunch money. Ciara wasn't overly concerned. On the days the library was open, it was manned by Eileen, a volunteer witch. Ciara was maybe eighty per cent certain they wouldn't try anything with witnesses present.

Ciara handed Cassidy a copy of *The Bitch* by Jackie Collins. 'Oh hey, I found your book,' Ciara said brightly.

'What is this? High school?'

'Well, you jumped me in the showers, so apparently.' Ciara looked deep into her eyes, scanning for signs that this *was* Cassidy and not a demon wandering around in her shell. Her pupils *looked* normal, but that might not mean much.

Cassidy checked that Eileen wasn't listening. The older woman was busy reading an Agatha Christie paperback. 'I shouldn't have done that. I let my personal feelings about Dab get in the way of the bigger picture.'

'And what bigger picture is that?'

The blonde American lowered her voice to a whisper. 'He spoke to us. It's time.'

Ciara looked to Eileen and realised the librarian wasn't just still; she was *frozen*. Her fingers were stuck, mid page-turn. 'The fuck is happening, Cassidy?'

'Levithan is rising. Like, now.'

'Yeah, I don't fuckin' think so.' Ciara started towards the exit, keen to see if whatever enchantment held poor Eileen affected anyone else.

Cassidy now shouted. 'This is your last chance, Ciara. Join us, and you'll be spared when the tides roll in.'

That was the third time she'd been offered that plea bargain: by Hale, and then Lucifer, and now Cassidy. Before she'd killed him in Manchester, Dab had said a new era was imminent. The dawn of Satanis. He'd said the witches who bowed before Satanis would evolve into a new form of demonic angel.

She could see why the likes of Cassidy would find that tempting. She'd gone from Daddy Kane to Dabney Hale and now Lucifer. It was mortifying that she herself had once sought solace in Dabney's arms, allowed him to feed and clothe her when she was at her lowest ebb. Patriarchy was so *familiar*, there was an idle comfort in it. It was easier to submit than to swim against its current.

Ciara was over submission. 'Tell my ex it's a no from me.'

'What a waste!' Cassidy called after her.

Ciara left the library for the relative safety of the Rec Room. This central atrium was where most inmates spent much of the day. There was a TV, and a pool table, and chessboards and the like. It was here she felt the floor shake. Gently at first, as if a huge eighteen-wheeler were passing by. The other inmates gathered at the tables looked only mildly perturbed to begin with.

Guards patrolled, both on the ground floor and on the mezzanine running around the perimeter of the hall. They stopped, alert.

The rumble grew stronger, and Ciara knew, intuitively, that Cassidy hadn't lied. The time was now.

'Take shelter!' Ciara cried. Dozens of pairs of eyes looked dumbly in her direction. 'Go! Move, you fuckin' eejits!'

The room went dark. The electric lights fizzed and faltered. Sparks rained down. Ciara turned her face to the four-sided glass pyramid built into the ceiling: the skylight. Overhead, thick purple-black clouds gathered over Grierlings.

One of the wardens activated an alarm and a wailing klaxon echoed through the hall. More inmates left their cells or workstations to enter the communal quad. 'Ladies, head for the fire escapes. Meet in the yard,' a warden called down over the railings.

With an ear splitting crash, the ceiling shattered. Ciara launched herself under the closest trestle table as shards of glass rained down. The screams started. The running started. From the library, Cassidy and Monika emerged, the only calm faces in the room. They looked to the skies expectantly.

Ciara poked her head out from under her shelter to see a slight form levitate in through the ceiling, carried on a pillow of ice-cold air. 'The fuck?' she uttered. To use that kind of witchcraft in here was impossible. She ought to flee with the others but found herself transfixed.

As the witch came in to a soft landing, Ciara saw how *young* she was – not much older than Theo. She had silvery white-blonde hair framing a startlingly pretty face and killer cheekbones. She was familiar, but Ciara couldn't place her.

Ciara scrambled out from under the table, making sure no one put themselves between her and the doors at the end of F Block.

The girl, slowly, turned her head to face her. Her bare feet, her cheeks, were streaked with blood, and dirt, and tears. When she spoke, it was with a male voice, deep and far, far older than her exterior. 'Feeble-minded girl,' he said. 'You could have been an archangel on high.'

Ciara knew the voice. *Belial.* And she realised she knew his vessel too. It was Snow Vance-Morrill, Helena's daughter. But she'd only ever met her as a baby, so how did she know that?

It was like her ears popping after landing on the runway. Her sentience! She could hear again! How? Actually, she didn't care how. It was like seeing light for the first time after months underground.

There were two voices inside Snow's head. One was Belial, as ancient and muscular as a mountain face, and the other was a petrified young woman, weeping and begging to be set free. Sheer panic, and such regret. Poor, poor Snow; a cornered animal in her own mind. 'What the fuck did you do to her?' Ciara's mouth was dry.

'She invoked me the same way her mother did. She is become the sword of Satanis. It was supposed to be *you*, Ciara Kelly.'

Blinding rods of lighting forked down through the chasm in the roof. Snow's body was illuminated for only a second before she unleashed whips of electricity in her direction. Ciara's instinct was to fly, but while her powers were returning, she wasn't there yet. She hurled herself, shoulder-first, across the floor, forgetting it was covered in broken glass. It hurt; scrapes and jabs in her knees and hands. She could only hope her healing would return too.

The hall stank of burning. Sure enough, blackened scorch marks pocked the white walls.

Ciara managed to crawl behind a cement pillar as Snow flexed her hands and released another bright white torrent at her. Ciara cowered, pulling her legs under her chin. Searing heat roared past her cheeks.

He meant to kill her. Kill *her*. Of all the fucking witches to take out, he chose the incarcerated one, the one with her powers muzzled. Perhaps she was just the first on his shopping list. Target practice. 'What do you want?' she screamed.

The barrage stopped but she daren't peek out from behind the post. 'Nothing can stand in the way of our ascension.'

Run was her only option. Hoping for some benefit of surprise, she leapt from her hiding place and behind the next pillar, the one nearest the F Wing corridor. Once more she felt flaming heat on the back of her neck. She couldn't stop. She ran down the hall, the fire escape door a pale square at the end of a long corridor.

She hadn't run far when the floor seemed to buckle under her feet. She overstepped and fell forwards, smacking her chin on the tiles. Behind her, Snow placed both hands on the ground. From her palms, the floor split and splintered, rupturing into jagged crevices. *Fuck.* Ciara, her chin bloody, climbed back to her feet and staggered to the wall to steady herself. Dust and plaster poured from above as further spiderweb cracks appeared across the ceiling, and again, she began to run.

He was going to crush her, bury her alive. Chunks of masonry smashed to the floor in front of her. Ciara squealed, ducking out their way. Acrid dust choked her throat and nostrils. Her eyes were dry with grit. The whole corridor churned and convulsed like some carnival funhouse from her childhood. She went down again, this time onto her knees.

Ciara Kelly, better than anyone, knew when she was fucked.

She rolled onto her back as a great slab of the level above lurched downwards. With an almost guttural groan, the celling caved in directly above her. Ciara couldn't even scream. She closed her eyes and waited for the pain.

It didn't come. She opened her eyes and was shocked to see her hands had instinctively shielded her chest. She was holding the slab about half a metre from crushing her. She let out a shaking breath. The concrete block hovered before her. She had enough room to slide herself along the floor on her back using her legs and still be able to levitate the hunk of stone. 'Shit,' she breathed, wriggling out from under it. As soon as she was free, she let it fall.

Head to toe, she was grey with dust. Through the debris, she saw Snow, still glowing, float over the wreckage in her direction. 'Fuck that,' Ciara said and threw herself at the fire doors.

What she witnessed on the other side of the doors very nearly made her turn back round and take her chances with Belial.

The yard between the men and the women's block was a battlefield. With the restrictions on their powers weakened, it was all-out carnage. 'Holy shit,' Ciara breathed.

Some inmates had enough strength to levitate over the barbed-wire fencing. For others, years-long resentments could now be fought the magical way: men against men, women against women and, for the first time within prison walls, men against women. Guards and prisoners and prisoners on prisoners.

The air reeked of sulphur; crackled with electricity. Bodies were hurled left and right; arms twisted backwards with a blink of an eye. Healers inflicted excruciating pain with the touch of a hand. So, this was what a prison riot looked like at Grierlings. It was fast and noisy and smelly. Screams and wails and bones snapping. The poor guards were doing all they could, but most of them weren't especially skilled witches or warlocks. The prisoners could now easily overpower them, although some wardens resorted to mundane tasers or batons. Some had guns; they yapped and popped, and women flopped dead like ragdolls.

Behind her, another part of F Wing collapsed noisily. The yard was thick with a smog of dust and smoke. Flesh cooked. People – men, women – shrieked as their skin peeled.

Ciara flinched and sprinted towards the high prison fence, lungs and calves straining under her first exercise in months. If she could get past the wardens, she'd risk levitation. She was so focused on a gap where there were no guards, she didn't see Cassidy step into her path. 'Going somewhere?'

'Oh for fuck's sake, not now.' Ciara swiped the smaller woman across the yard. She really flew, landing about twenty metres away. Ciara was almost impressed; she thought she'd be rustier.

Only then Monika pushed her hard on the shoulders. Ciara went down, her butt smacking painfully onto the tarmac. 'Come on!' Ciara shouted, glaring up at the boulder of a woman. 'This is your chance to escape! Why are you dicking about with me?'

'Our master wants you dead.'

'Why the fuck do you want a master?'

Monika answered by dragging her up by what little hair she still had. Maybe she should have gone for the buzzcut after all. Monika clamped a hand around her throat and squeezed. Ciara knew, somehow, that this was it. She'd had some near misses, but her luck had finally run out. Some Lithuanian woman was going to crush her neck. She'd hoped it'd be more poetic.

Silver speckles danced across her vision as she stared up at the wintery sky. She tried to send some sort of a farewell to Niamh, a feeling more than a message – a sense of *go well, sister*.

Only then she hit the floor, feet first. She folded like a marionette, quickly regaining her senses. Monika knelt next to her a moment, before slumping down.

Looming over them was a broad silhouette. She was familiar with those shoulders, with that bearded jaw.

Luke.

He held a stolen taser in his hands. 'Come on.'

She didn't need telling twice. He held out a hand, pulled her upright, and they ran.

The yard was almost impenetrable with a wall of smog. It was choking, but it also gave them cover. Ciara and Luke reached the brick wall next to the kitchen fire escape.

'Hold on tight,' Ciara told him.

'Can you do this?' he asked, looking up at the twenty-foot brick wall.

'There's only one way to find out.' She stood behind him and looped her arms under his. 'Sorry if I drop you, loverboy.'

'Yeah, thanks.'

She felt strong though. She lifted Luke off the ground and to freedom.

Luke swore loudly and she clung to him more tightly. He was as heavy as he looked. Below them, Grierlings was swallowed into fire and ruin. Good riddance to it. She watched as the towering chimneys of the Pipes collapsed in on themselves.

'Where are we going?' Luke bellowed.

'The last place you'd expect.'

ALL THE GANG, TOGETHER AGAIN

Elle - Manchester, UK

As far as Elle was concerned, she was at HMRC for moral support and because Niamh had asked her to be present for the scheduled multi-coven summit. She hadn't expected to arrive to a prison-riot-slash-jailbreak.

The open-plan offices on the third floor were in polite chaos, women just short of running around to attend to the crisis. Niamh ran a hand through her hair, an island in the middle of it all. 'Elle, what do I do?'

A witch thundered past Elle, clashing with her shoulder. She shouted a sorry as she hurried away. 'Well . . . delegate?' Elle said. 'You can't go there.'

'I could . . .' Niamh had sensed something was amiss before the first reports reached them. Elle had only just arrived in Manchester when Niamh had stopped dead and announced, *Something is wrong with Ciara*.

'Stop avoiding this meeting.' Elle knew Niamh too well.

'Correct.'

'You've already sent your scariest witches to Grierlings, right?' Niamh nodded yes. Apparently they were deploying *Sorbus* cannons that the Prime Minister had forced Helena to commission, *just in case*. 'So you've done everything you can.'

'Can someone get me an update? Can I get confirmation that my sister is safe ASAP?' Niamh asked no one in particular. All around them, phones rang and rang with no one to answer them. 'Elle, they think it was Snow.'

'It *can't* be.' In Elle's head, Snow was still a cherubic six-year-old, just like Holly was.

'She said she was going to come for me, Elle. Maybe she meant it.'

'You're a Level 5 Adept, I think you'll manage.'

'So I strike her down and kill her? She's sixteen.'

What would she do if Holly went AWOL? 'Have you rung her grandma? Do we know she's left Cornwall?'

'No. Good point.' Niamh flagged down Sandhya and asked her to do it.

Sandhya agreed. 'Niamh, I think you should head down to reception.'

'Has Leonie arrived for the meeting?'

'Not quite . . .' Sandhya's face hinted at further chaos as she headed off to find a contact for Lillian Vance.

Niamh asked if Elle would stay with her; she didn't see how she had a choice. Feeling a bit nauseous, Elle joined Niamh in the lift and they headed down.

Niamh had already explained that Leonie had called in the middle of the night to tell her that the legendary Calista had teleported from Aeaea of all places to warn them that Lucifer was about to make his move. Leonie had been banging on about the fairytale island ever since she got back. Obviously Elle believed her, but it was a *bit much*. Like Aeaea was what they'd put on their list when they did their Fortunes as teenagers. On a piece of paper, they used to each write four guys, say Leo, Skeet, Keanu or Will; predict how many kids they'd have together and *then* where you'd go on your honeymoon. They always started with Aeaea or Ibiza, that was the obvious choice for a young witch in the nineties, but they also knew that Aeaea was as fictional as the idea of marrying Will Smith.

If this Calista woman was a friend of Leonie's, they were probably about to embark on quite a Birkenstocky meeting. She was very likely 'a character'.

But as the lift opened onto the swanky lobby, Elle was first stunned, and then delighted. Waiting, sheepish and awkward in the centre of foyer, were Ciara and Luke. Both were filthy, grey with grime. Call her naive, call her an optimist, but Elle had spent those weeks in Hebden Bridge with Ciara as she masqueraded as Niamh. She was a different beast these days – and here she was, alive and safe! It was like old times.

Elle looked to Niamh, hoping for a cue on how to respond.

'OK then,' was what Niamh actually said and that wasn't quite the *Real Housewives* reunion she'd expected. Instead, she calmly exited the lift and walked through the security gates. Elle followed, letting her take the lead. It was her sister and ex after all. Just as long as Elle got to watch, that was fine. 'So you escaped from prison and came directly to the cops?'

'What prison?' Luke said. 'It's rubble.'

'Grierlings is fucked,' Ciara added. 'We came straight here.'

'Points for good intentions, I guess.'

'Was it Snow?' Elle asked.

'Yes,' Ciara said simply, and this all stopped being even dimly fun.

Elle felt responsible. Snow wasn't always an easy girl to like, but after what they'd done to her mother, they owed that girl a lot more than any of them had given. They'd failed her as a coven, but even more as aunties. She was supposed to be that girl's guide-parent. 'Is she OK?'

Ciara shook her head gravely. 'She is so fucking not OK. She invoked Belial. She'll be on her way. We won't have long.'

Elle was so disappointed in herself that she hardly realised Niamh was talking. 'Why would you come here? You know I can't just let you go.'

Ciara shrugged. 'Because I'm a Level 5 Adept and Satan is about to manifest on earth. You need me.'

'And what about you?' Niamh turned her attention to Luke. 'I don't need you.'

Elle tried to give him a low-key glance of encouragement. He'd lied. She'd lied. They'd all lied at some point. And he seemed sorry.

'I want to help,' he said. 'However I can.'

'Have you become a powerful warlock overnight?' Niamh said. She was punishing him, and no one understood that urge more than Elle.

'Niamh, we can't do this now.' He kept his voice steady and emotionless.

Niamh was about to spit a reply his way, but seemed to swallow it back. 'Don't get in the way, don't ask stupid questions.'

'I'll do my very best.'

The handsome outer doors to Her Majesty's Royal Coven swung open, flooding the grand pillars of the marble lobby with daylight. Chinara entered first, and then Leonie, Radley, Valentina, Kane, and then more men and women Elle did not recognise. As soon as Calista arrived, she knew it was her. She had to stifle a gasp as she cut through the crowd gathering in the foyer. What power. Even as a healer, Elle sensed the sort of radiance she'd only ever witnessed once or twice in her life. Her aura was almost hot on her skin.

She *was* wearing Birkenstocks, though, in that Elle was vindicated. They must deliver to secret islands.

Calista stepped forward from the pack, not waiting for introductions. Niamh met her in the middle. She bowed her head, deferential. 'Welcome to Her Majesty's Royal Coven.'

'There is no time,' the woman said with only a trace of a Greek accent. 'We have a lot to do.'

The Oratorium was Elle's least favourite room at HMRC, mostly because it was so freaking cold. She wrapped a blanket tight around her body. They had air con, why couldn't they heat it up a bit? It was February, for crying out loud.

At least the pews were tightly packed. She'd never seen it so busy. Even with the Supernormal Security girls sent down to Grierlings, it was pretty much the most witches Elle had ever seen at one time. But that wasn't a lot; she saw now that Hale's war and the casualties at Ciara's coronation had very much been a part of the plan. They'd thinned the line of defence. In this hodgepodge of HMRC and Diaspora and the Cabal, there were only about two hundred heads in the room. Oh, there must be many more witches and warlocks out there, but most couldn't float a Pop-Tart out of the toaster. This was it, the best witches in the UK.

Niamh let Calista speak. Elle thought that was Good Leadership because Helena would have absolutely hogged the microphone. Calista didn't even need one. 'Thank you for welcoming me into your coven,' she began. She sat on the cushions usually reserved for the Head Oracle. She looked so old; Elle wouldn't even like to guess at her age. 'We all knew this time would come, and in my homeplace, all the signs are aligned. The tide runs red and the sun no longer shines on our island. The wind sings a lament of things to come. It is time. Leviathan rises.'

Niamh, maybe wisely, had left Theo at home. Elle agreed that the time for arguing who was, or was not, the Sullied Child has passed. Theo was a child, but she wasn't sullied. Only the child part mattered.

'Do we know when?' Niamh asked.

'Soon.'

'How many of you survived the attack on Aeaea?' Niamh asked. Leonie's head bowed.

'Too few,' Calista said. 'We cannot hold him back alone. Aeaea was always in Gaia's plan. A home for us, and a prison for him.'

'Levithan is *there*?' Niamh asked, aghast. She was sitting next to her sister, and Elle couldn't deny it was lovely to see the twins side by side. It had been *decades*. It felt *right*.

Calista explained, eyeing Niamh with something like suspicion. 'His bones were cast in stone and rest in the deepest trenches of the ocean. His soul is . . . elsewhere.'

Niamh looked like she was about to speak, but changed course. 'What would you have us do?'

'You are the oldest coven in the world, but we are sisters all.

We have always been sisters, regardless of where we are born or where we reside. One nation of witches, and now we must unite.'

Niamh looked downcast. 'We will do all we can, but a lot of covens won't believe us. They think we're delusional.'

'We must show them. Gaia made only one home and it is theirs as well as ours. We must try.'

'You want us to come to Aeaea?' Elle spoke up.

Calista nodded. 'It is where He'll rise. Gaia forged us because she always saw this moment would come. We are her weapons.'

Leonie's hand went to her bump. Next to her was Radley. He caught Elle's eye a moment and she looked away, feeling herself blush. When she looked back, he was still looking. Elle didn't look again because, as far as her Year 7 memories went, looking three times might as well be having sex.

Luke was next to Radley. He'd slotted in amongst some warlocks, no doubt trying to blend in. He was laser focused on Calista, as she should be. Elle concentrated.

Calista appealed to them all. 'We are the line between humanity and demonkind. That is what it is to be a witch. If we do not act, He will devour reality and remould it in His image.'

Elle, Niamh, Ciara – can you hear me?

It was Lee, in her head.

Basically, I'll go if you go.

Elle was never the first to commit. Years and years of waiting for Helena to decide on her behalf were all too clear now. Niamh sighed deeply. *As long as Theo is by my side at all times, I'm in.*

Finally, Ciara spoke up. *Girls' trip!*

AN IMPOSSIBLE ASK

Ciara - Manchester, UK

Helena's old office was still sad and bare. Ciara had only used it a couple of times during her tenure as fake interim High Priestess, and it seemed Niamh hadn't had a second to make the room her own either. There were still pale rectangles on the wall where Helena's artwork had been.

'What are you going to do with me?' she asked her sister. The halls of HMRC were still bustling with the aftermath of the witch jamboree, but Niamh had singled her out for a private audience.

'I don't know. Honestly, I don't care what you do,' said Niamh. 'That's not why I asked to talk to you.'

'Is this about Luke?'

'Oh my gods, no!'

'Because if I'd known you weren't dead forever, I'd have never . . . you know.'

Niamh looked at her aghast. 'That's really decent of you after murdering me, thanks.'

It's a naff trope that twins have some sort of psychic connection, and most don't, but Ciara and Niamh really, *really* did. It had taken Ciara a lifetime to realise how much she thrived when she was in proximity to Niamh. Their energies volleyed between them. It was oddly energising. Ciara assumed Niamh felt it too.

'Look, this isn't an easy thing,' Niamh began. 'But I have a huge favour to ask.'

'Reasonable, I suppose.'

Niamh wouldn't look her in the eye. She closed the office door to shut out the hubbub. Her sister took a deep breath and said, 'I need you to kill me. Again.'

Ciara waited for the punchline. 'You've got to be kidding?'

'I'm not. You did it before, and you have to do it again.'

'Are you out of your fuckin' mind?'

Her sister sagged against the big desk, half-perching on the side of it. 'Ciara . . . there's something I haven't told anyone.'

'Well, don't tell me, I don't want your baggage.'

Niamh gave her a stony glare. 'This is your fault. Partly. When . . . when Theo brought me back, she didn't just bring *me*. And I think Calista knows. Maybe Theo too. Something about the way she looks at me.'

None of that sounded good. 'Rewind. What do you mean?'

'You know how Calista said Leviathan's body was at the bottom of the sea? Well, his soul was put somewhere even harder to find. In death.'

Ciara squirmed. 'OK. What . . . what did you see . . . over there? Were you aware?'

'Yes, no.' Niamh shrugged. 'It was like sleep, but I was fading away inside a single memory. It was lovely I suppose, but then there was something else . . . an abyss, just black and cold and empty and that was where I felt it. And since I came back, I've been aware of something following me.'

Ciara remembered her vision in the bathtub, months back, feeling something ice-cold brush against her legs in the dark expanse of water. Maybe twins *are* linked.

'What kind of something?'

Niamh's eyes glistened. 'Look at me.'

'I am.'

'Look at my shadow.'

Ciara humoured her. The vast office windows cast many shadows but her sister's did seem unusually long as it stretched over the ceiling. Even though Niamh's arms were folded defensively across the chest, her shadow's spindle fingers twitched at its side. It had needle-sharp talons. Ciara looked back and forth between the two. 'How is that possible?'

'It's attached to me. I can't get rid of it.'

'How . . . how does it feel?'

A tremoring sigh shook her voice. Maybe relief at finally offloading this burden. 'It feels like everything you've ever been scared of all at once: the crack in the wardrobe door, the hand coming out from under the bed, the cellar stairs, the man watching you at the bus stop. That's what it feels like. It's *Him*. This is why Lucifer did everything he did; it was all a way to get Leviathan back onto this side of the barrier. And we fell for it.'

Ciara paced the office floor, avoiding the additional shadow. She felt its wrongness deep in her sternum. 'Fuck. OK. But that doesn't explain why you just asked me to kill you.'

'Again.'

'Yes, thanks, I'm aware.'

Niamh drew a long breath. 'It's all I can think of, Kiki. This fucker's been following me around like a lost sheep for weeks. Maybe if I go, he goes.'

It hit Ciara. Niamh was actually serious. 'You don't know that.'

'I do. It feels like he's anchored to me.'

'Well, what if you die and then he's just floating around like a leech looking for someone else to latch onto?'

'Ciara, it's the only thing I can think of! Kill me. Forever this time. Bury me and salt the fucking earth. We've both seen what happens to the world if Satanis becomes whole.'

The oracles' vision filled Niamh's mind, and she reminded Ciara, pushing the images into her head. The rubble, the dust, the screaming. They had both seen Manchester levelled. And that would only be the beginning. Satanis had his eye set on reality itself. Air, water, earth and fire all up for grabs. The natural law rewritten.

'It has to be worth a try,' Niamh finished. 'I'm just one woman.'

'I'm not doing it.' Ciara didn't mean to sound as petulant as she did.

'You did it before.' She wasn't angry this time, merely stating fact.

But Ciara had never been surer. 'Niamh, I was *possessed*! Belial! Helena juiced me with Belial. Do you really, *really* think I'd have murdered you in cold blood?'

When Niamh said nothing, it really fucking stung.

'OK.'

Niamh looked her square in the eye. 'Our past doesn't matter anymore, this is the best chance we've got, Ciara. This thing wants Theo. She has her whole life ahead of her, and I'm . . . well, I've died once, I can do it again.'

Ciara turned for the door. This conversation was over. 'Then find someone else. But I'm not doing it. I would never.'

Her dramatic exit was ruined by a knock at the door. Ciara opened it to find a frantic-looking Sandhya poised to knock on the other side. She looked deadly serious.

'What's wrong?' Niamh asked.

'You need to get home. There's something wrong at the cottage.'

The twins looked to each other with a single thought: *Theo*.

34

THE BINDING

Theo - Hebden Bridge, UK

The symposium at HMRC gave Theo all the distraction she needed. She and Holly turned the lounge of Niamh's cottage into a ritual space, moving all of the furniture to the sides of the room. As the evening drew in, a low fire in the hearth illuminated their shrine. The cottage was as protected a space as they'd find in Hebden Bridge, fortified with Niamh's charms and spells.

'Are you ready?' she asked Holly.

'Not really, but you know I'm your ride or die.'

Theo really hoped it wouldn't come to that. She'd told Holly what Lucifer had shown her at the watermill. Both girls had agreed they had to do *something*. They knew things that the grown-ups didn't. They had to at least *try*.

They knelt on opposite sides of the shrine: a low table covered in tight bundles of lavender and parsley, black candles for protection. Holly nodded and placed her effigy onto the shrine. It was male-shaped, in the image of Milo. An ugly, lumpy thing; Holly had fashioned it from pillowcases, teddy-bear stuffing and twine.

'Mother Gaia, hear your daughters,' Theo started. 'Receive this homunculus in place of the demon Lucifer.' She flicked through the grimoire with her left hand, holding her right over the shrine. The candles felt hot on her palm.

'Theo, this is like a binding you'd do on an ex,' said Holly. 'Is it really gonna work on a demon?'

'I'm not an ordinary witch remember,' Theo told her. 'Just concentrate.'

She reached for the length of barbed wire she'd pilfered from the fields down the lane. The grimoire had specified chains, but Theo figured this would work just as well. She rested the wire across both palms and held it over the shrine. 'Mother Gaia, imbue these chains with the power to contain and constrict our enemy.' Then she picked up the little mannequin and started to wrap the barbed wire around it. 'Bind him, Gaia, from doing harm against your daughters. Hear my plea.'

She wound the wire tighter and tighter, the barbs digging into his cotton flesh. As she pierced its 'skin' little beads of scarlet blood soaked the fabric.

'Is it bleeding?' Holly gasped.

'It's working!' Theo exclaimed. 'Bind the demon Lucifer, take his powers, and render him weak.' Blood now dripped onto their shrine, falling in thick dots onto the herbs and runes. For a moment, she dared to think they'd done it.

Then the cottage windows shattered, blowing inwards. The blast reduced the glass to little more than dust. A gale tore through the lounge, extinguishing the candles and swiping away their little shrine.

'What's happening!' Holly cried. 'Is that you?'

'No! I don't know!'

She was answered by a loud crack. Niamh's paintings and photos fell from the wall before an ugly crevasse splintered the plaster. Theo dropped the doll and seized Holly instead, pulling her backwards towards the kitchen.

A chunk of wall was pulled away and a face from the past strode into the cottage.

'Snow!' Holly yelled over the hurricane winds.

Fucking hell. Theo had never liked her.

'Not quite,' a voice said. It sounded nothing like Snow, but Theo had heard it before, once on that fateful night in Hardcastle Crags. It was Belial.

'Holly, run!' Theo said.

No time to think, Theo reached out with both hands and flung Niamh's sofa at Snow. Snow's mouth opened and she spat a fireball at the obstacle before tossing it aside like a thrown pillow. The settee almost roared with flames, and soon swallowed the curtains as well. Snow just stepped through the blaze, not even wincing.

No! Not the cottage. Not her happy little home. She tried to summon rain, knowing even that wouldn't be enough. Maybe she could pull water out through the underground pipes and douse—

She had no time to enact this plan because Snow blasted her off her feet with a mighty gust of wind. Theo tumbled backwards into the corner of the kitchen counter. 'You were warned,' Snow said, toying with her. 'You were given a choice. This could have been avoided.'

Theo glared up at her. 'Tell that to your mother . . .'

Snow's eyes widened and Theo knew there was *something* of Snow Vance-Morrill left in here. She was distracted just long enough for Theo to raise a hand and bring a flaming wooden beam crashing from the ceiling onto Snow's head. This time, she went down, pinned under the hefty plank.

Theo hesitated a moment, deciding whether or not to pull her out. No. That wasn't Snow, not wholly – and Belial would kill her in an instant. Theo ran out through the open kitchen door and into the garden where Holly waited. 'What do we do?'

'Call Niamh! Quick!'

'My phone is inside!'

So was hers. Shit. A column of thick, choking smoke now coiled above the cottage like some fat black serpent. They were in the middle of Heptonstall village; surely someone would call the fire brigade?

Snow appeared in the back doorway, framed by flames. Holly whipped out a hand and summoned a garden fork from the flowerbed. She flung the implement at Snow, but the taller girl batted it aside. 'Pitiful.' Snow sneered and unleashed a bolt of lightning at Holly.

Theo screamed as Holly was pummelled to the rear of the garden, landing hard and rolling into the roots of the apple tree. Theo ran to her side and at once sensed life. She was alive but hurt. She shook her by the arms. 'Holly? Holly, can you hear me?'

Snow walked across the garden towards them, fluid as a panther. Theo held out a blackened hand and held her still. It should have been the easiest thing in the world, but she felt Snow push, push, *push* against her, until her wrist bent so far back she feared it might snap. Theo wailed in pain, but held on.

'Can I tempt you?' An all-too-familiar voice said. Lucifer, as Milo, leaned over her shoulder.

'Go away!' Theo sobbed. Hot tears ran down her cheeks. Her wrist throbbed. Snow's face was focused, murderous.

'Bless your little binding spell. It caused mild skin irritation.'

'Stop this,' Theo begged. 'Holly needs help. Please, let me heal her.'

'You can let go. Snow is mine. She won't hurt you unless I tell her to.'

Theo didn't know if she believed him, but it was too much; she had to release her. Her whole body sagged, spent. Snow remained in the centre of the lawn, crackling with little blue snakes of electricity. White hair circled her face as though she were underwater.

'Last chance, Theo,' Lucifer purred.

'No!' She shook her head miserably. It didn't matter what she did, he was better.

'Remember my offer. No one else has to be hurt. But if you don't . . .' Theo looked at his face, as open and jovial as it ever was. 'You mistake me for someone who can't cause damage on this plain. If you find a crack, you can get inside and cause great damage. See?'

She followed his gaze to where Snow stood. The girl lifted a metre or two off the grass.

'What are you doing?' Theo asked, suddenly very worried.

Milo smiled, his lips only inches from hers. She felt his breath on her skin. 'I want you to see just how harmless I am.'

Snow's legs bent forwards at the knee with a hideous crack.

'No!' Theo yelled, but it was drowned out by Snow's screams.

A ghastly, pained yelp, but only for a second. Snow's spine crunched backwards until her head collided with her rear. One arm went forward and the other back. He then twisted everything the other way, just to show her he could. Lucifer folded his human puppet into a pretzel. He then dropped her to the lawn, broken and bent. Her head turned backwards, Snow's dead face was frozen into something like surprise as a foul-smelling green fog flowed from her mouth and nostrils: Belial, fleeing back into the soil.

Theo stood frozen, too stunned to react. She couldn't look away from Snow's lifeless eyes and knotted limbs.

Lucifer dusted off his hands. 'Do you want me to do Holly too? It's like balloon animals. I could try a giraffe?'

'No!' Theo cried. She wasn't sure he could unless he possessed her too, but she wasn't going to risk it. 'Leave her alone.'

Behind him, the cottage continued to snap and crackle. She could feel the oppressive heat on her cheeks. And it was *noisy*; the inferno seemed to cheer itself on. Niamh's cottage was a skeleton inside the flames.

'I think maybe you forgot what I am, Theodora. I'm God of the Demons. There's nothing I can't do. So here are your choices for a final time: Either everyone you love dies as the world burns, or you can take them with you to our new kingdom. Which will it be? No more questions, no more games. Option A or B?'

Theo looked to the unconscious Holly, and Snow's mangled corpse. The roof of the cottage caved in with a deafening bang.

Lucifer held out a pale hand, and Theo Wells took it.

THE DARKEST NIGHT

Niamh - Hebden Bridge, UK

She had come to this cottage just shy of her tenth birthday. She had lived here with her grandmother, and then Conrad and then, later, Theo.

Now it was a charred husk. How it reeked. Even with Chinara's torrential rain cascading over them, some smaller fires still persisted within. There was nothing left. Her entire life was cinders and black sludge. At least the deluge hid her tears. She let it soak her, raindrops running from her hair over her face and dripping off her nose.

Leonie covered Snow's twisted body with a blanket.

Elle held Holly tight, healing her broken ankle and flesh burns.

Ciara and Radley searched the streets of Heptonstall for Theo. No one knew where she was. Niamh was scared to find out.

The shadow, the thing that had followed her since her return, followed her no longer. She'd looked, she really had. It was gone. Funny; its disappearance was all she'd wanted, but she suddenly wanted it back where she could see it. She had a horrible notion about where it had gone. To *whom* it had gone.

He had called her a *vessel*. The thought of that adipose thing entering Theo . . .

Niamh was aware of Luke's grand frame behind her. 'The dog?' he asked.

She didn't take her eyes off the smouldering ruins. 'He was at Mike's. Thank the gods.'

'Niamh, I'm so sorry.'

'Everyone got out,' she said, her words hollow given Snow's fate. Someone (her) would have to tell Lillian Vance that her granddaughter was dead as well as her daughter.

He wrapped a big arm around her shoulder, and she didn't push him away. 'I know what that cottage meant to you.'

'It's just a house.'

'No it wasn't,' he said, and she gulped back tears. 'It's OK.'

She let herself rest her head on his broad chest and it felt reassuring until she felt guilty for feeling so. She pulled away and looked to where the small form of Calista waited patiently in the rain. 'Theo?'

Calista nodded sombrely.

'Is she alive?'

'Yes. She's no use to him dead.'

'How do we get to Aeaea?'

With a swipe of her arm, a portal opened behind Calista in the fields beyond the cottage wall. From even her position in the garden, she could hear the rush of the ocean.

On the other side awaited the fight of their lives. The final war between the witches and Satanis.

PART II

LEVIATHAN WALKS

There was a star riding through clouds one night, & I said to the star, 'Consume me'.

—Virginia Woolf, *The Waves*

RETURN TO AEAEA

Niamh -

Aeaea, somewhere in the Mediterranean Sea

Standing at closed shutters, Niamh looked out over the island through the slats. The Temple of Circe stood at the southernmost peak of the island, and her bedroom offered the most magnificent view. She watched lightning lick the horizon, far, far out to sea. It'd be beautiful if it wasn't the apocalypse. It had been three long days and nights since they'd arrived on the small island, and the storm hadn't abated for a second. The sea was a dirty bronze, its churning somehow obscene. White spray crashed into the cliff faces, furious, and the little lighthouse on the Cecilia peninsula was barely visible though the lashing rain. Niamh couldn't see the whimsical island pathways Leonie had described, only surging brown currents flowing downhill. All in all, she'd been expecting something a bit more *Mamma Mia!*

The room was the biggest perk of being the High Priestess thus far. According to Calista, the temple had been constructed by the adherents of Circe, centuries after her death, *if* she'd ever lived at all. This suite was atop the temple, with a grand veranda leading off the shuttered doors. Apparently, Calista found it too ostentatious to use as her quarters. Niamh found it to be the exact right level of ostentatious: a veiled four-poster bed, a chaise draped in silks, and dozens of candles nesting in tiled alcoves built into the white walls. A marble effigy of Circe herself watched over the room.

On the downside, this *was* Greece, and even witches couldn't put toilet paper directly down the loo.

Niamh missed home already, but her home wasn't even there anymore. She sorely missed that novocaine numbness she'd experienced when she first woke from the dead. This was worse. Having to appear sane and in control, when she felt like she'd stepped out onto the M1 and been repeatedly knocked down by oncoming traffic. *You're alive again, BANG! Conrad's not dead, THUD! Theo's gone, SPLAT! Your home is a pile of rubble, BOOM!* Limping, she was limping through all this.

They needed a real leader. Someone with Helena's strain of deluded self-confidence and callousness to do whatever it took to win.

Maybe Ciara was better suited to the role after all.

There was a knock at her door, and she realised she had no concept of how long she'd been storm-watching. 'Come in,' she called.

She recognised the polite throat-clearing as Luke, and turned to face her visitor. He wore jeans and a faded Garbage tour T-shirt, washed almost to the point of transparency. 'They're ready for us,' he said.

Niamh picked up her phone. There was no signal out here, but she still carried the thing around like a security blanket, waiting for a call from Theo that wasn't going to come.

'Are you OK?' he asked.

'Luke, why did you come?' she snapped. Then took a breath. She hadn't meant it to sound so harsh. 'Sorry, that was uncalled for.'

He looked wounded but shrugged it off. 'Where else would I go?'

'*Your* flat wasn't just reduced to cinders.'

'I wanted to come.'

'Why?' she asked again, softer this time.

He shrugged wide shoulders. 'Penance?'

She dared herself to look at him properly. She'd been avoiding looking directly at his face because he had the most open, lovely blue eyes, and she'd fallen into them once before. She wouldn't again. 'Is it that easy, Luke? You do us a favour and we all forget what you did?'

He said nothing for a moment. 'I don't know, Niamh. I don't really know how the mechanics of forgiveness work, but I have to try.'

The others could wait another minute or two. It was her prerogative to be fashionably late – and it was past time to have this conversation.

She sat on the chaise and gestured to a high-backed wicker armchair. 'Come in if you're coming in.' He entered the room awkwardly, unsure of what to do with his big hands. 'Tell me the truth, and know that I can compel you to tell me everything, so do it right first time.'

He sat carefully on the antique cushions. 'I'll show you. How about that?'

Words were easier to fake than memories. 'If you wish. On your head be it if you reveal something you'd rather I didn't see – mundanes tend to think of the worst things they've done first. Can't help it.'

'I'm not a mundane, remember.' He gave her a small smile. 'I'm open. Wide open.'

Niamh sighed and let her mind attune to his. The first level was the aura he was giving off: receptive, welcoming. She went further than that, into the meat of his past. Soon she was no longer in the bedroom in Aeaea, but in a small, drab house in Sheffield.

The woman, his mother, was beautiful and warm. She wore her hair very long, and poker straight. She was petite. They had a cat, Trixie, and she used to drag a shoelace across the carpet for it to chase. In the wedding pictures, she had looked very happy, but considerably younger than her husband.

They must have been in love once, though Luke couldn't fathom why.

His earliest memories were filled of this woman. This woman was a witch. A box room; Thunderbirds wallpaper. She made his puppets and teddies dance or move using her mind. She would only perform these little shows if he promised to keep it a secret – especially from Daddy.

How he adored her.

Then a van; a scuffed Head holdall. Luke was pressed into the back of an oily van by strong arms. 'We're going away, stop asking questions.'

'Is Mummy coming?'

'Mummy isn't coming.'

They'd been in the new house, and the new school for a long time before Luke stopped asking where his Mummy had gone. She had 'gone away,' and that was that. At the start, his father was nicer than he had ever been. They went fishing. He taught Luke how to play darts, how to fix a motor engine. But his enthusiasm would not last. It was as if he'd found having a child draining, and could only keep up the Father-of-the-Year act for short bursts.

But Luke came to understand, through the stories his father told as they ate chips out of newspaper while Match of the Day *was on that his mum had left them because she was a selfish woman who chose another life. A life without them. A life with witches.*

Had Luke ever seen his mother do anything unusual? Yes, he had. This narrative checked out. His mother had abandoned him in this joyless home to frolic with her girlfriends. It didn't seem fair. This injustice metastasised within the little boy, growing solid and black in his chest. He no longer missed her; he hated her.

On his thirteenth birthday, Luke was taken to a smelly, beery basement club. Men of all ages clamped him on the shoulder, clapped him on the back and welcomed him. Skinny, gawky Luke felt inadequate and shy. This was where he learned the truth. When his father first suspected his mother of being a witch, he had been directed to this collective. They had shown him how to gather all the evidence they needed to prove she was guilty. On the day he had done so, Luke had been removed from the home he'd grown up in before she could bewitch or kidnap him.

They also told him that there were only two ways to cure a witch, and that was with water or fire.

They had drowned his mother.

But how had they disposed of her body?

There was a mass graveyard on a wasteland near Sheffield. Naturally, there were a number of police officers amongst the witchfinders, so it went unreported.

All the anger towards his mum dissipated. He could believe she was a witch, but she had not deserved to die for it. This realisation was slow, solidifying the more time he spent at the Working Men's Club. All they did was hate women over pints of stout and pork scratchings. They moaned and moaned, and blamed all their personal failings on their existence. There was nothing that wasn't their fault. By this point, he was fifteen or so and there were girls at school he admired a lot, female teachers too. It was becoming that much harder to believe that women were inherently devious, greedy, or out to exploit men using witchcraft if they were witches, or good old sexual wiles if they weren't.

Luke liked the company of women. No, that was reductive – women aren't all one way. He liked having male and female friends. Better.

He went to university, and, with a little distance, he began to pity his father. A man who could no longer love women. He had remarried – briefly – but Denise, while mundane, had only confirmed his dad's suspicions that women were lazy scroungers who want men only for their wealth. When that marriage ended, Peter dedicated himself solely to the witchfinders, eventually becoming their chapter leader.

Luke was a man now. Made redundant from his first job, he went about starting his own business, and that was when Peter had asked him to infiltrate Hebden Bridge. 'It's the new Pendle,' he'd been told. Luke had not believed this claim, despite a dossier of evidence.

'There's a coven keeping track of us,' Peter told him. 'They know our faces. We need new blood. I just need you to watch. With your new job, you've got a reason to go door-to-door, haven't you?'

Guilt. Parental guilt it was. Peter had 'raised him singlehandedly', and he was now calling in the debt.

Hebden Bridge was nicer than Huddersfield and had a rather more affluent client base, much more likely to pay for bespoke fresh veg, fruit and dairy produce. 'Go on then,' he'd told his father in 2018. 'Go on then.' Never had three small words caused so much pain. Except, of course, the obvious.

Had he been surprised at how many witches were in Hebden Bridge? Yes. In his first few weeks in town, he witnessed Lilian Vance float across the room to her wheelchair while delivering milk. He saw Sheila Henry seemingly hold a conversation with sparrows outside the chapel.

And Niamh. The first time he saw Niamh she'd been sunbathing in her garden. In a pretty summer dress, she had been lying on her stomach, legs kicked up. She'd drawn a daisy up out of the earth, one after the next, to make them into a daisy chain to wear in her hair. How very, very beautiful he found her.

And that was where she stopped. She rose from the chaise and pretended to fix her hair in the mirror on the dresser. 'Well, I knew all that.'

He looked crestfallen, and she felt bad at once. He'd just shared excruciating memories, and she'd repaid him in sass – something girls, sadly, learned from poor, male-written television in the nineties. 'OK,' she relented. 'I knew those facts, but I hadn't felt them. I am sorry for what happened to your mam, but it can't ever excuse what you did to Sheila.'

'They were coming for you and Theo.'

'That wasn't Sheila's fault.'

'I had to give them someone!' It was almost a wail. Sitting became too much for him to bear and he strode to the terrace doors, facing the maelstrom outside. 'I *swear* I thought she was going to fucking massacre them. She almost did.'

'I wish she had.' What a cursed feeling this was. Even now she wanted to comfort him, to forgive him, to square this awful circle in her mind. But how could she forgive his betrayal? As a witch; as a woman? 'You are not the man I thought you were. The man I needed you to be.'

'You needed me to be Conrad, and I wasn't.' As soon as he said it, she could sense he wished he hadn't. It was probably a fair enough assessment, though, so she couldn't be mad. He took a breath. 'I don't want to sound like Princess Diana, but . . .'

'There were three of us in our relationship,' she finished for him. He managed a wan smile. She returned the gesture. They were at a stalemate. 'The others are waiting for us,' she said, heading for the door.

'Niamh, wait. One last thing, I promise,' he said, following. 'Look, the thing with Ciara. I would never . . .'

She cut him off. 'I know,' she said, allowing herself to sort of pat his shoulder like he was a faithful St Bernard. 'Maybe I'm truly naive, but that much I knew.'

37

THE SUNEATER

Leonie - Aeaea, somewhere in the Mediterranean Sea

There weren't many women she recognised from her last visit. She couldn't bring herself to ask if that was because of the massacre, or if they'd simply moved on back to the real world. Who'd blame them after what happened? They'd been here for two days before Lee realised Nyssa, Calista's golden lioness, was missing. She'd soon learned Hale's thugs had mounted her head on a spike outside the temple. The sanctuary they'd been promised had been forever violated.

Of course, *right now* it was busier than ever with all the new arrivals. The place had the vibe of a sports hall in a hurricane. Everyone who she'd thought would join her had: her brother, Dior, Valentina and Sabrina, but some additional witches whom she hadn't. Madame Celestine, for one. Leonie was as surprised as anyone that she'd followed them from London. When asked why Celestine had joined them on their pilgrimage, she'd said because she wanted to be with the cat with nine lives – she must carry luck with her. Apparently, Leonie was that cat. She decided to take it as a compliment.

There were too many witches in the hall to fit around the banqueting tables. Women – and a few warlocks – sat wherever they could find space: up against the shrine to Circe, on the well-worn steps, around the tables and on rugs and pillows on the floor. This was the most impressive room in the temple – the intricate and epic frescos on the soaring walls were mercifully unspoiled following the attack. They depicted the origins of Aeaea and all the witches who'd sought sanctuary here over the centuries. The columns that held the painted ceiling aloft were painted in gold leaf, and minute marble tiles were intricately laid out in a spiral pattern on the floor.

Niamh, Calista and Luke descended the stairs together, each carrying huge leather-bound volumes in their arms. Leonie tried to read Niamh, but her defences were higher than ever. She looked tired, and older too. *Niamh* might be a reflection of how *she* looked. She felt a low-level nausea every time she smelled food, her boobs were both huge and sore, and her skin kept breaking out into painful zits. Pregnancy was *fun*.

Room was made for Calista and Niamh at the head of the banqueting table. Luke joined Sandhya and Ciara in perching on the stairs. Ciara looked frail after her time at Grierlings, but Leonie actually liked the pixie crop on her.

This was mad. This was all so fucking mad. Everyone she knew in the world was in a temple on a tiny Greek island, not for a holiday, but for the apocalypse. And she was fucking pregnant despite having never met a sperm in her life. It was so demented; her mind had almost shut down to it all. She was on a strange, amiable autopilot. Chinara seemed to be on tenterhooks, waiting for her to lose her shit, but Leonie felt more together than she had in a long time. Maybe it was Bump. She had to be an adult for Bump. Chinara was next to her on a plush loveseat, massaging her swollen feet on her lap. Her trotters currently looked like Cornish pasties. Pregnancy. Was. FUN.

Calista tapped Niamh gently on the hand. 'It's your coven, my child.'

'Is it?' Niamh asked before reluctantly standing. A hush quite naturally fell over the room. 'Thank you for coming, everyone. It means everything. There's a lot of power in this room right now, I can feel it.'

There really was. Pretty much everyone from HMRC had come

through the extraordinary water conduit they had created together. Only a skeleton crew remained back in Manchester.

'Have we found Theo?' Elle asked from her spot at the table next to Holly.

Niamh shook her head. 'I can't see her anywhere. He's got her really well hidden.'

'But you think she's still alive?' Holly was a twitchy, anxious mess, and who could blame her?

'He has plans for her. She will be alive for now,' Calista said.

'What do we do?' Leonie put in. 'We've been here for days and the waiting around is driving me up the wall.'

'Sunbathe?' Niamh said with a wry smile. The sun hadn't shown its face since they'd arrived. 'We've been studying these.' She opened the first of the ginormous volumes they'd carried down from the library. 'Calista says they're the most complete records of the prophecy.'

'Stories are older than writing, and this story has been told in every tongue, echoing down the generations,' Calista said. 'The story of the end times.'

Niamh cleared her throat. 'See as I see, sisters. Oh, and brothers.'

Niamh closed her eyes and Leonie did the same, waiting to receive the images or memories she was casting around the temple.

Niamh was a skilled sentient, and the pictures arrived with cosy finesse, almost as if she was dreaming on the verge of sleep. The book was full of detailed illustrations, and Niamh provided a narrative in those soothing Galway tones.

Gaia is Mother, and she birthed the world of herself. She willed it into being. She made form from formlessness. From nothing, there was. This newfound permanence was hard and soft, rocks, water, air. She made life, and she was fascinated by it. It was free and made choices. It survived and fought and persevered. The more she made, the more it grew and evolved and lived. There was a little bit of her in everything there was.

Alas, she did not exist alone. She brought her brothers and sis-

ters with her, and they did not like the touch, or taste, or smell or sights of this new state of being. Gaia tried as best she could to imprison and weaken these bitter entities, but they too grew and multiplied.

Gaia's creation was imperfect, but she loved it all the same. It was infuriating and stubborn and self-destructive, but also capable of great tenderness and beauty. She guided it from afar, offering kindness and compassion. The flaws in her great design only made her more loving towards it.

In time, Gaia knew her siblings, the demons, would rise up against her creation. And so she came to earth and imparted a taste of her power to some young women, who then shared this incredible gift with their sisters. These women became the first witches, and they were tasked with ensuring demonkind could not hurt Gaia's precious child.

Many thousands of years ago, in the old kingdom of Kemet, a great and powerful demon rose out of the Nile, a dragon who wanted to eat the sun.

The daughters of Gaia travelled from far and wide, for weeks and months. They were legion, and they were mighty. They took into their bodies all the power of the sun and the moon, of the seas and the skies. Gaia sent unto them daughters of ever greater power and skill.

A thousand and one women died, it is said, and the Nile ran red with blood. The Suneater could not be stopped, but the bravest of Gaia's daughters took a sacred blade and slit the dragon from mouth to gullet, and out slithered three foul eels. The witches named these writhing creatures after the three fatal weaknesses of humankind: hate, fear and want.

Like Gaia, these brother demons knew nothing of our chronology and cared not for time. They told the witches their return and reunion were inevitable, and when they did, a child would lead them out of the darkness, and once more they would swallow the light. The sisters banished the three demons and hid them where they could never find each other.

Stories have power, and the witches knew they must tell this story for all of time, because it would surely come to pass. They would wait, and they would commune to share their legends. This was how the covens came to be.

Niamh finished her tale by closing the hefty tome. 'So there we go. That's what we're dealing with.'

'A thousand and one women died?' Elle asked, nervously casting a glance around the Great Hall. Counting, no doubt. There were far fewer women here than that.

But that's not what Leonie took away from the story. 'There was a blade that could kill Satanis?'

'There was,' Calista said. 'Aside from the Seal of Solomon it is the treasure most sought by witches.'

'Do we know where it is?' Leonie asked.

'We do not.' Calista sounded downcast. 'Probably long since lost, or worse, destroyed.'

But Leonie felt a prickle of excitement for the first time in days because if something as real as a blade could cut Satan, that meant he could be killed again.

THE OWL AND THE PUSSYCAT

Theo - Out to sea

Time meant nothing anymore, and it had been days since she'd seen anything but water. She and Lucifer were alone in the little rowing boat. Somehow, she never grew tired, thirsty or hungry. The salt and sun did not burn her skin. It was *him*. There was a little bit of him inside her veins.

Lucifer rowed while Theo sat on the little bench at the rear of the boat. He no longer wore Milo's form. He looked like Luke, only Luke wearing a Captain Birdseye sailor's outfit. When she'd asked him why he looked this way, he told her, obliquely, that he only looked the way she wanted him to look. Theo could only think she subconsciously wanted a father figure in this moment, which made a sort of sense. A big, strong man to take you on a sailing trip.

The sky was as expansive as the sea, but both were much too calm. They'd sailed for what felt like an eternity, but never once had the winds or waves picked up. 'Is this real?' she finally asked. She'd been trying to not talk to him as much as possible. She didn't want to give him the satisfaction.

Luke/Lucifer smiled. 'As the three of us draw ever closer, our power increases. Reality is ours to bend. Already, dear one, you're fixing our fracture.'

She scowled at her captain. 'Do you ever just answer a fucking question with a yes or a no?'

'Not if I can help it.' His grinning teeth were somehow shark-like.

Gods. 'Will this be over soon?'

'Sooner than you think.'

'So that's a yes? Why can't you just say that?'

He flashed his eyebrows and carried on rowing.

The ocean was the best way to feel insignificant. She was a dot, so why did everyone give such a shit about her? It was absurd, her importance. Given a choice, she'd be at home, mindlessly plugged into brain-rot on TikTok, swiping from haunting legends of the Appalachian Mountains, to *Opinions about K-Pop Idols that Would Get Me Cancelled*, to some gross-but-cute little kitten that can't poop properly.

Only home wasn't there anymore, and neither was she.

She did have a choice though. 'You said that I could shape reality as I see fit.'

'You'll be a goddess.'

'OK, so what if I want to keep everything exactly the way it is?' She felt satisfied with this potential loophole she'd thought out.

'Whyever would you do that?'

'Maybe I like it here?'

He considered her with a wry smirk and she felt some fresh mansplaining was about to drop. 'I didn't have you down as so selfish, Theodora.'

'How is that selfish?'

He looked at her through condescending eyes. 'How lovely for *you* that *you* live with a supportive, financially stable and kind-hearted witch who took you in against all reason. Maybe you've forgotten how relentlessly cruel this world is?' She couldn't meet his gaze. 'Only a year ago you were a coiled spring of fury, waiting to strike. You torched your school. Your whole life you'd been abandoned, betrayed, abused and mocked. How easily you forget.'

'I haven't!' If only she could.

'Gaia!' he spat. 'The *thing* you call Gaia. Negligent, blind. Truly an unfit mother, utterly powerless to curtail the woeful failings of her bastard children. You're cannibals, eating her tender green flesh. Guess how many years this ass-fucked planet has left.'

'What?' Theo replied. 'I can't . . .'

'No, I wouldn't want to either, because it's terrifyingly few.'

The problem was, she believed him. It was scary, but in her heart she knew it was true. If she dwelled too long on it, it felt like she was going to burst. Better to pretend it wasn't happening, the way everyone did.

Lucifer continued his tirade, spittle flying from his lips. 'Humanity is an appalling virus. I wouldn't want them anywhere near my creation. In just a few hundred short years – a blink of an eye to us – they've raped the planet over and over until it's a dying husk. Why? Because they like big cars and cheap flights. They like flimsy garments that cost a pittance and they wear once. And this obsession with plastic – water, grain, fruit, there's nothing they won't wrap in it. They like making rooms colder, and gardens warmer—'

'Stop it! I get it.'

'Then you know why we have to end them. *They* are the problem. I don't see any other species burning fossil fuels, do you? The birds and the bees don't fly on private jets . . .'

She couldn't disagree. Gaia had made witches for one reason alone, after all. 'But Niamh . . . and the others?'

'A promise is a promise, Theodora. I will spare them.'

She nodded, and on they rowed.

DREAMS

Elle - Heaea

Funny where life takes you, Elle thought. The great hearth in the banqueting hall was pleasant, and the red wine – from the island's own vineyard – was exquisite, but this was all a bit surreal. It was the final part of some ITV drama she'd been following tonight. Would the Sky Box back in Todmorden record it? Would Sky TV even exist for much longer? A notion she couldn't wrap her head around; what would they do once the world ended? Nothing. Because there would be nothing.

And no one knew. All around the world, people went to work, or the gym, or the supermarket. They were busy making plans for the weekend, or booking summer holidays for a summer that might not come. Elle envied them their ignorance. In a world where she'd snipped ties with her friends, she could have been one of those lemmings scurrying towards the end of the world. She honestly couldn't decide who got the worse deal.

She became aware of a form looming over her. She looked away from the crackling fire and saw Radley approach. He brought with him a carafe, and she held out her stout tumbler for a top-up. 'You're up late,' he said.

'I'm knackered, but the second I get into bed I'm wide awake,' she told him.

'I've gotten to the point where I power-sleep. I can function on three or four hours a night.'

She smiled up at him. 'That, Mr Jackman, is very bad for you. Eight hours a night – nurse's orders.'

He asked if he could join her and she welcomed him onto her sheepskin rug. They clinked glasses. 'I *had* to come here,' Radley said. 'What's your excuse?'

Elle honestly hadn't thought about *not* coming. It had been a no-brainer. 'I can help. I suspect we're going to need nurses, don't you? And anyway, wild horses wouldn't have stopped Holly coming, so I never really had a choice.' Her daughter had already taken herself to bed, and after a few days here, Elle trusted that she was safe making the short walk down the mountain side to their little villa.

'I think you're right,' Rad said. 'Well, I'm glad you came,' he added more quietly. 'We can burn the midnight oil together.'

His loaded gaze awoke some long-forgotten giddiness at the sheer fizzy potential of a new flirtation. All those new firsts they might get to share. It was very odd. She was flattered by the male attention because she'd long harboured a fear that she'd *let herself go* or that childbirth had irretrievably rendered her hideous.

That said, while it was nice to know there *could* be men in her future, right now the thought of having sex, even *kissing* another bloke, felt alien. It'd be like making out with a dolphin or something. Her circumstances may well be ready, but neither her body nor mind were there just yet.

And, given all the doom and gloom, she might never get the chance.

It had been so long since she'd navigated this minefield, she wasn't quite sure what to say. She didn't want to be hysterical or presumptive, but she also didn't want to lead him on. 'You're a good friend, Rad.'

He sat up a little straighter. 'Oof!'

'Oh, goddess, am I that transparent?'

'I've heard this one before. I think all men have at some point. It's character-building. All those things they taught us in PE, but they never taught us to deal with rejection . . .'

Elle rubbed his arm. 'Then you've definitely heard the next one: it's not you, it's me. Only, this time, it *definitely* is. After Jez and Milo, I'm just so knocked down, you know? It's taking everything I've got to just stay upright and be there for Hols.'

'I understand.'

Elle was almost surprised at the clarity she felt on this. It was refreshing, a luxury, to have any time whatsoever to even consider herself in this much depth. 'It's tempting to look for a Jez replacement, it is, but I think that's a really bad idea. I don't think I want a fella, I think I want to piss him off. Or, like, *beat* him, or *win*? But it's not a race. I have to keep reminding myself.'

'That sounds wise.' Radley Jackman was very handsome studied this close; lovely teeth and full lips. Incredible skin for a man, and the suggestion of dimples. Elle knew *why* he was single – his steadfast commitment to the Warlocks' Cabal for one, but also the fact he was courteous and polite and kind. He was the man women would turn to only when they'd come to understand that so-called 'alpha males' will never settle for just one mate. His time would come, she was sure of it, because she felt that, in the end, women want a best friend.

'Do you know what I need, Rad? I need to be by myself.' This simple truth soared out of her as if she was uttering the most cursed phrase a woman can ever say. 'I need to prove that I can be. I have never been alone! Ever! I was *sixteen* when I met Jez, and all through my twenties, I was terrified of what I'd do if I was by myself. Like, who'd fix the car? Who'd take things to the tip? But you know what? I can literally pay people to do that shit.'

Rad laughed heartily. 'I thought you were going to say *I can do those things*.'

Elle grinned back at him. 'Come on, Radley, let's not get crazy.' They clinked glasses again. 'Anyway. We've got work to do. I want to help Niamh if I can.'

'You will. You are.'

'I want to hurt him, Radley. I want to really *fucking* hurt that bastard that pretended to be my son.'

Rad nodded grimly. 'You will. We all will.'

She was quiet for a moment, wondering at the need she felt to *share* with him. To explain – she could do *more* than they all could. She shuffled closer to her companion. 'Rad, did Lee ever tell you what I did to Jez?'

'No.'

'I turned him to stone.' She breathed the last word. 'How is that even possible? Watch this . . .'

Dotted at intervals around the banqueting hall were vast floral arrangements made with fresh flowers that had been harvested from across the island. Trapped inside during the storm, the bouquets had all started to wilt and droop.

Elle wafted a hand lightly, stirring her radiance like water in a bathtub. This wave sloshed around the room and, in turn, each vase was reinvigorated. Plump, creamy-pink petals flourished and stems stood tall and proud. Leaves unfurled, waxy and green.

The other witches and warlocks in the room stopped their chess matches and card games to witness this with surprise and delight. The best part? Elle had hardly flexed a muscle.

'Impressive,' Rad – another healer – remarked. 'Aren't you a Level 4?'

Elle shrugged. 'Supposedly.'

'Elle, you are *not* a Level 4. Clearly. And that's a good thing isn't it?'

'But . . . last summer I used my power to hurt.'

'We can do that,' Rad said quietly as if this was a great taboo. 'It's not about wanting to, but we can . . . Elle, go get him. Kill him. Do what you have to do.'

He looked at her in a way that no other man had ever looked at her, in a way she hadn't thought was possible: like he was seeing the witch in her . . . and liking it.

It had stopped raining, finally, by the time the fire had dwindled. Elle couldn't drink anything else or she'd puke. She was already feeling the dry-mouth and her legs were unsteady as she ventured out into a bloated humidity that was almost worse than the rain. So much for any idea she'd had of nibbling olives on a terrace somewhere. She hurried from the temple down the winding track through what the locals called 'the village'. In reality, it was just a cluster of clay huts built into the hillside. They were basic, but they all had running water and a toilet, so it could be worse. Not *much* worse, but . . .

As she approached their chalet, she saw candlelight still bobbing away through the slatted shutters. Holly must have fallen asleep with the lights on. She'd always been a greedy sleeper, even as a baby. She loved her sleep. Only then, Elle heard scuffling from within and she sobered up in a snap. Someone was moving around inside. 'Holly?' she said, but there was no response. She wasn't going to waste time getting the others. She could – and had – caused enough pain on her own. Taking a deep breath, she pushed her way into the compact space, only to almost collide with her daughter.

To keep the younger children busy, some of the local witches had given Holly colourful chalks to draw on the paving slabs outside the temple. Now Holly was standing on a chair, drawing on the walls with them. 'Holly, what on earth are you doing?'

Her daughter ignored her and kept grinding the chalk into the wall intensely. Her hand seemed to move with inhuman speed.

'Holly! Stop!' Elle took hold of her arm, and Holly's neck twisted to face her. Elle recoiled. Holly's eyes were pearly white and empty. 'Oh my gosh. Holly? Baby?'

As if she was in some sort of trance, Holly went back to her mural, the scratch of stone on stone the only noise in the villa. Holly had gone through a period of sleepwalking years ago, but never like this. Elle took a step back and took in her enormous design. Holly had turned the entirety of the wall into her canvas. Shapes took form out of bold, swirling loops of colour.

Elle covered her mouth with her hand. The subjects of her portrait couldn't be clearer. She turned for the door. She had to get Niamh.

THE LAST TEMPTATION OF CIARA

Ciara - Aeaea

Ciara glared at the buxom woman at the other end of the banqueting table. She cradled a younger woman's palm in her hand, reading her fortune.

Taking her mead with her, Ciara sidled down the table and scooched in alongside the young witch, bumping her down the bench with her hip. 'Do you mind?' she said curtly, not exactly offering much in the way of choice. The witch made space for her, and Ciara unfurled her hand before the palmist: Madame Celestine.

The look on her face was worth it. The women went stiff.

'Been a while,' Ciara said. 'So. You still torturing children?' Celestine went to leave, but Ciara riveted her to the long bench. 'Stick around, bitch.'

Celestine's face contorted into an ugly grimace. 'I never tortured no one.'

'Is that how you sleep at night?' Ciara fought a strange urge to laugh. Or cry; she wasn't sure which. 'My mother paid you to exorcise me and you took her fucking money. Did you know there was nothing wrong with me?'

Celestine nodded slowly. 'I told your mother as much.'

'Then you could have saved me from her.' Ciara fought to keep a tremble out of her voice. She would rather die than cry in front of this woman.

Celestine's face was impassive. 'But, sweetheart, I did see your future.'

'I was a child.'

The necromancer lowered her voice to a vicious hiss. 'A child who became a killer in cold blood. A woman who allowed herself to be the vessel of the devil himself.'

Ciara shook her head. 'It wasn't fair. It wasn't my fault.'

'Child! Who the fuck do you think you're talking to?' Celestine tapped cherry red talons on the wood. 'Fair! When was life ever fair? Lemme tell you about my life as a young witch back in Congo, and then we'll talk about fair.'

Ciara considered Celestine with a tilt of her head. 'You should be glad that I'm feeling less murderous these days, *Patricia*. But if I see you anywhere near a child ever again, I'll kill you. Am I clear on that?'

Celestine pushed herself away from the table. 'Fool girl, what makes you think any of us will live to long enough to taste the nectar of revenge?'

Ciara lay in her narrow bed watching lightning fleck through the slats of the shutters. Despite the wind and rain, it was still oppressively humid, and sleep felt miles away. Maybe it was lingering adrenaline in her veins after her confrontation. Maybe a bit of regret at how she'd spoken to Celestine? Fuck it, that bitch had it coming.

There was no point even looking at a watch, it'd only confirm how few hours of rest she'd get. They say the best cure for insomnia is to get up and do something else, but this was Aeaea – there wasn't any Netflix. There wasn't even Pinterest.

'I can't sleep either,' said a familiar voice.

Ciara rolled over and Jude was beside her in bed, a hand curled underneath his head, exposing one armpit. She fell out of bed and found herself not on cool terracotta tiles, but on the trodden cheap carpet of her student house in Durham. Rarely hoovered in a year, it was matted with red hair and rolling tobacco. 'Oh fuck off,' Ciara said.

'Charming.'

'Look, I didn't fall for Good Cop or Bad Cop, so why are you here?'

Jude, Lucifer, Whatever tucked his other arm behind his head. He luxuriated on their old sad single bed, where they'd spent many a night coiled like rattlesnakes to save pounds from the coin-operated meters. 'Maybe I missed you.'

'Jesus.' Ciara plonked herself on her ancient swivel chair. Yellow foam poked out from a rip where she'd picked at it.

'What? I've spent countless centuries around humans, and you're one of the best ones I've met. You hate the species almost as much as I do.'

'I won't argue with that,' she muttered. 'Look, what have you done with Theo? Give her back.'

He looked at her. 'You care about her?'

'Why is that such a surprise? I'm not a total fucking psycho. She's a sweet kid who's asked for none of this. Let her go.'

'I can't. I like her too, but I suppose I would; she's my greatest creation. Speaking of – Leonie Jackman is with child, I see.'

'*With child?*' She put on an ominous tone. 'She's up the duff.'

'Tell me about this child.'

'Get to fuck.' She rethought this, her grogginess subsiding. 'Why are you so interested in Lee's baby?'

At first, Jude said nothing, inspecting his fingernails. Only then he confessed, 'It was not foreseen.'

Ciara smiled. She could tell he didn't like that and was feigning nonchalance. 'You'll have to wait until it comes out like the rest of us. No spoilers.'

Jude sighed in annoyance and got out of the bed, stark bollock naked. Ciara made a great show of not looking over his body, however long it had been since she'd gotten laid. He stretched and slid on his old Calvins. Black with a red waistband. 'Don't you want to know how *you* turn out?'

'What?'

'Now that the end is close, the conclusion gains clarity. All the possible outcomes converge into me.'

'Do you see the one where we stop you?'

He laughed, and she remembered how much she'd cherished that noise. Jude Kavanaugh didn't laugh freely or generously, but he had always laughed at the things she said, and it had made her feel so special. 'That's not an option, I'm afraid. There's a reason your oracles have seen this for hundreds of years. It was always counting down to this. Nothing lasts forever, Ciara. Don't be sad.'

It niggled at her. She had no reason to feel sentimental, warm cosies about this world. She didn't have a reason to be here: no job, no man, no real purpose. This life had royally fucked her over since she was a little girl. AND YET. She didn't want this cunt to win either. Maybe that was it. Woman scorned and all that.

Ciara being Ciara, she knew exactly what she wanted to say: she wanted to tell him how they'd destroy him because together they were some of the most sensational witches this sorry planet had to offer. Witches had stopped him once before and they would do so again. But maybe Ciara was evolving because she knew anything she said might tip him off. If he hadn't known about Lee's sprog, there might be other details – like this fabled blade – he didn't know either. Best to keep schtum. In fact, that was probably why he was here; she was being singled out as the weak link. Good luck with that, toss-rag.

'Why did you come here, Ciara?'

'To a weird dream version of my student bedroom?'

'You know what I mean. Though if this doesn't work for you . . .' The walls of the damp terrace crumbled and Ciara gripped the edge of her desk as the ground shook. Blinding sunlight appeared through the spiderweb cracks in the walls. Her nostrils were greeted by salty air, and she heard the gentle sigh of the tide. Her walls parted, and she stepped outside the ruins of her bedroom and found white sand between her bare toes. They were on a tropical beach.

'I've never been here,' she said. 'What is this? Holiday brochure?'

'It's what you wanted, all those nights alone in your cell at Grierlings,' Lucifer said. 'I'd know. You wanted a mojito and a trashy beach read. Is this the limit of your ambition?' Yes, that sounded like actual fucking paradise now he mentioned it. 'A place with no rules, no responsibilities. No guilt. So why did you come to Aeaea?'

Ciara looked out at the endless turquoise waters – impossibly blue – and then back to the fringe of palm trees swaying with the lightest of sea breezes. 'I'd have thought it was obvious. I was running from you after you turned Snow into a human knot.'

'Liar.' He rushed at her and clutched her jaw in his hand. She swiped his arm away. 'You could have gone anywhere, but you went to them because you secretly crave their forgiveness. Your sister and her little friends. Do you think they'll forgive you? Really?'

How could she feel the sun on her face? This wasn't real. Felt real though, real enough that she was worried about sunburn. 'No, probably not,' she confessed, turning to the horizon. The sea rolled ahead of her for miles and miles until it met the cloudless sky. She wouldn't forgive herself, so it seemed a little rich to expect anyone else to.

'Then why bother?'

She sighed and looked back at him. He now wore swimming shorts and lay on a cushioned sunbed, sipping a salt-rimmed margarita. 'You don't understand family? Sisterhood?' she said.

'Not really.'

Something solidified inside her. An epiphany. '*That's* why you'll lose.'

For the first time, he looked at her with ice-cold eyes.

Ciara awoke covered in sweat. She pulled the thin sheet around her chest, feeling very naked even in her T-shirt and pants.

For reasons even she wasn't fully aware of, Ciara slipped on her jeans and Converse and headed for the temple. She didn't want to be alone, and didn't know where else she could go.

Ciara didn't know if she'd answer her, but at the top of the sanctuary, Niamh came to her door.

Her sister, hair like a nest, blinked at her a moment. 'What do you want?'

'Can I sleep with you?' Back in the day, if one of them had a nightmare, they didn't even need to ask. They'd just climb on in with the other and snuggle close.

'Whatever,' Niamh said and stepped aside to let her in.

Niamh's quarters were far nicer than her little hut on the hill and, while they didn't snuggle, Ciara felt finally at ease in the king-sized bed. Too hot, she lay atop the sheets, skin exposed to the night. 'Niamh?' She thought she ought to tell her about her most recent nocturnal visit.

'Go to sleep, Ciara.'

'I just saw Lucifer again.'

A pause. 'We'll talk in the morning.'

Ciara grinned into the pillow. Her sister had always liked her sleep.

Feeling safer than she had in many, many months, she had very nearly drifted off when she awoke to a loud rap on her door. Both sisters sat up and looked to one another. Niamh coughed to clear her throat. 'Hello?'

The door opened and it was Elle. 'Sorry to wake you up.'

'It's fine, what's up?'

'You need to come and see this. Both of you.'

'*Me* too?' Ciara squinted though the low light.

'Yes, you too.'

THE CHOSEN FEW

Niamh - Beaea

Holly's mural was beautiful and strange. They all gathered around it, as if they were appraising some new exhibit at the Tate Modern. Holly now slept, sent peacefully into restful slumber with a touch of Niamh's hand.

The sprawling image covered most of the interior of Elle's villa, from floor to ceiling. Niamh couldn't help but think of the news story from a couple of years back, when they'd discovered ancient cave paintings from the palaeolithic era in Spain and what these images revealed about the past. Holly was an oracle. What did her etchings tell them about the future?

There was a sun, and the sun smiled down on them. In tarot, The Sun was perhaps the most benevolent card of them all, a kind omen. Elegant golden rays travelled from the skies and into the bodies of five caped children. They were themselves cradled in the palms of five larger women – and both the girls and the women were undeniably them.

Like Gemini, the two redheads stood with arms and hair intertwined. Next to them was a pregnant woman – Leonie, clearly, with brown skin and tight curls. She had a sword for a mouth. Elle was next to her, depicted with a human heart in her free palm. Finally, there was Helena, crowned but weeping, and bathed in flames. All five rose out of a pond or a lake and, in that lake, was a great green serpent, coiled and contented.

Calista made a brief *hmm*. 'The child is very powerful.'

'Her grandmother was Annie Device, from Pendle,' Elle said, as if that explained everything – which, to be fair, it did.

'Is this the past or the future?' Chinara asked.

'I did Drama for GCSE, not Art,' Leonie said. 'Fucked if I know.'

'I think it's both.' Niamh tilted her head, excavating for extra meaning. 'I think we're holding ourselves at Oathtaking. The night we received Gaia.'

'So what?' Ciara said. 'Are we like the Chosen Ones? I don't wanna be fucking Buffy.'

'Well, neither did Buffy, that's sort of the whole point,' Niamh replied.

'She had destiny thrust upon her,' agreed Leonie.

It was an interesting take. None of them had chosen to be witches. Taking the oath *was* a choice, however, and they had *all* made it on that night twenty-five years ago. Holly's painting seemed to single the five of them out, though. Chinara wasn't in this portrait, and neither were Theo or Holly or Calista or Luke. Just the Hebden Girlies group chat.

'Helena was meant to be here.' Leonie reached out and touched her chalky face. 'We killed her. Or we let it happen. Potayto, potahto.'

The words hurt, like a stab in Niamh's lower spine, but it was true. They could have done *something*. *She* could have halted her trial. Now. she was confident she would have defied coven law.

Ciara spoke. 'Exactly. When Hale took me out of the coronation, he told me all this shit was a big plan to break us up. Helena, Annie . . . you.' She said the last one to Niamh very awkwardly. 'It was to take out the most powerful witches.'

Calista clapped her hands noisily. 'Don't you see? You are the most precious of Gaia's daughters.' She looked each of them over in turn. 'It's not coincidence. You took the oath under a blessed moon, when Mercury and Mars were in conjunction; the perfect balance of intelligence and logic, and of ferocity and passion. Gaia saw you that night, and chose her soldiers.'

'I'm no *soldier*,' Elle protested.

'Then leave,' Calista snapped, shutting her down.

Elle would *never* leave them, and maybe that did make her a warrior in her own way. 'If we're the chosen ones,' Niamh said, 'what are we chosen to do? Could Gaia have left instructions?'

'She did,' Calista said and promptly walked out of Elle's cabin.

The friends looked to each other, bewildered. 'Do we go with her?' Ciara asked, and Niamh shrugged. *Fucked if I know.*

They did follow her, and, as the covens slept, she led them deep inside the mountain. Luke, suffering the same insomnia as the rest of them, came too. Niamh found his presence reassuring, truth be told, like a piece of Hebden Bridge, of home, was with her.

The Temple of Circe was only the entrance to miles of catacombs: they had walked through a nondescript door, concealed behind a tapestry in the chapel. Spiral stairs circled deeper and deeper as corridors became caves, their way illuminated by flickering torches. Their party was accompanied by a trio from Calista's coven who lit the lamps as they went.

'Circe kept her secrets hidden,' said Calista as they walked, her voice echoing. The deeper they went, the more power Niamh felt tingle on her skin. The air was cold and crisp down here, wet and unbreathed. 'She had many visitors to her island, but these caves remained unspoiled by man.'

It was nice that somewhere was.

Calista looked to Luke. 'You will come no further, friend.'

'Fine by me,' Luke replied and duly stopped following their procession. 'I'll be right here.' Niamh gave him a nod. Something had unknotted between them, after their chat. She was *grateful*, she realised. Grateful he wasn't pushing the boundaries, and also just grateful that he was here.

They walked on without him, and Niamh lost all sense of time. She had no idea how long they'd been on their descent.

'This is pure mental,' Ciara muttered, falling in step behind Niamh.

'We're witches,' Niamh said by way of an explanation. Maybe they'd forgotten. With all their Gousto boxes and gel nails, and eggs benedict on sourdough, they'd forgotten that *this* was them. They belonged in musty, spooky caves with flaming torches. HMRC had taken something wild and corseted it. And for what? To blend in with Victorian England. Maybe there had been need, then. No longer.

'Down here.' Calista motioned for them to stoop under a low-hanging boulder. Niamh couldn't help but think of *Alice in Wonderland*. Vanishing into black holes rarely ends well.

She swallowed hard and ducked into the crevasse. Then inhaled sharply as, after a moment of pitch darkness, she emerged into a vast, dome-like cavern. 'Oh my gods . . .' Somewhere above them, the formation of the rocks allowed a column of sheer, silvery moonlight to slice downwards onto the surface of a pool. It was still as black satin, and just as inviting.

Gathered around the pond, carved out of the marble walls, were Amazonian statues of women. Five of them, serene; sentries of the underground reservoir.

'Look at them,' Elle breathed.

They were somewhat like the women depicted in Holly's mural, but these statues were faceless. The first held a sword; the second a scroll; and the third a lily, sensually, over her vulva. The fourth cradled a lamb; the fifth, a crown. Niamh knew what these sentinels represented. The roles of women: warrior, scholar, lover, mother and leader. Was this *them*? No. No woman is just one of those things, or *all* of them – at least, never at the same time. The pressure to be all five at once was what killed women.

'They're beautiful,' Leonie said. 'I'd put them in my garden, if I had one.'

'Water feature,' Ciara added.

Niamh heard Calista quietly tut at their irreverence, and Elle told the naughty schoolgirls off. 'Stop it,' she hissed. 'This is like their church.'

'Sorry, Mum,' Leonie muttered.

Niamh suppressed a smile, torn between deference and naughtiness. This was how they, as a clique, had always dealt with anxiety – they pointed at it, prodded it, made fun of it until it shrank. It was their way. Sorry, Calista.

'We don't know who carved these,' Calista said. 'They have stood for centuries, waiting. We have wondered why. Now we know for whom they waited.'

'It can't be for us,' Leonie said, jokes aside. 'It just can't. We're *nothing*.'

'You aren't,' Chinara interjected. 'Look at everything you've done. You already stopped Belial once. You stopped Hale. You stopped the attack at the coronation.'

'That was you as well.'

'Us then. We're not regular women anymore.'

'We are,' Niamh said loudly, over them both. Like the pond, her thoughts felt still and clear. 'It's just that *regular women* have more power than we've ever, ever been told we can have. What if the biggest lie there ever was was that women are weak? Why did men want us to believe that? So we'd think we needed them? So they could control us? Look how big they made these statues. They're fuckin' titans. What if *this* is what women are? Really? We're . . .'

'Women of Mass Destruction,' Ciara said. 'That's what Hale called us.'

'They're scared of us,' Elle said. 'Lucifer and Belial. That's why they're torturing us.'

'So we fight,' said Leonie. 'He hasn't won yet.'

Almost as though Satanis had heard their resolve, a low grumble started beneath her feet. Niamh rested a hand against a clammy granite boulder to steady herself. The entire cavern lurched drunkenly and dust rained down from overhead. She braced herself; if the cave collapsed, she'd have to form a shield around them. After a moment or two, the earthquake subsided. 'What was that?'

'Leviathan,' Calista said gravely. 'He breaks his chains.'

IN THE END, IT'S THE CHOICES WE MAKE

Theo - Out to sea

They rowed under a black-blue sky, stoned with an impossible smattering of stars. The sun yawned and stretched from the sea, the dawn was so beautiful that Theo shook with tears. Gaia's perfect and strange world was drawing to a close. And it was all her fault.

'Why do you cry?'

'Why do you think?' she sobbed bitterly.

'Do you truly believe our reality could be worse than this slow death?'

Theo said nothing. Then she noticed that Lucifer, still looking like Captain Luke, had stopped rowing.

'What are you doing?'

'We're here.'

'Where?' There was nothing around them save for miles and miles of rippling ocean.

'Wait and see.'

The boat rocked gently, and then less so, bobbing up and down until Theo was compelled to clutch the rim of the vessel. 'What are you doing?'

'Watch.'

The sea on the horizon swirled around, as though it were being sucked down some gargantuan plughole. A whirlpool the size of a football pitch drew them ever closer. 'Make it stop!' Theo cried. Lucifer only smirked.

The whirlpool seemed to bubble and slick rocks pierced the white, churning waters. Theo looked on as two symmetrical outcrops rose from the ocean. It took her a moment to realise they were curling horns, like those of a ram. They were joined in the middle by a rocky cranium. A whole rocky island emerged from the sea, dripping and pocked with barnacles and green with seaweed. Caves had been carved to represent eyes and a nose while the largest opening of all was a great, fanged mouth. The island cast a cold shadow over their puny little dinghy.

Theo would not show fear before the giant stone skull. 'Camp,' she said, deadpan.

Lucifer laughed. 'Quite. The witches who created it had a flare for the dramatic, I suppose.'

He continued to row them towards the gaping cave mouth. 'Is he in there?'

'Yes,' Lucifer said. 'It's where they put his bones. His soul, however, resides in you. Here they will finally be united. And then we can be one again. My brothers and I will reign eternal.' The little boat bobbed just outside of the jaws of the island. 'Are you ready, Theodora? To become a goddess?'

Eons ago, had Gaia welcomed this change? What if it had all been an accident? Perhaps, in the reality that had come before theirs, someone had sailed a different unwilling victim towards this fate. What if Gaia was a girl, just like she was, forced into eternal servitude?

Lucifer looked to the distance, like he was sniffing the air.

'What?' she asked.

'Nothing to concern yourself with. The witches are going to try to kill you.'

'I think that concerns me.'

He shook his head, unbothered. 'You'll squash them like ants. But for now, let's slow them down . . .' His eyes turned jet black.

His jaw seemed to unhinge itself, and his mouth opened unnaturally wide, grossly distorting his face. Theo covered her ears as he emitted a horrific screech, and a foul-smelling black gas rippled from the elongated slit. The rancid cloud poured deep into the ocean, spreading through the sea like an oil slick. The torrent finished and he licked his teeth clean. 'Let's see how they get on with that curveball.' He grinned, black saliva running down his chin.

THE GOOD FIGHT

Luke - Aeaea

The witches had gone on ahead without him. Maybe it should be mandatory for every cisgender man to feel this surplus to requirement at least once in his life, thought Luke. Never had there been a sparer spare part. It was healthy, though, to confront the truth: that women didn't need men in any practical sense, and that his role was only to help them however they thought he could.

He waited in the dank tunnel, hoping the flickering torches didn't die out. Unsure of what to do with his tree-trunk limbs, he half-perched, half-sat on a slick boulder and did his best to ignore the creeping cold sensation in his jeans.

He smiled to himself. His mother had always said that people who sit on cold floors get piles. Was that even true? He'd held it as sacred fact his whole life.

'It's not strictly true,' a female voice said from the shadows. 'But people who sit still for a long time might get them.'

Luke stood. 'Who's there?'

A host of extra torches sputtered aflame. Suddenly, the entire tunnel glowed as if it were gilded. Walking towards him in a simple white dress, her chestnut hair almost to her waist, was his mother. Just as he remembered her.

'You're not real.'

'Where else but Aeaea would the spirits of witches go to find rest?' She smiled and her eyes crinkled in a familiar fashion. She had always been a smiley woman, her skin laughter-lined.

Luke shook his head. His instinct was to run the way they'd come, upwards towards the temple crypt. But that would mean leaving Niamh. He'd said he would wait, so he would wait. 'The others . . . they said Lucifer came to them. To trick them.'

Angela Sawyer came towards him, hand outstretched as if to stroke his face. Luke flinched away from the ghost's touch. 'This is no trick, Luke. Consider it a gift from Gaia. From one mother to another.'

'Please don't.'

'I never got a chance to say goodbye.'

'Please, *stop*.' He had been six years old when last he'd seen her. This apparition even unlocked the memory of her scent: a gentle, airy rose perfume. She wore a silver charm bracelet. He remembered going to the antique jewellers with his father to pick out a new charm for every birthday and Christmas: a tiny teapot; a hand mirror; a frog.

'You've seen unbelievable things. Can't you believe this?'

'No.' Luke stood tall. 'Lucifer appears as the thing you most want.'

The woman grinned. 'The thing you want most is the leggy redhead . . .' He couldn't deny that. Angela, for lack of a better name, seemed to glow from within. His own, personal Blue Fairy. Her edges were hazy, ethereal. It was too perfect to be true. 'My boy, we don't have long. I just had to remind you of one thing.'

He said nothing; he wouldn't engage with this spectre. The witches hadn't been fooled, and nor would he be.

'You were born of love, Luke. Your father wasn't always the monster he became. He and I were happy once. You are the sum of that joy.'

Luke felt tears prick his eyes.

'You've seen such hate, that to love as strongly as you do is remarkable. It is your power.' Angela held out her hand again, and this time Luke didn't shy away from her. It didn't feel real, but it did feel warm. It felt like hope. 'You kept your heart soft. Love her, Luke.' She leaned in closer. 'She loves you, too.'

He was about to argue the opposite, when the array of torches blew out, leaving not even a whiff of smoke.

Voices echoed down the tunnel, growing louder. One by one, as they approached, the torches lit again. Niamh and Ciara emerged first into the dim light. Luke swiped a tear from his beard.

'You OK?' Niamh said.

'Fine.'

Niamh nodded. 'Come on, there's something wrong with the sky . . .'

They made their way down the zigzagging cliff paths that flowed towards the beach. The dawn sky was unnaturally red; not sailor's warning pink, but blood in water. A fierce wind continued to batter the island, sand stinging his eyes as they made their descent.

Niamh put out an arm across his chest to stop him. 'Wait,' she said. 'This isn't right.'

'I'll say,' he said under his breath.

The rest of the witches gathered alongside them, looking out over the bay. 'Do you feel it too?' Ciara asked. 'What is that?'

'I've never felt anything like it,' Leonie added.

'I have,' Niamh said. 'It's death. Dead things. That's what it feels like.'

Elle gasped. 'Oh my god! Look!'

She pointed to the shallows, where foamy surf rolled onto the shingle beach. It took Luke a moment to see what she was gesturing at, but then he saw a head emerge from the waves, staggering through the choppy waters. It lurched towards them, rags, seaweed and flesh and muscular sinew hanging from a skeletal frame. He saw salt-bleached bone: ribs and collar and skull.

'What in the fucking *Pirates of the Caribbean* fresh hell is this?' Ciara said loudly.

Calista took a step towards the edge of the ravine. 'Already the natural law is being rewritten. The dead walk.'

Luke saw a rusted blade in the corpse's bony hand. If it weren't so terrifying, it'd be fucking cool. Christmas Day, with his mum, *Jason and the Argonauts* on BBC2.

He felt a rush of wind about his ankles as Chinara took flight to his left. The hairs on his forearms prickled and the air turned noticeably more humid. A moment later, lightning flickered around Chinara, with a crackle and snap. She seemed to blaze from within as she raised her arms to redirect the lightning towards the beach. Her petite frame shook as she discharged, hurling blinding light at the walking cadaver. Luke shielded his eyes, but when she was done, only charred remains were burned onto the sand.

How sad it was that his father and his friends couldn't have just accepted how awesome these women were.

Chinara floated back onto the hillside. 'They burn like anything else.'

But already a further pair of zombified remains emerged from the tide. 'The sea has plenty of dead to offer,' Calista warned.

'Why?' Luke asked. 'Why are they doing this?'

'Because we're winning,' Niamh replied urgently. 'The cave. They don't want us in the cave.'

Calista took Niamh's hands. 'We must not delay further. Go to the caves, form a circle. Gaia will come to you.'

'You can't know that!' Niamh argued.

'Faith, sister. When has she failed us before?'

A gaggle of witches from the coven ran down the path to join their advance party. There were maybe thirty of them – the children safely back at the temple. One of the witches, an older woman with closely shorn silver hair, handed Luke a shotgun and some ammo. 'Make yourself useful, darl,' she said with an Aussie accent. 'Kiwi, not Aussie,' she told him, reading his mind.

He loaded the weapon with ease. Maybe his dad's bitter lessons would be good for something after all.

Calista didn't take her eyes off the invading cadavers. 'We will defend the coastline, buy you time. It has to be the four of you.'

'I'm not leaving Holly,' Elle said, shaking her head.

'She will remain in the temple with the children.'

'And I'm not leaving Chinara!' Leonie added vehemently.

But Chinara grabbed hold of her partner's shoulders. 'My love, you must. I'm much more use here.'

Even Luke knew that was true. He'd seen enough to know there was none more powerful than Chinara. Leonie had no choice.

Now Niamh turned to him. What she said surprised him more than Chinara blasting the shit out of the walking corpse. 'Go home, Luke. Use the water conduit.'

'No,' he stated.

'This isn't your fight.'

'Yes it is. You need to go. I'll make sure nothing gets into the temple.'

'Luke!' Niamh looked pained, and they didn't have time for a big heart-to-heart. She spoke quickly. 'I know you need me to forgive you, but I don't know if I can. I don't know if I ever can.'

That felt like a heel on his heart, but he shrugged it off and cocked the shotgun. 'Fair dos. I'll work on forgiving myself, how about that?'

'I can make you forget,' Niamh offered, and he detected a hint of reluctance in her voice. It made his heart surge with hope. 'Sheila, me, all of it.'

'Don't you fucking dare!' It came out more strongly than he'd intended. It was true though. Niamh was the love of his life, and that was not something a person just gave up.

Searching his eyes, as if to make sure he was certain, Niamh slowly nodded.

Ciara hovered further up the path, waiting for her sister. 'Niamh, come on!'

'We might die,' she said.

'We might not,' Luke said.

Finally, Niamh allowed him a delicate smile. 'Which is scarier?'

He winked. 'Let's find out when you save the world.'

They kissed. He wasn't sure who initiated it. It was fleeting, and Niamh pulled back at once, like she was surprised her lips had shot forwards. 'For luck,' she said, and hurried up the mountainside.

FIRST CONTACT

Leonie - Aeaea

I don't want to do this without you. That's what she had told Chinara on the hillside, their foreheads pressed together so hard it hurt. At the same time, she knew she had to. It was time to own it. The Leonie Jackman origin story. It wasn't the journey she'd have chosen, but no one gets to choose. *This* was where she'd come from; she was a daughter of Hebden Bridge, the same as Niamh, Ciara and Elle. This was their journey, and they had to finish it together.

Chinara was the most powerful elemental on Aeaea, perhaps the world. If anyone could defend that beach, it was her. Trust.

She, Niamh and Ciara waited on the margins as Elle said a tearful goodbye to Holly in the great hall in the temple. Elle was beside herself, but Holly was holding it together. That girl was boss. If their daughter was anything like Holly, Leonie would be highly satisfied.

Elle returned to the group, her face puffy and red. She wiped her eyes on the balls of her hands. 'Let's do this, before I change my mind.'

Leonie gave her arm a squeeze. 'You don't *have* to do anything,' she said, and meant it. Chosen Ones or not, consent is sexy.

'No.' She shook her blonde head resolutely. 'I'm ready.'

'You said that with some determination,' Ciara added.

'I want to rip that fucker a new arsehole.' The three of them just stared at her. Did *Elle* just say that?

'I'll drink to that,' Ciara said, grabbing a half-finished glass of ouzo off the table.

Leonie quickly rounded up three more glasses and they toasted before knocking back the aniseed liquor, pregnant or not. Fuck it, she'd quit smoking, she was allowing herself a shot.

They returned to the caverns, reaching the underground reservoir in silence aside from the scuff of Docs and Converse, as if they had agreed that this was too big for silly quips about Indiana Jones this time. The walk didn't seem to take as long; before they knew it, they'd arrived, and the black water and its marble totems waited for them, expectant. *Now what?*

'What do we do?' Elle asked.

'Is it a water conduit?' said Ciara.

'I don't think so.' Niamh held her hand over the pool. 'It doesn't feel like one.'

'Calista told us to form a circle.' Leonie tentatively placed a foot in the pond. The surface rippled and it was icy cold, but her foot found the floor. She advanced further, struggling to catch her breath as the water rose over her knees. 'Come on in, the water's Baltic.'

Ciara helped Elle in as Niamh cursed loudly. The four of them waded into the centre of the pool, the waterline settling just over their waists. If things weren't so fucking bleak it'd be quite funny. How was this any different to the 'Push a Push Pop' days when they'd peeled off their socks and shoes, and rolled up their Miss Sixty jeans to paddle in Hebden Beck?

'What do we do?' Elle asked.

'Form a circle and hope we get a text from Gaia,' Ciara replied, holding out her hand.

Leonie took it and closed her eyes.

'I wish it wasn't us,' Elle said.

Leonie nodded in understanding. 'But it is.' She shrugged. How she was meant to empty her mind and focus was anyone's guess. As if sensing this, Niamh almost forced her essence through her palm and up Leonie's arm. Very Niamh; no time to fuck around.

They had done this a gazillion times since they first met. It was like hearing the opening bars of your favourite song. No matter how long it's been, it takes you straight back, Do Not Pass Go, Do Not Collect £200. The familiar blend of Niamh's cornflower blues, Elle's sage greens and Ciara's iridescent violet swirled and mingled with Leonie's sienna. Such happiness swilled around her reverie. They could have been in the treehouse, or in Helena's bedroom, listening to that Dido album. Cackling together in the back row of the cinema, laughing at every death in whichever *Final Destination* had the rollercoaster. The past was a haven as well as a quagmire.

Now, as then, it was almost a game; how fast could they go? Together they were a battery, they could excite their auras, whip their innate energy into a whirlwind. The colours blended. They were one.

Leonie dared to open her eyes a crack. Around her knees, the black waters now swirled like a whirlpool. 'Is that meant to happen?'

'Concentrate!' Niamh snapped.

Leonie did feel that breathless *Final Destination* rollercoaster rush in her chest, the second at the top before the plunge . . . but nothing happened. The fall hesitated before them.

'It's not working,' Elle muttered.

Only then they fell.

Hard, and fast, as if the floor had gone from beneath them. Leonie plummeted chin first into the freezing water, no time to suck in a breath. She felt it rush up her nostrils and it was all she could do to not choke.

Hold on. Niamh's single command whipped between them. Lee gripped Niamh in one hand and Ciara in the other and clung on tight.

At first there was only cold and dark. Every instinct in her body told her to swim upwards, but down, down they went. After a moment, Leonie realised they weren't even in water anymore, and that she could breathe. They were falling, but slowly, as if held in honey or glue. Floating, not sinking.

Curious, she opened her eyes.

Light. There was light now.

In this feather-pale light, she saw only her memories.

She dropped a paving stone on Darren Greaves, the worst boy on the Belle Isle estate, when he called Radley the n-word. Darren Greaves cried.

Her mum made them jam sandwiches, cut into crustless triangles, for the car when the witches took them to Hebden Bridge. They went sweaty and sticky in the plastic bag.

Her dad smoked Rothmans King Size, but only in their Ford Sierra. He listened to Roxy Music and Sade on cassette.

In Hebden Bridge, Ciara hexed a townie boy who'd squeezed her breast. He convulsed on the cobblestones and pissed his Kappa trackies. It had been scary because she knew it was forbidden, but also *right*, so right.

She met Chinara in Wales, searching for rebel warlocks. She made sure she was on her patrol after that because there was no way she was letting that woman out of her sight.

The Somerset Floods; the siege of Hebden Bridge; the fountain in Bologna.

Ciara bringing a dead bird – briefly – back to life. Ciara on a tube train, kicking her feet against the seat.

Ciara and Niamh in their bunkbeds.

Wait. These were not her memories.

The twins, arriving with sad little suitcases at their grandmother's cottage. Ciara at a bus stop, high, until she was found by Conrad.

Elle and Jez dancing to '2 Become 1' at her wedding. Elle weeping as she held a dead infant in her arms, its skin purple and crinkled. Then crying different tears as a screaming Holly was placed in her hands.

How was this possible? These scenes *surrounded* her. Surrounded them.

Niamh and Conrad in Greece or something, watching the sunset. Niamh seeing Theo for the first time, like a spider in a web, pressed to the roof of a cage. Niamh and Luke making breakfast in the cottage.

Ciara placing a pillow over Niamh's face; Elle turning Jez to stone; Leonie trying to execute the Prime Minister at the House of Hekate.

All of their years now spun around them, a frenetic carousel. She felt sick, and dizzy.

HOLD ON.

Time. Time closed in on them. The images overlapped now; four reels rippling over each other in some sort of ribbon gymnastic display. All the days of their lives laid out for them all to see. Naked, exposed. It was much too much. Leonie screwed her eyes shut as the noise of their collective memories reached fever pitch. The laughter, the tears, the moaning and sweet, syrupy gossip was a cacophony. Leonie longed to let go of their hands and clamp her own over her ears, but knew she must not.

She braced herself and waited for it all to go away.

'Leonie,' Niamh said. 'It's OK. You can let go now.'

The air smelled different. It smelled of *holiday*, arid on her nostril hairs. It was sunflower yellow on the other side her eyelids. Leonie opened her eyes to a shimmering desert haze. Rippling dunes stretched out before, rising and falling in sensuous curves. 'This isn't real,' she uttered.

'I think it is,' said Elle, letting a handful of hot sand run through her fingers. 'It's like Dubai.'

Now wasn't the time for a lecture on the dubious morality of tourism in Dubai.

'If it was a trick, how are we all seeing the same thing?' Niamh asked.

'Are we all seeing *Dune*?' Ciara checked.

Leonie rose from her knees to her feet, unsteady on the shifting sands.

'Do you think this is your memory of Dubai?' Niamh asked Elle. 'Are we somehow in your past?'

'No.' Elle considered it a moment. 'No way. You'd be able to see the Burj Whatsit.'

A dry, hot wind blew sand in her face, and Leonie shielded her eyes. The sky and landscape were the same blazing orange. The sun was so hot, she could almost feel the freckles pop on her dark skin. Shit, pray for the gingers.

This was all familiar somehow, and not just from watching *Planet Earth*. It was like she'd been here too. Or a dream of a dream.

'What just happened to us?' Elle said.

Ciara seized her arm. 'Look!'

Below them, in what served as a valley in the dunes, a black chasm opened in the landscape, almost like they were in a giant egg timer and the sand was being sucked downward. Leonie, less keen these days to be the reckless one, let Ciara go first, but she did follow. They half-walked, half-slipped down the embankment towards the eddy in the sand. Niamh and Elle were close behind.

As they grew closer, Leonie saw murky water bubble up out of the sandy funnel. 'What the fuck?'

A low rumble, a growl, shook the ground beneath her feet. She clutched Ciara for support.

A murky puddle spilled across the plateau, gurgling and spurting from the waterhole. 'Stay back,' Niamh said. Leonie *knew* Chinara should have come; she could have stopped the flow.

As they backed away, the pool fanned out across the basin, growing wider all the time. Now reeds and vines started to emerge from the sand, forming a bank around this new, fertile, pond.

The women ducked down as shoots turned to trunks around them, providing very welcome relief from the blazing Saharan sun. An emerald canopy formed overhead, changing the light from gold to green. The temperature eased and, from somewhere, birds began to sing. Leonie even heard the rhythmic croaking of a frog somewhere close by. 'Elle, is this you?'

'No! I wouldn't know where to begin,' she said. 'It is magic, though. I can *feel* it. Can't you?'

'Yes,' Niamh said. 'It's like I'm recharging or something. It's in my bones . . . my skin.'

They now stood at the edge of a small lake at the heart of an oasis, and the unexpected growth spurt seemed to settle. It smelled . . . abundant: floral and fresh and *oxygenated*. Ridiculous, but true. Leonie had never breathed cleaner air. It was delicious. She rinsed out her lungs. It was all so . . . familiar. She *had* been here before, in a very specific dream.

And then this pocket jungle seemed to inhale and hold its breath.

'What's happening?' Leonie whispered, suddenly scared. The lagoon rippled. Something moved under the surface. Fast, and in their direction. A muscular shape almost breached and then dove.

Niamh flinched backwards as a head surfaced from the centre of the pool – a *human* head.

Human-*ish*.

'What the fuck?' Niamh breathed.

The form was female, bare-breasted, but covered in glistening reptilian scales. Leathery, segmented scuta covered her chest and abdomen like armour. At the waist, the scales thickened into a tail that remained under the water. Half-woman, half-serpent.

Like the statue in the temple.

Ciara was gripping her hand so tightly it hurt; none of them dared speak.

Then the snake-woman opened vermillion eyes. The needle-like slits widened as she considered them.

Leonie took a step forward and squinted at the figure. *Impossible.* Under the green skin, she *knew* that visage. Her wet curls were slick and hung down her back, but it was *her*. Her *face* at least. 'Senait?'

The serpent cut through the pool in their direction. Her lips didn't move, but Leonie heard her.

No.

'Then what the fuck are you?' Ciara said. So they could all hear her in their heads, not just Leonie.

I am the Avatar. I speak for Her.

They didn't need to ask who. Gaia's voice was as golden as Leonie had always assumed it would be. All four elements at once; it was both light and deep, warm and sparse at the same time. 'Why do you look like Senait?'

The child looks like Her. She made her in Her own image.

'Why? What? I don't understand.'

This moment always was. The time when the darkness would devour the light and the Mother would be no more.

'Who is she? Gaia?' Elle said.

She is Everything.

'Good thing we're not being vague,' Ciara muttered in her ear.

If He succeeds, everything you know, everything you are, and everything you love, will cease to be.

The Avatar looked directly at Leonie and she remembered the visceral fever dream she'd experienced that night on Aeaea. The vivid, almost neon, Tree Python that had entwined her body in the rainforest.

This was the place she had dreamed of.

And this woman was the snake.

The oddest sense of relief came over her, like concrete blocks lifting off her shoulders. She drew herself taller and breathed deep.

Leonie Jackman was still a Gold Star Lesbian. Phew.

'How do we stop him?' Niamh asked.

The weapon.

'My baby?'

The child is no weapon.

'The dagger,' Leonie said. 'The one the ancient witches used.'
The blade and the diadem.
'She means the crown,' Ciara said wearily. 'The Seal of Solomon . . . which I turned to dust on a whim and scattered over Manchester City Centre.'
Nothing is lost to Her. The coronet exists in time.
'I'm confused,' said Ciara.
'Join the club,' Elle added.
Niamh shook her head. 'What's the first thing we learn at Witch School? *Only Gaia sees everything.*'
Leonie's hands were already resting on her bump as the truth seeped into her brain. 'Oh my goddess . . .'
'What?' Elle said.
'That's the gift she gave us,' Leonie breathed. 'We didn't just move location. We moved in *time*.' She looked again to the Avatar, still serenely poised over the lake. It loomed over them, majestically feminine. The curve of her long body was almost sensuous. Leonie finally found the right question to ask. '*When* are we?'
The beginning. The day He broke free of his chains. One hundred and fifty thousand years before your time.
Too big a number to comprehend. Leonie felt a sort of vertigo kick in.
'Bullshit,' Ciara called.
But the serpent glared down at her, eyes burning. *Fire, air, earth, water and time. The fifth element, as natural and inevitable as the rest. She endows you with mastery of time. While you have the child, you have the gift. Go now. Go to where you need to be.*
Leonie searched for words that didn't sounds ridiculous, but came up short. 'So my baby is . . . pure Gaia magic?'
'Cool,' said Ciara.
Time is a river flowing past to future. She made it so. But She can bend it as a ribbon; make points touch. And now, so can you.
'Wait!' Leonie said, her gaze flicking back and forth from her bump to the goddess. 'How will I know where to go? *When* to go?'
She will know. You will get to where you need to be, each of you.

'Well, what does that mean?' That was a lot of trust to place in a foetus.

'Why us?' Niamh asked suddenly. 'She could have chosen any witches from all of time, but She chose us. Why?'

The Avatar now looked directly at Niamh before sinking back into the tranquil lake.

Because you loved each other the most.

The pond rippled, and her face dipped under the surface.

TIME AND AGAIN

Niamh

Gaia's Avatar had gone. The last ripple on the pond settled. On the horizon, three stick figures emerged over the brow of the dunes. Niamh squinted against the inferno sun, and saw three young women approaching, little more than girls. 'We're not alone,' she said.

'Who are they?' asked Elle.

Leonie examined them. 'I've seen them before. They're the first witches. This is the story my coven has shared for centuries. We're in Africa.'

'I think right now there's *only* Africa,' Niamh added. She remembered Conrad being fascinated by the evolution of humanity – how people had all fanned out from a common ancestor on this land mass, before the earth split asunder.

'This really is the beginning,' said Ciara. 'How it all started.'

Leonie looked over the horizon, transfixed by the new arrivals. 'Those girls come here, and Gaia gives them a tiny bit of her power.'

'Hello Grandma,' Ciara muttered.

'We should go,' Niamh said. 'I don't want to do the whole step on a butterfly and change the course of history thing.' This was already hurting her head. If Gaia saw all of time, had she always seen them being here? She'd got this familiar brain ache over *Back to the Future* too. Were they *changing* history? Or had they *always been* a part of history? She wished she could summon the snake lady out of the lake for some clarity on that.

'Go where?' Ciara asked. Fair.

'And how?' Leonie rubbed the bump. 'This thing didn't come with instructions. Am I a fucking time machine or summat?'

'Form a circle again?' Elle suggested.

'It must be the water,' Niamh said, hoping she sounded confident. 'Water bends space, why not time?'

'But I don't know what I'm doing!' Leonie flapped her hands on her wrists. 'This isn't even my power! It's hers!' she pointed at her leopard-print-clad bump.

All three of them looked to her and, once again, Niamh really missed Helena's decisiveness. 'We have to trust in Gaia,' Niamh said. 'She said, trust the baby. And the baby brought us here, didn't she?'

'To be clear . . .' Elle paced, hands on hips. 'We're going on a mission through time to find the Seal of Thingy and a magic knife.'

Well, when you put it like that, it sounds stupid. 'Yes,' Niamh muttered.

'OK, just checking.' Elle looked about as thrilled as Niamh felt. She missed the days when the ambition of her witchcraft was to float a pencil.

'Back to the water it is . . .' Ciara led the way into the desert oasis and they all gripped each other's hands and waded into the pond. This time it was mercifully warmer, the jungle air barmy.

They watched as the witch girls grew ever closer, headscarves wrapped over their faces to shield them from the whipping sands. Niamh wished them well. Those poor wee girls, chosen for a mission they hadn't asked for, the weight of the whole world on their narrow shoulders.

She was dwelling on their fate when the silt floor went from under her. She barely had time to scream *hold on* before her face was submerged.

They fell. At first the water was brisk, rushing up her nose, but it soon took on the same strange treacle quality and their plummet became more of a drift. Niamh screwed her eyes shut, feeling herself tip upside-down. She clung to Ciara's wrist, and mentally told them all *don't let go*, even if she wasn't sure her powers would work in this weightless abyss.

Her body felt immaterial. The things she held true – the head is joined to the neck; the neck is joined to the spine – suddenly felt less certain. It took all her effort to even place where her hand was. It required such concentration that she was only dimly aware of Ciara's grip loosening. *Ciara! Hold on!* But it was too hard, as if they were rolling down a sheer hill, building momentum, losing control. She wasn't even cognizant of when she lost Elle's hand, but she realised, with dread, that she'd already let go in her effort to keep hold of Ciara.

Ciara!

She slowed, alone again. For a horrid moment, she was back in that nether-region between the living and the dead. She wanted to scream, but found she couldn't.

She felt herself spinning, head over heels. She had let go and now she was adrift. She thought of Theo, alone with Lucifer; she thought of herself, how she'd failed. And, surprising herself, she thought not of Conrad, but of Luke.

And then bird song.

The air smelled wholly different to how it had in the arid desert or humid oasis. Here, it was all mulch and moist leaf litter. Moss and dew.

Niamh opened her eyes to see her home: Hardcastle Crags. She toppled forwards onto her knees and pressed her forehead to the damp ground. She wanted to know if it was real, and it was. She'd never been so pleased to feel wet soil on her face.

She wasn't far from the beck. She could hear chatty water brush over the pebbles, which meant she was somewhere on the sloping bank. It wasn't unpleasantly cold, but nor was it summer.

First question: Where were the others? She was alone. She'd been unable to hang on to them.

Next question: When was she? Normal rules didn't apply any

longer. Her clock on her phone – still wedged in her rear pocket in case Theo texted – wasn't going to help her, she suspected.

There was a noise in the undergrowth, and Niamh readied herself to fight. She was poised like a tiger when *her* Tiger came padding through the brambles. The dog registered an almost comical expression of surprise before giving her nostrils a lick. 'You good boy! What are you doing here?' She scratched his ears and he rubbed up against her.

Only then she heard a voice on the wind. 'Tiger! Here boy!'

The dog looked as confused as she did. Is there anything worse than hearing your own voice? It conjured memories of practising French at school with Elle, and the sonic horror of how shrill and reedy her voice sounded on the cassette recorders.

Niamh, instinctively, held on to Tiger's collar. She squatted further in the shrubbery and peeked up the embankment. She caught a flash of red hair in a topknot – *her* red hair. She – the other her – wore a wax jacket and Niamh could also see a hint of her Hunter wellies. The expression on her (other) face was strained. 'Tiger! Here! Now!'

Oh this was honestly too much. Niamh remembered this. Every dog owner has it: the day you lose the dog. The sheer dread of it. It's your fault – you let the thing off the lead – but the fucking thing always comes when you call. Until he hadn't.

'Tiger!' Niamh heard, and remembered, the rising tide of panic in her gut.

Of course, Tiger had returned, and that was not what this particular Sunday walk in Hardcastle Crags had been notable for. Far from it.

Any second now.

'There's not actually a tiger, is there?' a deep, booming male voice said.

Luke. This was the very first time she met Luke. He was walking a neighbour's dog – a chocolate Lab called Bouncer, as she recalled.

Why the fuck had the baby brought her here?

'I've lost my dog,' she told him. Niamh remembered how she'd instantly been struck by his height, his broad shoulders – but most of all his kind eyes. How foolish she'd been.

'I'll help you look,' he offered.

Niamh knew now that she'd been a mark. He'd probably borrowed that dog with the sole purpose of stalking her. God, was that even a neighbour's dog? Come to think of it, she'd never seen it again. Fucking men.

'You don't have to do that,' 2019 Niamh told him.

'Don't be daft, 'course I will. Tiger! Is he all right with blokes?'

Niamh felt Tiger's coarse fur between her fingers and realised the enormity of this moment. Shit-motherfucker-shit. Was this a test? If she released Tiger now, he'd flee uphill to the other Niamh, and she would have never spent a fraught afternoon with Luke. She'd have never asked for his number. They might have never . . . crouching in the bushes, Niamh found herself in the position of changing history, which took her right back to her previous conundrum.

They were either here to alter history, or affirm it. *Only Gaia sees everything in eternity.* Luke had refused her offer of a fresh start, but now it was her turn. She could remove him from her life by letting the dog go. And what would that do? Save Sheila? Maybe. But she also knew from her sister that Luke had, essentially, saved the world last year. Had it all been necessary?

Fuck.

If she and Luke had not begun their slow courtship ritual, he wouldn't have been around to protect Theo. She definitely wouldn't have plucked up the courage to visit Ciara in the safehouse. That would mean preventing Leviathan from coming over from the nether-region, but it would mean she wasn't here now to do this. A true conundrum.

More than that, her time with Luke had been . . . healing. She was ready to admit that. Movie nights at the Picture House. When she'd gone to his place and they'd . . . and the summer. Last summer. She wouldn't want to be without last summer.

Perhaps *that* was why Leonie's child had brought her here. Luke wasn't a complication in her love life. He was *vital*. He was part of her story now, just as she was part of his. For better or worse, they . . . *were*.

So she decided to go with Option B: she had always been here and had ever been the reason she lost her own dog for a day.

Trust in Gaia, if not Luke.

Niamh held on to Tiger's collar until long after the voices had disappeared into the forest. Niamh knew Tiger would come running back to her as the sun was setting, as if nothing had ever happened.

And now Niamh knew why – he had spent an hour with his mother, squatting in a bush all along. That was good news for Tiger, but left her with a new riddle to solve: How the fuck did she get back to the others?

THE GUARDIANS

Chinara - Heaea

Chinara walked back into the strange crimson daylight to find Luke still in position outside the temple entrance with his shotgun. 'Did they get back to the cave?'

'Yes,' she said. 'And I sealed the door. I bought them some time. Now,' she told him, 'you remain here. If anything comes within ten metres of this door, shoot it dead. Even if it's me.'

'What?'

'Don't trust anything, even your own eyes. We're dealing with Satan here, my friend.'

He inhaled through his nostrils and nodded slowly.

Chinara hesitated. She was unsure about leaving her beloved's fate in the hands of any man. 'Do you love her?'

He met her eyes in full. 'Yes,' he said without hesitation.

It would suffice. 'Good, then I know you'll do whatever it takes to keep those women safe.' She gave him a brusque nod of her head. 'They need me on the beach.'

She dimly heard Luke called good luck after her, but she was already bulleting into the sky in an arc towards the coast. As she made her descent, she saw the witches were mostly holding back the corpses that came out of the surf. But there were so many of them, scuttling over the beach like rats. The skeletons were in various stages of decomposition, some just bone, others swollen and bloated, their pink flesh torn and chewed. They were only distinguishable by what clothing remained: diving suits, vestments, naval uniforms and clothes from every era Chinara knew. All were filthy, rusted and ragged.

These zombies were dead, but they were fast. And silent. The empty eye sockets and skinless smiles were malevolent, not just because of her innate aversion to dead things, but because of the dark magics which animated them.

Chinara's feet touched down on hard, wet shingle. She hadn't had to fight like this since the war, and even then, only once or twice.

'Get back!' she cried to the front line of defensive witches. They were mostly sentients, punching the corpses backwards into the sea. Chinara let her hands grow hotter and hotter. They felt itchy at first until they almost fizzed and then, with a rush to her head, immolated. She dealt with the ones closest first, hurling whiplashes of fire at them. Her flame roared. The clothing they wore caught at once, but the cadavers kept juddering in her direction.

This wasn't going to be easy.

Since she was a little girl, people had told her to hide what she could do. Because she was a witch, and in Nigeria, that put her in danger. Even when she later found herself at HMRC she was encouraged not to 'show off'. Not everyone liked that a Black refugee – an uppity lesbian with a law degree, no less – was better than them. She had made herself small.

Now it was time to be very, very big.

With smoke and burning flesh acrid in her nose, she changed tack. She summoned the winds down off the mountain, buffeting the hideous forms backwards. She felt out until her mind reached the familiar tang of salty water. Directing the wind to the water was easy enough, but she needed a lot of wind and a lot of water.

Chinara braced herself, widening her stance and bending her

knees. She held her arms out wide and flexed her fingers into stiff claws. She didn't even realise she was screaming. Her shoulders ached, but she did it, twisting tornados over the water. Great columns of water held the sky aloft. There was something almost sensual about the way the pillars danced over the sea, spinning around and around. The funnels sucked up the ocean into coiling, slinky waterspouts which, in turn, pulled the dead into their grip. She watched as the corpses spiralled skyward, their spindly limbs torn from their sockets.

She would kill them all to protect Leonie and their daughter.

Chinara Okafor clamped her molars together and let the full force of Gaia surge through her petite frame. Cadaver upon cadaver crumbled.

If the wind hadn't been so loud in her ears, she might have heard the young witch screaming, begging her to look behind her. But Chinara did not. In fact, the first she knew of the sleek figure was a blazing pain in her lower back.

She looked down and saw a rusted, needle-thin blade jutting out from just above her hip. It hurt so much, she couldn't form a noise; her mouth just gaped open. She lost control of the sea, her waterspouts collapsing. It was all she could do to stay on her feet.

With a wet squelch, the blade slid out. Blood gurgled from the open wound and she slapped both hands over it, feeling heat seep through her fingers. She couldn't place her legs and down she went. She hit the sand and saw her attacker wore a ripped buccaneer's coat in scarlet red. The skeletal sailor was raised aloft before being ripped apart into three segments by a sentient somewhere. Good, at least it was dead.

It didn't hurt anymore. Chinara couldn't feel anything at all. Her breaths came in short, shallow gasps.

She would never get to see her daughter.

She was so ready to love her, too. She'd wanted her, all her life. Would Leonie know? Would Leonie know to tell her about her other mother, who had loved her so much? All the things she had pictured: teaching her how to walk, how to read, how to be a witch.

As her eyes closed, she saw women gather around her, their panic, their sorrow. She tried to say the word *healer*, but it was much too late.

47

TIME TRAVEL IS A MOTHERFUCKER

Ciara - Ankara, Turkey

They had lost her sister.

'We have to go back!' Elle shouted as they stomped over the rocky foothills towards the ruins.

'Go back to where?' Leonie threw her hands up. 'She could be anywhere. Any-when.'

'Do you think she's . . . ?' Elle didn't finish the question.

'No,' Ciara said firmly. 'I can feel her. Can't you?' She looked to Leonie.

Leonie closed her eyes, as if searching. 'Yes,' she admitted, opening them.

'OK,' Ciara said. 'Now, where are we?'

Leonie told them this was the place where the Seal of Solomon had been unearthed. 'I just focused my mind on where the Seal was, and here we are . . .' she'd explained. It gave Ciara some hope that if *Lee* was now steering the ship, it meant they could also search for Niamh.

'Let's get this fucking thing and get on it.' Ciara led the way to the dig site. She hoped if she acted with enough authority, no one would remember the only reason they were *on* this little quest was because she'd turned one of their only weapons against Satanis into pixie dust.

Turkey was disappointingly un-Turkish. In fact, the mountainous archaeological site could well be a quarry in Swindon if she weren't so frigging sweaty. Dry heat surrounded them. What feeble breeze there was felt like a hairdryer and offered no respite.

Leonie and Elle trailed after Ciara as she descended the ladders into the dig site. The sun was setting behind the mountains and everyone seemed to have gone home for the night. A chain-smoking security guard and his dog had been easy enough to bewitch: the man was patrolling elsewhere, satisfied he was alone.

Leonie, the only one of them who'd been to the sunken temple before, pointed to an area covered by a blue tarpaulin. 'There should be a door under there.'

Ciara whipped it clear with a fan of her fingers.

'Careful!' Leonie said. 'It's like a gazillion years old.'

'If it survived being *buried* in an earthquake, I don't think a gentle breeze is gonna bring it down, do you?'

Leonie snorted. 'Fair.'

It was an ancient stone gateway, with what looked like snakes carved into the masonry. Stick women worshipped the serpents, which she found rather phallic, even knowing what she now knew. 'It's the temple of Sheba,' Leonie explained. 'The Queen of Sheba was a witch.'

Ciara stuck her head into the tunnel beyond.

'We need an elemental,' Elle said. 'It's pitch black in there.'

'Mundanes have their uses, too.' Ciara smiled, holding up a torch. 'The security guy lent me this.' She switched it on and cast it around damp, stony walls.

Leonie told them it was a bit of a walk and, as they ventured deep under the mountain, Ciara was grateful of the others' company. This would be scary as fuck if she was alone. After so many years locked into the confines of her comatose body, small spaces seemed to constrict around her in a way they never had before. She couldn't rid her head of the notion that the air was thinning in the narrow tunnels. Was it her imagination or was it actually harder to breathe? Leonie, reading her, reached for her hand and gave it a squeeze.

Eventually they came to a stop. Scaffolding secured the end of the passage. Ciara cast the torch over a mound of rubble.

'Oh shit,' Leonie said.

'What?'

Leonie's eyes skittered as she worked it out. 'I got it wrong. We're too soon. They haven't got to the tomb yet.'

'But that's good, isn't it?' Ciara said. 'Like if we got there after them, your woman would have already taken the Seal back to Aeaea?'

Lee frowned and massaged her temples. 'Oh I don't know, this time travel shit blags my head.'

'No that's right. We have to get it before . . .'

'Zehra.'

'Before she does. And then have to we put it back so she can discover it. That way we don't change the future and become apes or whatever.'

'What?' Elle's voice came from the dark.

'Planet of the Apes?'

Elle grimaced. 'Not for me.'

Ciara suddenly wished she had a whiteboard and a pen to draw some sort of diagram. 'If time doesn't exist for Gaia – or if she *is* time – this was always the way it was. We were always here, and there, and then. Everything that happens now always happened.'

Leonie shook her head. 'Nope, lost me.'

Ciara sighed. 'Don't you, like, *read*?'

'Not if I can help it,' Leonie said.

'I like a Sophie Kinsella on holiday,' Elle added.

OK, so that put Ciara in charge. 'We just have to be careful is all I'm saying. We can't risk the future. Now, let's get into the crypt.'

'I can move the rubble,' Leonie said.

'I'll try to turn the stone into dust,' Elle said. 'Would that help?'

'You can do that?' Ciara looked to her.

Elle looked at the debris with a little more despair than Ciara would have liked. 'I think so.'

Ciara nodded. 'I'll make sure the tunnel doesn't collapse on our heads.'

'Teamwork makes the dream work.' Leonie positioned herself ready to excavate the tunnel.

And it did. Leonie was precise in her tunnelling, removing bite-sized chunks, piece by piece, while Elle duly reduced them to sand and then nothing at all. They spoke little, focused on their task. Through thick dust, the mound cleared and a gasp of crisp, earthen air greeted them. It was as if they'd pierced a bubble. As the debris settled, Ciara saw they'd unearthed the upmost part of an arched entryway.

'This is it,' Leonie said. 'We had to crouch to get in, I remember.'

Leonie went ahead, and Ciara followed. The air inside the tomb was oddly liquid, as tart as champagne. Unbreathed for thousands of years.

'Look!' Leonie said once Ciara was upright. She swept the torch beam across the chamber until it landed on a mighty statue: a woman atop an elephant.

Leonie stared in shock at the monument.

There was nothing on the Queen of Sheba's head.

'Where is it?' Ciara asked.

'I . . . I don't know,' Leonie said. Ciara wondered if they all shared the same sinking feeling. 'Zehra said this was where they found it.'

Elle told her to shine a light on the sandy floor, in case the crown had slipped off the effigy during the landslide that had buried it. They set about searching on hands and knees, digging and sweeping, but there was nothing crown-like amongst the urns, trinkets and treasures the queen had been interred with.

'This is fucked!' Leonie cried. 'It was here! It had to be! How else would Zehra have got it? I thought Bump was supposed to get us to where we needed to be!'

Something had gone awry. Already. Ciara stood, hands on hips. *Think.* She'd worn the fucking crown, felt its devastating force. The diadem had told her its story; built by King Solomon for his consort, and the Queen of Sheba had deemed its power too great for any witch to possess. It had been sealed within this temple . . . or had it?

What she hadn't factored in was their part in the jigsaw. *Who had stored the crown here?*

Ciara turned to Leonie. 'Who put it here?'

'What? I don't know. Like Sheba's coven?'

'What if *we* did?' She looked between her friends, waiting to see if the penny had dropped. 'We have to go *back*.'

'Back where?' Elle asked.

'To when it was made.'

THE KIND SCOUSER

Elle - Halifax, UK

She had let go, and now she was lost.

They had returned to the water conduit on the outskirts of the dig site; a pathetic stream running down the mountainside, little more than a trickle. Leonie had focused on going back, going *way* back. Difficult to picture a place you've never been, or even read about. All three of them had said their prayers to Gaia.

Once more they had fallen, only this time, it had been too much. She had thought about Holly, about how far away she was. She had panicked about getting back. The tumult inside her tummy had somehow manifested outwardly and she had jolted out of Leonie's grip.

The last thing she remembered was Leonie's voice filling her head, begging her to hang on as they spiralled down and down through time. Elle had closed her eyes, assuming it was the end. She braced for impact . . .

But it never came. Instead, she merely . . . arrived.

Though she doubted this was King Solomon's ancient empire. Because *this* was a hospital toilet. She was on her hands and knees, panting heavily as the panic subsided.

Elle would recognise the smell of the detergent anywhere. Hospitals have a very specific smell: the fake flora of the cheap NHS cleaning products somewhere between sweet and sterile.

From this position, she could see underneath a row of toilet stalls. A pair of slippered feet sat on the loo, and she recognised the pink Uggs. She heard a sharp intake of breath, a muffled sob, and suddenly knew precisely where she was. Calderdale Royal. *Bloody hellfire, not this.* For a moment, Elle was too stunned to move, but then gathered herself enough to scramble into the neighbouring cubicle and lock the door. She put the seat down and sat on the toilet, instinctively pulling her feet up onto the toilet in case the person in the next stall looked underneath. Her hands were clamped over her mouth as she tried to quiet her own hitching breath.

Because the person in the pink Uggs was *her*. Of course, this episode in her life was all a blur – partly because of the number Lucifer had done on her – but mostly because she'd been exhausted, on morphine, and half-starved. She'd been unable to stomach any of the hospital food they'd tried to force upon her – even the jelly. To this day, she couldn't touch the stuff.

She felt it was probable she must not be seen – least of all by herself. Ciara had said something about paradoxes, and while Elle didn't quite know what that meant, it didn't sound good. And anyway, even in her befuddled state, she was pretty sure she'd have remembered meeting herself in a toilet.

Elle heard the other Elle trying to stifle her tears. She remembered it like it were yesterday. Jez had kept telling her how strong she was, and how well she was doing, so she had hidden here so he didn't see her cry. It had only been three days. They were desperate to discharge her, but Elle couldn't contemplate going home without her baby in her arms.

Future Elle remembered all the cards that were waiting for them on the coffee table. All the neighbours who'd pop over to see how she was getting on. For weeks Elle had to tolerate their wide-eyed sympathy, their home-cooked Tupperware offerings. She didn't want a lamb biriyani, she wanted Milo. She'd felt it all again, so recently. Milo had been pressed out of her dough, and the cookie-cutter shape would never, ever be filled, because the little boy she was supposed to have was gone. It was still there, the absence of what should have been; a hollow on her soul.

The next thoughts arrived all at once, getting wedged in the doorframe of her brain.

1. A kind Scouser had looked after her that day, passing loo roll under the stall.

2. *She* was in the next stall.

3. She remembered what Ciara had said about them always being part of this sequence.

4. Oh, for crying out loud.

With a deep sigh, Elle unspooled a handful of toilet roll from the Kimberly-Clark dispenser and made it into a bouquet before reaching into the gap under the wall. 'Here you go, doll.' Her Scouse accent was a GCSE Drama mixture of *Brookside*, Jodie Comer and Sporty Spice. Elle had got a B. She clung to the fact that her Liverpudlian accent had been convincing enough to fool a grieving woman sixteen years ago. Mortifying, honestly.

'Thank you,' a sniffly voice said as the loo roll was plucked from her fingers.

Elle couldn't remember precisely how this conversation had played out, only that it had. Now she had to retrace those steps. 'You all right, love?'

'Yeah. Sorry. I'll be fine.'

Elle wanted to punch through the wall and throttle herself. *You don't have to be fine, your baby just died. Tell the world, tell the world that this is the greatest pain anyone has ever felt, and you don't give a flying fuck if your ugly, noisy misery makes them uncomfortable.*

But that wasn't how it had gone.

'You will be, you know.'

'Sorry?' The woman on the other side blew her nose.

'I, um, I'm sure you're going through hell right now, but . . . you know, it does get better.'

There was a long silence.

'Are you there?'

'Yeah.'

'I lost a baby too,' Elle said, and saying it aloud now was as awful as it had been then.

Another sniff. 'How did you know?'

'Why else would yous be crying on a maternity ward?' Actually, that wasn't quite accurate. She'd cried buckets of exhausted tears after Holly had been born, too. Breastfeeding her had proven impossible, and she'd wept many a time over that. There's always something for a mum to cry over.

She heard more tears. 'I'm sorry.'

'Don't be sorry. Don't ever be sorry. You didn't do anything wrong. I swear down.'

'If I had *made* them listen though. I knew something was wrong, I did.'

Elle winced to hear how raw she sounded. That pain had hardened to steel over the years. 'They did listen, doll, they just didn't believe yous. Same old story. The doctors think they know your body better than you do. You coulda said anything and they'd have all been like *you just take it easy, Mrs . . . Comer.*' Better than nothing.

'What am I gonna do? Everyone wants me to get on with it like nothing's happened.'

'You'll get on, because life gets on, doesn't it. But you won't ever forget,' Elle said, because though her memories had – for a short while – been taken from her, she had always retained that weird indent where her baby ought to have been. The devil himself couldn't fill that void. 'And that's good, because would you want to?'

'No! He was my baby boy . . .'

'I was the same. But it, um, like becomes scar tissue. And I became a mum again – so will you.'

'No, I can't do this again.'

Elle's heart broke. It had been that bad. 'Babes, you're a *mumma*.'

'I'm not.' The noise Other Elle made was almost animal, like a dog being kicked.

'Oh yes you are. You wanted him so much, and you were ready, body and soul,' she said warmly. 'That's a mother that is. You always will be.'

Other Elle blew her nose again. 'Thank you. God I'm a mess.'

'Let it all out,' she told her. It was comforting in a way, to be in this position. There was so much joy ahead for the woman in the next bog. Horrific days lay ahead, too, but infinitely more happy ones: the wedding, and Holly, and nights with her friends. Farfalle pasta sprayed gold, sparklers and mittens, shite nativity plays where Holly cried because her tinsel halo was itchy.

A thought occurred to her: losing Niamh on their journey through time had been no accident, and it hadn't been an accident that she ended up here. Gaia had said the baby would take them to where they need to be. That meant she need to be here. That Gaia had sent her here.

But why?

And that's when Elle felt it. That *iron* inside. The space where Milo's loss had been had filled with ore and solidified. She was *not* the same woman who had sobbed in the toilet almost seventeen years ago. She had gotten *through* it. She'd needed the reminder. And suddenly Elle felt *strong*, stronger than she had ever felt in her entire life.

Elle Device was ready for revenge.

THE QUEEN OF SHEBA

Leonie - The Ancient Kingdom of Solomon

They had lost Elle. It was all they could do to stay hidden and keep a lid on panic. They were in their own set of trouble: there was no explaining their clothes, here.

Leonie and Ciara worked to keep themselves totally shielded as they observed, wide-eyed, where Lee's baby had taken them.

This was incredible, just unbelievable. The only thing she could liken it to was a theme park – when you join the queue for the rollercoaster and it's all fibreglass blocks designed to look like an Aztec temple or a volcano or something. Only this time, it wasn't fibreglass – it was *real*.

What blew her mind was that it didn't look ancient in the way that the temple on Aeaea did; under a jolly turquoise sky, everything was new, and clean, and, in a way, modern. It was, after all, a palace.

There were in a bustling courtyard before mighty palace steps. It was a marketplace; traders were allowed through the imposing portcullis and into a sprawling forecourt. She and Chinara had been to Morocco, and it was a little like that with the haggling, and dealing, and noisy bartering. The main trade seemed to be in livestock – goats and sheep – but she also saw silks, and fabric, and spices. Some obnoxious teenage boys made stupid hooting noises in a misguided attempt at impressing some giggling young women. Nothing ever changes, she thought. It was twelve thousand years ago according to Ciara's maths, but give them a smartphone and it could be now. People just peopling.

Since they'd arrived, they'd searched every nook and cranny of the bazaar for Elle. Like Niamh, Leonie could still sense her essence . . . but so distantly. With enough time, and some peace and quiet, she felt confident she and the baby could locate them both. Was the word symbiosis? It wasn't that she could *steer* this gift, but she felt at one with it.

This is insane. Ciara's voice filled her head. *Where do we start?*

We need to get inside the palace, Leonie told her. With two sentients it really shouldn't be an issue.

Leonie weaved through the crowd to a stall selling silks. Strongly suspecting they didn't take ApplePay, she slid a length of magenta silk off the tradesman's table once his back was turned. She wrapped it over her head, and then took another to tuck around her waist, hiding her jeans. She then handed a peacock blue silk to Ciara. *Put this on.*

It's not my colour, but whatever. Ciara did as she was told. It was giving Claire Danes in *Homeland*. *We charm the guards?*

Exactly. Leonie let her defences drop and both women became visible. In the thrum of the marketplace, she was confident they hadn't drawn any attention to themselves.

Why don't we just stay shielded and fly over the gates? Ciara asked.

Because she was exhausted, for one – she didn't know if she could hold that magic for so long. Before she could share the thought, they were interrupted by a shrill fanfare and the townsfolk fell quiet at once.

She turned to witness a procession of leather-clad, hulking guards file from the palace gates. An entire troop flooded the souk, deathly sharp spears glinting, winking in the midday sun. The men began to bark orders at shoppers and merchants, driving back the crowd. Leonie couldn't translate the words they were saying, but she could read their thoughts, and one word – an image – was clear.

Queen.

Leonie gripped Ciara's arm. *What is it?* Ciara demanded.

Witches! Make yourselves known! You will not evade us.

Their target had sought them out. 'They're looking for us!'

Ciara looked left and right. 'What do we do? Do we run?'

Behind them, the portcullis was lowered, sealing them inside the palace gates and the crowd surged, growing tighter packed around them. Leonie placed her hands protectively over her bump, fearful of a stampede.

'But we want to find her, right?' Ciara said. 'Right?'

'Right. Oi!' Leonie pealed at the top of her lungs. Would she greet them? Or behead them? 'We're here motherfuckers!'

The sentries cleared a channel through the crowd, flanking a path. Down the centre of this channel came four gargantuan guards, shirtless mountains of men, carrying an ornate golden litter on their vast shoulders. Its inhabitant was protected from the harsh sun on all sides by gossamer drapes. At the heart of the carriage sat a serene, lone silhouette. A lithe, female form.

'Obsessed,' Ciara muttered as the caravan headed directly for them.

Leonie ignored her. 'I don't think they're rolling out the red carpet, Ci.'

In a sort of pincher motion, Leonie found they were surrounded by guards; some of them warlocks. They weren't fighting their way out of this one. 'Kneel!' one guard said in English. There wasn't time to dwell on that now, not with his hand on the hilt of his sword. Leonie pulled at Ciara's wrist and they both knelt on hot, sandy cobbles. 'Lower!'

Leonie pressed her forehead to the stone in submission.

The guards placed the litter on the ground with a clunk. Leonie heard them withdraw the dainty drapes concealing the queen and she dared to glance upwards. The shimmering corona partially occluded her view but, on a throne within the litter sat a slight figure, dressed in creamy silks, her throat and wrists glistening with emeralds and rubies the size of marbles. She wore gold cuffs and a veiled crown. With a perfectly manicured hand, the Queen of Sheba reached up to withdraw her veil.

There was a moment where Leonie's brain couldn't make sense of it. A glue-brained second of recognition, then denial, then acceptance.

Senait sat on the throne.

She grinned down at her. 'What are you doing? Get up off the floor! Sorry about the guards, they take it all dead seriously.'

Leonie dusted off her knees. 'What the hell is going on?'

The young woman looked almost disappointed by the question. 'Oh, OK. I thought you might have figured it out by now,' Senait said.

'Figured what out?' Leonie gritted her teeth, swallowing back the desire to punch her out of her carriage.

Senait sighed. 'You better come on inside. We've got a lot to talk about . . .' And she finished on one word. *'Mum.'*

SISTERS

Niamh - Galway, Ireland

Like in *A Christmas Carol*, the ghosts were not being kind to Niamh. From the beck in Hebden Bridge, she'd found herself in a far less welcome river: the River Corrib on the night her parents died.

The water was icy cold and the horn shrieked from where her father's chest was jammed, dead, against the steering wheel.

Niamh did not want to see. The car was almost on its side, half in and half out of the water where it was run off the road. She knew, because she'd read about it many years later, how both of them had been decapitated. She could not see that and survive.

She sat at the roadside, some distance away, watching the emergency services diligently work to free the bodies. *Why here? Why now?* This was the last place she wanted to come, and Gaia knew it. She hugged her arms tight to her ribs, trying to rub some heat into her body. She was worried if she got any colder, the paramedics and firefighters would see through her shield.

So she took herself to the back of an open ambulance to get out of the biting January air. She was warming up nicely – until a body bag was stretchered in. She ought to have seen that one coming, really. Niamh pressed herself into a tight corner on the floor, tucking her feet out of the way. This was cruel.

The rear doors were slammed shut. And now she was stuck, alone, with the mangled corpse of one of her parents.

The ambulance drove away from the crash site. Niamh suspected her hunch about Lee's unborn child using water conduits was correct. Water seemed to link the various places she'd materialised: the cave pond, the desert oasis, Hebden Beck and now the Corrib. She could use that; water was her element. She would find the nearest body of water and hope Leonie could summon her back. Niamh *could* feel her friend's aura still. At school they'd once made a 'telephone' with two yoghurt pots and a length of string. It hadn't worked, of course, but this felt the same; Leonie was *there*, at the end of a very long string. Now, how to reel herself back?

She couldn't do anything from the back of a moving vehicle and so Niamh waited for the ambulance to arrive at what was *now* University Hospital. Back then, it was still just Galway Central.

The second the paramedic opened the rear doors; Niamh made her escape, sidling out alongside the stretcher. She didn't want to know which of her parents was in the black bag, it was too awful to contemplate. She vaguely remembered that the hospital was close to the canal. She would make her way there and try her luck.

'Girls! It's this one! Come along now, quickly.'

Niamh turned into the wind and saw Belinda Friel hurrying two small redheads into the huge glass A&E entrance further down the block. *Oh fuck.* How had Niamh forgotten this?

That night – *this* night – they'd come to the hospital. There had a been a horrible misunderstanding. Galway was a small town and someone had seen Mum and Dad's car at the scene of the accident and informed Belinda, the girls' babysitter for the night, that they'd been *hurt*. Not knowing what else to do, Belinda had rushed us to the hospital to greet them.

Niamh felt lightheaded. She wasn't sure her shielding charm was working anymore. Was this why she'd been brought here?

Surely she wasn't supposed to *meet* her past self? She wasn't big on science fiction, but Conrad had been. She'd sat through enough bottom-shelf-of-Blockbuster DVDs with him to know that you're *not* supposed to do that.

But what other possible reason would there be?

Her feet walked her towards the spinning doors. Niamh joined a rotation and entered unseen. It was mercifully warm, but chaotic: Someone was getting angry with the woman on the front desk about how long he'd been waiting. An elderly woman pressed a bloodied tea towel to a man's head wound. The moulded orange seats, rows of them, looked stiff and unwelcoming and there was an air of sticky, fidgety impatience.

Niamh looked around, but she couldn't see where Belinda had taken the children. Niamh strained, trying to remember that night. She had tried hard to forget; it wasn't her most cherished of memories. They weren't here though; she'd have remembered all the carnage and gore. No, she recalled a quiet, private room. A big square TV was affixed to the wall, showing a film she was too young to watch.

Warmer, Niamh affirmed her shield as she passed the kerfuffle at the reception desk. Past them, down a long, starkly lit corridor, were a series of private rooms. One was marked FAMILY ROOM, and that felt feasible.

From inside, Niamh heard shrill raised voices. The door burst open, and Ciara raced out of the room, weaving through the crowd like a fox. Niamh covered her hand with her mouth. If she remembered correctly, her sister had just called their babysitter a miserable fat cow. Instinctively, Niamh pressed herself to the plastic trolley bumper on the wall to get out of her way as she headed towards the revolving doors. Niamh peeked inside the room and saw herself, over twenty-five years ago, gawping up at the TV absentmindedly.

Brenda Friel, a hard-faced neighbour – and a low-level healer – spoke to her younger self. 'Niamh, you stay here. I'll get your sister. That child has the devil in her, I swear.'

Not far wrong. The older woman exited the family room, but strode in entirely the wrong direction – heading further into the department. Niamh thought to redirect her, but it was too late. Ciara was already out of the front door. She felt the need to go after her – and then, it was like a light turned on in her head. She was *meant* to be here, and she was starting to think she knew why.

Niamh let her shield fall out in the corridor. There was no one too close and the hospital staff seemed to be actively avoiding making eye contact with anyone. On a plastic wheelie trolley, someone had left a stethoscope idle. She took it and looped it around her neck, hurrying after her little sister. Younger Niamh would be fine, although watching *The Accused* that night was how she'd learned what rape was.

She stepped back into the grip of the cold and scanned the drop-off zone. She couldn't see the girl, but she did see the diligent paramedic reloading her gurney into the ambulance in which Niamh had arrived at the hospital. That gave her an idea of where her sister could be. She knew Ciara well; she knew Ciara wouldn't wait.

She had gone in search of her parents.

No, no, no, no, NO. Niamh rushed down the side of the hospital building, shielding herself as she went. The paramedic had left via an anonymous port to the right of the grander public entrance to A&E. Niamh slipped through the gap in the double doors before they could close, and tried to make sense of the busy reception area.

Nurses and porters and doctors swarmed efficiently around their hive, and Niamh pressed herself against the wall. How old were they? Nine? There was no way Ciara would have been able to make herself *invisible* to these mundanes, but she *was* small and bold and highly sneaky. Maybe she hadn't needed to.

Niamh was a vet, not a doctor, but she could make sense of the NHS signs – in English and Gaelic – on the walls; Resuscitation Bay 1–5, ICU, Theatre 1–3 and, on the floor below, Mortuary. Most children would be deterred, but not her sister.

Avoiding human traffic, Niamh tiptoed downstairs. Thankfully, the lower level was much quieter. Quiet, in fact, as a crypt. The windowless corridor was long and sickly with greenish-white light. A lanky porter whistled the Cranberries as he wheeled an empty trolley towards the lift at the furthest end away from the mortuary.

She waited until the elevator doors sighed shut before she let her spell fall. Checking that the stethoscope was still around her neck, she proceeded to the morgue.

Sure enough, standing slap bang in the middle of a row of industrial refrigerator doors, was a very shocked little girl. She leapt back, caught in the act.

The morgue was as cold and clinical as Niamh would have expected: three stern steel slabs felt very final in the centre of the apple-green linoleum floor, while cold storage lined one entire wall. Mercifully, there was no sign of the body bag she'd ridden in with; she assumed the porter had stored it in of these cabinets.

Niamh instinctively understood that Ciara mustn't know who she was. She put on her very finest *Bridgerton* accent. 'And just what on earth do you think you're doing, young lady?'

Ciara's jaw hung open and Niamh knew, without the need to use her powers, that her sister was cooking up a lie.

'You shouldn't be in here,' Niamh continued in her English clip.

'I . . .' her sister started, and then deflated. 'I think my mam and da are dead.'

A doctor was just about to break that news to them. How could she know? 'Even so, this is no place for little girls. You need to go back upstairs. There's a frantic lady looking for you.'

Ciara at least had the good grace to look a little ashamed. 'Are they though? Dead?'

Her face was crumpled, and Niamh saw she was about to cry. *Oh, hell.*

Niamh knelt to her level. 'Hey now . . .' She almost said *it'll all be OK*, but, honestly, it wouldn't be. Not for a long time. 'What's wrong?'

'It's my fault,' she whispered.

'What is?'

'What happened. The crash.'

'I . . . I don't think that's true.'

Ciara looked into her eyes. The same as they were now, green, flecked with amber. The same as hers. 'I wished for it.' A tear ran down her face. 'I fought with my mam and I wished . . .'

Niamh couldn't embrace her without giving herself away. She rubbed her arm instead. 'There, there.' She almost forgot the voice. 'We all think a lot of silly things when we're cross.'

'But . . .' her sister said, her expression hardening. 'I meant it.'

Niamh could see now what she hadn't been able to see, not then. Her mother, their mother, had *hurt* this child. Ciara, nine years old, was worn down to a stump. How had she never realised this at the time? They spent half their lives in each other's minds for fuck's sake. This tired little girl, and her punctured heart, had wished her mother would die, and meant every word.

'I am sorry,' Niamh said, meaning that too. 'You have a sister, don't you? Upstairs?'

Ciara nodded and Niamh steered her away from the fridge doors.

'Let's get you back to her, shall we? She'll look after you.'

'She hates me,' Ciara said.

'She doesn't!' Niamh said, perhaps too forcefully. 'I have a sister too, and we fight all the time, but that doesn't mean I don't love her with all my heart.'

'Really?'

Niamh bowed to her level again. 'Listen. A sister isn't the same as a friend. The love goes all the way to the core, like a peach stone. Whatever you say or do to each other, it stays the same; hard and strong. No matter what.'

Ciara considered this, but said nothing as they left the morgue. Niamh placed her hand between the girl's shoulder blades and guided her down the gloomy corridor.

Niamh had to hold in her own tears all the way back to A&E. No small feat – because how she wanted to wail.

SENAIT

Leonie - The Ancient Kingdom of Solomon, ninth century BCE

The palace was palacing. It was as palatial as you'd want an alcázar to be: towering marble pillars, statues in bronze, gold-woven tapestries, and palm fanners, and actual live peacocks just roaming around willy-nilly. Honestly, ridiculous.

From the courtyard, they had been led through soaring halls and atria until they arrived at a private sanctum, where sunshine spilled as magnificent columns through skylights in an ornately painted dome. It was a throne room of sorts, and Senait had draped herself over the fur-covered throne as soon as they'd arrived. She was attended by five women in similar opulent dress. 'It's OK, this is just my coven. I don't let men in here. We can talk about whatever. My girlies don't speak much English anyway, to be honest.'

Leonie heard Ciara's thoughts *very* clearly and echoed them. 'OK, then. What the actual fuck, Senait?'

She huffed. 'I knew you'd be like this.'

Hands on hips, Leonie glared at her. The only other chairs were scatter pillows and – if she sat down there in her current state – she'd never get back up. 'Can I sit down, please?'

Senait vacated the throne and gestured at it. 'Knock yourself out.'

Leonie flopped onto it, thoroughly knackered. 'You said I'd be like what, exactly? Totally fucking bewildered? Because, yes. I'd fucking well say so.'

'Please don't swear, it's cringe. And it's freaking me out.'

Ciara took charge, gods love her. 'Leonie's your mother?'

'Uh-huh.' One of her handmaids returned with an overflowing platter of fruits. Senait plucked a grape from her and fell back onto a pile of pillows. 'Thanks, babe.'

'But *how*?'

Senait held out her hand. A different handmaid brought her a very standard WHSmith ring binder in violet and Senait flicked through pages in plastic wallets.

'What's that?' Leonie asked.

'The spreadsheet you made me way back when.'

She rubbed her ever-expanding bump. 'This is you?'

Senait didn't look up from the file. 'Uh-huh. Pretty weird seeing you like this, to be honest, but it was always gonna happen I guess.' She kept on leafing through the pages in her folder. 'Yeah. It says here that Mum is gonna come to ninth century BCE, and that's when I'm allowed to tell you the truth. So that's what I'm doing? You didn't give me a script, so I'm just, you know, doing my best.'

Ciara interjected. 'How long have you been here?'

'A year or so. Pretty sweet gig. Sol is a decent bloke.'

'Sol?' Ciara paced, agitated.

'That would be King Solomon.' Leonie thought she might genuinely faint.

'You married King Solomon?' Ciara said.

'Sure!' she said, as if it were the most casual thing in the world. 'Once you get past the language barrier, he's a babe, so why not? Nobody said I had to, but the vibes were vibing, so . . .'

Leonie winced. If there was a polite way to ask an intersex person if she could have kids, she didn't know it. Leonie has seen Senait's naked body in Bologna and . . . it seemed . . . unlikely. 'I thought . . . I thought the Queen of Sheba had children? I . . . well . . . can you even have children?'

She grimaced, lips curling. 'Ew! No! As if actual King Solomon has one wife! He's a king!' Senait rolled her eyes. 'What? You didn't think ENM was invented by fuckbois in Hackney did you?'

'Ethical non-monogamy,' Leonie told Ciara.

'Oh.'

Senait's tone grew more serious. She crossed her legs, lotus-style, and sat up straight. 'Mum, I did what you have always told me to do. I came here, with the ancient stones from Aeaea and offered them to the king. Obviously, he went mad for them and agreed to a trade if I accepted his hand in marriage. I've been here since, waiting on you.'

Leonie looked to Ciara, who could only offer a shrug. 'Can these girls get us something a bit stronger than water?'

Senait gave her handmaiden a nod and off she went. 'This is the end of the book though. It's almost the end of the line. I had to be here to make sure you got the Seal, and then I'm a free agent. Again, your words, not mine.'

This was a deeply unnerving sensation. To converse with someone who claimed to know your future was nauseating. She'd clung to the quaint notion that she was – that they *all* were – the sole drivers of their destinies and yet here was proof to the contrary. But her future self *had* made decisions for Senait, and that only added to her bone-deep unease.

A different handmaid, this one built like a brick shithouse, approached Senait with a jewelled case. She presented to her a very basic-looking crown that Leonie had last seen on Dabney Hale's bonce. 'Oh, there she is,' Ciara said. 'You wanna be careful with that thing.'

Senait smiled. 'That's one thing both you and my husband agree on. It's a headfuck. Literally.'

Leonie stood and held her hands up in surrender. 'Can we just take a minute, please? I'm struggling a bit.'

'You told me you would. You warned me that you wouldn't believe me to begin with.' Senait flicked through her ring binder again. I have some pictures of us somewhere . . .'

Leonie was quite certain she didn't want to see a polaroid of her future, and held out a hand to stop her. 'Stop! Let's start at the beginning. *My* beginning,' she added before Senait could butt in. 'When I first met you in Italy . . . ?'

'I knew who you were, yes,' Senait admitted. 'Didn't you think I was acting a little off?'

'Well, I dunno. Maybe.'

Senait finally moved her arse and came to Leonie's side, perching on the arm of the throne. 'My whole life, you taught me the story. We called it The Plan. I know The Plan like the back of my hand. Where I have to be, and when.'

'You can time travel?' Ciara asked, highly sceptical.

'Sure. Gaia gave me a bit of her power. You already know that, keep up. It's pretty cool. I'm one-of-a-kind, as far as we know. I can see the river of history and sort of . . . move up and down it.' When they stared gormlessly at her, she said, 'You can *fly*, why is time travel so unhinged?'

Ciara went on. 'But that means you can see into the future too? Do we win?'

Senait took a breath. 'The future is like a blob. You know I said time was a river? The future is where it meets the ocean. I can see it all clearly, but it's too big. I can't see the details.'

'OK, that makes sense, I guess.'

'How old are you?' Leonie asked her.

'Twenty-two.'

Leonie rubbed the bump again; she couldn't help it. 'So what happens between now and . . . here?'

Senait shook her head. 'You told me to just give you the crown and send you on your way. If I say too much, it might change how you act and that could bring the whole thing crashing down.'

'What's that supposed to mean?' Ciara said. 'If you can help us, just fucking tell us.'

Senait straightened up, and for the first time Leonie saw a queen. This wasn't the lost little girl in Domino's club or the wide-eyed child who'd travelled to Turkey with her. And yes, in this light, Leonie saw herself in her. Her nostrils flared and she stared Ciara down. 'No. You need to shut up and listen to me. I'm, like, the expert on this. I cannot fuck it up. It's like a Swiss clock: everything is very, very finely calibrated. If one tiny cog is out of place, all of time is fucked. There is a way for you to defeat Satanis, and there is a future where you do, but it is hanging by a thread.' She took a breath. 'But when the time comes, you'll decide for yourselves. I can't tell you how to act, and neither can Gaia. It has to be you. Both of you.'

She gave the Amazon a nod and the giantess brought Leonie the crown in its casket.

'There. I can tick that one off my list.'

Leonie took the crown reluctantly. 'And when we're done?'

'Leave it to me.'

She nodded. She knew exactly where poor Zehra Darga would unearth the artefact in centuries. No wonder the seal was in such good nick – it took the express lane to 2022. 'Wait. We can't just leave you here.'

Senait looked puzzled. 'You don't.' She turned to the final page in her ring binder. 'I'm about to . . . go and tell you not to have an abortion in London.'

'That hasn't happened yet?'

'Not for me. It's on the list. I'll get to it. I'm guessing it works out because . . .' She waved a hand at Leonie's abdomen.

Ciara shook her head. 'Chronology is fucked,' she muttered.

'Senait,' Leonie said. Her mind was just beginning to accept this information. The dough was rising so to speak. 'You're my *daughter*.'

'Yep.' She smiled broadly. 'My whole life! I'm glad I can be honest this time. Pretending was the *worst*.'

Leonie allowed a brief laugh to slip out. From their first meeting, she'd adored this girl, even when she'd been a lot to take. She'd felt so comfortable around her; so protective of her. So trusting even when Hale told her . . . and that was a fair point, actually. 'Hale.'

Senait's gaze dropped. 'I'm sorry. You and Calista told me it had to happen.'

'You know Calista?'

'I've known her my whole life too.' Senait raised a finger to her lips, as if she'd given away too much.

Leonie recalled how Calista had led Senait out of the olive garden on the night before the massacre. She'd known. She'd known what was about to befall the island. 'But why?'

'It had to happen. It was The Plan,' she said, as if that explained everything. Leonie knew, because, for the first time, Senait was allowing her to read her unfiltered, that if they now tried to retrospectively pick up any fallen domino – Annie, Helena, Zehra, *any* of them – it would disrupt the chain of events that might lead them to their shot at victory. That so many women had to die for them to succeed against Satanis didn't feel fair.

'So we just go?'

'You just go.'

'But I don't want to leave you behind.'

'What?' Senait sounded confused. 'You don't. I haven't been born yet, silly.'

Ciara muttered *fucking hell* and went to explore the tapestries.

'Mum, you have to go back to your time. Like, now. It's really vital that you go.'

Leonie frowned. There was something ominous about her tone. 'Why? What do you mean? Don't fuck about.'

Senait's eyes widened. 'It's Mama.'

'Mama?'

'You're Mum, and she's Mama. She needs you now.' She added more quietly, 'You have to be there for her.'

There was a feeling like plummeting in her stomach, the ground rushing up at her. Time stopped dead. 'Chinara? Why? What's happened to her?'

THE AVOCADO BATHROOM

Niamh

The water was icy cold and then scalding hot. Niamh breached the surface, gasping for breath. Her elbow clonked something smooth and plasticky. She gripped the rim of what she quickly understood to be a bathtub. The water was just too hot to stand, although perhaps welcome after the shock of the canal in Galway. Clumsily, she hauled herself out of the water and flopped her legs over the side, rolling onto a threadbare, damp-smelling bathmat.

As she recovered from the shock of the water, Niamh looked up at an Artex ceiling, black with mould – familiar. She'd seen this place, *smelled* this place, in her dreams. Or rather, in *Theo's* dreams.

She heard her before she saw her. The child, a wee pink jelly-baby of a thing, screamed and screamed, half-swaddled in a beach towel next to where Niamh lay. Her little wrinkled fingers clawed at thin air. She'd witnessed this scene from a variety of angles, but she'd always been outside of it, watching over it like a spectre. This time, she was here.

Soaked, Niamh took a smaller, damp hand towel that hung next to the sink. It was stained but better than nothing. She quickly dried her hair off and then attended to tiny Theo. She tucked the towel around her flailing limbs. 'Sssh, shush now. You're OK.'

The infant was wet and raw and Niamh knew what had just happened. She'd almost been drowned in the tub.

She took Theo in her arms, but froze as a figure appeared in the bathroom doorway.

'Who the hell are you?' The woman was hardly a woman; she couldn't be much more than seventeen or eighteen years old. She wore a limp velour tracksuit on her much-too-thin frame. The skin Niamh could see was mottled and patchy with sores and scratch marks. 'The fuck are you doing with my baby?'

Niamh held Theo closer. 'What were *you* doing?'

'Give him here.' The woman reached for Theo with pale hands.

'No!' Niamh held her closer. 'I know what you did.' In those nightmares, Niamh had seen her holding her baby under the bathwater.

Theo's mother gave a guttural scream and first punched the wall before twisting towards the bath and pulling down the shower curtain. The whole plastic rail came loose, clattering into the tub. 'You don't understand!' she sobbed.

'Then why don't you tell me?' Niamh used her most conciliatory tone, sending soothing subliminal thought waves her way.

'Who the fuck are you?' The girl's eyes were wild. Niamh recognised this expression from a thousand cornered animals at the vets. 'Did *he* send you?'

Niamh shook her head. 'No one sent me. I'm a witch. I'm a healer. I can help you.'

If this girl was surprised to hear her admission, she didn't exhibit any shock. Instead, she gripped fistfuls of her lank hair and shook her head in despair. 'You can't help me.'

'I can. Why did you want to hurt your baby?'

'*That* is not a baby!' the girl said and pelted out of the bathroom.

Niamh knew what came next, but she clearly wasn't sent here to stop her from trying to drown Theo as that had already happened, so there had to be some other reason. She gently laid the howling infant back down on the bathmat. Now that Theo was swaddled in the towel, the shrill howl had dimmed to a whimper. 'It'll all be fine, Theo, I promise,' she whispered.

Niamh entered the dingy hallway and found the girl rummaging through a drawer in the kitchen. She saw a blade glint in the low light. 'You can't stop me,' she cried, and Niamh backed off at once.

'Just don't hurt the baby.'

The girl left the kitchen, but Niamh barricaded her path to the bathroom. Theo's mother screamed again and almost flung herself into the living room. Niamh knew from memory they were in a high-rise flat. Judging from her accent, they were in Scotland somewhere.

'Tell me your name.' Niamh cautiously followed her into the living room.

'Why should I?'

'I don't know? You look like you need a friend?'

The girl considered her through the curtains of greasy hair. Gods, putting to one side the wear and tear, she looked so similar to how her daughter would eventually look. 'My name's Milena.'

'I'm Niamh.'

'How did you get in here?'

'Like I said, I'm a witch. A really powerful one.'

'You from HMRC?'

Shit, how to answer that? 'I guess I am, yes.' High Priestess, now you ask.

'Then you can get to fuck.'

'No! I'm not here officially . . . I'm just here to help. That's all. Please put down the knife.' It was only a vegetable peeler, really, but she could do some damage if she put her mind to it.

'It doesn't matter. He'll kill me anyway.'

Niamh took a step towards her. Milena hopped from foot to foot. The girl was shivering. 'Who will? Lucifer?' Milena looked at her, and that confirmed it. 'I've seen him too. Who did he come to you as?'

Milena shook her head. 'You don't want to know.'

'I do, you can trust me.'

'My stepdad.'

Well, that was bleak. She wished she hadn't asked. 'Whatever he's told you . . .'

'You dumb cunt, he didn't tell me shit. It's what I *did*. The coven . . .'

'Which coven?'

'The Cult of Satanis,' she whispered. 'They told me . . . they needed a vessel.' She began to cry. 'I was so fucking stupid.'

'They took advantage of you, Milena. This isn't your fault.'

'I needed – I needed to get out. And He came to me, as Asmodai. He came out of the sea and . . . they said Sonny – my baby – would be the vessel. That Leviathan would rise and I would be . . . I would be a queen,' she pleaded with Niamh. 'But I can't get him out of me. I see his face when I close my eyes. I can *taste* him on my tongue. You have to let me do it. That wee baby will kill us all.'

'She won't. He won't.' Fuck. 'That child is an innocent baby.'

'He is the Sullied Child.'

'I'm sorry but I don't believe in all that. That child . . . is going to grow up and be the loveliest little thing. Kind and sweet and loving.'

Milena scowled. 'How do you know?'

'I, um, oracles. The oracles at HMRC. We've seen that child. They grow up. You don't kill that baby.'

She now wept freely, and Niamh sensed real aquamarine relief under all the turmoil. She believed her. 'What kind of a mother am I?'

'One that needs help! Let me help you . . .' At the same time, Niamh knew they couldn't rewrite history. If the story was to unfurl correctly, Theo had to live and find her way to Hebden Bridge via the long, painful days in the care system. It was horrible, but true.

'There's nothing of me left. I gave myself to the demons. They're in me now. My bones are black and full of holes and there's maggots in the holes.' Her expression hardened and her pupils widened, unnaturally so. 'I need to kill him. I need to kill my baby . . .'

Niamh raised a hand and threw the slight girl across the lounge. 'I'm sorry but no. That's not how this goes.'

'You stupid bitch! He'll kill you all. He will fucking eat the whole fucking world!'

'I'm not gonna let you hurt a baby.'

The girl convulsed on the floor, crawling back onto her feet. Milena hobbled to the sliding balcony doors. They opened with a rusty screech. 'I cannae do this. No more. I can't do this anymore. I'm sorry, I'm so sorry.'

'Milena! Please!' Niamh tried to protest, she really did, but she had seen how this ended. She knew what was about to happen, and that she wouldn't stop it.

'Stay away!' Milena's hair blew across her face. 'I'm sorry.' She laughed bitterly. 'All this because of what *he* did to me.' Once more Niamh saw her stepfather's leering face in the girl's mind. 'I killed us all. It's all my fault . . .'

'Milena!' Niamh cried, but it was all so fast.

Milena almost rolled off the rail of the balcony. Silent, she fell into the night. By the time Niamh reached the edge, Milena was already splayed on a corrugated garage roof eight storeys down. Niamh could make out the twisted doll-like form, motionless.

Niamh knew how the story went. Stealing some clothes from Milena's bedroom, she concealed her red hair under a beanie hat and put Theo delicately inside a Head sports bag, wrapped in the throw she took from the settee.

She knew exactly where she had to go. From the high-rise, she shielded the pair of them so they could get past the police cars and ambulances that had come for Milena, and carried the baby through the wintery streets of Glasgow. It was trying to snow, half-hearted wisps of powder fluttering around the streetlights like dandruff.

She wandered the streets of the city centre, utterly unfamiliar to her. She relied on crinkled maps posted on street corners to find her way to Glasgow City Council on Albion Street.

This was the most awful thing she'd ever done, but she clung to the knowledge that Theo *did* survive this night. This was where her story began.

Checking the street was clear, Niamh tucked the baby into the arched doorway of the offices. She had dressed her warmly, layering her in a babygro and coat and booties. She stroked Theo's chubby cheek with a finger. 'Theo, it's Niamh.' The baby looked up at her with big blue eyes. 'You're gonna be fine, yes you are. You're going to grow up and become the most beautiful girl – inside and out. But I'm sorry my wee darl, it's gonna be real fucking tough. Some shit is gonna happen to you along the way, but stay soft, little one. Stay kind, and stay open, because one day, I am going to *love* you. There's a whole coven waiting for you, my sweetheart.'

Niamh's tears started to fall on the poor girl. She was consigning the girl to fifteen years of abuse, and misery, and confusion. For a moment she allowed herself to imagine a world where *she* raised her. Where she told her every day that there was nothing she could do or say that would make her love her less. Theo's childhood could be one of unconditional love, and total acceptance. A perfect transgender witch.

She could take her *home*.

But no.

By now Niamh knew that, in this life, there is no such thing as The Easy Way. There are infinite ways, but they are each Hard. The promise of an Easy Way is a cul-de-sac only fools head down.

She wiped her cheeks and strode away before she took the baby back with her and ruined the future for them all.

MEDUSA

Elle

Elle stood amongst the ruins. She'd given up screaming. There was no one else here.

A doleful wind howled through what was left of the town. The sky was chalky white and the rubble was white and the trees were white and bare. She didn't know where she was. There were no clues to guide her. What ruins existed were little more than bone fragments; chunks of tooth and jaw where once buildings stood.

It felt like hours since she'd made the water conduit back at the hospital. She'd clogged a shower cubicle with toilet roll, letting it flood before stepping in. She'd tried to send a message to her sentient friends, like a summoning beacon, and she had fallen back into the strange vortex, only to find herself in this . . . wasteland.

Elle walked. There had to be *someone* here. She felt as far as her powers would allow, searching for any sign of life. There was nothing. No birds in the sky, no blades of grass, not even a nettle or a dandelion. This awful place, wherever it was, was lifeless. A charred husk. It was the most awful thing she'd ever felt.

The wind was harsh, sulphuric, and she couldn't begin to fathom *when* she was. This could be a million years ago. This could be some war-torn desert or nuclear holocaust. Why would Gaia choose here of all places? Elle knew that Niamh and Ciara had seen premonitions of the world once Leviathan rose. Was this her turn? Or were they simply too late? Elle looked around for any sign that this was Aeaea. Any sign of Holly.

Just as she was about to lose all hope, she felt a glimmer of someone's aura.

There.

She ran towards it, slipping down the cracked, parched basin of a river. The stumpy remains of a much-eroded bridge remained on either side. Her pretty dress was already ruined, what was one more stain at this point. She made her way up the opposite bank on all fours, in search of the faint life-sign.

Only traces of civilisation had been left standing: Tetris-like formations of bricks and doorframes; burnt-out shells of cars and malformed human statues. Perhaps she was in the remnants of a museum or sculpture park.

'Hello?' Elle ventured again.

How could anyone live here? Nonetheless, the aura she felt was human; too complicated to be an animal or plant. It was difficult to see through the gritty wind, but a structure came into view. It was slightly more intact than those around it; something of a tiled roof remained, although a huge chunk had been bitten off the upper corner, exposing the house's innards to the elements.

In the endless gale, something creaked. Elle held her hand to her brow and dared to glance upwards. Over the door of this lone building was a rusted pub sign. It was caked in thick white dust, but she could still decipher two mammalian faces and some lettering. She'd seen it a trillion times.

This desolate shell was the Lion and Lamb in Hebden Bridge. She was *home.*

'What the hell happened here?' she muttered.

Just then, a figure emerged from the dust storm.

'Hello!' Elle cried, but the stranger just continued towards the pub, bowed head concealed by a rough cape. 'Can you hear me?' This was all her nightmares at once; no one able to hear her no matter how loudly she yelled. 'Hello!' she now screamed.

There was something familiar about her gait, her uneven stride. 'Annie?' Elle felt tears prick her eyes. She'd give anything to have another day with her grandmother. 'Gran? Is that you?'

'It's not her,' a new voice told her. 'And she can't hear you.'

A second body stepped round the side of the pub. Elle recognised her at once. It was her daughter. At least, a *version* of her daughter. This Holly was a woman in her twenties. She had a shaved head; lyrical, swirling tattoos up both arms; and a foul ring through her nose like a bull. Elle felt herself swoon at the sight of her; what had she done to herself? 'Holly?'

'Well it figures, doesn't it?' she said kindly. 'Of course *you'd* want spoilers.'

'What?'

'This is the future, Mum.'

'What? How?'

Holly gestured at her white jumpsuit. 'Guess who's Head Oracle now?'

'Are you serious?'

'Aren't you proud?'

This was much too strange for Elle to even think about Holly's career at HMRC now. 'Where the hell is this?'

'Come on. You know.'

'It's Hebden Bridge.'

The cloaked figure finally reached the Lamb and Lion. She was close enough for Elle to witness an ancient woman, lined and hunched. Her eyes were pearly with cataracts. 'Is she OK?' Elle asked.

'Blind and deaf,' Holly said. 'She doesn't know we're here.'

'Are we even here?'

'You are.' Holly followed the old woman into to pub. 'I'm back at HMRC. I'm in your head. I'm casting myself forward in time.'

Elle trailed after her daughter. The interior of the pub wasn't much better than the outside. Sure, the hefty wooden beams had withheld whatever storm had befallen their town, but the windows were mostly shattered and everything was covered in the same impenetrable white dust.

With arthritic hands and filthy nails, the old woman took a can opener to work on some label-less tins she'd scavenged out in the wilds. The wilds of Hebden Bridge? Elle couldn't process this. 'Hols, you better tell me what's going on right now . . .'

'Gaia sent you here. As a warning.'

'Of what?' Elle barked. She was getting pretty sick of Gaia's road trip to hell.

Holly looked confused. 'What do you think they are?'

Her daughter stood aside and she saw another statue in the centre of what was once the den. It was an ugly thing, open-mouthed and wild eyed. Its frozen arms went to cover its face. 'I don't know,' Elle said.

'Mum, that's Auntie Niamh.' Holly expression was soft, apologetic. 'The ones outside were Luke . . . and me. We came to stop you. And failed.'

Elle considered the statue. This was nothing like when she'd transformed Jez. He'd looked like a craggy boulder. This one had a shapely torso, flowing hair. Flowing hair like Niamh.

She turned on her daughter. 'How is this the future? How do we even have a future if—'

'We win.' Holly took a cautious step towards her. 'Mum, we win. But that's only the start.'

Elle watched the old woman scoop what looked like cat food out of the tin with her fingers and shovel it straight into her puckered mouth. 'The start of what?'

She heard tears tremble in Holly's voice. 'You change. In order to kill Lucifer, you . . . evolved.'

'Into what?'

Elle already knew the answer. 'Into her.' Holly pointed at the crone.

'You can't stop, Mum. You get stronger and stronger until . . .' She gestured at the husk that was once Hebden Bridge. 'And it's not just here, it's everywhere.'

'No,' Elle breathed. She sat in the skeleton of an old armchair, threadbare and springs exposed.

Holly crouched at her side, eyes wide and pleading. 'You know it is. You're a Level 7 witch, Mum. But it's not too late, you can still stop this from coming true.'

'No,' Elle said again. Slowly, deliberately, she looked, truly looked, at the younger woman. 'I meant *How fucking stupid do you think I am?*'

'What?'

Elle snapped her hand out of Holly's grip. 'Did you think I'd fall for the same bollocks twice?' Her daughter's face hardened. 'I might have fallen for Milo, but I think I know my own daughter. I'm not that bloody stupid. Nice try, love.'

'Mum . . .'

'I mean it's very convincing. I can smell that cat food from here. Once upon a time this would've been my worst fear. Ending up a mad old hag, all alone. Clever, but not as scary as it used to be.'

With a guttural creak, like the earth shifting, the older crone turned to stone and then crumbled into dust. The sediment swirled around Holly like a dirt devil and Elle slipped out of her armchair to take cover behind what was left of the bar.

As the fog settled, Lucifer looked like Milo once more. 'Aw fuck! You got me, Mum! I so nearly went for Annie too. Damn.'

It made her feel sick to see him again, but she wouldn't cry in front of him. The utter bastard. That's what he wanted, and she wouldn't give him the satisfaction. 'Are you going to kill me?'

'What makes you think you're that special?'

'You tell me. You chose me.'

'Level 7, ha! The only thing you got Level 7 in was cycling proficiency. You were, however, close to the *actually* powerful witches.'

Inadvertently, perhaps, but he'd only succeeded in reminding her she *was* powerful. She *had* turned a man to stone. 'Sorry,

I don't buy it. You're trying to scare me out of using my powers. Why? And how did you get me here? Where am I?' she babbled.

Milo grinned again. 'I figured out what you naughty little ladies were up to. It's not just Gaia who exists outside of time, you know. You're poking around for the means to destroy me so I intercepted you. Sorry, but I will not have my ascension spoiled by a clique of simpleton women. Now, back in the day, *those* witches were formidable. Warriors. Look at you, your head full of air fryers and gel nails.'

She didn't see why that was a bad thing. Jez could list every World Cup winner since 1966 and no one minded that. 'Let me go.'

'I don't think so.'

Elle reached for the half-eaten can and threw the cat food in his face. He barely flinched. He wiped the lumpy jelly from his eyes and scowled in a way she'd seen him do a thousand times. 'It's not the fucking *Wizard of Oz*, Mum.'

In a rush of ferocity, she gave up entirely on magic and darted round the bar to give him a good *shove*. He felt solid; fleshy and muscular. Surprised, he stumbled back, giving her the chance to get past him. She flung open the pub door, ready to flee across the fake wasteland until she found water, only to step right back inside a mirrored version of the crumbling Lamb and Lion.

'Nice try. I made a little hell, just for you.'

'Let. Me. Go,' she repeated. 'If I'm really no threat to you, what are you so afraid of?'

Lucifer shook his head. 'I'm going to pick you off one by one. If you can't get back to Aeaea, who's going to stop me?'

Elle made a silent vow. One day, soon, she was going to really, *really* hurt this twat.

Milo's smile grew wider, too wide; it split the sides of his face, revealing rows and rows of pincer-like teeth. 'You're going nowhere, Mummy. You're mine now.'

Elle would not flinch. 'My friends are going to *spank* you, you little shit.'

He shook his head no. His head split all the way open and the gaping mouth swallowed the rest of his body until he had vanished and she was alone in this impossible trap.

His voice remained. 'Two down, three to go.'

CERRIDWEN

Ciara - Hebden Bridge, UK

Falling, then spiralling. Ciara felt herself being drawn away from Leonie, her limbs like syrup. Further and further she fell, and it was all she could do to break the surface. She couldn't stand this, the feeling of incompleteness. It was all too familiar. Those years suspended in the tar pit of her coma; there, but not.

With a cry, she pushed her head through the water into the cool night air. She felt sharp, hard stones under her rear and, wiping her eyes, she recognised the canopy of Hardcastle Crags. She was sitting in Hebden Beck. The water coursing around her crotch was most disconcerting and she clambered to the riverbank. Her hands and feet slipping on mud and reeds, Ciara hoisted herself onto dry land.

The forest was ripe, or she was. Everything smelled too much; too leafy, too swampy, too nature. Fuck being a witch, Ciara wanted to be a basic bitch with a white Land Rover and Chanel husband. A tiny dog. She'd dress it as a bee. Or maybe she was simply cold and hungry.

Why here? Why Annie's fucking cottage?

With a groan, Ciara got to her feet. Now, on top of everything, she had to figure out how to get back to the others. That was all of them now, scattered across history. Had Gaia meant for that to happen, or were they in deep shit?

She was worried about Niamh. She could feel her, just, but it was like she was a billion miles away, at the bottom of the deepest ocean trench.

Ah well, only one way to figure out *when* she was, and that was to ask. Depending on the era, she figured she could be herself or Niamh; wasn't like Annie could actually see her.

Ciara squelched round the side of the watermill until she reached the rusty old gate and beat her way through the bramble jungle to Annie's front door. She gave it a knock and waited until she heard a voice telling her to enter. Oh, how she'd missed that voice. Earthy and filthy as Yorkshire itself.

Judging from Annie's lined face, this was in her latter years. The sight of her filled Ciara's heart with a rare warmth, immediately followed by an intense sadness. Grief: a shot of love and a chaser of disappointment. Annie wore a candyfloss pink wig and a lemon-coloured mohair cardigan. 'Hey, it's Niamh!'

'No it isn't. I spoke to your sister on the phone earlier. Come inside, Ciara.' The elderly woman scribbled something on her journal and set it aside.

'How did you know?'

Even blind, the oracle gave her a withering glare. 'How do you bloody think?'

'Fair.' Ciara plonked herself down on the settee opposite Annie in her favourite armchair. That thing had a perfect indent of her buttocks. 'I'm wet, sorry.'

'Well water conduits will do that for you. Not least ones that have brought you through time *and* space.'

'So you knew this was going to happen?'

Annie smiled slightly. 'Oh, something like this *really* jumps out. Witches defying the flow the time? All those oracles at HMRC were so fixated on their Sullied Child, they never took much time to consider an equal, nay, more brilliant, force for *good*. Did I not used to say to you girls that everything in nature is about balance?'

'You did,' Ciara conceded.

'Well there you go. If Satanis, or whatever you want to call him, conjured up a weapon, then it stands to reason Gaia would too. What is it? How are you able to move through time?'

'Would you believe it's Leonie's daughter?'

'Come again?'

'It's not a *thing*, it's a girl. Leonie is pregnant.'

Annie clapped like a much younger girl might. 'Well I never! Marvellous! Oh, that is good news! After all these centuries, a new breed of witch. I shall go happy knowing that.'

Ciara frowned. 'What do you mean?'

Now Annie sighed. 'You're not the only visitor I'll have tonight, love.'

It took her a moment to understand. 'Helena?' Annie nodded. No tears and sadness, just a grim stoicism. 'I'll fucking kill her.'

'Ciara Kelly, you'll do no such thing.' Annie's lips drew tight. 'Days must be allowed to play out or you being here now might not happen, and it must. You wouldn't even be here if it weren't for Helena.'

'Oh come on! I can definitely take her.'

Now Annie smiled. 'Some things never change, do they? But alas. In days gone by they called us Seers because that's our lot. We weren't called Changers.'

Ciara reached over and took Annie's papery hands in her own. 'But I don't want you to go,' she whispered.

'Darling girl, I'm already gone.' Ciara said nothing in reply because she was worried she might allow out a strangled sob. 'And we had this Brucie bonus, didn't we? More time than you thought you were getting.'

That brought precious little comfort. 'How long have we got?' Was there time for a cup of tea? A game of chess? Ciara used to read her *TV Quick* magazine as a teenager so she'd know what was on the telly.

'Not long,' Annie admitted. 'And I still need to give you a gift.'

'What? You knew I was coming?'

'I knew it was a possibility – one of many. Honestly, Kiki, at this point it's like trying to pull a very long, single strand of spaghetti out of a bubbling pot with naked fingers.'

'So what have you got? Will it help?'

'I wish it was as easy as that. It's not something I can just give you. You'll have to go get it. But you need it, if you're going to win.'

The penny dropped. 'The dagger. The one that split Leviathan.'

Annie nodded. 'You've used it before . . .'

The memory entered Ciara's head without finesse or permission. Disguised as Niamh at Summer Solstice, she'd hexed their former High Priestess, Julia Collins. The night she'd started the war. She'd invoked the demon Naberius – eating a crow's head in the process – and travelled to that year's induction ceremony in the Pendle Hills. It had been painfully easy to mingle amongst the partygoers.

From a safe distance, Ciara had cast her spell. The middle-aged witch, dignified with her blow-out and claret cape, had stopped swaying to the beat from the drummers. She'd picked up the ceremonial blade they used to induct young witches into the coven from the altar and sliced it across her throat.

A fine mist of blood had erupted from the carotid. For a moment, no one'd noticed. And then the screaming had begun.

Ciara dragged herself out of Annie's reverie and back into the cosy living room at the watermill. 'How do you know that?'

'Because you remember it all too well.'

'I wish I didn't,' Ciara spat.

'What's done is done, and you need that blade.'

'Why would I need that fucking thing?'

'Cerridwen.'

'What?'

'That's the name of the blade. It was a gift from the Irish coven in 1869 on the foundation of Her Majesty's Royal Coven.'

'They probably didn't want to be colonised,' Ciara muttered.

Annie chuckled. 'And isn't that what you and your sister were for us. A gift from Ireland. Cerridwen was used at every oathtaking until . . . well.'

'So what? I don't want it.'

'It's a powerful blade, Ciara. It predates the Morrigan herself. It came from the time of the demons.'

'It can hurt them?'

'Once there was a blade that severed Satanis.'

'The Suneater,' Ciara said. 'Leonie told us the story.'

'That scythe was smelted down into ore from which ironmongers made five daggers for five covens. All in case . . .'

'All in case he came back. And is this Cerridwen one of them?'

'So the story goes.' Annie urged her, 'Find it, Ciara.'

'Where is it?'

'That's the tricky part. It's in the archive at HMRC.'

'You're kidding right? What am I meant to do? A heist?'

Annie turned her head towards her, her blind eyes piercing all the way through her. 'Guess who's on her way. If anyone can do it, Ciara, you can. The girl who got backstage at a rock concert.'

Ciara smirked. 'Busted. And I blew—'

'I don't need to know that part. Now go. She's almost here. You'll find what you need in her car.'

Ciara's heart sank lower than she'd thought possible, somewhere far below her ribs. 'But that means . . .'

Annie nodded. She squeezed her hands, and no further words were necessary. Ciara pulled the wise old woman into a tight hug and latched her chin over her mohair shoulder. 'I love you,' she breathed.

'Oh, Ciara Kelly. You are loved.'

Crouched amongst some sprawling umbrellas of rhubarb leaves, Ciara watched as Helena Vance descended the hazardous forest steps that led to Annie's cottage. She scrutinised her face for murderous resolve, but all she saw a sickly pale woman, gaunt and exhausted. Ciara wondered if Helena had been very unwell, afflicted with some sort of rot in her brain.

Ciara waited until Helena was almost at the watermill before darting uphill towards the road to Heptonstall.

A vintage Jaguar was parked askew in a layby. Helena's father's pride and joy if she recalled correctly. Naturally it was locked, but this was hardly the first time Ciara had used telekinesis on a vehicle's mechanism. She popped the actuator and opened the driver-side door. Helena had left her Mulberry handbag on the passenger seat. Careless. Taking care not to make it look as if there had been a robbery, Ciara's fingers dipped into the contents of the bag until she felt the hard plastic of Helena's HMRC lanyard.

This is what they deserved for having such antiquated security. She had told them herself during her brief stint as acting-imposter-High-Priestess. She pocketed the pass and then helped herself to a crisp twenty-pound note out of her purse. Helena could more than afford it and Ciara was starving.

With that, she lifted herself off the muddy road and high, high, high into the night sky.

The 'flight' to Manchester was exhausting. Ciara could scarcely remember the last time she'd eaten and, more than once, she felt herself dipping off her trajectory. She had to stay aware and she had to stay shielded. In her own muddled timeline, she knew she was soon to be awakened from her decade-long slumber, and she was pretty sure she'd have remembered if she'd read about the flying woman over Lancashire.

This was mad. Somewhere below, her body was tucked up in bed at the Manchester safehouse, just waiting for Helena and Belial to rouse her. This distracting thought almost caused her to plummet over the city centre.

OK, if she was going to do the *Ocean's Eleven* bit, she was gonna need a Whopper. She almost flopped down outside the closest Burger King to York Street and took a moment to fight the wooziness in the back alley. Thank Gaia for the humble rat; the well-fed little pals were just ripe with abundance and Ciara was able to use theirs to bring herself back to something resembling human, and then wolfed down a veggie whopper and some disappointing fries before approaching the grand façade of Her Majesty's Royal Coven, energy restored.

It had been a hot fucking minute since she'd done an old-fashioned glamour. In witching terms, it was the equivalent of doing a funny voice. She wasn't about to change her skin and bones; she was going to create a subliminal suggestion – a psychic lullaby. As a sentient, she was more able to achieve this than most. Basically, the Jedi Mind Trick.

Feeling a lot less loopy with a burger in her belly, Ciara focused on Helena Vance. Her sleek hair, her prim clothes, the Tory rod up her ass. The pass would grant her access, but she couldn't alert anyone else in the coven. A coven full of elite sentients trained to see through such rudimentary spells.

Fuck. She clung to the mission. She'd fooled them all before, hadn't she? She owed Gaia. She owed Annie. She owed Julia fucking Collins. She owed every single witch in every single coven. She had been used. She had done Satan's dirty work in destroying the Seal. Securing Cerridwen would be her penance.

She tapped the pass on the keypad outside the ostentatious double doors and entered the coven. At this time of night, the great lobby was mostly empty. Federica, a burly night watchwoman, sat with her feet up on the reception desk. On seeing her, she quickly sprung to attention. 'High Priestess!'

'Don't put your feet on the desk.' Ciara invoked the tone she imagined Helena would have used.

'Sorry, Helena.' The glamour was working then. Federica was a sentient. Not a powerful one, but still. 'Are you here about the haul?'

'The haul?'

'The stuff from Rye.'

Why not? 'Why else would I be here?'

Federica squirmed. 'I think they're checking it all into the archive.'

'Good.' Because that was exactly where she needed to be.

Ciara took the elevators to the basement level. She closed her eyes and fortified the illusion. Emerging, she walked away from the gym space and into the archives. She heard voices. Jen Yamato and Sandhya Kaur. Both wore their HMRC capes. They look surprised to see her. They greeted her as High Priestess.

'We brought everything back from Sussex,' Sandhya told her. 'They'll be assessed and checked into the vault tomorrow.'

'Very good,' Ciara said. 'Dismissed.'

They did as they were told and trotted out. Truly Helena was feared in this place. Well, they were right to be scared.

Now alone in the windowless archive, Ciara let the glamour dissipate and got to work. There were maybe fifteen document boxes piled on the central desk, each labelled with that day's date and MERMAID INN – RYE. She turned on a lamp and prised one open. Books; boring. Another contained antique contraband: goblets, jewellery and amulets. As she rifled through the box, her hand suddenly blazed with pain.

She yelped and withdrew her arm at once. 'What the fuck?'

More carefully, she examined the contents of the second box. Gingerly placing each item on the desk, she actually saw a chunky, silver man's ring idling at the bottom of the container. She lifted it out by a paper luggage tag attached by a yellowed string. '*Beast's Girdle*,' she muttered to herself. It was a handsome enough ring, but even holding it by the label, Ciara felt its power. She certainly recognised the dull rubies held by prongs at the head of the piece.

This was Belial's ring. This stone contained all the power she'd needed to steal Niamh's body.

A sudden thump made her drop the ring back into the box. She froze, making sure she was alone. After a moment she allowed herself to breathe once more. She quickly placed the gold and bronze loot back into the box. Ciara made sense of the events of the night: Helena had sent HMRC to Rye to find the tools she needed to invoke Belial and, in turn, resurrect her. The ring had to be left where Helena would find it, or this whole timeline was fucked.

She was about to turn her attention to the locked vault when she heard a thump again. It was close by, muffled. She checked under the desk itself, feeling faintly ludicrous. She was alone. Ciara surveyed the scene again.

On the desk there was one crate unlike the others. This one was far older; a suitcase-sized leather trunk sealed shut with rusted clasps. On the luggage label it said *Crank's Panini – Do Not Open Under Any Circumstances*. She placed her ear closer. Nothing. She realised how ridiculous she must look, listening to a suitcase. What was she expecting? Paddington? She dismissed it with a loud tut.

The vault was located at the far end of the archive where books and artefacts were stored in the original, glass-fronted apothecary cabinets. They were largely for visitors. Anything with any real firepower was secured behind the enchanted Cold Iron doors to the vault.

Ciara pressed her pass to the scanner and the display prompted her for the code. Oh motherfucker, what was it? She'd been briefed during her time as Niamh. 20061869. The date the coven had been created. The positive little bleep the vault made was the best sound she'd ever heard. The circular metal door slid aside to grant her access, the inner lights pinging on at the same instant.

Now, *this* was more like it.

Ciara swept into the treasury. The walls in front and to the side of her consisted of drawers and shelves; the uppermost requiring a wheeled ladder to access. She didn't have long to find this thing. In her favour, she was at least familiar with the relic.

She was grateful to see the vault was organised alphabetically and quickly located the shelves marked *C–D*.

The Lore of Caspar; Coins, Miscellaneous; *Corona De Angeles* . . . and there it was. *Cerridwen*. Like all the objects, it was stored in a simple brown box and labelled with a barcode. Ciara took it down from the shelf and took off the lid. Wrapped in plastic was the ceremonial dagger. It hadn't even been cleaned; there was a rust-brown residue on the blade.

Blood spurting from Julia's throat like an aerosol.

Ciara felt a wail bubble up in her throat. Her regrets were getting physical.

She was yanked from her guilt by a louder thud outside of the vault. 'Hello?' she called, shoring up her disguise. 'Who's there?'

She took only the dagger in its plastic wrapper and placed the box back where it was. She tucked the weapon into the back of her belt and crept out of the vault and into the archive room.

It was darker in here, but she saw a dark shape on the floor. Edging closer, she saw it was the leather trunk. *Crank's Panini.* It had evidently tumbled off the worktop and now lay open. The interior of the crate was lined with fuzzy red velvet, like her old clarinet case. 'Who's in here?' she demanded, reasserting her disguise. 'Come out right now. This is your High Priestess.'

She reached out psychically. There was *something* in the basement with her, she could feel it. It wasn't quite like anything she'd felt before. Sort of human, but sort of . . . not.

She crouched aside the fallen trunk. An envelope had slid across the floor and under the table. She pried it out with her fingertips and pulled out the documentation that came with the trunk.

> Rene Diavolos Crank [D circa 1476 Paris] was a fifteenth-century alchemist and warlock. Consumed with the quest for immortal life, he spent his later years perfecting the dark art of soul transfer. It is said his chimpanzee familiar, Rocco, enclosed, was the intended recipient and subject of his experimentation.

Ciara knew before she heard the footsteps.

It had all been too easy, hadn't it?

She became aware of quiet, raspy breaths. Hysterical somehow, almost like a throaty chuckle. Then footsteps; gentle, scurrying. Ciara rose to her feet, scanning the dark archive. Too many nooks and crannies.

Then she gasped. There it was. Hidden by shadow, a hunched little figure – the size of a toddler – stood between her and the door. It jerked forwards, limbs spasmodic, and Ciara stepped back, her heart thundering in her chest. As it lumbered into the low light of the vault, Ciara got a good look at Crank's monkey. It was hideous. The wasted, mummified body was frail and leathered, over five hundred years old. Yellow, fractured teeth were fully bared in a terrifying imitation of a grin, and its eye sockets were black and hollow. Its nails were razor sharp, dragging on the tiled floor. A furless tail trailed after it like a snake.

Ciara backed further away, trying to estimate if she could get into the vault and seal herself in.

Only then its skinless lips moved. *'Ceeraaaah.'*

The chimpanzee was trying to say her name.

'Ceera.'

'What the fuck are you?'

Its raspy voice gurgled in its throat. *'Frum Jood.'*

From Jude. Ciara's blood went cold. He knew. Lucifer knew where they were and what they were up to. Ciara reached for the dagger tucked beneath her belt, but it was too late.

The hideous creature launched itself at her with a feral screech. Ciara covered her face with her arms but, as it made impact, she fell onto her back and heard the blade clank over the tiles.

Teeth and claws tore at her flesh. Ciara screwed her eyes shut, fighting, but it was useless. It took a chunk out of her arm. What else could she do? Ciara screamed and screamed and screamed, but down here, in the soundproofed, airtight vaults of HMRC, there was no one to hear.

A WOMAN'S PLIGHT TO CHOOSE

Leonie - Aeaea

Leonie was meant to be the most powerful witch there ever was. She had the ability to change the past, the future, the present.

Well, who gave a florid fuck.

The beach was carnage. The corpses of the sea weren't as strong as the witches, but there were simply *more* of them, and they moved so quickly – broken limbs almost rolling over heads and shoulders as they swarmed the shoreline. Their rotten bodies were easily broken; as Leonie raced over impacted sand, she used her mind to lacerate the forms at the waist. The severed halves were still animated, crawling over the sand like crabs, but there wasn't time to pulverise them further.

She had come back in the nick of time; in the distance, Chinara was alive, and battling, only Leonie had emerged from the sea too far down the coastline. Her lover was a speck, maybe two hundred metres further down the beach. This was a type of running Leonie hadn't done in her entire life. She had her period every PE lesson. She'd strolled around the perimeter of a pitch for five years. Now, her thighs burned. With what little strength she had left, she levitated herself off the ground and hurtled forwards.

And then she saw it. The skeletal form in the redcoat lurching behind her. Chinara was preoccupied, controlling twisting columns of water to soak up the corpse army. She cried her name – with her voice and with her mind – but Chinara didn't look her way.

'Chinara!'

To her, Chinara Okafor was the most important woman in the world. Losing her had never even entered her head. They were going to be together forever.

She saw the blade jut through her waist.

'No!'

Redcoat drew it back and Chinara folded to the sand. How? Chinara was made of steel and concrete. How could something so strong crumble so fast?

Near enough now, Leonie lifted Redcoat off its feet and tore its body into three pieces. It made an inhuman shriek before the limbs flopped to the ground. Leonie threw a shield around them. 'Healer! I need a healer! Help her!' Leonie scarcely recognised her own voice.

She fell at Chinara's side and clutched her face. 'Babe, babe, it's me. Can you hear me? Open your eyes, love. Please? It's me.'

Chinara did not open her eyes. Her breathing sounded wet, bubbly, and her tank top was black-red.

'Leonie!' She turned and saw Luke outside of her barrier. 'This way! The healers are off the beach!'

The mundane was filthy, sweaty and had a deep cut to his forehead. He held a shotgun before him, scanning for further assailants.

Leonie waived her shield and he ran to her side. 'Help me lift her,' she told him. 'I'll shield us.'

Had Chinara always been this tiny? Luke lifted her with no effort whatsoever and Leonie cast her strongest psychic field around the three of them. *Anyone* who came close would get a headache worse than death.

She let Luke lead the way. 'Holly and the girls made a shield around the whole temple,' he said. 'So I figured I'd be more use as a human ambulance.'

Leonie couldn't speak. Chinara could not die. 'Hold her tight!' She gripped Luke and lifted all three of them off the dunes.

'Fuck!' he yelled as his feet left the floor. 'That one! The hut on the hill!'

She skimmed his mind and knew which one he meant. She scooped them up in a mighty arc, dropping them towards the makeshift hospital bay and alerting the healers within; a screaming siren in all their heads.

They hurtled towards a domed clay hut, the walls brilliantly white even in the storm, the roof cobalt blue. Leonie lowered Luke to the hillside before allowing herself down. She didn't let go of Chinara, keeping her afloat as they entered the villa.

'Help us!' she announced, failing to keep shrill hysteria off her voice. She sounded like a madwoman.

A trio of witches had cleared a space on a cot. Calista stepped forward to greet them. 'Here. Quickly, child.'

Leonie steered Chinara's form onto the bed. Luke hung back, letting the women work. 'Heal her.'

Calista gave a nod and held her remaining hand over Chinara's heart. 'Leonie . . .'

'She isn't dead. She is not! I can feel her.'

Calista reached across Chinara and took Leonie's hands. 'My child, she's dying. She's almost gone. You know what that means. A witch doesn't interfere with nature. Everything dies.'

Leonie couldn't help but think this was her punishment. For failing to save Annie, or Helena, or Zehra. This was her price to pay. Why should she get a happy ending when so many others grieved so deeply?

Chinara's breaths came to her in shallow, rasping gasps. Her eyes were open but were glassy and unfocused.

'Let her go, child. There isn't a healer on earth who could help her.'

Leonie looked to Luke; the human pincushion. Elle had brought him back from the brink more than once. 'Yes there is.'

She stood and placed her hands on her swollen abdomen. She was getting used to it now, this strange new gift. Senait had told her she could *fold* time like a ribbon, nip different points together as she wished. Why shouldn't she use it to save Chinara's life? What else was it good for, if not this?

At school, Mrs Finch had once told her to 'stop showing off' in a drama class. All her life, she had watched girls be told that it was unladylike to revel in their talents. Don't brag, don't outshine the boys, don't draw attention to yourself.

Leonie Jackman was one of the most powerful women on this clapped shell of a planet and she was done, just fucking over, doing as she was told.

She rose off the floor and smashed through the ceiling of the little hut. She exposed herself to the sky, the rain and the wind, hovering above the coastal cliff. Gaia on her skin. Gaia in her tummy. She could stop time, *stop actual time*. She could slow the turn of the earth – and she did. Just for a moment, there was stillness. Perfect, luxuriant pause – truly the gift every woman craves the most. A moment to herself.

The witches on the beach; the witches on the hillside turned their faces to her like she was the sun and they were sunflowers. Leonie connected with every witch on the island of Aeaea. Now, or then, in some when, these women would meet, or had met her friends. Together, they could find them.

Hear me. Niamh, Ciara, Elle. Follow my voice. Follow me home.

With Senait's power at her disposal, she reached out with her mind; not geographically, but chronologically. When were they? She felt Ciara; she was the closest. She was in distress, fighting, struggling. Niamh was dimmer. She was sad, so sad. And Elle was . . . scattered in a way she couldn't fathom.

Girls! Follow my voice! Come here you cunts!

'Leonie!' Someone called her name.

Arms out, she twisted herself round and saw Helena Vance standing on the rim of a rocky outcrop, her chestnut hair wet ropes across her face. 'Stop!'

She had her hand around her brother's throat, his feet dangling helplessly as she held him aloft. There was a nasty gash to his brow. Leonie scanned them. While the female form was oddly blank, it really was Radley. No tricks this time.

'Let him go!' Leonie called as she descended towards them.

'I will,' Lucifer said with Helena's voice. 'But leave your friends where they are.'

'Why?'

'You can't have it all, Leonie dear . . . but that's very you, isn't it?' Helena's mouth curled into a sneer. 'No compromises, no concessions. Poor little Leonie had a grotty childhood so now she wants the moon on a stick. The rest of us are meant to, what? Pay reparations? Feel guilty? Apologise for the sins of the past? Well now you have to choose, my love. Which is it? Your lover or your brother?'

Radley scowled through the lashing rain. 'Save Chinara, Lee! She can't hurt me.'

'Darling, please!' Helena said and outstretched her arm as if Radley weighed nothing. His legs flailed over the ravine.

He looked to her, unable to speak. *Just do it.* He told her.

Leonie would not choose. She shook her head and screamed over the wind. 'Not today, Satan. You picked the wrong face to wear, because if Helena taught me one fucking thing it's that there's nothing wrong with a woman wanting it all.'

Helena scowled and let her brother fall.

56

SPLIT SECOND

Leonie - Aeaea

The drop was very high. As Radley's arms and legs cycled in thin air, she guessed she had around ten seconds.

Leonie found she could do a lot with ten seconds.

Senait's gift was truly the most extraordinary power. No wonder only one witch had ever been blessed like this because it was inhuman. Leonie was a *goddess*.

She looked forward and backwards down a seemingly endless river of time. She found she could move up and down it at speed, flicking through days like pages in a phonebook. More than that though, she could navigate it. Finally, she had mastered it. She wasn't falling, she was *flying*.

She could sense them. Like a bloodhound, she followed the auras she knew she needed. First Elle, because she was the one she needed most. She was the hardest. She was in the future, and the future existed in infinite tributaries – some similar and crowded, but some eons apart. But there Elle was, trapped in a version of Hebden Bridge.

Leonie materialised in that flimsy reality for only an instant. She grabbed Elle and withdrew to the stream. As they travelled, Leonie smelled *everything*, all the scents of humanity: petroleum, sewage, lobster pots, chip shop chips, cumin, Chanel No.5 and armpits. Colours flashed around them in a crazy strobe. Leonie closed her eyes and focused only on where they needed to be.

The little hut on Aeaea.

If the other witches – and Luke – were surprised at her sudden return, they didn't show it. After all she'd only been gone for a single breath as far as they were concerned. Dust was still falling. Rain now poured through the hole she'd – somewhat impetuously – torn in the ceiling. The whooshing in her ears ceased and she felt solid ground under her feet. Chinara was on the bed before them, covered in a sheen of sweat.

Lee turned to a baffled Elle. 'Help her.'

She didn't stick around to explain. Radley was still falling. Down, down, down. Eyes wide, mouth surprised.

In the same way she'd always been able to move herself through space, Lee now moved herself through time.

Boom.

Where am I?

A dark room, library smell.

Ciara, on the floor, wrestling with . . . a thing.

Leonie raised an arm and, as she did, the horrid goblin rose with it. Leonie made a fist and the creature – a *monkey*? – creased up like a ball of waste paper.

Ciara scrabbled to her feet. 'Lee!' She was bleeding profusely, though already healing herself.

'The fuck happened to you?'

'Possessed chimp.' Ciara swept a plastic-wrapped item off the floor. 'The dagger.'

Leonie nodded and grabbed her wrist. 'We move.'

Six seconds. Radley still fell, serrated rocks and fizzing surf growing closer and closer.

Niamh was in Glasgow, and further back, about sixteen years prior. Leonie and Ciara appeared before her as she walked down a lonely city street, snowflakes drifting in the curbs. Niamh seemed resigned. She'd been crying. 'I had to do it, right? I had to leave her there?'

Leonie read her and saw what Niamh had just done.

'Babe, you had to.'

Niamh just nodded. Leonie held out a hand to her, urging her to join them. 'Ciara got the knife. I got the crown. Anything else we need?'

'I think we're done,' Niamh said sadly, looking over her shoulder at a grim council building.

Leonie clung to them tightly, able to manoeuvre the rapids expertly. It was as if she was riding some cresting wave. Impressive because she'd never been able to master surfing. She'd always stood on the beach, clapping Chinara's attempts.

Chinara.

All this meant nothing without her.

They were back in the villa.

The twins embraced her at the same time. 'How the fuck did you do that?' Ciara asked, holding her tight.

Four seconds.

'It doesn't matter,' Leonie said. 'Please. Help Elle.'

Niamh crouched at Elle's side. Ciara went the opposite way. 'We'll give her everything,' Niamh said.

Three.

The healer and the adepts joined hands and radiance began to emanate from their skin, flowing into Chinara's body.

Two.

'Don't let her die. I'll be right back.'

One.

Leonie arrived on the rocks at the foot of the cliff, and fought to steady herself on the slick surface. Icy spray spritzed her face and she was soaked at once. She braced and looked up to see Radley plummeting towards her. She raised her hands and waited until she could feel his essence.

With clenched teeth, she caught hold of him with her power. She wobbled, but her foot held its ground. Suspended above her, she lowered him as gently as she could onto the treacherous surface.

Radley was dumbstruck for a moment, blinking sluggishly. She gripped his arms to stop him slipping into the surf. 'How . . . how on earth did you do that?'

Leonie shrugged it off. 'Oh, come on, you didn't think I'd let my little brother get smushed did you?' She pulled him into a hug. 'As if.'

'You are the most impressive person I've ever known,' he breathed into her hair.

'I know,' she said. 'Now we have to go . . . come on.'

'Go where?'

Leonie found it hard to say the words. 'I . . . It's Chinara. She's dying.'

THE SULLIED CHILD

Niamh - Beaea

Send my love.
What a meaningless phrase, until now.

For now, Niamh was pouring her affection for her patient, direct – channelling her radiance into Elle, the most powerful healer amongst them, who in turn siphoned their collective energy into Chinara. Rain dripped onto them, from the hole Leonie had torn in the cabin roof, but Niamh cared not. The water kept her alert.

She wiped some rain from Chinara's clammy face. She admired Chinara deeply; she wished she knew her better. And she loved what Leonie had become because of her. Calmer, content, more selfless. *Balance.* Isn't that what makes love work in the long run? They weren't the *same*, they were *equal*. Their love had spawned a great evolution in her best friend, and she *never* thought she'd see the day when Leonie became a mother. Now it made perfect sense.

She would make sure she had time to get to know Chinara better. And that Chinara and Leonie had more time, period.

On cue, Leonie – this time with Radley – materialised in the hut. 'How is she? Can you save her?' she asked at once.

Elle looked to Lee, face blotchy and flustered. 'I don't know. Her insides are so red, almost black.'

'Please . . .' Leonie clutched her belly. 'I need her. I can't do this alone.'

Niamh noted Lee's bump was now huge, her soaked T-shirt

straining across her skin. What's more she could quite clearly *sense* the infant within. A little person, with an aura of her own. There was no denying it; Leonie was simply more pregnant than she'd been back in the caves. Not as if this was a normal baby though. What was nine months to her?

'I need more power,' Elle said. Calista began to argue about the natural law once again. Elle's eyes glowed like molten amber, silencing her. 'It can be done. I just need *more*.'

Calista relented. Niamh saw the older woman defer to Elle. 'You are powerful, healer. All our strength comes from Gaia. Draw energy from her now. From the sky, the wind, the rain.'

The older woman gestured that they should take Chinara in their arms. Niamh helped Ciara draw Chinara's shoulders off the cot. The four women embraced her tightly, and Niamh did feel some weak transfer of energy. There was life in her. She could heal, but it needed to be *now*.

Above them, in the mauve sky, veins of lightning flickered. *Use it*, Calista told them internally. *She's an elemental.*

Elle looked to the skies, her entire body shimmering with golden radiance. Niamh wasn't an elemental – she didn't know how to steer the weather. All she could do was what she did best: talk. *Gaia. Help her. We need you.*

And Gaia heard. Another gift.

Tongues of lightning lashed the cottage on the hillside. It was blinding. Brilliant white light erupted all around them. She clung to Chinara and it was as if the witch absorbed every drop of the heat from the bolt.

Don't let go! It was Ciara, in all their minds.

I feel it, Elle said. *It's working. She's coming together now.*

Niamh hung on for dear life. She pressed her forehead to Chinara's cheek, rocking her back and forth like a baby. She didn't feel the lightning as it hit them. She closed her eyes and felt it ripple through her skeleton. The golden lifeforce within Chinara grew stronger and stronger, trickling through her bones and flesh and skin.

Suddenly, Chinara's whole body convulsed and Niamh heard an almighty inhalation of breath. The woman tried to fight them off. 'What's happening?' The cry was Chinara's deep, rich voice.

Niamh let go as Leonie broke through with a sob. 'You're OK! You're OK!'

Niamh and Ciara helped an exhausted Elle to her feet. She looked pale, worn, her own strength distilled into her patient. She wobbled, and the twins guided her to a now damp empty bed.

'Nailed it,' Ciara told her, kissing her cheek as Niamh told her to rest.

Niamh turned her attention back to Chinara – she might not be out of the woods yet.

She had rested her chin on Leonie's shoulder. 'What happened?'

'You got stabbed by a zombie.'

Chinara could only manage a twitch of an eyebrow. 'Makes sense.'

Niamh scanned her over. There were still muddy, ketchup-colour splots in her aura, but they seemed to be receding, and there was nothing to suggest internal damage. Elle had brought her back from the brink of death, and they had all lived to tell the tale. She allowed herself to breathe at last.

'Niamh?' It was Luke. He lingered by the door and had an ugly gash on his forehead. He must have been fighting.

'Here,' she said, attending to his wounds, but he caught her hand before she could heal him.

'That's not what I was going to say . . . look . . .' He pointed up through the gaping hole in the roof.

'What?'

'The storm. It just stopped. Like someone turned it off.'

Niamh looked to her sister, who just shrugged. She headed past Luke and outside to the hills.

The sky was now a strange sandy-orange hue. The night sky right before it snows. She couldn't hear a bird or a breeze. It was oddly still, like the island was holding its breath.

Luke stood at her side. 'Look at the sea.'

Niamh held a hand to her chest. 'That's impossible.' The tide had stopped. The water was dead still, not a wave or a ripple on its steely surface. 'What the fuck?' She turned to Luke and, to his visible surprise, wrapped her arms around his chest. He was safer with her, she figured. 'Hold on tight.'

'Not again . . .'

She lifted him off his feet and swooped them downwards towards the beach, ready to fight anything that might rise up out of the sea.

Instead, as her feet hit the sand, she saw only confused witches. The husks that had risen from the ocean bed were little more than heaps of dust on the beach, blowing away like leftover barbecue ashes. She looked to Luke. 'I don't get it.'

Ciara landed alongside them. 'Why did they stop?'

Luke just raised an arm and pointed out to the horizon. 'That's why . . .'

Niamh followed his gaze. 'Oh shit.'

She was a speck on the horizon, but coming closer.

Theo walked on water, her boot-clad feet touching the surface of the sea lightly. Each footprint caused only the gentlest of centric ripples. But this wasn't the Theo she remembered. The girl now looked like a young woman. A warrior, no less. Her raven hair fell to her waist in perfect waves, and her alabaster skin was flawless as marble. She wore a fitted armour of steel and leather, something from another time, a time of fire and iron, but she carried it effortlessly, one foot in front of the other. Her eyes . . . her eyes were as black as onyx. She would be so beautiful.

If her expression wasn't so entirely full of malice.

Her walk was elegant and poised, unhurried as she coolly surveyed the chaos on the beach. She reached the shoreline and stepped onto the sand with no more ceremony than one would have disembarking an escalator.

Niamh went towards her. Whatever this was, wherever she'd

been, they could fix it together. They'd both been through worse.

'Theo—'

'Stop.'

Niamh stopped, unable to take another step.

'Kneel.'

Niamh fell to her knees, no control over her limbs. Behind her, Luke, then Ciara, and then every other witch on Aeaea collapsed to the sand, heads bowed in supplication. 'Theo, please.'

'Theo Wells is no more, witch.' The warrior woman looked to her with those hollow shark eyes. 'Now bow before Leviathan.'

THE AWFUL TRUTH

Ciara - Heaea

On seeing this formidable new incarnation of Theo step out of the ocean, Ciara did what any sentient would do: she read her mind.

She wished she hadn't.

A second inside its head and she vomited canary-yellow bile on the sand. She couldn't help it. It was every fearful moment she'd ever experienced all at once: lurching turbulence on a flight to Majorca when she was six; standing on the rim of the highest diving board at Halifax pool; watching Hale flood Somerset. It was like that amorphous feeling had taken physical form, and it was cold, and gluey, and stank of shit. Both gelatinous and barbed on her tongue somehow. Slugs and thorns.

She withdrew her feelers at once.

She'd been looking for Theo. Theo had the most beautiful aura – something akin to mother of pearl – but she couldn't see it inside that being. Not even a hint of her.

Theo was all gone.

She switched her attention to standing up. Nope. No good. Her hands were welded to the hardpacked sand. It strained her neck to even look at her, as if gravity wanted her forehead pressed to the ground as well. She fought it.

Leviathan was as beautiful and deadly as the sea he'd risen from. Ciara didn't envy Theo this fate. In fact, looking at this avatar, she felt *embarrassed*. What a fool she had been back then, to believe this entity was the answer to her formless, girlhood dissatisfaction. Growing up, she had felt powerless and so had craved power. But *power* wasn't the answer to the fact that she felt lonely and unlovable. *If you won't love me, I'll make you fear me instead.* Stupid little bitch. It seemed so obvious now.

'Where's Theo?' Niamh shouted at the avatar, kneeling alongside Ciara.

The black-eyed woman glowered down at them. 'She was the vessel. She has fulfilled her divine purpose.'

Ciara risked another look within, searching for any trace of the poor wee girl. She felt such intense fear it wrung her spine. 'Is she dead? Is she gone?'

Leviathan looked to her as if she was an imbecile. 'She is Leviathan. She is everlasting.' Her voice was silken, deeper than it ought to be.

'What happens now?' Luke asked them both.

The demon answered for them. 'You will be rewarded with life eternal. I am true to my word.'

Ciara couldn't think of anything worse. Just one rainy Sunday afternoon in March was intolerable, imagine *forever*. Absolutely not.

'Don't do it,' Niamh said. 'There are seven billion people on earth.'

The eyes seemed to say *and?* 'As the sky falls and the sea rises, their fear will be delicious.'

'What then?' Ciara said. 'If there's no one left to fear you, what even are you?'

Leviathan sniffed the air. 'The universe will be ours to define. A vision of pain and torment. I shall feast eternally. Never dying, only sweet suffering.'

'Hell on earth,' Niamh said.

And isn't that what hell is? People suffering eternally. Milton, and Pullman, and every writer who'd ever described hell had foreseen this moment.

Suddenly, Ciara found she was able to move. Next to her, Niamh and Luke flexed too. She looked to her left and saw one of the sea-zombies had dropped a verdigris-crusted cutlass. She lifted it with her mind and hurled it at Theo.

Niamh screamed. 'Ciara, no!'

She didn't intend to slay the beast, not while there was even a chance Theo resided in there. Her attempt to incapacitate him was futile anyway. Leviathan caught the blade with catlike reflexes, fingers wrapped around the sharp end. Confused, he took the hilt in his other hand and examined his palm. Where he had seized the cutlass, there was now a bleeding gash. Inky-black blood ran down his metal sleeve. The demon king looked puzzled, almost childlike. 'What is this sensation?'

'Pain,' Ciara growled. 'Get used to it.'

Alas, the wound glowed and sealed itself. Theo had been a healer, after all. Ciara cast a quick glance at Niamh, however. It didn't need saying. The demon had *form* now. She had hurt it. That was worth knowing.

Once more, her body was frozen, the demon regaining control. Now Leviathan raised her arms. 'Join me, brothers of mine.'

From the sea, two entities joined Leviathan. The first was a reptilian form weaving through the water like an eel with spines running down its back. It reminded Ciara of a Komodo dragon, but not quite. As it crested out of the still ocean, it coiled and transformed into the avatar *she* recognised: Jude Kavanaugh, tall, muscular and naked, striding through the shallows. He gave her a wink as he padded through the surf to stand alongside Leviathan.

The final figure was a hulk of a creature. First the bull's head rose from the sea, followed by muscular human shoulders and a barrel chest covered in coarse hair. Belial too was naked. A thick tail flicked angrily at his rear and his legs ended in cloven hooves.

The sky was now ruby red. The air singed her nostrils, harsh, like ammonia.

Leviathan, Lucifer and Belial. This was never supposed to happen. *This* was the reason for them, for witches. Ciara wished she could take her sister in her arms because they both knew it. They had *failed*. Thousands of years of witches had kept these three motherfuckers at bay, and it was them, the millennial witches of West Yorkshire, that had fucked it.

Gaia must be so ashamed of her daughters.

And that made her *mad*.

Ciara was almost surprised at the level of delusion in her tank. She wanted to destroy these cunts, and for some reason she really believed they *could*. After everything she'd been through, she was an optimist, who knew?

'Brothers,' Leviathan began. 'The time is finally at hand. We shall be one. Satanis will be whole again.'

'*Atomic Kitten*,' she mumbled.

'Ciara,' Niamh muttered. 'Is now the time?'

Yes. Because she had to remember who they were. They were *them*, and they were fabulous. 'We're gonna stop them,' she told her, and – fool she was – she meant it. With great effort she pushed her right hand through the silt to touch Niamh's little finger and a jolt of radiance pulsed between them.

Leviathan offered Theo's hands to the demons on either side of him.

'Ciara . . .' Niamh said, and Ciara heard the fear in her voice.

'They didn't even get the joke.' She offered her twin a sly smile. 'Losers.'

As the trilogy of Satanis joined hands, their bodies collapsed. At first, Ciara thought they'd turned to blackened ashes, only then they swarmed upwards, transforming into a shifting cloud of fat black buzzing flies, accompanied by the smell of rotting meat. Able to move once more, Ciara ducked as the noxious mass flew overhead.

The shape seemed to disperse towards the hillside and Ciara finally gripped her sister close. For a second there, trapped in the past, she thought she'd lost her again. 'What was that?'

'I don't know.'

Luke added, 'Maybe the merger isn't instant or something?'

'Maybe,' Niamh agreed. 'I'm guessing whatever is happening, it's using all their energy, which is why they had to let us go.'

'So it's weakened right now?' offered Luke hopefully.

Maybe? Made sense – in as much as any of this made sense. 'I hurt it,' Ciara said. 'I made it bleed. You saw. It exists in our reality and that means . . .'

'Ciara . . .'

'That means we can kill it.'

Niamh gave her a dark glare. 'It's *Theo*.'

'Is it? Was it? Did you read the fucking thing? It looked like her . . . but there's nothing of her inside. I – I think she's gone . . .' Maybe she should have used Cerridwen while she'd had him right in front of her. If that was their one shot, she'd blown it.

Niamh shook her head, defiant. 'Come on, let's get to the others while we can move our legs.'

What remained of the coven gathered in the temple. No one commented on how obviously fewer they were in number; there had been untold losses on the beach, and no one could face counting the corpses. Ciara did three laps of the banqueting hall and saw that Madame Celestine had not returned. Some nasty voice in her head told her she was glad, but that streak of inner piss only made her feel even worse.

Leonie, now cumbersome and struggling to move for her belly, searched amongst the survivors. 'Where's Valentina?' She grabbed the young black witch from her coven, the gorgeously queer one. 'Kane! Did you see her? Valentina?'

They shook their head. 'I couldn't help her . . . she's on the beach.'

Leonie swore so loud it felt like the temple shook. She punched a pillar with such force she tore the skin on her knuckles, and Elle had to step in to heal her.

There was the odd sniffle of tears, but there was mostly stunned silence. Ciara shook it off; they had to, all of them. Gaia only knew how much time they had before the Megazord demon turned up. She looped her arm through Leonie's and pulled her towards the banquet table. 'Lee, we have to focus.'

But Leonie couldn't stop sobbing. 'Fucking Val, man. I fucking loved her. What am I gonna tell her fucking boyfriend?'

'I know, but we have zero time. There won't be a boyfriend to tell!'

'Enough!' Calista snapped, tired of waiting at the table. 'Did you get them? The Seal and the sword?'

Leonie exhaled and composed herself a second. Chinara was seated beside Calista, battered and bruised, but well enough. 'Yes, I got the seal,' Lee said.

'From your daughter,' Ciara added.

'What?' Chinara looked bewildered.

Ciara. Leonie gave her a death glare. *Don't you dare. Not now.*

'Lee can explain later,' said Ciara. 'And I got this from HMRC. Annie told me where to look.'

'You saw my grandma?' Elle gasped, tearful.

Ciara nodded and placed the ceremonial dagger on the table.

Niamh winced 'Is that . . . ?'

'The knife I used to kill Julia Collins? Why yes, it is. The irony isn't lost on me.' Ciara looked around the table. 'Why is everyone staring at me?'

'So now we have two McGuffins and a magic baby,' Niamh said. 'Great. But we can't kill Theo. No way.'

'I'm with Niamh,' Luke said.

'As if you get a vote, witch-killer,' Holly spat over the table.

'Oh grow up, as if we haven't all killed witches,' Ciara shot back and the girl visibly shrunk inwards like a tortoise. Fucking Gen Z.

Elle looked surly for a second. 'What did I do?'

'Hello, Helena?' Ciara rolled her eyes. 'Gods, you know what this means, don't you? Fucking Helena was right all along. You all could have stopped this in Episode One. If you'd have just let her little band of TERFs kill Theo, none of this would have happened.'

Niamh glared. 'I wouldn't have changed a thing.'

'Me either,' Leonie added.

'I'm not saying *I* would have . . . just an idle musing.' Ciara protested.

Niamh went on. 'The fact remains Theo is totally innocent in all this. See as I see . . .'

Niamh's mind opened itself to all of them and Ciara saw that fucking awful flat again, the one in Theo's dreams. This time the memory was solid, less gauzy. She saw the young woman more clearly, and now a name: Milena. Niamh had met with her. As a group they watched as Theo's tormented mother had tried to kill her own baby to see off the prophecy.

Calista's voice broke the spell. She spoke quietly, in Greek.

'What is it?' Leonie asked her, voice croaky. Her eyes looked red and sore.

Calista clutched at a delicate silver locket around her throat. 'Milena. My poor Milena.'

'You knew her? Where was that? When was that?' Elle said.

The old woman shook her head. This was the first time Ciara had seen her flustered. 'She's my granddaughter, my sweet, foolish Milena. My daughter died young, killed by her own husband. I raised Milena here, but I failed.' Niamh asked what she meant. 'She was a wildcat and I could not contain her. Even as a girl this island was much too small for her. She wanted a great bigness. She wanted danger.'

Ciara knew that childish urge only too well. When life deals you a shitty hand, you go all in. If you're in pain, the whole world ought to feel it too. 'And that woman is Theo's mother?'

Calista was sombre. 'I knew not. That child was hidden from sight.'

'Her father was Asmodeus,' Niamh said gravely.

Ciara knew him well. Pure lust, pure sex. She'd been there, not that she could really remember it. Imagine an orgasm so powerful it renders you unconscious. Somehow, they'd made him flesh for long enough to create a human child. Fucking terrifying.

Elle looked on, confused, trying to catch up. 'So wait. You're Theo's great-grandma?'

'It would seem so,' Calista said and then she seemed to gather her wits, chuckling wryly. '*Theo*. Of course. My name, back when I needed one, was Calista Theodorou.'

'No way!' Holly exclaimed.

'A part of her knew her name,' Niamh said softly. 'Theo is still in there. They went to a great deal of trouble to make her. They need her.'

'I couldn't sense her,' Ciara admitted. 'I tried.'

'Please, Kiki. I know Theo. She'll *fight*.'

Ciara said, very gently. 'I think she fought already, and lost.'

'Ciara, I love her.' Luke took Niamh's slender hand in his big man paw, and she didn't resist.

'Mum!' Holly cried. 'They're talking about killing Theo! Tell them!'

Elle clutched the girl. 'Love, I know, but that . . . thing might not be Theo. It was just . . . wearing her body.'

Everyone now looked to Ciara. Of *course* they'd expect her to be up for the worst deeds possible. She felt the burn of frustrated tears in her eyes. 'We'll try. I promise.' She scooped the dagger off the table. 'If we're going out, we're going out with a fight.'

Their conference was interrupted by a young witch racing into the temple lobby. 'Come!' she cried in an accent Ciara didn't recognise. 'Come and see!'

Fucking hell, what now? Ciara followed Luke and Niamh out of the grand double doors onto the fountain courtyard. Behind them, Leonie and Elle supported Chinara down the sloping temple steps. Calista and Radley brought up the rear.

A brisk wind now pummelled the piazza. The young witch just pointed upwards, and words were needless. The sky was now an intense black-red, like roses, like blood. *Red sky in the morning, sailors' warning.* 'Oh shit,' Ciara breathed.

There was an elliptical slit in the sky and surly clouds were being sucked towards this rupture like rainwater drawn to the gutter. Beyond this wound there was an impenetrable blackness;

a void. How could *nothing* feel so deep and dense? Ciara could hardly look at it; it filled her with that same crushing dread.

'This is it,' Leonie said. She clutched her bump, shielding it.

'This is what they always wanted,' Ciara confirmed, remembering her insights on top of the Beetham Tower when she wore the Seal. 'The end of everything Gaia made.'

Her sister looked to her. 'So that would be the end of *everything*, then? Period.'

'Yep.'

THE CAVE

Theo

The water was icy, and her jeans clung to her legs. The boulders were razor sharp under her bum. There was no dreamlike gauze to this, it felt *real*. Was that that same as it being real?

And yet. Though they had sailed into the cave together, body and soul, only her body had left.

Still, she somehow had form. At least, she believed she did. Theo could still hear the sigh of the waves as they rolled in and out, the rhythmic, echoing *plop* as water ran off stalactites – stood to reason she had *ears* then, didn't it? It was pitch-black there, deep inside the cavern, but even in the darkness, she could see a grey hand. Chipped glitter nail polish. What did that mean? Were there two of her now? All she was sure of was that the doppelganger that had left her here wasn't her; it was malevolent, and as it left, it had taken all her hope with it.

And she had let it. For she had consented to this. Theo felt sick with guilt. How selfish she was. Every other family on the planet would perish so that she could keep hers.

Deep down, she feared this was another of Lucifer's deceptions, but all she could do now was wait to see what their new future looked like. Perhaps *this* was their hideous new purgatory and she'd spend the rest of eternity in this dank sea cave. The cold was bone deep, coming from inside out. She would never feel warmth again. And perhaps that was all she deserved for selling out the human race.

She had figured out Lucifer's catch. There's always a catch, right? Theo realised there was nothing in his pact that forced Niamh and the others to go along with her bargain. They might fight.

In fact, she banked on it – and *that*, she was sure, Lucifer hadn't caught onto. She could only repeat her little prayer, her mantra, her manifestation. That they would stop him. Niamh and the others. If that meant destroying her body, then so be it. She'd accepted that outcome when she agreed to Lucifer's trade.

All she could do now was wait and see if she'd successfully tricked the devil himself.

Then she heard a voice from the darkness.

This isn't real, it said.

'Hello?' Theo said aloud.

Theo strained to see who had spoken. The warm, kind female voice sounded familiar, but she couldn't quite place it. 'Hello?' her own voice rattled around the empty cavern. Theo honestly couldn't be sure if the woman was inside the cave or inside her head.

This is where they put you, but you're still you, and you're still powerful. Break out of the prison they made for you.

'Who is that?'

That matters not. They took your body.

'I don't know how to get it back!' Theo wailed.

They took your body, she said again.

Theo sniffed. 'You already said that.'

I would think you of all people would know that the power was never derived from your body. It always came from within. You are *the power.*

This was absurd. She really must be dreaming. Because she finally placed the soothing, hot-chocolate tones: they had accompanied her from afar for her whole life. Late at night, even in the worst care home, Theo had *felt* this voice, telling her to hold on for one more dawn and see how things looked in the light.

It was the voice of their Mother.

The voice of Gaia.

And if *she* was offering help, maybe the tables could be turned.

Tears pricked Theo's eyes as she felt for the first time in a long time, *hope*. Was she saying that she didn't need her body to stop Leviathan?

And the hope solidified into *fight*.

Maybe there was still time on the clock after all.

POETIC JUSTICE

Niamh - Aeaea

'Ta-dah,' Lee said wryly as she set the Seal of Solomon carefully on the banquet table next to the dagger – 'Cerridwen', according to her sister. The crown was rather less bling than Niamh had anticipated, just a very simple band of bronze, with ancient script engraved both inside and out. She held a hand towards it, but it was as if it were repelling her. It set her teeth on edge, made her elbows itch. There was intense, complex magic on both of these items: a choir of ancient spells were smelted into the metal. Niamh could only think *that* was how these items had eluded Lucifer for over a millennium.

'I can't do it,' Ciara got in first. 'I don't trust myself, and you'd be mad to trust me to. I'm a junkie.'

Niamh sighed. 'What does it do? You're the only one who's worn it.'

Ciara looked up at her wearily. 'You absorb every demon entity for miles around like a sponge. They flow through you and your power just goes through the roof. It's like you can turn them into energy or something.'

Chinara fixed Niamh with her steeliest glare. 'Niamh, it has to be you.'

'What? Why me? You're the Level 6! I'm a meagre Level 5!'

'Chi almost died!' Lee rebutted.

'I *did* die!' Niamh protested in vain. She'd already accepted the selection. Ciara was as strong as she was, but she was damn right to not trust herself with that much firepower. There was only one fatal flaw. 'I can't kill Theo if it comes to that. I can't. Worst person for the job.'

'You might have to,' Leonie said gravely. 'I know, I know! But one girl or the rest of the world? It's an ass or mouth situation, but it's a pretty obvious choice.'

'Then you do it!' Niamh snapped.

Holly said nothing, but, grim-faced, pushed her chair away from the table and stormed out of the great hall.

'Niamh, fuck, I'm pregnant! And this baby *has* to be born safe and healthy or the whole fucking tapestry goes to shit. Senait *has* to live so that we can be here now with these weapons.'

'You're High Priestess,' Elle reminded her softly. 'The coven trusts you to decide . . .'

Niamh slapped both palms against the table. 'I fucking hate this!'

'We all do,' Ciara said, taking her hand. 'But I think Theo would want the same. I think she went to Lucifer knowing we'd stop her.'

Yes, Niamh thought, because she was fundamentally a good girl. It wasn't fair. It was the easiest thing in the world for Niamh to favour one sixteen-year-old over the rest of the human race, because she loved that one young woman. They'd baked apple and blackberry crumble together with fruit from the garden. The custard had turned out like scrambled egg, but they hadn't minded. Niamh had introduced her to the joys of *Clueless* and *Mean Girls* and *The House Bunny*. In return, Theo had taught Niamh how to blend bronzer in such a way that she didn't end up looking like she was in the chorus of *Cats*.

But wasn't that just the issue? If Niamh could see Theo for who she was, she could empathise that every other ant in the human ant farm was as complex and wonderful too. *Every* house or flat or caravan or tent had a favourite film, a favourite pudding, an amazing skill.

Seven billion Theos, or just the one *she* loved?

'I need time to think.' Niamh left the table, but took the crown with her. Just in case.

She took it upstairs and out onto her veranda. The wind was still strong and the black slit in the scarlet sky seemed to gape wider. It was worsening. Reality swirling down the drain.

Alone, she felt the Seal in her hands. It was as warm as flesh, as if it was a living thing – and oddly muscular somehow. It would, she implicitly understood, make her strong. And now, once again, she needed to be. Niamh was so fucking sick of it. Her parents died (*be strong for your mammy and dad*); her fiancé seemingly died (*you'll get through this, you're so strong*) and her sister had languished in a coma for almost a decade (*I don't know how you do it, you're ever so strong*). Niamh wanted to not be strong. She wanted to lie on a bed while someone fed her rice pudding and jam on a little spoon.

With flawless timing, Luke joined her on the terrace. She faced him. 'Tell me you've come to feed me rice pudding and jam.'

He looked rightly puzzled. 'I haven't, but I would, if I could. I reckon you've probably earned it.' He stood at her side, looking out at the apocalyptic vista. 'So this is the end of the world. I sorta assumed it would be global warming that got us, and that we'd be dead long before, if I'm being honest.'

She appreciated the mirth, but she couldn't muster a sassy comeback. 'I can't do it, Luke.' Her throat was needle tight.

He didn't need to ask what she meant. 'Then don't.'

'What?'

'You're in charge, do what you want.'

She almost laughed. She'd never even considered that she had a say in the matter.

He went on. 'I love your sense of duty, obviously, and it's probably why they made you High Priestess – but when was the last time you did something because you wanted to, and not because it was *the right thing to do*?'

She ran a list in her head. She'd let Conrad go. She'd taken

Theo in. She'd accepted this new role under duress. Honestly, she couldn't recall her last wholly selfish choice.

'You don't want to kill Theo,' Luke said.

'Well of course I don't!' she snapped. 'But maybe this time I really don't have a choice, Luke.'

'You *always* have a choice, believe me.' He gripped the edge of the balustrade and rocked his body almost over the edge. 'I made one. I killed for you. And it is killing me. I don't think I'm ever going to get past it.'

Niamh felt a familiar sour sensation fizz across her middle. *Don't you pin that one on me, you motherfucker.*

'Sorry, I don't mean that it's on you. I made my own bed. What I mean is this: if you kill Theo, you might save us all, but kill yourself in the process.'

It was odd, because this was not the point of his anti-pep talk, but she felt herself harden. People were forced into awful choices all the time. She ought to be getting better at making them. Choosing Theo over Helena; leaving Conrad in Wales, in the past. She was a vet for fuck's sake. How many days had she watched pet owners choose to end the suffering of a creature they loved like a child? Life *is* sacrifice. All of them practised sacrifice every single day.

With everything she'd seen, it was almost quaint that she still believed in happy endings. How many books had she found comfort in after her parents died? Too many *Sweet Valley High*s to count. All of them had been big on poetic justice: Elizabeth, pure of heart, is rewarded by the universe, and Jessica, ambitious, mischievous, gets what's coming her way.

Am I a good person?

'Yes,' answered Luke without hesitation. Her thoughts were so loud, even he could hear them.

She looked at his handsome face and it reminded her how much she missed Hebden Bridge. 'Are you sure, Luke? I almost murdered my sister. I *did* destroy her mind. I couldn't save Annie.

I let Helena die. I failed to protect Snow and Theo. Maybe I don't deserve the Happy Ending Package.' He shook his head in protest.

She took the deepest breath she could muster. 'I have to do this.'

'Niamh, are you sure?'

She stepped back from him.

'Niamh . . . don't.'

Even as torrid gales whipped her hair over her face, Niamh placed the Seal of Solomon upon her head.

THE DEMON QUEEN

Niamh - Aeaea

She could see them.

Demons, in their truest form.

Even here, on the hallowed ground of Aeaea, there were entities everywhere. Like wraiths they slithered out of the cracks between the tiles under her feet, and down from the roof of the temple like autumn leaves. They were gaseous, translucent, but they whispered and wailed and simpered in nasal whines. They begged her to see and acknowledge them. Their faces were repellent, as if they'd been designed to revolt human eyes. Fetid skin sagged, and slack mouths gaped. Eye sockets were black and empty, or lined with yellow teeth. Soon, a cyclone of these forlorn spectres circled them.

'Do you see them?' Niamh breathed.

'See what?' Luke said.

She was relieved he was spared the monstrous sight, but it made her feel very alone all of a sudden. 'It's working,' she told him. 'Luke, go. For Gaia's sake, just run. I don't want you to get hurt. There's so many of them.'

He didn't argue, just backed away. 'I'll get the others.'

Niamh didn't need to wonder where Satanis was. She could feel him now, like the burning July sun on her face. She turned to the northernmost tip of the island, where the mountains were highest.

'Tell them he's gone there, to the north mountains,' she told Luke before taking flight.

She hovered over the temple of Circe. This was virgin territory for her. Yes, Ciara had used her body for some messed-up shit – the white stripe in her hair was testament to that – but Niamh had never invoked a demon in her entire life.

Almost like she knew, Niamh looked down and saw her sister far below in the fountain courtyard with Leonie and Elle, Luke racing down the temple stairs to join them. Ciara squinted up at her, recognition in her eyes. *Just let them in. They want you. They need you. It's not the other way around.* And then she added, *Trust me.*

The phantoms had followed her skywards. Their coldly moist fingers gingerly reached her for skin, looking for the entrance. Niamh looked up to the pink sky, tilting back her head. *Go on then*, she told them.

She'd never imagined what it would feel like if a demon passed through the flesh, but – if she had – this is *precisely* how she'd have described it. A bone-deep chill, a shiver like snow injected into her veins. She felt her body try to shake it off, a judder. Her neck spasmed; her toes cramped.

Then, as soon as the cold gripped her, she felt an itchy-hot buzz crackle across her skin, as if a current flowed through her. The Hulk analogy was apt because it felt as if she was expanding. There was a weight to her, as if she could crush the world like a satsuma in her palm.

The mountain.

Wasting no further time, Niamh rocketed from the temple towards the north of the island. There was Satanis, overseeing his handiwork from the highest vista. A king on his mountain throne.

Niamh came into a smooth landing. The flight was the most effortless she'd ever done. The mountaintop was brutish and exposed to the elements. The promontory overlooking the ocean was a rocky plateau thatched with parched yellow grasses and shrubs.

The demon king Satanis turned to look at her. His face was still Theo's, only now he had horns – Belial's great ebony horns, curling around her face. Lucifer's golden hair fell in opulent curls down his back. And Leviathan's bottomless black eyes remained, staring back at her now. 'You cannot hope to stop me,' he said, voice deeper than ever.

Niamh raised a hand and it was if she was raising a hundred hands. She took hold of the slight figure with her mind and pulled him – for his aura was no longer anything near to Theo's – close. His booted toes scraped over the rocky summit.

'Nice crown.' Satanis grinned Lucifer's grin, before swiping a fist across Niamh's face. The force was such that it punched her clean off her feet and she tumbled, head over feet, across the table of the mountain.

She rolled to a halt not far from the edge, buffeted by the patchy ferns and grasses. The air was thinner up here, and Niamh more keenly felt the thirsty suction of the abyss high above them.

Satanis taunted her. 'You cannot beat me, witch. Those beings inside your veins are my children. I am their source. You're asking minnows to defeat a river.'

Niamh licked coppery blood from her lip. 'We'll see.'

She took hold of a mighty boulder and ripped it off the cliffs. With everything she had, she hurled it at him. It was so fast, it bowled Theo's body back down the hillside, pinning it down. With satisfaction, she heard a pained *oof.* Only then the great grey rock turned into a flock of crows and took flight, cawing as they went.

Satanis floated back up the hill to greet her with the feathered grace of a ballet dancer. 'Reality is mine now. Forget everything they taught you about the natural order. Gaia's rules no longer apply . . .'

The slate under Niamh's feet turned to a porridge-like slop, and she started to sink as if she was on marshland. Clawing at blades of grass, she was soon immersed to her chest.

Fighting not to panic as the lumpen mush rose around her cheeks, Niamh felt for life around her. The demons in her head knew *everything* and they knew that a breed of daisy was indigenous to Greek mountaintops. Niamh summoned them to her now. The flora sprung up through the cracks in the rock, little white petals flowering before her eyes. They grew towards her, thicker and thicker, writhing over the terrain like worms. She grabbed hold of their stems in fistfuls, using the 'ropes' to haul herself out of Satanis's tar pit.

'Nice try,' she told him, dusting herself off as she rose to her feet.

'Innovative,' he conceded, and the sludge turned to a fine dust on her clothes.

Not waiting to give him another chance to attack, Niamh did something she'd always wanted to do: she summoned *fire*. She'd seen Chinara do it and it had looked cool as fuck. She imagined her fists to be matches and struck them against the air. Her palms burst into flame, and she threw fireballs at her rival.

Satanis cast an invisible shield around himself, so Niamh intensified the blast, directing columns of flame at him – great, blazing whips of it. He had to plant his feet and for the first time, she saw she was testing him. He bit his lip, and she drove him further towards the edge.

Niamh!

She froze.

She heard her.

Her. Theo.

It was like a voice coming from the bottom of a well, but it was still Theo's true voice she heard, over the roar of the inferno.

Theo! Hold on!

Niamh's fire turned to water and splattered over her shoes in a great slop. 'See, that's the problem,' Satanis said, dusting off his hands. He looked almost disappointed in her. 'You won't hurt me because you're terrified of hurting the girl. Your heart is a chew toy.'

It was true, and Niamh found she couldn't lie. 'Please, just let her go. I heard her, she's alive in there.'

He shook Theo's lovely head. 'We need a vessel.'

Niamh winced. 'Why are you bleeding?' Black blood, like oil, gushed from Theo's nose and mouth, dripping off her chin. Satanis raised a taloned finger to their lip and looked genuinely puzzled. Something was amiss. She could use that. 'Something's wrong, isn't it?'

Niamh. Her voice, again.

Niamh allowed herself a brief smile. Internal bleeding, baby. Theo, the real Theo, was fighting back *from the inside*.

SACRIFICE

Theo

What she was trying to say was 'Goodbye'.

Theo had figured it out. Clearly Satanis needed her – he'd gone to an awful lot of trouble to get her. He'd also left some trace of her alive in this freezing, salty cave. Why leave this pilot light burning unless absolutely necessary?

Well fuck him. Fuck him all the way up the bum.

The water was black, and deep, and cold, but Theo wasn't afraid.

Lucifer had told her, right before the ritual to revive Niamh, that everyone had to make sacrifices. Niamh had offered up her powers to make Theo a woman. Ciara had slain her sister to regain life. Annie had accepted her fate to save this timeline. Luke had forgone Sheila Henry to protect her and Niamh. Everyone had made life-shattering choices to protect her – Elle, Holly, Leonie, Ciara and Niamh most of all.

Well now it was time to cash in all these favours.

They had all fought so hard for her, and now she would save them. Satanis had chosen her and had chosen her *now* because she was a *child*. The Sullied *Child*. Why does any grown man fuck with a younger woman? Because they know they can dominate them. They'll do as they're told.

It was time to show Satanis that he'd picked the wrong traumatised transsexual witch to fuck with.

Now, Niamh. Kill him now.

There was a silt beach of sorts within the cave. She waded into the shallows. Gaia had told her this wasn't real. If this was all a pocket within her psyche, she felt she could weigh herself down with all the regrets, and guilt, and shame, and self-loathing, and disgust, and despair she'd accumulated over her sixteen years. No one did messy like her.

If she had sold her soul to Lucifer, she would now destroy it. Theo kept walking into the black tide until it washed over her face.

She took her last breath and went under.

THE WYRM

Ciara - Heaea

They could see the fire from the temple. The furthest tips of the mountains were now capped with thick black smoke. Ciara looked to the others. 'We have to help her.' Even with the crown in her sister's possession, Ciara figured it couldn't hurt to tag team the motherfucker.

They had gathered on the balcony that ran round the top tier of the temple to get a better view; Luke, Chinara and Lee, Elle and Holly, and Calista. They'd all seen. Niamh had flown faster than Ciara had ever seen a witch fly. Ciara remembered the euphoric feeling the Seal had given her and was briefly jealous until she remembered the fact she'd almost crushed Manchester underfoot.

'I'll come,' Elle said, surprising Ciara. 'What? I want that bastard to pay.'

'Leonie?' Ciara said. They could carry Elle between them with ease.

They turned to look at Lee, but a deep frown creased her brow. 'OK, you know I'd normally be down for whatever, but I can't.'

'What's up?' Chinara asked her.

Leonie looked pasty, her top lip sweaty. 'This is so Christmas Day special, but how do you know when a baby is coming?'

'Are you fucking serious?' Ciara said.

Leonie glared. 'No, I thought it'd be a great time for a gag? Of course I'm serious, you twat.'

Elle switched into nurse mode, attending to Lee's bump. 'Does it feel a little like period pain?'

'Maybe? I sort of have a cramp in my back and thighs, too . . .'

'How?' Chinara said, still nursing her stab site. 'You're nowhere near nine months.'

'Our baby can time travel, Chi, I'm not sure she's that fussed about a schedule.' Suddenly Leonie winced and inhaled sharply. She steadied herself on the balustrade. 'Yep, I think this is it.'

'No offense, but your baby is kind of an asshole,' Ciara said. Lee rolled her eyes, but didn't disagree. 'It's OK, I'll go alone.'

'Chinara will go with you,' Lee said.

'She won't,' her partner said resolutely. 'I'm staying with you.'

Calista stepped to Leonie's side. 'Elle, go with Ciara. I have delivered countless children over the years. Go.'

Elle nodded before turning to her daughter. 'Holly, I want you to stay with Auntie Leonie, OK?'

The girl clutched Elle's sleeves. 'Mum, no. I want to go with you.'

'You must be kidding! Young lady, you will stay right here.' Her daughter was about to argue, but Elle cut her off. 'I can't fight him and worry about you. Help your auntie. I have to help Niamh and Ciara. I want to watch Lucifer die. In a lot of pain.'

Holly gripped her tight. 'I like this scary you.'

Ciara told Elle it was time to fly. 'Hold on tight.'

'I know the drill from when you kidnapped me, thanks.'

Fair.

'Wait!' Calista commanded. She slipped a suede pouch from around her waist and offered it up. It was the dagger. Cerridwen. 'You will need this. Your sister went without it.'

Ciara took it, no longer fearful of its past. 'I'll make sure she gets it.'

She secured the scabbard around her waist, looped her arms under Elle's, and then they were up and away. Ciara didn't speak, concentrating on keeping their bodies aloft. Difficult to do with Elle screaming like they were on a rollercoaster – and when her mind kept straying to Niamh and whatever was happening on that mountaintop.

As they came into view, Ciara saw Niamh doing everything she could to pummel Theo, but, even from here, Ciara felt her heart wasn't in it. Who could blame her? It definitely wasn't a coincidence that Satanis had mostly kept Theo's form.

Stay back, Niamh told her. Without taking her eyes off Satanis, she must have sensed their arrival. Grateful, Ciara began their descent some way short of the apex.

'Why are we stopping?' Elle shouted over the wind rushing around them.

Safe distance, she told her.

She brought them down on a well-trodden mountain path. Ciara wasn't sure if Satanis had seen them approach, but it was safer to assume he was aware of everything. 'What do we do?' Elle said.

'You should hang back.' Elle went to argue, but Ciara cut her off. 'Ellie, if one of us gets hurt, you're our best bet. Come only if you have to.'

Reluctantly, she nodded. 'Good luck. Love you, babe.'

'Duh.' Ciara winked and hurried up the winding path. She hoped to sneak up on him from behind. While Niamh distracted him, she'd snap his skinny neck. It had worked real well on Dabney Hale. That thing is NOT Theo, she told herself. He was Satanis. She had to do this. She'd done worse.

Pressing her body low to the rocky edge of the precipice, Ciara poked her head over her parapet. Niamh levitated a few inches off the ground, arms splayed. She seemed to have the demon locked in place in some sort of mental battle of wills – but still, Ciara saw, she would not kill her – *him*. This thing was NOT Theo.

Ciara stood. She could help with that. If Niamh could not kill this abomination, she would. She was already the bitch twin, so her reputation could hardly be worse.

She went to snap his neck. Her eyes widened; it was as if the beast's neck was now made of iron girders. She couldn't budge him a centimetre.

Ciara. A voice swirled around her mind. It was Theo's voice – or at least it sounded a lot like her. *It's me, the real me. I'm going under. I'm dying. I can make him weak. Finish him. Just do it. Niamh can't.*

Oh gods. That made it so much worse.

Theo was on their side, though. The girl was brave; she knew what needed to be done even if Niamh didn't.

Ciara planted her feet wide and threw everything she had at Satanis. This time he did stumble. Only then, his head twisted one-eighty degrees to face her. Ciara gasped at the abomination. 'Oh, the evil twin, nice try.'

He merely blinked and she was lifted clean off her feet. She was catapulted over his head and hit her sister like a bowling ball. She felt it keenly in her ribcage and they both went down together, landing in a heap at the very edge of the precipice.

'Are you OK?' Niamh asked, helping her up.

I can hear Theo, she told her, hoping Satanis couldn't eavesdrop.

Me too.

She's fighting him.

I don't want to lose her, Niamh said.

She's trying to save us all.

Niamh pleaded: *What if she can fight her way out?*

Ciara felt this was only delaying the inevitable.

When I say pull . . . PULL!

Ciara knew exactly what her sister meant to do. Niamh tugged on his left side, and Ciara on his right, as if to split him down the middle. If they could weaken him in this physical form, perhaps Theo could find a way to assert herself mentally.

'Pull!' Niamh screamed aloud.

Satanis's head swivelled to face them as his arms snapped outwards as if they'd seized his wrists and yanked hard. His feet left the floor and he hung, Christlike, arms outstretched.

Ciara gave it all she had. She didn't even realise the scream she heard was coming from her throat. Her skull rattled as she focused her entire mind on hauling him away from her now – much – stronger twin.

The slight figure was wrenched to the left, and he rolled over once before steadying himself like a cat ready to pounce. They had succeeded in ruffling him. He had to pant to get his breath back. It was working.

'You cannot beat me!' he cried, his voice deeper still. 'I AM A GOD!'

He turned his face skywards. Following his gaze, Ciara looked to the black wound in the sky. Only now, something emerged from the gash. 'Fucking hell,' she shouted over the wind.

'What *is* that?' Niamh cried.

It was *foul*. At first she thought it could have been a dragon or a snake, but it possessed twitching segmented legs like those of a centipede. Each leg was shaped like a chubby little infant's arm, each with wriggling fingers on stumpy hands. A curved, spiny body continued to pour from the incision until its tail tapered to a sort of fin. It stank. The putrid funk of shit and puke and pus filled Ciara's nostrils and she fought the urge to vomit on the spot.

As the creature flew ever closer, the head resembled those *Blue Planet* fish that live in the darkest trenches of the ocean: an array of uneven eyes almost glowed with their own red light. It opened its jaws, and wet, fleshy lips peeled over sharp, piranha-like teeth. From within its mouth, a second, smaller head emerged, and it was screaming; a shrill, pained wail.

Ciara held on to Niamh's hand. Because the second face was a cruel mockery of Annie Device's; rotten and decaying, the flesh falling from her skull.

'I told you,' Satanis said, more calmly now. 'I am a god. Creation is mine. I call this the Anniewyrm. Do you like it?'

The serpent twisted and coiled mid-air and changed course directly towards them. The stench grew worse, and this time Ciara did throw up.

Niamh stood her ground. 'I can stop it.'

'No, you can't . . .' Satanis taunted.

She held out her arms and Ciara could only duck at her side, praying the Seal would do its job. 'Niamh . . .'

'I can do this . . .'

Everything went dark as the Wyrm bore down overhead. 'Niamh!' Ciara shrieked.

Too late. The creature barrelled into her sister, clamping her in its massive jaws. Like a shark, it plucked Niamh off the ground and carried her off the rim of the mountain. It happened so fast, Niamh didn't even scream.

Ciara scrambled to the edge of the cliff in time to see the beast drop her sister from its mouth. She fell. She was now too far away for Ciara to see if she was conscious or not. Had those teeth bitten her in two? Jesus fucking fuck. Her heart raced; her skin was hot and tight.

She faced Satanis, who waited, poised. 'One to go,' he said.

SACRIFICE (CONT.)

Theo

This wasn't so bad.

The water was warm now. Was that a good thing, or a bad thing? Who cared. The important thing was she'd found a way to fight him.

Who's a little bitch now? The thought amused her.

There was no seabed, and she kept sinking, down and down and down. Black and airless. She felt sleepy, head all full of cottonwool, right on the verge of tumbling to unconsciousness. Only it wasn't sleep, it was death.

Theo welcomed it.

Forevermore, her legacy would be this: The Sullied Child brought Leviathan out of the sea, but then she killed him. Let the oracles tell *that* story.

OK, she'd be dead – sucky – but at least she'd die a hero, and not a pariah.

This was the most in control of her life, and her body, that Theo had ever felt.

She'd loved Niamh and the others. *I am lucky*, she thought, *that I got to love at all.*

And I think they loved me.

So that's nice.

THE OFFER

Ciara - Heaea

Ciara prayed for a final finale. *Fin.* She couldn't stand the notion of going back to that purgatory she'd toiled in, all those years in the hospital bed. If this was death, let it be a full stop; a little black dot of nothing. Peace.

Satanis strode towards her, ready with a death strike. Ciara braced. Only then, his leg twisted painfully at the middle and he fell to a kneel with a yelp. Ciara took the bonus moment to regain her composure and got back on her feet. The demon too tried to rise, but fell again, this time rolling onto his back.

Ciara reached out for that distant essence of Theo she'd heard. Nothing . . . no, not *nothing*, but the candle was going out. A glowing wick, and little else, but still, something of her lived . . . for now.

There was a scream from above. Ciara looked up and saw the Wyrm disintegrate into blackened ashes. Satanis writhed, arching his back in pain. 'You don't have the power to sustain it,' she told Satanis. 'You're dying.'

'You wish, witch. I have the Sullied Child. I will keep her eternally.'

Ciara shook her head. 'But *she's* dying too. I can feel it. She's fighting you, but you need her, don't you?'

To see the great demon king like a beetle on its back, fighting to get onto his hands and knees was beyond satisfying. Ciara strode forward and delivered a swift kick underneath his chin.

The momentum rolled him over. His eyes were no longer jet black. The expression was softer. 'Ciara . . .'

It was Theo. Or was it? This could be one more of Lucifer's tricks. This *was* what she wanted most, after all. But she couldn't help herself; she ran to her aid. 'Theo?'

'I can't hold him back,' she cried through bloodied teeth. 'I tried to die, but he won't let me go.'

'Fight him!'

'I can't! Please, just kill me. Quickly. Do it now.' Ciara reached for the dagger at her waist. It should have been easy; she thought she was ready. Her hand clutched the hilt, but she found she couldn't withdraw it from her belt. 'Ciara! Quick! He's coming back! Just do it!'

'Stop!' Ciara yelped. 'Just shut up!'

'You have to.' Tears ran down Theo's face. 'This is what we have to do.' She fell forwards, face down into the dirt.

Ciara stood. In a way, she wished she *was* the natural born killer everyone assumed her to be, but the world had her wrong. She'd even had *herself* wrong. She wasn't nearly as cool as she'd thought she was when she was seventeen. And thank the goddess for that, because she had been such a mardy cunt. Being that fucking angry at the world took energy, and frankly she was too tired to care with that sort of fury anymore.

Where there once was a cauldron of sizzling rage, there was now the hearty soup of forgiveness.

Ciara had *forgiven*. The world; her mother; *herself*.

'I can't do it,' she gasped, tears in her eyes as she failed the world. She couldn't do what needed to be done. Theo had her whole life ahead of her, who was she to take it.

When Theo raised her head, she wasn't Theo anymore. The eyes were black and the expression hard. 'What a disappointment you are.'

'Fuck you. You're the one who can't fucking stand up.'

Satanis continued to limp and stagger, fucking Bambi learning to walk. Theo, still in there somewhere, wouldn't give up. Satanis toppled to his knees again.

'Here's an idea,' Ciara said. 'Let her go.'

'Never,' he snarled.

The words felt like bricks in her throat, but she coughed them up. 'Take me instead.'

His eyes narrowed. 'Nice try, witch.'

'Your vessel is fucked,' she said with growing verve. 'She's a kid. A skinny little girl. She lives on bubble tea and McFlurrys.'

Satanis ignored her. 'This is what she was made for. Part human, part demon. She is the bridge between worlds.'

'*Every* witch is part human, part demon. Isn't Gaia just a big demon too? We treat her differently, but she came to this world and placed a bit of herself in the first witches, and every witch since.' His silence spoke volumes. 'Babe, you're on your *knees*! I'm just as strong as she is. Stronger. Older. Wiser. Typical of a man to think youth tops experience.' She allowed herself a small smile as she goaded him. 'Level 5 Adept, at your service. And you *know* I can take a demon. I've had 'em all. You already know me, Satanis, inside and out.'

The demon said nothing, but considered her with a slow tilt of the head, like he was measuring her body up for size.

A WOMAN'S RIGHT TO CHOOSE

Leonie - Aeaea

The contractions weren't fucking about. Why they called them *contractions* Leonie wasn't sure because it mostly felt like her entire cunt was about to lift off. And also like she might, at any moment, shit herself.

She'd indulged bucolic notions of water births or forest clearings, but there wasn't time. She found brief solace in leaning over the foot of the bed on all fours while Chinara rubbed her back. She had taken all her clothes off because at one point she honestly thought her clothing was conspiring to strangle her.

She'd once seen a viral clip of a panda bear shooting a baby out of its fanny like it was a ping pong ball. Hers wasn't a mundane pregnancy. The thought that little baby Senait might pop out of her painlessly was all that was keeping her going at this stage.

'You're doing amazing,' Chinara kissed her hair.

Calista returned with some mint tea. That's what Leonie had wanted ten minutes ago. *Now* she wanted an ice cold Peroni with a slice of lime. Labour was a *ride*.

The healer placed the tea at the side of her and stroked her face. Leonie felt the radiance ripple through her, and, briefly, the throbbing in her womb eased off.

It's time, Calista thought, and Leonie heard all too clearly. She wasn't referring to the imminent birth, either. 'I know,' she whispered, and then more loudly, 'I *know*.'

'You know what, baby?' Chinara said softly.

'We have to go,' said Leonie. She went to pick up her clothes, wincing as another cuntpunch hit.

That got Holly's attention. 'Go where? You can't! You're giving birth!'

'I had noticed.' Leonie grimaced.

It clicked for Chinara. 'We've got to go back.'

Lee gripped her girlfriend's wrists, clinging on for dear life. 'And I can only take us back while she's inside me.' She screamed out, just once, and turned to sit on her rear. If she could reach in and yank her out, she would.

Holly joined them, pointedly maintaining eye contact, bless her. 'What do you mean?'

Leonie started, but found she needed to focus on breathing. Calista stepped in. 'Senait was born twenty-two years ago, right here on Aeaea. I delivered her myself. For the story to play out as it must—'

'We have to go back . . .' Lee finished.

Chinara stood and rubbed her brow. 'No, wait. I need to think about this. We know our daughter can move through time. It doesn't matter where – sorry, when – we have her. She'll get herself to where she needs to be.'

But Leonie had moved across eras the same as Senait had, and she knew first-hand how fragile those gossamer threads were. Time played by a specific logic, and it couldn't be messed with. 'It has to happen how it happened.' She gasped. 'Or who knows what else might be different? How the future will change?' She gripped Calista's arm, draining some more vitality from the healer.

'Leonie is right,' said Calista. 'Any other path threatens the here and now. What if you take the child to London and she is . . . struck by a bus?' No one said anything, and Calista continued, eyes wide but steady. 'You have to trust me. I lived it. We hid Senait on the island for over twenty years without the forces of evil seeing her.'

'Anywhere else they might,' Leonie finished, swallowing a scream. Her body was shifting, expanding, trying to deliver the child. How utterly fucking incredible the human body is. 'There's no choice.'

'You always have a choice,' Chinara said, more angrily than she intended perhaps. 'When have you ever, *ever*, done as you were told?' she added more gently.

Leonie cupped Chinara's cheek with her clammy palms. 'My love, that's because I'm a selfish brat. Always was. It's not just me now though, is it?' She rested a hand on her bump and felt the child within fighting her way out. She knew Senait as a young adult, and adored her, but this was more than that. Under all this agony there was *glee*. Any second now she'd meet Senait for the first time and would love her with everything she had. She already knew; she would do *anything* for this baby. Give up anything.

And that included Chinara. If she had to.

'I'm going,' Leonie said. 'You can stay if you want, I'd get it.'

'Oh don't be stupid, you daft cow, of course I'm coming.'

Leonie laughed until Chinara kissed her mouth. Leonie felt something like a rush in her abdomen. 'I don't think it'll be long.' It had to be *now*. Once Senait was born, there was no more time travel for anyone except their daughter. She was consigning them to the past. Leonie wondered if this was parenthood; sacrifice that didn't even feel like sacrifice.

'You did Gaia proud.' Calista kissed her crown tenderly. 'I'll see you very soon, a long time ago, my fair child.'

In the absence of a heartfelt goodbye scene, Leonie cast a psychic farewell to Niamh, Ciara and Elle, sort of an XOXO into the foundations of Aeaea.

Leonie told Chinara to hold her. Chinara wrapped her arms around her and Leonie pulled her tight. Together they sandwiched the little girl that was about to come out of her; a cocoon of pure love. Leonie screwed her eyes closed and reached out psychically, teasing the long ribbon of time into a ripple.

When she opened her eyes, she felt the kiss of cold water on her toes. Bubbles of surf. The beach. It was dawn. The sky was infinite and gold and lilac with wisps of cotton clouds. White foam lapped over her bare feet, and it was precisely what she needed. She got the message.

Gaia, you're welcome.

'Are we here?' Chinara said. They were in the same loving knot, kneeling on the sand.

Leonie was about to answer when a further contraction gripped her entire spine. Chinara held her tight, guiding her out of the sea onto the sand.

When the pain passed, she looked up to see two women walking over the sand towards them. The first was Calista. She walked upright, both hands at her sides. It took Leonie a second to recognise her companion: Zehra Darga, here a striking woman of thirty or so, a far cry from the middle-aged archaeologist she'd met last year in Turkey.

Last year, in two decades' time. Same difference.

The pair reached them and knelt in the sand. 'Do you know who we are?' Chinara said.

'No,' Calista admitted. 'Though we knew you were coming, sisters. Our oracles told of the women who would come from the sea.'

'I'm Chinara. This is my lover, Leonie.'

Leonie looked up into Calista's eyes and pleaded. She exposed her swollen middle. 'And this is our daughter, Senait. We have to protect her.'

Calista smiled kindly. 'Then we shall.'

67

HOW ELSE?

Niamh - Beaea

Don't you dare, Niamh Kelly.

She heard Elle loud and clear. She felt very warm and toasty, as if she was wrapped in sheepskin. Radiance. It was Elle's radiance.

She didn't know how long she'd been out for, and only vaguely remembered the Wyrm clamping its jaws around her torso. She'd passed out almost at once. 'How bad was it?' she managed to ask.

She opened her eyes to see exactly how concerned Elle was. She lay in a grassy verge, about a hundred feet down, in the shadow of the mountain's summit. 'You were a chew toy,' she said ruefully. Just as Satanis had.

'Thanks for patching me up.'

Elle slapped her gently on the top of her arm. 'You almost snuffed it. Again. What's going on up there?'

Niamh tested her limbs and found she was able to sit up. The Seal was still on her head and she adjusted it. As she did, she felt the alien bodies inside her ripple. She was fine – better than fine. There were even more entities swarming close to her. She absorbed more as she floated to her feet.

'Steady on!' Elle said.

'It's the crown,' she told her. 'I'm strong.' Elle nodded her agreement from down below. 'I have to get back. Ciara's alone up there.'

'Do it,' Elle said. 'Whatever it takes.' Her eyes drifted to the ever-expanding void overhead. 'It's getting bigger.'

Niamh gave a curt nod and levitated upwards, towards the rocky outcrop. Ready to blast the motherfucker out of Theo's body, she arrived to a scene she wasn't expecting.

Ciara stood over Satanis. He looked to be out cold, splayed on a solid stone slab, a flat boulder near the summit. Alive, although the essence was dim. Niamh slowed to an easy landing and walked to Ciara's side. 'What happened?'

She felt it before she saw it. Her sister was *so* cold.

Repelled, Niamh took a step away before Ciara turned to face her. Her eyes were black and her skin was so white it was eggshell blue. As Niamh watched, Ciara's cropped hair grew back from her scalp, over her shoulders and all the way down her back. Auburn, thick and luxurious. Her cuts and bruises healed. She grew taller, more muscular. A pair of onyx-black, ridged horns twisted from her skull, like a ram.

For a moment, Niamh could not speak. She forced some clod words out. 'Ciara, what did you do?'

'She made me an offer I couldn't refuse.' Satanis examined his hands, as razor-like talons grew from his fingers. 'Oh, this is *much* better. She was right.'

Ciara, are you in there?

The beautiful face scowled. 'Nice try, Red, but unlike Mopey the Emo Tranny down there, Ciara Kelly was a *willing* vessel.' He raised his hands to the sky and almost wrenched the cut wider. 'Fits like a glove.' With horror, Niamh watched as the ocean itself was sucked upwards in a twisted waterspout.

'Stop!' Niamh cried, almost feeling the scream of the earth at her core. She threw herself at Satanis and he batted her away like a fly. She crashed onto her rear.

Satanis circled her. 'This is wonderful, don't you think? Sister versus sister, witch versus witch. Any other ending would have been such a let-down.'

This version of her foe was so much *sexier*, prowling like a leopard. It made her sure there *was* some of Ciara left in there.

The whole mountaintop seemed to revolve drunkenly around Niamh and she was forced to steady herself. 'What are you doing?'

'Well, if the Kelly sisters are going to fight to the death in the rematch of the century, I thought we needed an appropriate setting.'

The revolution sped up, Aeaea spinning so fast it made her woozy. Niamh screwed her eyes shut and clutched her temples, trying to rid her head of the dizziness.

When she opened her eyes, the dramatic landscape of Aeaea was replaced by something familiar on an almost unbearably intimate level. Enough for a sob to fill her throat. She swallowed it back so as not to show weakness.

Fuckin' Leisureland.

They were at the funfair in Galway – where their da had brought them every other fuckin' weekend. Where their mam had bought them ice cream cones or toffee apples or candyfloss from the vans. Where they'd had their first crushes, on the sprightly lads with muscly arms who spun the waltzers. Their Irish home away from home.

It was night, and the fair was sound asleep, but with a snap of Satanis's fingers, the attractions around them came alive. Jazzy multicoloured lights came on at the same time as the waltzers started waltzing to her left. The Ferris wheel groaned to life. The witch outside the ghost-train began to cackle. Ultra Naté's 'Free' boomed from the funhouse while the carousel had its own calliope. It even smelled how she remembered: sugar; engine grease; hormones. Was this real? Was it now?

Satanis grinned with Ciara's teeth as it read her thoughts. 'Oh, it's real, and it's now.'

Niamh shook her head. 'Don't do this.'

'It's all going down the plughole, Priestess. But first I want you to see your home reduced to dust.' He held out a hand, and the funhouse burst into flames.

'No!' Niamh cried as the Ferris wheel collapsed in on itself, the metal struts almost screaming as they bent and snapped. Not Galway. Precious sweet Galway. She'd kept her memories of this city pressed like flower petals in her mind. It was quaint, charming and perfect to her, as perfect as memories of butterscotch Angel Delight and Sherbet Dib Dabs.

She fought back. She punched out with the full force of the Seal of Solomon.

Maybe she'd taken him by surprise, but he did reel backwards, tumbling onto the roof of the ghost train. He crashed through the fake, fibre glass tiles. She heard an electronic ghost wail from with.

It was only seconds until Ciara's form rose out of the wound in the roof. He was poised, uninjured. He hovered alongside the green, hook-nosed witch, giving her a nod of solidarity. 'Hey, sis, looking good.'

Ciara had to be in there. She just had to be.

He idled back down to the muddy pathways between the attractions, and insouciantly plucked a pair of dodgem cars clean out of the ride. The demon hurled them at Niamh and all she could do was block them, shattering them into smithereens. She shielded herself from plastic splinters as Satanis strode closer.

What could she do? What did she have to hand? Looking left to right for inspiration, she saw a game stall housing a row of gleaming water cannons. She'd played it a hundred times; you fired at targets to make dolphins race towards a finish line.

Water. Niamh flexed her newfound control of the elements to draw as much liquid up through the pipes as she could. There were demons in the subterranean water, so it was hers to master. The hoses snapped around on their pedestals to point towards her sister. Niamh fired them; seven powerful blasts of water shot towards the demon.

Niamh wrapped the torrent around Satanis like a lasso and,

once he was completely encapsulated, froze it solid. An iceberg in Galway. It felt like nothing was beyond her now. She took a brief satisfaction in this. Helena would have been proud.

Her elation was short-lived. The ice turned to icing sugar. She could taste it on the wind. Satanis stepped out of the white mist, shaking Ciara's horns clean of powder. 'Why aren't you learning, you fucking imbecile? I am the creator of this reality now.'

If she couldn't outfight him, her only hope rested in outsmarting him. *Think, Niamh, think.* The Prince of Lies ... lies. 'Really?' she said. 'Then turn *me* to sugar. Do it!' She had a feeling that if he could do that, he already would have.

'Where's the fun in that? I relish the fight.'

Bullshit, thought Niamh. No one likes effort. Everyone takes the shortcut. Belial was in there though, the demon behind every war and conflict on the planet. Even though ... 'Do it. If you can do it, do it.'

'I don't have to prove anything to you, witch.'

'Because I can do this.' Niamh opened her hand and Satanis burst into flames. Her sister's throat screamed. It was only for a second or two, but it was terrible to hear.

Satanis extinguished the fire with an almost bored expression on his face. 'You couldn't bring yourself to kill the girl. You're hardly going to kill your twin sister.'

With a flick of Ciara's wrist, he tossed her, like a ragdoll, onto the carousel. Niamh landed on the wooden planks on the outer rim of the ride. A carnival of horses cantered around her, each with a golden pole through their middle. From flat on her back, their painted eyes looked deranged and wild.

Get up, she told herself.

Satanis floated onto the carousel and rode a horse side-saddle to where Niamh had come to a rest. He hopped off his steed and delivered a kick to her midriff. She rolled into the wooden rail at the edge of the attraction. Her ribs throbbed. She felt the crown will her to stand.

'Get up, you pussy,' Satanis leered. 'Fight me like a girl.'

Niamh levitated herself at the devil. She wrapped her hands around his throat. 'I killed you once before.'

She pushed him up through the circular derby and up against the intricately painted central column, where the controller would operate the carousel. Niamh pushed Ciara's skull against the flashing amber bulbs.

Alas, she only felt a glimmer of the rage she'd felt ten years ago. Back then she'd believed her sister had slain Conrad. She knew better now. She knew Ciara better now.

'Then do it again.' The demon's black eyes bulged.

To sever a demon. Did it work like severing a witch? To do that, one asserts their own psyche into that of another like a wrecking ball. It's quick and artless; a ram raid; a smash and grab. Niamh slid into Satanis's mind.

It wasn't nice.

Starving children, corrupt priests, raping soldiers, paedophiles, thieves and abject misery. Inside him was a human stain. Every awful thought and feeling Niamh had ever had lingered in his mind; every jealous sour; every depressive belch and ache.

She had to withdraw.

Satanis laughed in her face, but in a way it helped. This wasn't Ciara. 'You could have been my queens! You could have served eternally in the kingdom of Satanis, and you chose mortal death! You chose to rot like meat. You don't deserve to call yourselves witches. You're nothing more than flying humans . . .'

Do it, a voice whispered, as Satanis continued to rant. A message under the noise.

The real world slowed down.

Ciara?

He can't hear me. Don't say a word.

'Where do you want to die, High Priestess? I shall save you and the bitch child until last so you can see the pain and . . .'

Listen. There's the dagger in my – his – belt. Cerridwen. Use it.

What?

The blade is Irish. It contains the power of the Irish coven, and like a fucking eejit he brought it home. Use it. He needs form in this reality – you can kill him.

He'll just use someone else.

No, Ciara said, *I'm playing dead. I'm stronger than he thinks. I can contain him – all three of him. I can take him with me.*

Niamh tightened her grip on her sister's throat. Satanis continued to laugh and laugh, but now he sounded strangled, gasping for air. In this world, even demons need to breathe. Niamh screamed a frustrated scream and hoped it drowned out their internal conversation.

Take him where?

Ciara didn't answer, and she didn't have to. Niamh had already been to the black gulf that waited beyond this reality. She knew only too well where they were all headed. Towards a deep dark nothing.

Niamh, this is it. We have one shot.

I don't want to.

When did either of us get what we want?

Niamh admitted something she never ever thought she'd say. *But I only just got you back.*

In these few days together, it had become clear to her how much she'd missed her sister. A paltry few days. She wanted more. A lot more. Even as Niamh wrung her sister's neck, she could imagine them, just the two of them, talking. Here, this night, picking at candyfloss as the calliope played its jaunty tune.

Niamh. Ciara paused. *Do you forgive me?*

Niamh fought the urge to laugh because the issue had always been if she'd forgive herself. She wished she'd seen that before. When they'd had more time. *Yes!*

Then please, Ciara urged. *Let me go. This way I can't fuck up a good thing. Let me go out on a high. Tell everyone I did one good thing.*

It wasn't fair. Niamh was finally ready to admit she'd always got the better deal. She'd got the cottage, the fiancé, the adopted daughter, the girl squad. Ciara had got the shitty end of the stick her whole life.

Let me do it, Niamh said. *It should be me. I died once, I can die again.*

But it's not you. He's inside me. I've got him Niamh. Do you trust me?

A pause. *Yes.*

Niamh looked up.

Satanis's black eyes widened and there was a gasping noise like he was choking. His whole body went stiff for a second and then his head jerked side to side, front and back, impossibly fast. Niamh heard his neck click and clack and then stillness. His head lolled forwards before he rose it steadily.

The horns were still there, but Ciara's eyes were grey-green again. There was a faint smile of triumph on her lips. She did it; she had him. She said aloud, 'Now! Fucking do it now! *Right in the peach stone.*'

The exact words Niamh had used in the mortuary.

What? Had she known? All this time.

'Forgive me,' Niamh breathed.

Ciara pressed her forehead against her sister's for a moment. 'Already done,' she said.

Niamh reached around Ciara's waist and felt where she'd stowed the dagger. She clutched the hilt and whipped it free of the belt in one fluid motion. Ciara's eyes were black again but that made it no easier. Satanis wore an expression of faint puzzlement that turned to horror as he saw what she held.

Drawing her elbow back, thick tears running down her face, Niamh plunged the blade at her sister's heart.

It was dreadful, and fast. Ciara's breastbone gave no fight as it sliced through skin and flesh and bone. Niamh only stopped when she felt metal scrape against the wooden panel of the ride.

No horns, no blackened irises, no claws. Ciara's pale fingers teased the hilt jutting from her chest, before flopping to her side. She said nothing, but her face was briefly ecstatic, and then slack. Niamh felt her body go limp and fold forwards. She withdrew the blade.

Niamh wrapped her arms around her sister and they both sank to the gangplanks between the horses. They continued to circle as the stallions galloped up and down in graceful arcs. The music played on. Ciara breathed, but in horrible wet, rasps as Niamh cradled her – holding her sister's head to her chest, burying her nose in her hair.

Then Ciara breathed no longer, and Niamh was alone, truly, for the first time in her whole life.

SWEET

Elle - Heaea

Milo was beautiful, and tranquil as he slept. He was as naked as the day he was born. Elle wasn't sure where he came from. One second he wasn't there and the next he was, splayed on a patch of wild grass a few metres further down the hillside from where she'd been hiding.

The fearsome wind abated, all at once, replaced by a mild breeze. The gulls started to call again. It would soon be dawn. Elle looked up, and the violent, ugly slit had gone from the sky. She wasn't wholly sure what that meant. Had they won? Or were they all dead? Is that why *he* was here?

Elle had studied *Paradise Lost* for English A-Level, and she'd always been obsessed with the black-and-white illustration of Lucifer; naked aside from a loincloth, winged and muscular. Her son reminded her of that drawing now. Even unconscious, there was a considered beauty to the curve of his arm over his head, the arch of his heel.

Elle knelt at his side. She poked his chest. He was *human*, and solid, and his chest rose and fell as he breathed. She ran a hand a few inches above his torso and she didn't register any internal injuries.

She placed a finger to his temple and woke him gently. His

eyes fluttered open and he still had his father's eyes. He always had, everyone said. 'Where am I?' he said.

'It's OK,' Elle told him. 'You're safe, back on Aeaea. I don't know where you came from.'

'She did it,' he stuttered. 'The witch beat me. I fled like a coward as my brothers drowned.' He spoke to himself more than her. He seemed to take in his surroundings, and then her. His expression softened to one she recognised very well. Her son, in need. 'Mum, I fucked up. Can you forgive me?'

He sat up and threw his arms around her shoulders. As she had done a million times in her dreams, she rubbed his back. Soothed him.

'You're not my son,' Elle said. A tear ran down the side of her nostril.

He looked at her, face so sweetly boyish. 'I am now. Mum, I'm just a boy now. I'm *Milo*.'

And he was. He needed her.

'You were a wonderful mother.'

Elle nodded slowly. 'I know. I am.'

She stroked his sandy hair off his forehead. And then she seized his skull with both hands. Didn't hesitate for a single second. Elle had been saving up her pain. She'd stored seventeen years of grief, and betrayal, and frustration away for a rainy day.

Now it poured.

She channelled every drop from the spaces between her stress-knotted sinew, out through her palms, and into his skull.

Lucifer was a silent for a second and then screamed. He howled. He gripped her wrists, but she held on tight.

'Mum! Mummy!'

No. 'You are not my fucking baby boy!' She screamed like she had never before screamed. He had a brain now, and lungs, and bones and a heart. Elle rotted them, turned them black and cancerous until they dripped out of his nose and mouth and eyes like oven grease.

She held on until the boy went limp and silent. Then she dropped him. Like rotted fruit, brown and bruised, he lay slumped over the rocks, slack and lifeless.

Smarmy piece of lying shit.

Elle stood and drew a deep breath through her nostrils. She smoothed down her dress and drew herself taller.

Satisfying, she thought.

A NEW DAWN

Niamh - Aeaea

There was such oneness between herself and the crown, that Niamh didn't even need to consciously think about getting back to Aeaea. One minute they were on the carousel in Leisureland, and the next they were back on the craggy mountaintop. She'd held on to Ciara's body throughout.

Niamh laid her sister flat and stroked the hair off her face. A cliché, but she did look peaceful. She also looked small, and frail. It was painful to see the truth of her; Ciara had always made herself seem bigger than she was. A feral cat hissing and puffing out her fur.

'Is it over?' A familiar voice spoke, and Niamh turned with a gasp of surprise and relief. She took hold of Theo's face and examined her – inside and out. She was just her again, only more confused, and freezing up here on the summit. She still wore the ceremonial armour, but looked lost inside it now. Niamh pulled her into a bear hug. She needed it, and was sure Theo probably did too.

Niamh removed the Seal of Solomon from her head. Finally, quiet.

Theo hesitated and then asked. 'Is she . . . ?'

Niamh nodded. She'd cried all her tears, and yet still felt damp inside somehow. Her voice was similarly waterlogged when she finally spoke. 'And before you even think it, *no*.'

'Don't worry, I've learned my lesson. No more raising the dead.' She stroked Ciara's cool cheek. 'She took him down with her. I don't doubt I could revive her with the Seal, but I'd only be bringing him back too.'

'Back from where?'

'That place. Wherever I was.' Niamh sighed. 'She's gone.'

'I'm so sorry,' Theo said. 'I kinda loved her, you know?'

Niamh managed a brief chuckle. 'Everyone did! I wish *she* knew. She never knew. Because I didn't tell her. I pretended I was so angry with her, but . . . There should have been another way.'

That hung between them. Niamh just held her. She didn't want to let go. Oh, Ciara. What would she have done in her forties? Her fifties? Beyond? She didn't know because her brain wasn't as nimble as Ciara's had always been.

Her sister's entire adult life had been blighted by shit choice after shit choice. For about five optimistic minutes, Niamh had seen something more for her – had allowed herself to. The world needed women like her sister, women who didn't give a dry shit what people thought of them, who acted on instinct, and without reservation.

Ciara had spent so long – too long – trying to be like Niamh. Maybe, if there was a lesson to dig out of all this rubble and dust, it was that she ought to be more like Ciara.

Niamh leaned over and planted a tender kiss on Ciara's forehead. *Farewell.* She pursed her lips and gently blew on her skin. Ciara's body turned to a golden dust, and scattered to the wind like sand, returned to the elements and to Gaia. The cloud lingered on the breeze a moment, and then she was gone. The sky was whole again. Indigo with golden clouds, dawn just on the horizon. There would be a tomorrow after all. Far away, and soon, the people of the world would be waking up, and heading to their Nespresso machines. They would remain blissfully unaware as to how Satan almost unravelled the rug of reality from under their feet.

'Leviathan will rise,' Theo muttered.

'I wish they'd been clearer on the *then He will fall* part,' Niamh said ruefully.

Theo took her hand. 'What do we do now?'

Niamh looked out at miles and miles of rippling sea. Gaia, beaming up at them. She was back, and she was grateful. Niamh could feel it. She was in the air and the breeze and the dew. She was in the tide and the light.

'Whatever we want,' Niamh said.

They met Elle a few metres from the summit. She stood over Milo Pearson's dead body. His blue eyes were vacant and his skin was pruned and grey. 'I killed him,' Elle said. 'He said Ciara killed the other two.'

'Good,' replied Niamh. Something of want, hate and fear would always live in every human heart, but that's where they'd stay. Hopefully.

They, all of them, needed some time, and so they walked the zigzag trail down the mountain in companionable silence. It didn't need saying that the breaking dawn was the most beautiful any of them had ever witnessed.

In the distance, Niamh saw two figures waiting for them in an olive grove on the promontory overlooking the bay and the lighthouse on the island. They waited patiently and Niamh couldn't find it in her to rush. As they came closer, she recognised Calista's gait. Her companion was less familiar, though she had seen traces of her within Leonie's mind: the young woman, Senait.

She greeted them with a knowing smile. The morning sun turned her curls to pure gold. 'Well done,' she said. 'Nailed it.'

Calista embraced Niamh, stroking her hair. 'We have known such loss,' the old woman whispered in her ear. 'But you more than most.'

Niamh said nothing. Calista turned her attention to Theo. 'And there she is. I did not dare hope we might have this moment.'

She rested a wrinkled hand on Theo's cheek and told her

everything she needed to know with that touch. 'You know me?' Theo said, eyes wide.

'Oh yes, I raised your mother.'

The information wove its way into Theo's understanding. 'You're my great-grandmother? No way . . .'

It was with great sadness that Niamh realised she was going to lose Theo too. The lost sheep had finally come home to her flock.

'But that means . . . you can tell me who I am?'

Calista smiled kindly, stroking a lock of raven hair off the girl's face. 'All in good time, my child. Theodora Theodopolis.'

And then Theo looked to Niamh, a glint in her eye. 'Um, no.'

'Yeah, that's awful,' Niamh agreed.

'Theo Kelly, I think,' Theo said. 'If Niamh will have me.'

It didn't need saying, of course she'd have her. There, a little bit of something good in the distance. The future and its warm promise.

'I have to be going,' Senait gently interrupted their little moment. 'I've done my job and I need to get the Seal back to the right place and time before it's too late.'

'What do you mean?' asked Niamh.

Senait sighed, a little sadly. 'All good things . . . I guess Gaia couldn't let me have this gift forever. Can you imagine if I fucked something up, or started going around killing Hitler and stuff?'

'I don't get it,' Elle said.

'I'm running out of steam,' Senait clarified. 'I can feel it. Each trip gets harder and harder, and takes longer.'

'The circle is almost closed,' added Calista. 'Once the Seal is placed back in the Shrine of Sheba, everything will be as it should be.'

Theo figured it out before Niamh did. 'But will you get back?'

Senait nodded. 'I always find my way home. Here. Aeaea is in my blood.' She gave Calista a lingering hug and kissed both cheeks. 'I'll see you soon, Auntie Cal.'

'Travel safe, my child.'

Senait held out her hands and Niamh handed over the seal. 'Careful with this thing,' she told her. 'It packs a punch.'

'Oh I know.' She gave them a wink. 'I gave it to my mum thousands of years ago.'

Calista slapped her playfully. 'You must stop doing that, Senait.' She half-apologised, laughing as she did so.

'You're Leonie's daughter?' Elle asked. 'You look like her. Like Chinara too.'

Gaia doesn't make mistakes, Niamh thought.

'I feel like I know you all,' Senait said, the sea-breeze lifting her cloud of curls into ever-shifting shapes. 'Growing up I heard so many tales about the Hebden Bridge witches and their adventures at Her Majesty's Royal Coven. Wish I'd been there.'

'You don't,' Elle and Niamh said in perfect unison.

Senait smirked and it was a hundred per cent Lee's smirk. 'I'm glad I got to meet you in real life . . .' As she said the final word, she dissolved in a golden shimmer, teleporting herself back in time.

'Mum!' Holly's voice cracked the tranquillity of the dawn. The girl charged down the temple path and threw herself at her mother. 'Are you OK?'

'I am now,' Elle said.

Further down the path was Luke, still dirty and bloodied from the fight on the beach. He walked with a slight limp. It figured that he hadn't wanted to bug the healers in the aftermath, but Niamh felt it was time to heal Luke. She went to him and touched her fingers to his cheek. She said nothing, but he nodded and she let her radiance flow into his skin.

His cuts and grazes healed. 'Thank you,' he said.

No pain can last forever, she told herself. *It can get to the point where you don't even feel it anymore but you tell yourself it's there all the same just to have something to hold on to.* She wasn't mad at him, even if she ought to be.

'Where's Leonie?' Elle asked Holly. 'Does she need my help? Did the baby come?'

Calista simply turned to the sea. The sun was all the way out of the water now, heading for the sky. It made a perfect black silhouette out of the little boat coming from the lighthouse on the archipelago towards the main island dock. The motorboat chugged towards them, leaving a chevron in its wake.

Leading the way, Calista started downhill to greet the boat. Confused, Niamh took Theo's hand and followed.

There were two figures on the boat – one waving, as the other piloted the craft. As they came closer, it was clear the pilot was unmistakeably Chinara. And the waving woman sported wild Diana Ross hair, blowing like a sail in the wind . . .

'What?' Elle said. 'I don't get it.'

Niamh squinted against the rising sun. So the hair was silver, and there were a few more lines and wrinkles, and her figure was fuller, but she was somehow even more beautiful and vibrant. Niamh forced herself to close her mouth and hide her shock.

This woman, clearly well into her fifties, was Leonie Jackman.

A BRIEF HISTORY OF SENAIT OKAMAN

Leonie - Aeaea, 2001

The lighthouse on the archipelago known as Cecilia's Island had been built originally in 1590, all beams and clay and open fires. Now it was to be their home. With the sound of the ocean just outside their window, Leonie hadn't experienced such restful slumber in her entire life.

Senait, for the first year of her life, slept between her and Chinara in their bed. Even as an infant, Leonie felt her potential buzz like a hummingbird's wings. Her daughter was a witch like no other.

It was not yet summer and, of an evening, they needed to light a fire. One such night, by the stove in their kitchen-cum-living-room, Leonie shared her fears with Chinara. 'Is it fair?' She looked at the perfect little baby in her basket. 'That she was born to be a weapon?'

'She will bring peace.' Chinara idly stroked the infant's tender head. She had an outrageous amount of hair for one so young. 'What weapon ever did that?'

'But she's just a little girl,' Leonie said. Senait had been born intersex – as, of course, they had known she would be. It was complicated to assume her gender, but Leonie *knew* how she chose to define herself in the future. Still, she hoped it wasn't she who imposed that decision on her, some self-fulfilling prophecy.

'Every other little girl in the world has a gazillion possibilities in front of them. Senait only has one.'

'She is special,' Chinara conceded. 'So we will have to be very special mothers.'

They kissed, and it sealed a promise.

Time was different on Aeaea. They had the same twenty-four hours, but life was no longer split into work and home; it was more a case of light and night. With the Greek sun on her skin, Leonie felt charged by solar power. Exactly why had she toiled on that rainy little racist rock her whole life?

During the daytime hours they'd take the boat over to the mainland and help the other witches with the gardens or in the temple kitchens. There were other children for Senait to play with as she grew older. There was Tamar, a witch who'd once been an infant-school teacher, and she gladly ran a sort of creche most days. Leonie often assisted, not wanting to miss a second of Senait's development. Calista's lion cub, Nyssa, arrived within days of Senait's birth, almost as if the beast was sent by Gaia to protect the child.

It was a daily miracle, watching their little human grow and change and learn. Their daughter was bright and funny and precociously chatty, somehow mimicking Leonie's Yorkshire accent. She quite literally ran before she could walk, launching herself across the lighthouse tiles, confident to the point of reckless. Leonie could only think it was genetic.

Chinara used her advocacy skills to approach other women around the globe that the oracles had flagged as being in danger. She told them the story of Aeaea; of how there was a secret island where they could stay for as long as they needed to ensure their safety. Occasionally she would use the water conduit system to reach these witches, although she couldn't return to the UK, not while there was a younger Chinara Okafor studying and training at HMRC. Nor could they risk leading the agents of Satanis to their home.

They'd maybe been on Aeaea for two years when the tension knots in their shoulders unclenched. Senait was a bubbling toddler and they were safe. This was their life now, and they needed neither fight nor flight.

When Senait was about four years old, Chinara and Leonie made some raspberry ripple ice cream with her and asked if she wanted to be a boy, or a girl, or neither. The child looked at them as if they were both raving lunatics and said 'GIRL,' as if it was the most obvious thing in the world. And that was the end of that.

Once Senait didn't need her mothers so constantly, things began to shift between Leonie and Chinara. A lot of things happened at once.

Sex. It's wild to expect sex with one person to be consistently surprising, which was why they, as a couple, had always been fairly open to the idea of novelty with other partners. But, in the years following Senait's birth, their sex life had morphed into sexless life, in that they kissed and cuddled and spooned, but orgasms were few and far between. This shift happened so slowly that neither of them really noticed until Leonie, as she supervised Senait and some other children digging a pit on the beach, realised it had been almost a year since they'd had sex.

Lesbian Bed Death comes for us all.

Around this time, it also became fairly clear that Chinara – now forty-four – was not, in fact, routinely having tiny heart attacks. She was perimenopausal, which went some way to explaining things.

The final thing to happen was Zehra. She had come to the island from Madrid about two years before they did, fleeing her ex-husband. As the coven drank wine or ouzo in the olive grove or in the temple, Leonie started to find herself wishing that everyone else would fuck off so she could be alone with the archaeologist. The woman was incredible. The shit her brain knew was wild. Philosophy, and religion, and cultural history. Leonie's grandma came from Barbados as part of the Windrush Generation, but Zehra knew so much about how her ancestors had travelled from Africa to the Americas, and their tribal roots.

Moreover, Leonie couldn't deny their mutual desire. It was obvious for everyone to see, including Chinara.

'What are we going to do about this?' Chinara finally asked one night in bed. The crickets were cricketing in the grasses outside their shuttered windows.

'I don't know. This isn't London. Zehra is our friend.' That being said, lesbian London was so incestuous, Leonie didn't see how it would be worse to start something on such a small island. Any gay woman gathering in Stoke Newington was certain to host at least two of their exes.

'You love her.'

Leonie propped herself up onto an elbow. 'I don't love you less. You and I are one. We are forever. I wouldn't be without you, not ever.'

Chinara kissed her. Her teeth glinted in the dark of their bedroom. 'So let's do something about that.'

And so Leonie starting dating Zehra, and married Chinara. They were two different women, and as such, her relationships with each were their own thing. She always came home to Chinara and Senait. She would not sleep away from either.

Calista blessed their union in a coven ceremony in the olive grove at sunset. Senait, then five, acted as a flower girl and bridesmaid. Both brides wore simple white linen slips and held native posies tied in twine.

'Leonie? Do you commit to Chinara for as long as it feels good?'

'I do.'

'And, Chinara, do you commit to Leonie for as long as it feels good?'

'I do.'

And with that, Leonie and Chinara *Okaman* made it as official as any witch ever does.

For another five years, things continued in this vein. The routine of getting Senait off to her lessons, tending to their community, seeing Zehra for exquisite massages and sex, spending lazy evenings with Chinara once Senait was asleep, cooking or reading. Gods, when had she last read a novel? In school? She *finally* got round to reading all those books she'd previously pretended to have read: Toni Morrison, and bell hooks, and Octavia Butler, and Zadie Smith, who wrote about women who looked like her! It was a revelation.

Leonie thought often about her other self, quitting HMRC to found Diaspora. With fondness she remembered that whiplash ambition, the pyromania with which she'd burned bridges. Her ambitions were still there, certainly, but were often eclipsed by her more pressing goal of getting Senait to eat a fucking vegetable with every meal.

It was not that her previous aims were less important than her role as a mother, it was that she'd valued *love* less than *success*. Allowing herself to luxuriate in her affection for her child, her wife and her lover now felt as rewarding as money or seeing her coven grow. She felt foolish for writing off emotional wins as feminine or weak. She wanted both.

There was one dark cloud over the island: Leonie knew Zehra would die on her 'first' visit to Aeaea in fifteen years' time. She also knew that the future could not change, not when the risk was existence itself. The foreknowledge took a heavy toll on Leonie, and Zehra, a sentient, could feel it.

There was a thermal bath deep within the caves below the temple. It was somewhere Leonie kept sacred for them. 'When you're with me, there's always just a little shot of melancholy in you,' Zehra said as they swam naked. 'Is it guilt?'

'Not at all!' Leonie told her. 'You know where I came from.'

Zehra swam close so their nipples touched. 'The future is dark and full of terrors.'

'You have no idea.'

She knotted her hands at the back of Leonie's neck. 'So then this sadness does not bode well for me.'

'You know I can't say. If I change anything . . .'

Zehra kissed her lips. 'My darling. There is not one thing I would change. I was so trapped, and now I am so free.' Zehra didn't speak of her horrific ex-husband, but Leonie had seen her nightmares. 'How can I regret any of this? What a fucking gift, to know what real love feels like.'

But Aeaea was too small for Zehra Darga. Leonie saw it coming a mile away, and she wasn't even an oracle; Zehra eventually wanted more. She wanted to study for her doctorate, and so off to Oxford she went, and Leonie felt worse than she'd felt since they'd arrived here. Her girlfriend was happy and fulfilled, but now on the path that would lead to her death.

Maybe one day, the fog of sadness would go. It hadn't yet.

Menopause came for Leonie too, and it was fucking horrific. About twice a week, she literally felt like she was going to fall off a cliff – a sort of breathless rush in her chest; the rest of the days, she felt like the layer immediately under her skin was on fire. Brutal. Luckily, a kindly pharmacist witch ferried HRT through the water conduit or Leonie would have considered early death.

On Senait's thirteenth birthday, they decided it was time. Chinara and Leonie took her to Calista at the temple, because they wanted this moment to feel reverential. 'Why are we here?'

'You know you're special, don't you?' Chinara told her. The four of them were alone in the great banquet hall.

'Is this about my penis?' The teenager had, perhaps unfortunately, failed to inherit Chinara's filter, leaving her mouth much more like her other mum's.

Leonie laughed. 'Not this time.'

Calista helped them out. 'Sweet Senait. When you were born, you were a great gift. From Gaia herself.'

'Fuck off.'

'Senait!' Chinara snapped.

'Sorry, Mama.'

Calista continued. 'And now I have to quote a very wise person: *With great power comes great responsibility.*'

'Isn't that Spider-Man?' Leonie asked.

'Indeed it is.'

That night in the temple changed everything. Of course Senait rebelled – she was thirteen. She didn't want a divine crusade; she wanted an iPhone. There was a pain barrier to push through. The oracles showed her, as best they could, the ruination Leviathan would bring upon the earth, but what a responsibility to place on her young shoulders.

There followed months of silent treatment or tantrums if her unique fate was mentioned over the dinner table. There were only three doors in the whole lighthouse and they were all slammed, repeatedly.

In the end it wasn't showing her death and destruction that helped Senait come to terms with her role; it was *stories*. Stories about how her mothers met on an HMRC mission in North Wales during a skirmish between rival factions of witches and warlocks. Stories about five girls in a treehouse the night before their oath-taking ceremony. Stories about women that could fly, or turn cheating husbands to stone. Stories of laughter and tears and the Spice Girls.

Leonie showed her the world of friendship outside of Aeaea. The things Leonie lived for. Something else Senait had inherited from Leonie was a sense of adventure and her task was now a vocation.

Training began in earnest. Every witch on Aeaea devoted themselves to getting Senait ready for the day she would leave the island. A true coven. The banquet room in the temple became a war room of charts and maps, displaying where Senait needed to be and when. An ageing actress from Notting Hill, Harriet Mullan, taught Senait in the arts of improvisation and role-play. The girl who'd only experienced island life would have to be, in no particular order, a runaway from Bolton, an exotic dancer, and the motherfucking Queen of Sheba.

They made a book for Senait to take with her. For her, and her only, life would be linear. 'And whatever you do,' Leonie told her one night, 'you make sure I don't get that abortion, or we're all fucked.'

'Language,' Chinara told her from the armchair next to the fire.

It all came round so fast. The older you get, the faster time seemed to ebb away. Increasingly, Leonie found she was trying to claw back the minutes like she'd lost something in the sand.

Leonie, of course, knew only too well the time and place she met Domino: the trafficker who would imprison her daughter in a twisted travelling circus for the best part of six months. 'I hate this,' Leonie said the night before Senait had to go. None of them would sleep that night, but she tucked Senait into her bed regardless. Her walls were covered with posters of Drake and Pete Davidson and Harry Styles. She was still a girl, a girl of twenty years.

'It's how it has to be, Mum.' Senait was now the young woman she'd met all those years ago in Bologna. Beautiful, gregarious and fierce. She was ready, even if Leonie was not. 'But I'll see you soon. You won't know it's me, but hey ho.'

Leonie held her closer than ever before. 'Wherever you go, know that you were so loved.'

'I know. How lucky am I to know. Never ever had to question it because I've felt it my whole life. So, yeah, thanks for loving me.'

As the sun rose the next morning, a very brave Senait left them via the water conduit in the temple fountain, off to her fateful meeting with Domino in Ibiza. Chinara held Leonie in her arms, both of them sobbing.

Her departure signalled the end and the beginning. The loop drew tight like shoelaces.

The massacre at the temple had to happen for Hale to capture Leonie.

Zehra returned to Aeaea after she located the buried temple homing the Seal of Solomon, and Leonie and Chinara went into hiding within the caves. They couldn't risk being seen by the younger Leonie or Hale. There was also the risk Leonie would blurt something out in a bid to spare Zehra, and she knew she must not. It would bring the precarious Jenga crashing down.

But the night before the massacre, Zehra came to see them in the catacombs. Perhaps she was more psychic than they realised, or perhaps she'd spoken with oracles. Either way, she knew. She forgave. 'I will protect you, my darling. I will make sure they don't get to the villa where you sleep.'

Later that night, as Zehra kissed thirty-two-year-old Leonie in the olive grove, Calista brought Senait to them in the caves. After a tearful reunion, they spoke. 'Was it awful? Keeping it a secret?'

'Yes, but harder that I was like a stranger to you. I wanted to squeeze you to death but you didn't even know who I was! And I had to sell you out to that cunt Hale.'

'Don't you worry,' Leonie said ruefully. 'Your Auntie Ciara is gonna twist his head off any day now.' That chapter felt like a very, very long time ago, and – to them – it was.

They spent the night, and the awful morning, together in the caves. They could do nothing as Hale and his warlocks ravaged the coven. Leonie took only scant comfort in knowing the coven survived through her actions. But one dead woman is a woman too many.

After what felt like days Calista, her scarlet wrist crudely bandaged, came for them. The coast was clear. All they could do was tend to the dead and wounded, hose the blood into the bushes.

That terrible night in the caves was the last time Lee and Chinara would see their daughter for years. She could not stay; after all, she had her work to do.

The last four months had been the worst somehow. Zehra had died, and Senait was gone, and their coven, depleted. A funereal mood lingered as winter came. Leviathan was awake, Leonie could feel it. From the top of the old lighthouse, she watched the ocean, waiting for the day that he would rise as prophesied. She was fifty-four now, but what was age to her? A witch; a woman outside of her time. She'd let her hair grow grey, let it grow long.

The Greek sun puckered her skin, but it felt like a blessing to have made it this far.

And then, one day, the sky turned crimson-black and the battle came to Aeaea. Chinara could help a little, hinder the demons with bad weather, but they couldn't cross paths with their past selves in any way that might change the outcome of that day. Leonie *had* to give birth to Senait amidst the fire and carnage. There were no guarantees of a victory. But as they watched, the monster that came from the sky disintegrated and the slit in the sky sealed itself shut. The sun rose out of the sea, and Leonie understood Gaia was back in the building. She looked to her wife. 'It's time. The boat?'

What a giddy crossing it was. It only ever took fifteen minutes, but they were the longest of her life. They should have flown, but she realised a part of her was anxious and stalling for time. Her life was about to resume, without her having missed a single day.

She saw them gathering at the quaint little port. She saw Luke first – too tall to miss. Then Calista's silver locks, and Elle's white hair, and Holly, and Niamh and Theo. Where was Rad? And what about Ciara?

The boat reached the dock. She saw them stare down at her. She dreaded to think how fucking old she must look to them.

'Leonie?' Elle said, unsure. She was precisely as Leonie remembered her. Cherub-faced. Not an inch of dark regrowth at her roots.

'Don't you fucking say a word about my hair, Elle Pearson.'

'It's Elle *Device*. And you look absolutely beautiful.' She smiled.

Leonie took Luke's hand and climbed onto dry land. She gave Niamh a bear hug, but quickly turned to Calista because she couldn't hold it in anymore. 'Where's Senait? Is she back?'

'She just left to return the crown. She has not yet returned.'

Leonie nodded. Chinara took her hand and gave it a squeeze. Their daughter would return when her work was done. This certainty was the closest Leonie had ever felt to faith.

'I don't get it,' Holly said. 'You got old . . . er.' She added the last part very quickly.

Leonie laughed and gave the girl a hug. It was so funny how she could still remember her too-sweet perfume, even after all these years. 'Come on Hollybobs, let's get a big fuckin' cup of tea, because we have got twenty-two years to spill . . .'

PART III

· ○ ◐ ● ◑ ○ ·

COVEN 4EVA
18 MONTHS LATER . . .

We are friends for life. . . . When we're together the years fall away. Isn't that what matters? To have someone who can remember with you? To have someone who remembers how far you've come?

—Judy Blume

REFORMATION

Niamh - Hebden Bridge

Some days the nerves could be so much that even a bowl of Coco Pops was unthinkable. But then, she also knew that if she didn't have any breakfast she'd potentially get up on stage and vomit all over the front row.

A banana! There's always room for a banana.

Luke entered their dusty kitchen-diner, already in his overalls. He gave her a fleeting kiss, although Niamh suspected it was merely an excuse to reach past her to get to the cafetiere of coffee behind her. 'I think the en suite will be good to go today,' he told her.

She almost swooned like a Hollywood heroine, right into his arms. 'Don't you lie to me now . . .'

'I wouldn't dare.'

They were living in the newly renamed Old Watermill in Hardcastle Crags. *Her* grandmother's cottage in Heptonstall village was beyond salvation, of course, so Elle had forced her mother to pull Annie's out of a sale in order to sell it to Niamh; all was fair in love and real estate. Luke had *gutted* the old, cat-shitty cottage. There was a kitchen extension, all glass and light, and now, after several false starts, the attic conversion was finally ready for them to move into. It was to be the boudoir of her dreams, complete with a skylight so she could watch the stars from her bed. Luke had built her fantasy home.

Sometimes in the night, Niamh panicked and inwardly scoured for whatever horrors she'd forgotten, only to realise there weren't any. The battle was both lost and won. The human condition: the eternal ache of the stupid things we've said and done in the past, healed with the ointment of the promise that'll we do better from now on.

Luke too harboured such pain, but together, they were healing.

He was secretly planning to propose. She vowed to act surprised. She had already decided, many months ago, she would say yes. She didn't even look Conrad or Cari up anymore on socials. She found she was no longer interested beyond a cosy *good for him* sensation.

She gave Luke a longer kiss, and did draw a little confidence from him. She needed it.

Theo joined them in the kitchen. Now in Sixth Form, she no longer had to wear the grotty St Augustus uniform. 'Aren't you late?' Niamh chided.

'Free period,' she said, going straight for the Coco Pops. 'Are you sure you don't want me to come to Manchester? Or is it one of those brave things you have to do alone?'

Niamh took a sip of ginger tea. 'Darl, I won't be alone.'

As far as mundanes knew, the conference was a celebration of International Women's Day. In truth, the GMEX Centre (because no one would ever refer to it by its new name) was that day hosting Coven Con UK. Yes, Coven Convention was something of an oxymoron, but that was just how it had been for decades.

The conference centre opened to delegates at nine for welcome coffee and croissants, and the keynote speech was to start promptly at ten. The main hall was packed and buzzing. Witches, warlocks and High Priestesses from all over the world came to the annual convention, and for many it was the only time they saw each other. The hotel bars surrounding GMEX would be *messy* for the next three nights.

Niamh always thought of the bit in Roald Dahl's *The Witches*, only they never turned any kids into mice. Fuck, that book was hateful on reflection.

In the wings, a sound engineer told her she was good to go, and Niamh walked onto the stage, imagining pinching a pound coin between her shoulder blades to strut upright and sat back in her hips the way Helena used to say Naomi Campbell did it. She barely heard the applause for the blood pumping in her skull. She drew strength from the women closest to her: Leonie and Elle. Also up on stage with her were Head Oracle Emma Benwell, Shadow Cabinet liaison Selina Fay, Sandhya Kaur and Radley Jackman. Seats were arranged behind a long desk, microphones on bendy stick things before each one. Niamh settled into her position and poured herself a glass of water, fighting to stop her hands from shaking. Her throat was tundra dry. Oh fuck a duck. Here went nothing.

'Good morning, delegates.' In the front row, she got a wink from Chinara. Next to her, Alyssa Grabowski looked rather less impressed, sitting alongside various High Priestesses from around the globe.

'So here it is,' Niamh said, all one big exhale. 'I know there's been a lot of gossip and speculation over the last two years, but today we finally set out our vision for the future of Her Majesty's Royal Coven.'

Another deep breath.

'There is no future for Her Majesty's Royal Coven.'

It was a stunt-queen move, and sure enough the conference hall erupted. Her statement only confirmed what people had been saying privately, but here was their confirmation.

Under the desk, Elle gave her knee a squeeze. Leonie, her silver hair now in locs, told her. *You're smashing it.*

'Today, we unveil something we think is better.' Niamh waved a hand behind her and the logo she'd spent no less than one week and four meetings approving with the board appeared on the video screen behind her. 'I present the NUC.'

THE NATIONAL UNION OF COVENS

More giddy chatter amongst the witches and warlocks. Alyssa looked like she might keel over at any moment.

'For a long time, it's been clear to many of us that HMRC was not fit for purpose. In 1869 the founders were essentially blackmailed into serving the government. We were forced to do their bidding, or risk being persecuted as we were in the Bad Times. Well, no more. Times have changed. Leonie?'

Leonie was still the High Priestess of Diaspora, even if Kane Dior Sanchez mostly handled it day-to-day. They, too, sat with Chinara at the front. 'When I established Diaspora, it was because one coven does not fit all. We need covens, plural, that address the needs of witches in our communities.'

'And so many UK witches are already in local groups,' Elle said, jumping in to back Lee up. 'HMRC was just . . . *there*. And none of us really questioned it. I didn't until I started the Healers Network.'

Niamh nodded her agreement. 'Of course there will always be a need for witches to collaborate with the government, and that's why Selina Fay and her team will continue to head up the Shadow Cabinet.' Niamh thought Fay was a bit of a cunt, to be honest, but she worked hard. There was yet *another* new prime minister since Milner had been forced to step down in an expenses scandal. This latest one was Labour, not that you'd know it from her policies or haircut. 'And it's my great pleasure to reveal that Radley Jackman will continue as High Priest of the Warlocks' Cabal for another term.' He gave a polite nod. Niamh now looked to her old assistant, Sandhya. Oh, she'd come a long way since those lessons at her kitchen table. 'And finally, I've appointed Sandhya Kaur to a new role. She is from here on the High Priestess of a new coven: Fortress. A group of witches and warlocks dedicated to establishing lasting peace, and harmony with our environment. Now, more than ever, we need an end to global conflict and to expediate urgent action on climate destruction. Fortress is a modern coven for the world we live in now.'

Sandhya gave her a brief smile. *Let's do this*, she told her. Her protégée was more than ready.

'And what about me? Well, I'll still be High Priestess, but I'm more interested in helping you start and maintain your own regional covens. Tell me what you need! Is it funding? It is people power? Do you need security? Help with legal representation? *That's* what the NUC is going to be about. We are totally independent and have no ties to government, finally. You don't *have* to join, but in the words of my wise friend Leonie . . .'

'Join a fucking union.'

There was a ripple of laughter around the hall.

Niamh finally exhaled. 'OK. Any questions?'

Oh, and there were.

END UP HERE

Elle - Manchester, UK

Holly, talking to Theo, had a glass of champagne in her hand. Chilling to see her looking so grown up, honestly, but it was a champagne reception after all. One glass wouldn't hurt. When *they'd* been seventeen, they'd been doing much worse at bus stops and in graveyards. At least they were in the ballroom at the Lowry.

This was, Elle thought, very nice indeed. Excellent use of coven money. Even the big American witch seemed to have lightened up a bit, talking with Niamh across the room. Elle ensured she kept one eye on Holly and Theo as she chatted with some of the women in her Healers Network.

She wouldn't tell anyone, because she liked sympathy, but setting up her coven had been pretty easy. There are witch doctors and nurses scattered around the NHS. It was mad that they hadn't come together sooner, really. All she'd done was set up a private Facebook group. The rest almost did itself. Last year, she'd gone to Niamh to ask for a bit of money so she could give up some hours on her day job and that was what had inspired the shift from HMRC to NUC.

Across the ballroom, she saw Vish chatting to some of the Cabal lot. She had to say he scrubbed up rather well. He normally lived in the standard physio uniform of track pants and aertex

T-shirt. He clocked her staring and gave her a sly wink. She shook her head. It wasn't time to tell people just yet.

She plucked a mini burger off a passing silver tray and shoved it in her gob. Of course this was the moment Lee patted her on the shoulder. 'Having fun?'

Elle nodded and swallowed fast. 'I am! You?'

'We're gonna head off soon, I think. I'm an old lady now.'

'You ruddy are not! Stop it!'

Niamh joined them, holding Luke's drink while he was in the loo. 'What are we talking about, ladies?'

'Leonie is bailing.'

'No! We have to celebrate!'

She rolled her eyes. 'Twist my arm, go on, I'll have one more! One! Enablers!'

'If you told me one day Leonie Jackman would be the first to leave a party, I'd think you were possessed,' Niamh said.

They'd not changed, not really. Yes, it had taken a few weeks to wrap her head around Leonie ageing twenty-two years overnight, but she was absolutely the same woman. The feeling between them was the same as it had been in the treehouse on the night before their oathtaking. Call it vibes, call it chemistry, whatever. However many days or weeks or months went by without them seeing each other, not a single thing changed. Not a stitch was dropped. They knew the feeling would be there waiting for them when they got back together again. That, Elle thought, was the mark of true friendship.

Elle leaned in closer, conspiratorial. 'If I tell you girls something, do you promise to keep it a secret?'

'Is it about the strapping young physiotherapist?' Leonie said without flinching.

'Vish,' Niamh informed her. 'Cute, isn't he?'

'Oh for Gaia's sake!' Elle exploded. 'I've been trying so hard!'

'We're *very* psychic,' Lee said.

'Well don't say anything to our Hols.'

'You know she's very psychic too, right?' Niamh put in, doubt written all over her face.

Elle looked over at her new beau. He was tall, *Love Island* muscular, and his beard was almost too perfect. One whole arm was covered into tattoos of leopards and palms and vines. 'He's *twenty-nine*.' She could hardly bring herself to admit it.

'So?!' Lee laughed.

'I feel like a nonce. Am I a MILF?'

'I'd shag you, so yes,' Leonie said far too loudly. 'Kidding! Sorry, Elle, that'd be incest. Gag!'

Elle rolled her eyes. Ironically, perhaps, she'd been introduced to Vish through Radley Jackman not long after she'd started the network: *I know a young NHS warlock in your neck of the woods who's interested in your network . . .* Turned out he was interested in a lot more than her network. 'What do I do?'

Niamh plucked an errant strand of hair off her lip gloss. 'Elle. Does he make you happy?'

'Does he make you cum?' Lee added.

'Yes. And yes,' Elle said.

'Then there's your answer,' said Niamh.

'Repeat after me,' Leonie told her. 'We deserve joy.'

Elle raised her half-empty glass of bubbly. 'We deserve joy.'

They were clinking when Chinara ploughed across the dancefloor to join them. She was out of breath, but aside from a few silver hairs, the woman had barely aged a day. It was infuriating.

'What's up? Is the cab here?' Leonie asked her.

'No! I just got a phone call . . . from somewhere in Whitstable.'

'Where?'

'Kent coast.'

'What about it?'

Chinara's eyes glistened. 'It's *her*, my love. I found our daughter.'

THE SCENIC ROUTE

Leonie - Whitstable, UK

Senait had once told her she saw herself living by the sea, of hearing the tide on shingle as she fell asleep. It could only be that she dreamed of this.

The beach was busy with dogwalkers, and there were queues for coffees, or fish and chips, or whelks and jellied eels from the various huts and food trucks along the promenade. There was nothing else in the world like the British seaside. Seagulls dive-bombed or shat on tourists who weren't smart enough to hide their vinegar-soaked chips.

'There she is,' Chinara said as they waited outside the pre-agreed tearoom.

Leonie turned and knew her wife was right. She gripped Chi's hand for dear life. They had been forewarned that she looked different, and she did. It was a surprise to see her looking *so* elderly, but her aura was the same as it had always been: almost silver, like mercury.

A beautiful young woman pushed the wheelchair towards them down the seafront. Senait's time-lined face lit up on seeing them, and Leonie ran to meet her. She crouched before her as Senait held out her arms and Leonie pulled her into an embrace. Her mohair cardigan was so soft, and her skin was like silk paper. 'Mum.'

'My baby, oh my god.' Leonie withdrew and let Chinara have a turn at holding their daughter a moment.

By her – admittedly quite shit – mathematics, Senait was now ninety-two years old.

She was still quite beautiful, and there was a familiar naughtiness in her eyes and dimples. She was also very chic in her turban and pearls. She had aged flawlessly. But Leonie had *so* many questions.

They sought refuge in the chintzy tearoom on the beach and ordered tea and fruit scones. Jam and clotted cream. The tables had wipe-clean PVC covers featuring different fruits. They were on the lemon table. 'You need to eat something proper,' the pretty carer told her. She was British-Asian, and called Aurora. Leonie sensed she too was a witch. 'She lives off ruddy cake.'

'If something has to kill me, I want it to be a scone,' Senait replied.

Leonie smiled, her mind wistfully wandering. 'I used to hide carrots inside your mash.'

'And I still fished them out. Foul things. *That* I remember, although you must forgive me if I don't remember everything. Mind like a sieve.'

'Senait, where have you been?' Chinara said, fighting to keep her voice level. Leonie took her hand under the table.

'I've been right here,' she replied. 'Since 1953.'

'What?'

Senait took a sip of her tea before beginning. 'Oh, Mama, it all went tits up. I went to return the Seal, but I got it wrong. I left the crown where it needed to be, but my powers went haywire. I fell backwards to 1900, and I was fucked if I was gonna live through *two* world wars, so I managed one last push and got myself to 1953. Could be worse, I thought. I needed time to regain my strength so I could get back to my time.'

'Yes, and?' Leonie looked at her in exasperation. Clearly she had *not* got herself home.

She at least looked sheepish. 'I met our Graham.'

Senait told them the tale. One unremarkable night at a jazz club in Brixton, the old Brixton Leonie dreamed of, Senait had been alone at a small table, half-lost in a maze of the music, when a handsome man tapped her on the shoulder. He asked if she wanted another drink – a whisky sour. She'd come for the music, but with his gentle demeanour and kind eyes, she couldn't help but be instantly intrigued.

She'd left him that night with her lodging-house telephone number on a napkin. He'd left a message with Mrs Brahmachari before she'd even got home. The rest, as they say . . .

'He loved me for me, Mums.'

'He was lucky to have you,' said Leonie at once.

'And I was lucky too. A kind, funny, brilliant man he was. A musician; there wasn't an instrument he couldn't pick up and fathom. He died during the first lockdown.'

Chinara told her how sorry she was.

'I made a choice.' The older woman twiddled the plain golden wedding band on her finger. 'And a good choice it was, because we were together – not without our ups and downs – for sixty-eight years.'

Leonie didn't want to cry, but fuck, thinking of the ache she had felt, the fear of the past years without her daughter – she was going to. 'I'm sorry,' she said. 'It's . . . the last two years. We thought something had happened to you.'

Senait smiled – all her own teeth she'd informed them. 'Something did. Something *good*. Mum. Mama. Listen. I remember the day you told me who I was and what I had to do. I remember being a little bitch about it.'

Both Leonie and Chinara laughed, fondly. She had been.

'My childhood on Aeaea, looking back, was paradise. You loved me and prepared me for what was to come. But, when I met Graham, he felt like the first thing I had ever chosen for myself. No more fate or destiny . . . just good old-fashioned lovey-dovey stuff.'

Leonie nodded. 'I understand. I just wish we'd been there to see it all. To share it all with you. I wish we'd met Graham.'

'You'd have loved him. And I thought of you constantly as I watched my own sprogs grow.'

Now Leonie grabbed Chinara's arm. 'What?'

Aurora flailed, remembering herself. 'Oh my gods! Sorry, I thought you knew – this my Granny Sen.'

'How?'

Senait smiled. 'We went to Vietnam in '68 with some other witches to help those who were displaced by war. We adopted Rora's mum and her little brother. We travelled for a while and then settled here later.'

'By the sea.'

'By the sea,' Senait said. 'Somewhere along the way I forgot what year I left you in. Sorry. I'm not as sharp as I was.'

'Wait,' Chinara said, rubbing her temples. 'Does that make us great-grandparents?'

Aurora smiled. 'And my brother just had a baby, so you're actually great-*great*-grandparents.'

And that made *her* mother, still up in Leeds, a great-great-*great*-grandmother. Leonie looked to her wife and said nothing, only beamed. How wonderful, after everything they'd been through, that there were still surprises left in this miserly world.

'So don't you worry,' Senait said, spreading clotted cream onto half a scone. 'There's plenty of opportunity for you to watch your acorns grow into trees . . .'

Leonie Okaman rested her head on Chinara's shoulder and felt all of time stop, just for her family. How far they had come, how fast they had run, and now they could finally stand still.

74

GOODBYE

Niamh - Hebden Bridge, UK

'Are you sure you don't want me to come? Or I could get the coven to teleport you?'

They stood next to Theo's third-hand red Skoda, on the road above the Old Watermill. The car had been a gift on her eighteenth birthday. She grinned. 'I think I'll be fine. I drove to Glastonbury, and that was further.'

Niamh stroked her hair. 'I know, I just want another three hours with you.' Niamh was already suffering dreadful empty nest syndrome, and Theo wasn't even gone yet.

'I'll be back in twelve weeks.'

The Bethesda School of Dance beckoned for Theo. She didn't seem remotely nervous. Niamh figured she'd been through worse. So much worse. How bad could a dance college for witches be?

Elle and Holly had come to see her off, too. Holly was ugly crying. 'Hol, you know WhatsApp works in Wales, right?'

'I know! I don't know why I can't stop crying.' Luckily, Holly's – gender-neutral term for a girlfriend or boyfriend – was with them too. Rae had been on the scene for a few months now – they'd met at a teen witch camp over the summer. They seemed like perfectly good craic. They were a big fan of piercings and dungarees from what little Niamh knew of them.

Elle took her turn to hug Theo, and then Luke – who'd booked the morning off especially. 'What am I gonna do without your shite music?' he told her.

'I made you a playlist.' Theo grinned. 'Didn't want you to feel left out.'

He rubbed yet more plaster dust out of his hair. 'Why do I know so much about Korean teenagers?'

'And witches.'

'That too,' he said with a smile. 'I love you, kiddo.'

'I love you too.'

And finally, it was her turn. Theo couldn't edge any further towards the car without hitting it. Niamh held her tight. 'I don't know what to say.'

'So don't say anything. It'll sound like *The End*, and it isn't.'

'Of course it fucking isn't. This is your home.'

'*You're* my home,' Theo said quietly.

Then she got into the driver's seat, slammed the door, and started the ignition. All of Hardcastle Crags immediately shook with K-pop. Theo only turned it up further as she pulled out of their driveway, waving as she went.

Both Luke and Elle wrapped their arms around Niamh as she waved Theo off, the car getting smaller and smaller as she drove downhill towards Hebden Bridge. 'I'll be OK, just give me a minute.'

Theo was right. Niamh thought about everyone she had and drew a little bit of strength from these cherished faces in her mind: her friends; her fiancé; her witches.

Wherever these people were, she was home.

She followed them inside, in the direction of the kettle.

VIVA FOREVER

There is a secret island of women.

And off that island, there is a sea.

And in that deepest trench of that sea, there is a tiny black sapphire.

And in that sapphire, there is a sky.

And under that turquoise sky, there is beach.

And on that beach, there sits a flame-haired woman on a rattan sun lounger, never getting sunburned.

Ciara took a sip of piña colada. Delicious. And refreshing. She never tired of them.

Nor did she tire of *him*. Presently, he walked through the surf in his tight little swimming shorts, as blue as the sky. Gods, the thighs on him. With a tinkle of her fingers, she beckoned him over. Her lounger was positioned alongside her beach bar, and her cabana.

She'd had very little time to throw this all together, but she was delighted by whatever whimsical impulse had meant her tiki bar was staffed by life-sized trolls like the ones she'd had as a kid – pink hair standing on end, and wearing little felt smocks. They didn't speak, just smiled and blinked. Perfection.

Jude joined her, dripping on the sand. His dick was clearly visible through the lycra trunks. 'How much longer are you going to insist on keeping this up?' he asked, perching alongside her.

'Oh, forever and ever!' Ciara said gleefully. The motherfucker had tried to flee at the last moment, but she'd kept enough of him to satisfy herself. He was powerless, at least in the demonic sense.

She held out her empty glass, and a troll brought her another without needing to ask.

The plan had occurred to her before she'd accepted the trade with Theo. The demons had vowed to make *her* a goddess. A goddess like Gaia, with the power to create a pocket universe all of her very own. What a stupid thing to do! Imagine giving *Ciara fucking Kelly* the keys to all creation.

In her dying breaths, she'd created an eternal beach holiday where she could read tatty *Sweet Valley High* paperbacks while listening to the Cranberries and Garbage. In an evening, she could have her own outdoor cinema screen showing *Cruel Intentions* or *Heathers* or anything she fancied that night.

A magic mirror she could use to look in on her sister and her friends whenever she wanted.

A hot guy who'd fuck her when she was horny and fuck off when she wasn't.

But that's the thing with creating your own personal heaven: it's not for everyone. Her prisoner, her paramour – whatever – scowled a second, but she found he never stayed mad at her for very long.

'Welcome to Hell, Lucifer.' She slipped a hand around his neck and pulled him in for a long, slow kiss.

She took her time. They had eternity.

THE END

ACKNOWLEDGEMENTS

In 2018, in a hotel room in Melbourne, I had an idea: *Desperate Housewives*, but they're witches. Back then, Leonie was a barmaid, and there was no Theo at all. How far we've come! Six years and four books later, we arrive at the end.*

There are so many people to thank. First up is YOU, dearest gentle reader. For most of my career, readers would come up to me and say, 'Thanks for . . . everything you do' or, 'I'm a fan of your work', which I suspect meant *Thank you for being visibly transgender at a time when it isn't very pleasant to be so.* But now, more and more, readers greet me with 'IS NIAMH ACTUALLY DEAD?' or 'NOT ANOTHER FUCKING CLIFFHANGER.' I can't express fully how joyous it is to be able to luxuriate in the world of HMRC with you. I feel so much less lonely (and unhinged) as a result. It is ours.

Over the years, so many people have worked tirelessly to get these books into your hands. First and foremost are the UK/US editing duo of Natasha Bardon and Nidhi Pugalia. The books wouldn't exist without them. A shout-out also to Helen Gould for

---

*The coven never ends. As long as there are women, there will be witches.

her invaluable editorial guidance, and Andrea Schultz and Margaux Wiseman for bringing the coven to the US initially. Special thanks to Fleur Clarke, and Holly MacDonald and Lisa Marie Pompilio, who are responsible for the design of the stunning covers.

Between HarperVoyager and PRH, there is a small of army of people to thank – not to mention the ever-growing list of houses around the world where the coven is available in translation. I don't want to single anyone out because I will absolutely forget someone vital and want to die. Instead, a sincere thank you to everyone who has worked on these titles: the publicists, marketers, copyeditors, translators, sales teams. As they say a lot in the US: I appreciate you.

So many of you discovered HMRC through the audiobooks, so an enormous thank you to Nicola Coughlan. The busiest, most talented woman in the world made time, and that means everything.

Finally, I owe so much to Sallyanne Sweeney and the entire team at MMB Creative, especially Ivan Mulcahy and Marc Simonsson. Thanks too to Katelyn Dougherty (not least for babysitting me in New York when I was on the verge of a nervy b) and Samar Hammam for taking the coven global.

JUNO
Dec 2024

Go back to where it all began.
Read on for a selection from
Juno Dawson's novel
Queen B,
available now.

19 MAY 1536

LADY GRACE FAIRFAX

The Tower of London

The Tower and the sky were the same hopeless grey. When the moment came, all was quiet. So quiet, in fact, that they could hear the head hit the wooden platform they'd erected on the green. *Thud.* It bounced once, and rolled once. Appalling, and undignified.

No provision had been made for her burial. She had been a problem to be solved, and now it was done. No man had prepared for the immediate next, and so it fell to the women.

For now, it was enough to get her away from the watchful ghouls at the scaffold on the centre of the courtyard. The ladies-in-waiting took the head and body into the chapel and wept. Their vulgar display was quite ghastly, and the men left. Just as the women had known they would.

Only six witches remained in their coven.

For weeks, they had been detained in the royal lodgings,

sharing in the queen's isolation. It had not been hard to convince Cromwell to allow them to share these final weeks in captivity with the queen; they'd scarcely needed magic. A man preoccupied with self-preservation above all else.

And so they had attended her until the very end. It was their duty, but more than that, they loved her. Clothed in black and grey, they had marched the final procession to the gallows.

Struggling to keep her stiffening limbs aloft, the women now lay the queen's body to rest on the floor before the altar. It was day; the candles were not yet lit. Absurd and unsure, Lady Grace Fairfax cradled the head as a babe. As the others looked to her, she placed it next to the exposed collar. Eyes closed and lips parted, she didn't look like Anne at all; so slack and unrefined. She didn't look *at peace*, she looked *dead*, some wet trout at a fishmonger. Grace tugged the white cloth from the altar, a golden cross clattering to the floor. She placed it over her face.

The women drew close, formed a circle around the body. Now, a dreadful quiet.

Grace looked to her fellow witches. Why was no one doing anything? 'Well?' she said impatiently. 'Revive her.'

The viscountess, Lady Rochford, clasped the silk blindfold to her breast, her knuckles white. 'Heresy, sister. We cannot.'

Grace ignored the outburst, instead turning to the old woman, the healer. 'Nan, can it be done?'

Nan Hobbs dutifully held her papery hands over the body. After a moment, she shook her head. 'There is nothing to heal, child.'

QUEEN B

'She is the *queen*,' Grace spat. Sour bile burned under her breastbone. She knew this coarse conduct was beneath her, but how could someone of Anne's magnitude be gone with such scant ceremony? After days of torturous waiting, and weeks of slow decline, it had taken a casual second.

Lady Jane Rochford, now, Grace supposed, their de facto leader, passed through what thin daylight filtered through the stained-glass windows of St Peter ad Vincula. She sighed. 'She is queen no longer. Seymour's girl will be upon the throne by week's end.'

'No queen of mine,' Lady Margery breathed, crouching at Grace's side.

'Nor mine,' agreed Grace.

There followed yet more silence. The air in the church felt oddly relaxed, and Grace found it disrespectful. The nerve of the world, turning when hers had stopped still. The column of meek sunlight advanced across the slabs. In these turgid minutes, Grace reckoned with the truth. Anne was gone, and no witch would bring her back. She was a fool unmasked, because she had not allowed herself to believe it, not truly. How she had courted some divine intervention, if not from the king, from the Mother. She'd have entertained, in her darkest moments, the treacherous tongue of Satanis himself.

And guilt. Such guilt. She could have stopped the blade. Any of them could have. Anne could have, instead of reading her carefully rehearsed lines so dutifully. She could have made the executioner plunge his blade into his own chest. They could have shown the world, at last, what it really was to be a witch. Alas, a display of their nature would bring a rain of fire down upon all witchkind. That, or they were cowards. Grace felt the air around her skin fizz. It was tempting to turn this fury outwards, but for what? *She* could have saved her. She had not.

The church door whined open, breaking her from her stupor. Isabel and Temperance, returning from the White Tower, carrying between them a plain wooden box. 'What is this? Where is the coffin?' Jane said, her face still ashen.

Grace did not much care for the viscountess, but she had not yet seen the woman weep, and she respected her grim resolve in the face of this grinding misery. She looked weary, her eyes sunken and cheeks hollow. Her husband *and* her sister-in-law, gone both, in a matter of hours. Their swift downfall was just that, a terrible fall, a plunge. Perhaps Jane's grief was yet to catch her up. Grace knew a dark tide would engulf her eventually. This was only the start.

'My lady, there is no coffin,' Temperance said, unable to meet her gaze.

'What?' Grace blinked in disbelief.

'This was as good as we could find,' Isabel, the youngest in their coven, said as they set down the grimy arrow box.

'They mock us,' Grace snarled. 'Killing her wasn't enough. Now they defile her.' She looked to the sky beyond the windows, feeling her eyes turn black. She summoned howling westerly winds. Grey clouds, irate, pooled around the Tower.

This day, this city, would mourn Anne Boleyn. They would hear the Mother scream in righteous fury.

Lightning lit the chapel, soon followed by a doleful rumble of thunder.

Jane Rochford clamped a hand on her shoulder. 'Lady Fairfax, I implore you. Reserve your vengeance. You shall require every last drop for the traitor.'

Indeed. There was only one cure for a witch who betrays her coven, and it was purifying fire. Grace Fairfax would find the witch that forsook their gracious queen, their high priestess, her Anne, and she would eviscerate her.

She would avenge the woman she loved with blood.

ALSO AVAILABLE

HER MAJESTY'S ROYAL COVEN
A Novel

At the dawn of their adolescence, four girls took an oath to join Her Majesty's Royal Coven, a covert government organization established by Queen Elizabeth I. Now Helena is the only one still in HMRC: Niamh's a country vet, Elle is pretending she's a normal housewife, and Leonie started her own more inclusive coven. When a dark prophecy centered around a warlock starts to unfold, the friends must decide where their loyalties lie.

THE SHADOW CABINET
A Novel

Niamh is dead, and Her Majesty's Royal Coven prepares to crown Ciara as High Priestess. Suffering from amnesia, Ciara can't remember what she's done, but her past—including former lover, renegade warlock Dabney Hale—hasn't forgotten. Hale is seeking a dark object of unknown power, and if the witches can't figure out Hale's machinations, all of witchkind will be in grave danger—along with the fate of all (wo)mankind.

QUEEN B
The Story of Anne Boleyn, Witch Queen

It's 1536, and the Queen has been beheaded. Lady Grace Fairfax, witch, knows that someone betrayed Anne Boleyn and her coven. Wild with the loss of their leader—and her lover—she will do anything to track down the traitor. But the betrayer was one of their own, and King Henry VIII has sent witchfinders after them. If Grace wants to find her revenge and live, she will have to do more than disappear. She will have to be reborn.

 PENGUIN BOOKS

Ready to find your next great read? Let us help. Visit prh.com/nextread